When Madeline Was Young

ALSO BY JANE HAMILTON

Disobedience
The Short History of a Prince
A Map of the World
The Book of Ruth

When Madeline Was Young

A NOVEL

JANE HAMILTON

DOUBLEDAY New York London Toronto Sydney Auckland

PUBLISHED BY DOUBLEDAY

Copyright © 2006 by Jane Hamilton

All Rights Reserved

Published in the United States by Doubleday, an imprint of
The Doubleday Broadway Publishing Group, a division of
Random House, Inc., New York.
www.doubleday.com

DOUBLEDAY and the portrayal of an anchor with a dolphin are
registered trademarks of Random House, Inc.

Special thanks, as always, to the Ragdale Foundation, for peace,
quiet, and time.

Book design by Pei Loi Koay

LIBRARY OF CONGRESS CATALOGING-IN-PUBLICATION DATA
Hamilton, Jane, 1957 July 13–
When Madeline was young : a novel / by Jane Hamilton.—
1st ed.
p. cm.
1. People with mental disabilities—Fiction.
2. Domestic Fiction.   I. Title.
PS3558.A4428W44 2006
813'.54—dc22
2006040238

ISBN-13: 978-0-385-51671-6
ISBN-10: 0-385-51671-1

PRINTED IN THE UNITED STATES OF AMERICA

1 2 3 4 5 6 7 8 9 10

FIRST EDITION

For my mother

Fabrizio thought of Clara. When he thought of her thighs and breasts he sighed; weakness swept him; he grew almost ill. So he thought of her face instead. Gentle, beautiful, it rose before him. He saw it everywhere, that face. No lonely villa on a country hillside, yellow in the sun, oleanders on the terrace, but might have inside a chapel, closed off, unused for years, on the wall a fresco, work of some ancient name known in all the world, a lost work—Clara.

—ELIZABETH SPENCER, *The Light in the Piazza*

When Madeline Was Young

EVERYONE WHEN I WAS GROWING UP HAD A DOG OR A BROTHER or a cousin, someone close by, called Buddy. The Buddy in my life had been christened Samuel Schubert Eastman in 1946. Certainly he deserved a dignified name, and yet we boys knew that for everyday use "Samuel" was too grave for a person like Buddy. Our cousin, as heroes must be, was the specimen among us. He was graced with sandy hair, green eyes, a dusting of freckles on his sunburnt nose, and thick gold lashes that matted in triangles against his cheeks after swimming. My mother used to say that his delicate features and those starlet eyelashes in his athlete's body were what confused the girls, the poor things sure he was tender. When he was fourteen, he told me part of what he guessed was a family secret, drawing me in one night with that piece of overrated information, the cheap start, the chocolate with a boozy liquid center. Buddy didn't yet know that there are a limited number of secrets in the repertory, very few of them worth disclosing, most of them good only for the quick thrill of stopping the pulse: suddenly you are not who you think you are. Despite his revelation and his alarming suggestion, it was even then his use of the word "secret" that seemed most vulgar.

We were sitting on the end of the dock at Moose Lake in northern Wisconsin. The house far up on the hill was not an ordinary Moose Lake cottage, the usual clapboard structure with uneven floorboards and a screened-in porch. No, the Maciver family house was made of granite and oak, walnut, copper, and English brick, a fortress with seven fireplaces and fifteen bedrooms, each with a sink scrubbed clean in the corner. Five of the rooms had their own sleeping porches, with faded cotton hammocks from Barbados strung across, the place the girls napped on the hot afternoons. There was also an icehouse, a pump house, a summer kitchen, a boathouse, and a barn. We were all proud to have an estate, which, we were called to remember, was the fruit of our dead grandfather's labor. That he was related to us seemed implausible—a man who had grown rich manufacturing glue? He had shot a buffalo on the range, the rug in the parlor as proof, but also with that nimble trigger finger he'd mounted and labeled and framed his butterfly collection. We loved to look at the petticoat wings and the sad balding thoraxes, the part that embarrassed us. Our forebear, the captain of industry, the great hunter, the lover of beauty, had been clever enough not to lose all of his fortune in the Depression, had made it possible for us boys of the glue dynasty to spend our days under our grandmother's direction in the boot camp of summer idleness. On her schedule we swam, we played tennis, we fished, and we chopped wood.

Buddy mentioned the putative family scandal to me one night, after we'd finally been released from the evening game of charades, all of us slow to get my grandmother's *Sapphira and the Slave Girl*. He and I were sitting on the rough wood slats of the dock, as we often did, moving our feet through the water, Buddy reviewing what had just happened or telling me what we might accomplish next. As if the idea were just occurring to him he said, "Hey! You know Madeline, pretty Madeline!" He was singing her name. "You could feel her up and it's not like you'd be a pervert. And if you knocked her up—say you knocked her up—she'd have a drooling mongrel that looked like you, but there's no way it would be a real half-breed."

When I didn't answer, he nudged me with his elbow. "What's the matter? You mean you don't know about your"—here he drew out the word, hissing in my face—"sister? She's fair game, Brains, that's what I'm telling you. Everyone should be that lucky, to have the opportunity right here in the home."

I knew about mating, my father's word, and I had the vaguest sense from dreams that my tallywhacker, as my mother fondly called the part—although it was unruly and had unreasonable hopes— might even so be a source of pride to me someday. In my waking hours it scared me to think of that someday, and I couldn't in much detail imagine how another person could participate in my privacy. The mechanics, then, the logistics of feeling a girl up, were impossible: not only how and of course where, exactly, but *why?*

"Madeline's not related to any of us!" Buddy cried, cuffing my shoulder. "The big secret, pal."

"I know it," I lied.

She'd probably really appreciate the, uh, attention." He laughed into his chest, my worldly cousin enjoying his own joke.

I suspect that my parents had told me about Madeline in some fashion when I was little, so that I'd always held the knowledge that strictly speaking she was not a blood relative. But she behaved as sisters do, and my parents treated her as one of us, and because she was perennially young I never thought of her as anything but sister. My parents were raising Louise and me, and always Madeline, educating us according to our abilities to be thoughtful, useful, and loving, keepers of the New Deal.

Later that night, in the boathouse, where all the boys slept, I lay awake brooding over what Buddy had told me. There was no electricity in the building, nor were there lights around the lake. The rough pine walls were dirty from decades of kerosene smoke, and the sheets that had once been white were dull from our heat and sweat. The darkness was complete. I had a hazy understanding that Madeline was some kind of relation—exactly how eluded me—who had been injured as a young woman. I was horrified even starting to think about her, against my will, in the way Buddy had directed. Everyone else in the room was asleep, and although I would have liked to go outside I felt that I shouldn't get up or move around. My stomach began to ache, as it often did when I was with Buddy for long. I could never repeat what he'd said, not to anyone, and most of all not to my parents. For the first time I wondered if they had to worry about Madeline, if she was ever in danger from the neighborhood teenagers, some of them nearly as adult as Buddy. My cousin surely wouldn't have hurt Madeline, and by "hurt" I meant kissing. But the way he had laughed into his shirt made me consider and reject and wonder again if he might have done something to my sister.

Madeline was in fact my father's age, forty-one that year. If Buddy had told me right off that Madeline had once been my father's wife, what would I have said or done, sitting on the pier, my legs in the water? Would I have laughed out loud? Would I have given a few kicks, splashing my cousin, making sure to get him all wet? Maybe I'd have argued, saying that a person who wasn't capable of doing logic puzzles past a second-grade level could hardly have been a *wife*. Or, as Buddy spoke, would my heart have abruptly begun to beat in my chest, hard, loud thumps—that overburdened muscle always the organ that registers the truth?

I suppose it's odd that for the length of my childhood Madeline never looked any different to me. I'd heard it said by the women on our block that she was a beauty—"a real Princess Grace," one of them called her. Despite Madeline's height and her regal charms, I always thought of her as a girl, first someone who was my older sister and then, forever after, when I'd bypassed her intellectually, as my youngest sister. She was long-legged and slim, with a silky blond ponytail, each day a fresh ribbon, a new color around the rubber band. Every other night, after her bath, she sat on my mother's bed under the Lady Vanity hair dryer, imperial in the shower-cap device, the diadem that was puffy from the hot air blowing through a fat cord. She did have a high forehead and notable cheekbones, and, by rights as a princess, a rosy mouth that puckered so prettily into a pout, what could be the precursor to a squall. She was a firm believer in outfits, so that if she was dressed in an ensemble as simple as a pair of turquoise-and-yellow-checked pedal pushers and a sleeveless yellow shirt, her socks were bound to be just that yellow, and her tennis shoes, some-how, miraculously, were exactly the turquoise of her slacks. Twice a year my mother took her to a charity resale store, where Madeline, in a fever of excitement, updated her wardrobe. She was a girl who laid tops and bottoms on the rug before she went to sleep, and who insisted that Russia, the cleaning lady, iron her play clothes.

I say she seemed a girl to me, but I also knew she was of her own kind—Madeline, the only one of us outside of time. I was old enough to understand the strange, mournful noise that came from her lonely bedroom, the sound of adult pleasure a person was supposed to stifle. I didn't want to think about any of it as I lay awake at Moose Lake. Somewhere in the middle of the night I realized that what was disturb-ing me most had nothing to do with my own family. I sat up suddenly, fumbled around on my windowsill, and struck a match. Madeline, my father, my mother, and even Louise and I—our lives were not to be made into stories for Buddy to tell. I lit the candle in order to look at him, unafraid then of waking anyone. His full, smooth lips were open against his pillow, his freckled back rising and falling. Before me was the boy who had the rest of his unending life to be the Maciver bard, to alter our history to suit himself. It surprised me, standing so close, that his breath was as sour as any of the other boys' familiar stink. Of course I had smelled him every summer, smelled his particular sweat mixed with the faint tang of Old Spice, but I hadn't realized that I didn't like it. I was unaccustomed to feeling insubordination with Buddy, and yet I was sure that in a minute I would effortlessly tip the flame to his soft, worn sheet and set him on fire.

Chapter Two

BUDDY AND I DIDN'T DISCUSS MADELINE AFTER THAT NIGHT at the lake—not because he'd expired in a plume of flames before my eyes, but because the topic didn't present itself again. We went on during the vacation as if the conversation hadn't taken place, or as if I had gladly soaked up the scant communication and had no further questions. He used to jump me from behind, always a big joke, and we'd tumble down the hill wrestling. As I remember, right after the revelation I did resist him with more force than usual and also almost pinned him, something I rarely was able to do. Still, it would never have crossed his mind that because of our talk it was he I might think of in a different light, rather than Madeline. She was not after all a girl you could consider for very long, weighing this part of her personality against that part. You spent your time with her fighting boredom, the way you would if you were told to watch little children. Even though in Buddy's character there was more range, although he was not simple, surely he would have had no idea that anyone might lose admiration for him.

That summer he introduced me to alcohol, and under the influence of the small amount of beer he was able to pilfer, we gambled with nickels instead of pennies. Our bad behavior is quaint now, adorable even, but at the time I thought we were in the most serious danger; I was certain that the discovery and our punishment would be so shaming, our characters so besmirched, that we would never really recover ourselves. We drank up in the woods in the dark, the one bottle going straight to my head, and afterward we'd stumble into the boathouse for cards with the younger boys. It stood to reason, then, that Buddy should have retained his luster. He instructed us as a group about "women," he called them, always pursing his lips as if he were whistling right before the "wo," and smiling hard on the "n," humming the final sound, in case the importance of the word should escape our notice. Our goal, he told us, was to get the goods from women with the least amount of trouble. His advice by and large ran toward pacification as the means to maintaining the upper hand, a general principle beyond our reach.

"Say you've snagged yourself a woman," he'd say, taking his time to arrange his cards. "Once you've got her, you want to make sure you tell her she's foxy, a doll face, a biscuit, but don't go overboard, you understand? You flirt with other women just enough to keep her on edge. You act like you're listening to the whining, you keep your peepers on her, you wrinkle your eyebrows." He demonstrated, head cocked, skin creased, the paragon of attention. "Why do you do this, boys?"

He couldn't really expect us to know the answer, could he? We all looked at the floor.

"Why?" he asked again. Cousin Nick coughed, and Petie accidentally dropped the rock he'd been holding. "Because," Buddy finally said, "you are concerned."

We nodded solemnly, hopeful that when our moment with a female came we could do exactly as he said. Although he had the sense that beer was too adult for the others, he had us all smoking cigarettes.

"Let me tell you something"—he'd take a drag no-handed as he slapped his cards down, the cigarette lifting when he drew in, the thing somehow staying firm on the ledge of his lower lip as he exhaled. "Getting pussy, it's like buying a car. You make your offer, right? The salesman counters, you make another offer, the salesman comes back with a bum deal." He surveyed the circle. "What do you do?" Again, that quiet. "Do you take it?"

"What's pussy?" said Cousin Petie, who had only recently been allowed to sleep with the big boys.

We laughed, most of us with the heartiness of discomfort, unsure ourselves of the details.

"You do not take the deal, you hear me? You hit the trail. Nine times out of ten, the hustler is at your heels, begging for your business."

Not long ago, I remembered that simile of Buddy's with my cousin Nick. We both recalled being confused enough to wonder which a person should do first, buy a car in order to get a girl, or get the girl so that purchasing the Chevy would be second nature. We marveled at Buddy's ease, the confidence in his delivery. "What you've got to realize, gentlemen," Buddy would say, "is that every single cupcake—unless she's a twatless freak of nature—has a pussy. Don't forget that. You fall for a certain broad, you start thinking she's the only one to get you all dick-brained. That happens, you might as well kiss yourself goodbye." He'd had real experience and he'd taken the time to consider his encounters. We knew his wisdom was hard-earned.

Cousin Nick pointed out that Buddy's father, Bill Eastman, had been a boozer and a womanizer, the divorcé with advice to give. Buddy, often fresh from a visit with the old man, was probably parroting him. It struck us both how relatively decorous Buddy's language had been: a boy with his swagger might have cursed like a sailor. That was the thing about our cousin, how he sometimes surprised you with what could nearly be called class.

That summer before I turned thirteen, I was, as always, at Buddy's side through the strict schedule wherein we fished in the tin boat and sailed in the sea boat and felled tall trees and swam across the green lake and played tennis in the old grass court in the upper pasture. As was my habit, I filled buckets with amphibians and rodents, jars with spiders and moths, boxes with jawbones and rib cages—those collections something Buddy would much later remember with contempt. At night, surrounded by my pails of scratching creatures in the boathouse, we had our den of sin with the boys. What were the adults thinking, that they entrusted the younger children to Buddy and even to me, a hundred yards away from the main house, in a tinderbox structure that we kept stocked with candles, some of us smoking until we fell asleep? He and I always excused ourselves for our midnight ritual just as the crew was drifting off, the two of us sitting on the dock under the shooting stars, talking in our way, man to man. If he'd been a reader, if he'd been literary, he might have said about Madeline that the mad wife in our family had come down out of the attic and taken up residence in the playroom.

When I look back, it seems surprising that it took Buddy to make me think I should somehow protect Madeline at the lake and at home from people who might prey upon her. Where had my brotherly chivalry been before that? Madeline seemed happy enough on the periphery of the little girls' gang, but I felt that if I were actively good I should build Lincoln Logs on the porch with her, or organize a Ping-Pong tournament for her group, none of whom could hit the ball twice in a row, the single return usually a fluke. Still, they would have been filled with self-importance and excitement. At the least I should have inserted myself into "Mother, May I?" during the adults' happy hour, staying next to Madeline as we took our no-risk baby steps. Even if Buddy leered and poked me in the ribs at dinner, I should have both shielded myself from him and shown him his suggestions meant nothing to me. I told myself, I insisted it didn't matter how or why my parents had adopted Madeline; she was my sister, a girl I hadn't paid half enough attention to over the years, a girl who was so pure of heart and silly she worshipped me. There was nothing Buddy could say, no matter how he talked, no matter how he jeered or winked, nothing at all that could make me ashamed to have someone like Madeline in my family.

It was shortly after Buddy's little talk on the dock that Madeline became ill. Although it turned out to be a harmless flu, my mother was so concerned that I became sure my sister was near death. She had a high fever, hot flashes that drenched her sheets, chills that made her teeth chatter. My mother was a nurse, but there were limits to her knowledge and confidence. Near dusk one night, she phoned Dr. Riley, a small-town physician of an era long past, a professional who could be counted on to treat large animals if the veterinarian was over-booked. When he got out of his car and came across the lawn, using his cane, and with his battered leather bag in hand, the children silently parted the way. My mother called down to me from the window of the south bedroom to show him up, and also, while I was at it, to bring her ice.

"Timothy," she cried, using my Christian name, something that happened so seldom I hardly recognized it. She must have realized her error because she began again. "Mac! Mac, get me a dish of ice, will you please?"

When I came into the room, she was propping the invalid in a sitting position on the bed with herself as the leaning post. She kissed Madeline's hair as she made the adjustments. There had been plenty of times when she had been alarmed over events—it was as if the end of the world were nigh when the Russians shot down one of our reconnaissance planes, and when President Eisenhower had to send troops to Little Rock she wept—but I had never seen her frightened for one person. She didn't say anything, saving her mouth, I guessed, for those prayerful kisses, and she didn't look at me, either. She made no comment about how I was upstairs, in a place the boys were forbidden, and she didn't ask after all for the ice. I remember knowing I was there because I could see in the long mirror my knobby knees, the awful brown fawnishness of my young self, my wide brown eyes, my brown hair in need of a cut, my uncertainty.

The doctor right away felt Madeline's lymph glands, smoothing his fingers down her neck. She had just enough energy when he did that to lift her chin and slowly close her glassy eyes. She was going to die. Right there in front of us, slumped against my mother, she was going to take one last little breath. And then what would we do? Would my mother cry out, suddenly insane like one of the tragic Greek heroines? Would she shriek at anyone who threatened to take the body away? I looked hard at Dr. Riley: *Say she'll live, say she'll live.* If she died we wouldn't believe it; and so it was up to the doctor to make the story true. For a minute, as I stared, I forgot the patient and the death and the panicked mother. It was as if I were in the room alone with the doctor, as if he were speaking to me while he attended to Madeline, as if he were telling me to step into my future. He had glanced at me just once, but in that look he had seemed to say, Watch. And I thought if you were going to pass on, it wouldn't be so terrifying with his hands moving gently over your face and throat, and if you were going to live, suddenly because of that cupped hand on your cheek, you'd be glad you were staying. He touched Madeline's forehead, he made her take a sip of ginger ale, and then he listened to her heart; he stared dreamily at the floor, tuned into the intricacies of her particular glub-glub, the whisper that seemed to tell him her history. As he removed the earpieces of his stethoscope, he said to Madeline, "The flu always seems worse in summer, doesn't it, young lady?" I recall noting that he would call her "young lady" because he was feeble and old. Anyone, compared with him, was young. He patted her leg. "You're just about over the hump, even if it doesn't quite feel like it." To my mother he said, "I don't see signs of scarlet fever, nothing dangerous here. She should feel better in a day or two."

Soon after he left, I went into the woods to sit on a stump in the near darkness. I was often crying in those days, and it always embarrassed me even in private, even as I couldn't help it, the girlishness of it. The shame made me cry harder, stuffing my fist in my mouth to keep from making noise. The doctor had said that Madeline was going to get well, that the worst was over, and so there was that relief. I thought I was for the most part grieving for Madeline, for her brush with death. Although she would survive, I was sorry for my neglect of her through the years, and sorry, too, for the wretched games I'd played, pretending she was the dog and I the master, she the servant and I the king, she the wife and I the commanding husband—Madeline, always the one who barked and fetched and scrubbed. I sobbed with useless contrition. Without knowing I was probably also crying because never again would I feel awe for Buddy in the thoughtless way a younger boy idolizes someone else. It seemed terrible that he had spoken about her to me—*the big secret, pal*—and then she had almost died, perhaps a cause and effect, his words somehow infecting her. And it seemed especially harsh to be miserable in a place that had always held the greatest of happinesses. I would have thought it worth weeping, I'm sure, if I'd understood that those summers would not come again, that Buddy and I would never be together at Moose Lake as we'd been all those years before.

Much later, when my sister, Louise, and I were both at Oberlin College in Ohio, I told her about that night at the lake, when Buddy informed me that I could, with impunity, have my way with Madeline. I explained that I'd figured out the pieces by talking to our aunt Figgy and also the cleaning lady, Russia. Louise said, "But Mac! You knew about Madeline. We've always known. I remember looking at the photo album with Mom when I was little, how she pointed at each person and explained." Louise repeated, "We've always known."

I understood again that it was Buddy who had made the story seem like a sensational deceit, a tabloid headline. When, in fact, our parents had absorbed Madeline's tragedy into everyday life so seamlessly it was unimportant to dwell on the circumstances. They had the balanced sense of both the absurdity of existence and the importance of using our gifts, of finding the work we were meant to do. Hardly the stuff of soap opera. It had taken me years to see that Buddy had told me about Madeline for no other reason than to impress his kid cousin in the moment: Buddy Eastman knew what it was to feel up a girl. That was all he'd wanted to tell. I stood like a dolt in Louise's dorm room at Oberlin, having revealed the great lie, the substantial weirdness I'd trumped up at the center of the Maciver clan. Only to find there was no secret and no pathology. "Maybe," Louise suggested kindly, "you were way too young when Mom told you and couldn't make sense of it."

Somewhere along the line, Buddy, in his superior wisdom, might have spelled it out, might have explained that my father, Aaron Maciver, had married Madeline Schiller on March 27, 1943. Did Buddy spare me that information because he knew I would not have wanted to hear such a thing out loud? Did he know that I was the type of boy who found it hard to believe that my parents hadn't always lived under the same roof? Even as I held the knowledge in a far fold, a neural nook and cranny, that Madeline had once been my father's wife, I was also sure that, despite the evidence about my parents' separate upbringings, they had actually been born married and loving each other. Buddy's news, if he'd carried on with it, would have been full of complications, but most probably I would have entertained none of them. I had no wish to think about how my father had extracted himself from one union in order to make another. Ridiculous! No doubt I had rejected my mother's account, told to me as one tells a three-year-old a strange fact of his life so that it is reduced to normalcy. At some point, however, I must have been scared to death and therefore rejected the story, relegated it to the world of make-believe. Because, if Madeline had been my father's bride when she was only a girl, or seemed so, that meant that I might already have gone to war or left home or not been my parents' child, and all without realizing it.

So—the facts, what stands as truth. In 1943, my mother, Julia Beeson, was a junior at Radcliffe College, not yet having borne either Louise or me in any other dimension or lifetime. She was invited to Aaron Maciver's wedding in Chicago, never having met him, because she was the roommate and good friend of my father's sister, Figgy, née Fiona, the maid of honor. Figgy would have demanded my mother come to her brother's wedding to meet a rich cousin, a poor relation, a handsome brute, a homely sailor—anyone at that late date would do to put a little romance into Julia Beeson's schoolmarmish life. The event had been scheduled to coincide with Radcliffe's spring vacation, the bride, so said Figgy, having gone to great lengths to accommodate the scholars. Figgy understood that it was essential to find an important man in order to become important herself; she wished that her closest friends would ultimately land boyfriends from the same echelon, so that years away they would find themselves seated next to each other at a State Department dinner. But first, for Julia Beeson, a man, any man.

According to my aunt Figgy, Aaron Maciver's bride wore a silk sheath that so conformed to her long, slim body that you imagined the silk was her skin, her skin the silk. At the altar, before my father and Madeline said their vows, the minister, standing a step up from them, put his hands on the shoulder of the bride and groom, and made the unfortunate remark clergymen sometimes can't help making in the heat of the moment. "If you two," he said, "could see twenty-five years into the future, you would not have the courage to make this commitment." He said the line tenderly, and many of the couples in the congregation laughed knowingly. Madeline and Aaron smiled quickly, privately—how little the minister understood the depths of their love! My mother, in the back pew, may have smiled, too, thinking herself adult enough to realize the hazards of matrimony. My father, overtaken by emotion during the vows, could hardly bleat out the required "I do." He did cry easily, a habit I knew I came by honestly. Figgy maintained that when he married Madeline, tears slipping down his cheeks, the women in the congregation, single and otherwise, were sorry not to have nabbed him for themselves.

I've learned most of my parents' history from Figgy and the cleaning lady, Russia, both women who don't check their hyperbolic tendencies. Nonetheless, it's probably fair to report that Madeline was the kind of woman who steps into the room and at once is the center of attention, the kind of woman who knows she has that effect and pretends it's nothing. "Miss Madeline," Russia intoned in her husky Mississippi accent, shaking her head, her lips pursed, "Miss Madeline in those days, in a sundress! Just like a queen, and she always, she always get what she want." Russia spoke admiringly, as if the work of realizing that sort of feminine potential took a great deal of strength. It's not hard to imagine that Madeline, the only child, the woman with allure, was compellingly haughty. She was probably not easy to please, and so for her suitors there was the continuous enticement, one challenge after another, one more offering to make, another promise to deliver. Before the marriage, my poor father wrote to tell her that she was all light and grace and goodness, confusing her beauty, perhaps, with her character.

It was after the ceremony, in the receiving line, that my parents first met. My father, fair and freckled, was wearing a light-gray suit with a white rose at the lapel. My mother was as ever herself, a person who made no attempt to be fashionable, who didn't strain to highlight her assets. She never wore makeup, she never spoke about reducing, and she had no interest in clothes beyond keeping herself warm in winter and cool in summer. It's possible she was vain about her hands, her long fingers and perfectly oval nails, but I say so only because she had the right to think them elegant. She had blue eyes, small but penetrating, a perfect short nose, a generous mouth that allowed for her brilliant smile and what I loved best about her, her wide-open laugh. My father once said she was the most irreverent serious person he'd known. But in the first encounter she was no doubt straightforward and earnest. In her plain blue suit, her sensible pumps, with her short frizzy hair around her face, she probably gave a solid handshake and told him she was pleased to meet him, and also that she wished him the best happiness in marriage.

Madeline would have been next in line. "Julia Beeson," my father might have said, passing her on, "this is my wife." My mother was as vulnerable to beauty as the rest of us, and she may well suddenly have felt shy. As if she were a dowager aunt, someone far older rather than a few years younger than her new acquaintance, she took both of Madeline's hands in hers.

"Figgy's friend?" Madeline turned to her new husband to make sure she'd heard correctly. "It's very nice to meet you. And what a pretty brooch." Before she greeted the next guest she'd forgotten the plain woman, forgotten her name and the great-grandmother's garnet brooch, an ornament years later she was often urging my mother to wear.

Julia knew only what Figgy had told her, that Madeline had gone to a dreary little college in Chicago and studied home economics with an emphasis on fashion design. Figgy's biography of Madeline was on the whole the story of Figgy's dissatisfaction with her future sister-in-law and her disappointment in her own brother for marrying down. The Maciver family had once been a significant Chicago dynasty, going back to the fur traders; they had their place still on the Social Register. Who was Madeline Schiller? There was the no-name college, not to mention the groveling parents who were denied membership at the country club, who had had to prostrate themselves to get Madeline into the Junior League so she could go to the cotillion. They'd had the gall to discourage Madeline from marrying Aaron Maciver, suggesting she could do better.

My father was legally blind without his glasses and during the war had been sent to work in a munitions factory in Wisconsin. After he tripped over a wire in the parking lot and broke his foot in several places, he was discharged. That is to say, the Schillers may have had their own reasons for worrying about their daughter's choice. By trade he was an ornithologist, and for most of his professional life he was the curator of birds at the Field Museum of Natural History in Chicago. He wore binoculars around his neck the way librarians wear their glasses. At least once a year he went away for months to collect specimens in mountains and forests marked with red dots on our globe in the living room. He always returned with suitcases of birds neatly packed in foreign newspaper, laid in crosshatching rows. I like to think Madeline's love for him was a sign of her native intelligence.

Despite the relatives' concerns, the photographic record bears proof that Mr. and Mrs. Maciver were happy, the two of them generally shoulder to shoulder, clear-eyed, and grinning into the sunlight. Right before the wedding, Madeline had quit her job at the dress shop in order to learn to be a wife. Every morning, Mrs. Maciver sat at the kitchen table reading the *Joy of Cooking*, that primer of Jell-O rings; scalding, simmering, and poaching; stuffings, dressings, and forcemeat; oyster soufflés; and the elusive milk-fed veal. She had been stricken by the fever of domesticity, something else that repulsed Figgy. Her fantasy was not modest in scale: eight children she wanted, four girls, four boys. On the curator's salary, they'd move to a large house on the lake, the little ones circling their mother in the nursery, Mother never losing her figure or her steady temperament, always unstained and unflappable in the center of the cheerful fracas.

It was peculiar, Buddy perhaps wanted to tell me, what lay at the heart of our middle-class white Anglo-Saxon Protestant life. There is a picture of my father and his bride heading out together from their apartment on the North Side, in Rogers Park, for a Sunday-morning ride on their upright bicycles with wicker baskets. It's possible the photo was taken on the day of the accident, an hour or so before my father decided for some reason to turn back ahead of Madeline. She wanted to go farther along the road by the lake, to visit her parents, and they separated, he promising to pick her up in the car to spare her the six-mile ride home.

The calamity and its aftermath have never been a story in the family, no recounting of those formless days in the hospital waiting for Madeline to wake, the first months of small and great hopes, the guarding against the clarity of future despair. No one had seen her lose control of the deep-blue Raleigh; there is no accounting for how she found herself on the pavement, the wheels crashed against the stone fence, the frame obscenely bent. The person who discovered her, who called for help and probably even resuscitated her, apparently was forgotten in the rush to the hospital. Madeline may have fractured a few ribs, losing blood into her chest occultly, low blood volume stopping her heart. There may in addition have been a blow to the skull, acute subdural hematoma, the compression affecting her judgment and abilities. I can only guess in crude terms what happened, as was true for the doctors of that time, too. If we are in the dark ages now in the history of our understanding of the brain, the 1940s was a geologic age, somewhere in the middle of the Paleozoic, the quiet years before dinosaurs thundered over the earth. There were as yet no assessment scales for the stages of coma and recovery, no brain scans to identify the areas of damage; there were as yet no comprehensive rehabilitation facilities for the impaired. "She was out long enough to return quite less than herself," is how Figgy explained the consequences of the smash-up. Madeline had suffered traumatic brain injury, resulting in memory loss, cognitive deficits, personality change, mood disorders—quite less than herself. There has always been privacy around the subject of her accident, something, I maintain, that is altogether different from secrecy. I have the habit of explaining to my wife, again and then again, that that kind of privacy goes hand in hand with dignity. Figgy herself was unsure of the details when she was telling me about the disaster, the summer before I went to college.

My father went out for a bike ride with his wife and sometime later brought home from the hospital a twenty-five-year-old woman who would forever have the intellectual powers of a seven-year-old. A fine tale with gothic possibilities, a good story for Buddy to consider telling in the dark night to his cousin. What, I wonder, did my father's colleagues say to him about this piece of bad luck, or call it carelessness on the part of the husband? He'd abandoned his wife on the trail, turning back for what important business? What studying or house project would have been so critical that he couldn't ride on to say hello to his in-laws?

My grandmother rushed in to be of service, hiring a nurse so that my father's work and graduate studies would not be disturbed. It was she and also my mother in those years who made it possible for him to get his Ph.D. and thereafter secure the curator job he'd always wanted at the Field Museum. Madeline's parents, curiously, astonishingly, moved to Florida, to Naples, as far from the disaster as they could get. Mr. Schiller, who had doted on her, behaved as if his only child had died, as if by relocating they could erase her memory.

I am a doctor now in a small town in Wisconsin, and I see ordinary tragedy often enough. When someone I hadn't known well passes away on my watch, I go through the paces of giving comfort and I make myself in the moment imagine the suffering. It never fails to be affecting: coming upon a group gathered by the bed, all of them freed from the hold of night and day in the hospital's eternal light, all of them suddenly having to take a part in the great drama of their family. Still, my sympathy is admittedly frequently an exercise, one I can take up at will and usually set down.

My father's sadness comes to me unbidden and at odd hours. His future was shattered, and yet day after day the ghost of that future sat stolidly across from him at the breakfast table. I knew Madeline as a woman who had moved into her injury, who seemed to inhabit her limitations, a woman who was fixed in her self. But what of those months and years after the accident, what of that long period of becoming? It's notable that neither Figgy nor Russia felt free to rhapsodize upon the Macivers' private affairs—Russia, the cleaning woman who observed us for generations, who could make a story out of very little material. Not even Russia would trespass, never volunteering a word about that in-between phase, Madeline wife but not wife.

My sentimental father might lie staring up at the ceiling at night, too stricken for tears. He might have gotten carried away by the old joy, let himself be hopeful when there could not be hope. Stupid! Maybe even brutish. He'd been fooled by the holy silence in which she'd always given herself, which was in some ways just as it had been before the accident. He'd never slept with anyone but Madeline, so how could he know the difference, if there was any, between their own

religion, this art of theirs, and what was the natural response of the average female? What had seemed spiritual about sex when she'd been
right had probably not required her mind or even much of a self. Did
she still have a self? Of course, of course she did. But maybe, after all,
there had been no profound understanding between them in their year
of marriage, open eye to open eye as they'd moved together, she
clasping his hips, she—the first time, what a shock!—turning around
on hands and knees, his Madeline, now sweet, now surprisingly fierce.
He had not imagined, for example, that they would share, and so ecstatically, their animal shame.

Very occasionally I let myself think of that kind of thing. I suspect
that not long after the accident my father knew he couldn't continue
the old communion. There was the canopy bed, excessive in lace
and ribbon, that he and my grandmother bought to entice Madeline
away from him, a garish little-girl delight to seduce her to her own
room. It is an embarrassment to recount that detail, my grandmother
in those early days setting the tone for the household, shopping for the
changed Madeline, doing what she could to ease the strain. Figgy
through the years pestered me with the idea that they were wrongheaded, re-creating Madeline's childhood, forcing upon her a young
girl's tastes and enthusiasms. We used to argue about it, she saying
that Madeline deserved the respect of an adult, that, even if she was in-
capacitated, she didn't have to play with dollies and puppets and finger
paints. I contended that Madeline gravitated to comforts she could
grasp. And, furthermore, she used brushes and tube paints and a
palette. I see now that it is a fair question, to ask how much of Madeline's disability was imposed upon her. In fairness, too, it is a question
that should be answered in terms of intention. Although the particulars are gruesome—the pink wallpaper, the vanity table with gold
trim, the shelf of toys—my father, my grandmother, my mother
meant to care for their charge the best they knew how; they meant to
help her hold still in her new self.

* * *

IT WAS A FEW MONTHS after my father's marriage to Madeline that my mother had quit Radcliffe and come back to her native Chicago to get a degree in nursing. Figgy tended to highlight the farcical, but my mother also wasn't a reliable narrator, she who thought her own life unremarkable. It is either fantastical, then, or an ordinary coincidence that my mother was the nurse's aide who bathed Madeline and changed her sheets in the hospital after the accident. During those weeks at the Evanston Hospital, Julia Beeson and Aaron Maciver ate dinner together—the closest Julia had ever come to having a date, Figgy said. In the cafeteria they ate tough roast beef coated with a thick, dull gravy. "Imagine it's caramel," my mother advised. I suppose they spoke about Madeline's prognosis, they spoke about her strength, her endurance. It's also likely that they discussed the invasion of Normandy. There may have been talk about the difficulty Julia had had at Radcliffe, the intense snobbery there, all those Winslows, Cottings, and Cabot Lodges. The wealthy Quakers and Unitarians had been so cool in their generalized liberal kindness, and she couldn't escape the feeling that she was a charity case, the match girl on a scholarship in her ragged stockings. When she had to leave Radcliffe to care for her ailing father, it was something of a relief, an excuse for escape. She confessed that to Aaron, confessed that her father's illness and death had saved her from the oppression of her classmates and the family expectation that she be a colossus of knowledge. What a deliverance, she said, to do honest work, to pay for her own college education toward a useful degree. Aside from that intimacy and the balm of sympathy as the crisis went on, surely what sealed my parents' bond was their mutual affection and veiled scorn for Figgy. My father, but softly, imitated his sister's capacity to work through a room of men until she'd lassoed the most eligible bachelor, and my mother, with such fondness, impersonated Figgy cozying up to the professor and at cocktail parties becoming chums with the president of the board.

After the patient was safely home, Aaron invited Julia to the museum to show off the collection to her, drawer by drawer. He was not yet curator, but he had a position in the bird division, making skins and assisting with the cataloguing. Because of Julia's genuine concern, she had soon, inevitably, become one of Madeline's constellation of caretakers. Why not, as a kind of thanks to her, extend the invitation to see the remarkable collection, the behind-the-scenes splendor? Over those birds that were presumed to be extinct—the great auk, the ivory-billed woodpecker—Julia nearly wept, and over many of the others—the indigo bunting, the chickadee, the hooded merganser, the common junco—she bent low and held her throat. He had thought she would enjoy them, but her reaction was beyond his expectation. Her appreciation for the dead was so great he couldn't resist asking her into the woods to show her the variety of the living in her own city. She was a quick study, and when she went to the nearby state park with him the following spring, to see the migrating warblers, she had done her lessons well, spotting without his help the chestnut-sided, the magnolia, the black-and-white, the Wilson's, the bay-breasted and golden-winged. Eventually, with the aid of a tape-recorded tutorial, she came to know the songs almost as well as he did. Although he'd been taught that comparison is odious, how could he not remark to himself that Madeline had never been interested in his work, that, for all her decorating sense, her artistry when it came to arranging flowers and furniture and putting suit with tie and shoes, she had not been seized by the magnificence of the birds? In the woods she had always grown cold, or she was dying of heat, or she was eaten alive by mosquitoes, frailties he had done his best to love. My father was impressed by Julia's quiet appreciation of beauty, by her stoicism when she was uncomfortable, by her intellect, and by her empathy for those who suffered, by her plans to become a nurse, to work in Appalachia or with Negroes in the city, a place where the need was acute. All that in addition to my mother's sly ridicule of his loudmouthed sister.

In the years before their marriage, my mother came to the apartment to cook a meal, to read to Madeline, to play Go Fish, to look at fashion magazines, to dress paper dolls. Julia would hold Madeline's face and speak to her, making a loving tableau. She told her stories, she tried to stretch her memory, gently, gently, so that Madeline, her head to her shoulder, as if in contemplation, didn't always become enraged by the challenge. My mother understood that a woman who had once been athletic, who had shot archery and enjoyed swimming, more than anything needed to be worn out, that it was important to keep the body moving. Julia may have known, before research began to bear the evidence, that exercise is important to cognition. Madeline had come out of the accident with a hitch in her walk, with an ungainly stride. It was, if I had to guess, a result not of the brain trauma but of a wrenching of her limb in the wrecked wheel. You had to look three times at her—once as a matter of course, and then at that odd lope, and again to see that it really was a lovely young woman. In summer my mother took her to the beach, and together they'd sink down out of the July heat into the cool water, Julia moving Madeline's arms to remind her of the strokes she'd used in synchronized swimming. She was with Madeline through her hysterectomy, a surgery the doctor had suggested in order to make Mrs. Maciver's life easier. As Figgy told it, my mother's attorney cousin arranged for my father to be legally separated from his wife. It was my mother, then, according to the lore, who orchestrated the divorce.

"ONLY A DESPERATE MAN would have taken your mother seriously," Figgy told me not long ago, when we were up at Moose Lake. "How else," she said, "could Julia have landed herself a husband?"

"Figgy," I said wearily. It wasn't the first time she'd spoken to me about my mother in disparaging tones.

"Mac! Sweetheart, come on!" My aunt leaned forward on the porch, after all those years still showing off her cleavage in her low-cut blouse, the withered bosom and her pearls at last giving her a patrician elegance. She said, "Your mother saw her chance and went after Aaron. Good for her, is what I say. I'm all for that kind of capture. But on a level playing field there would have been no competing with Madeline. The glamour-puss made her own slips, her own camisoles, her own winter coat—she was that particular. So what if she was no intellectual giant? What hot-blooded man cares about that? Madeline had powers beyond the standard dumb blonde—genuine star quality, that calculating femme-fatale lustiness beneath the cool platinum purity. I'm telling you in her own way she was a deep thinker. But had she ever read anything more difficult than a fashion magazine?" Figgy rubbed her hands together with the thrill of this part of the story. "Say there hadn't been an accident. Your father would have died a slow death, a cruel death, if he'd stayed married to that gorgeous twit, absolutely. He would never have gotten a divorce, never!" She threw her head back and laughed. "He'd have taken to drink!"

Because I made no comment, she seemed to think she had to elaborate. "Look-it. Your father, even with those thick glasses, has always appealed to women. He's one of those killingly thoughtful men—nothing showy, but if you happen to take a fourth glance you're smitten. Madeline was your father's real love, the passion of his life. He knew he'd never find someone to fire his jets the way she had—and let me tell you, as quiet and dignified as your father is, he couldn't keep his hands off her. She had this way of acting as if she tolerated his devotion, a total come-on, don't you think?"

"Yes," I said.

"Once she was out of the picture—so to speak—your father figured he might as well take a wife with broad hips." Figgy held her hands three feet apart, as if that distance had been my mother's girth. "And those sagging breasts! Those ill-fitting brassieres! She was a dead ringer for a Salvation Army matron. There was a hardy girl for you, someone who wouldn't slip off a bike and smash her head to pieces. A woman who was so hopeless she'd care for another man's wife. Wife Number One, Wife Number Two under the same roof—so Oriental!"

I had only to raise my eyebrows.

"You don't think so? Oh well, when we were roommates in college I always thought I could save Julia from frumpiness, bring her up in the world. Her big fat spanky pants drying in the bathtub gave me the giggles every morning. Don't mistake me, I loved the woman, you know that. Her secret playful streak, her intelligence—she was a walking reference for things historical, and she could recite poems stanza after stanza. I loved her like a sister."

Julia had been dead for a few years when that conversation with Figgy, one of our last, took place on the Moose Lake porch. As had become usual in my talks with her, I'd been filled with the outrage of a good son. As always, I'd remained the well-brought-up nephew. In the early 1970s, the two of them had had an argument from which they never recovered. I did try to remember that Figgy was probably still trying to justify herself, still trying, as she ranted at me, to make Julia see the light. I regretted, as I had often done, that I'd never gotten my mother to speak about the early days of her marriage to my father. She always brushed my questions off, as if taking on a burden like Madeline was something anyone would have done. I would have liked to tell my aunt that her friend Julia had become more beautiful as she'd aged, radiant in a way Figgy would never have understood. Julia grew rounder and rosier, and even frumpier than she'd been, if that was possible in Figgy's book, as the era of the girdle gave way to the salubrious days of the sack dress and sweat suits. Like a child, I wanted to shout at Figgy that my mother was better! Wiser! Smarter! Deeper than Figgy could fathom. Although Julia wanted to do good works on a large scale, organizing and assisting in an Eleanor Roosevelt fashion, it's not hard to imagine how she could easily have been drawn into my father's life, how she, with her store of sympathy and grace, might have thought that in the Maciver household there was in fact a need equal to her love. If I'd said so to Figgy, she would have laughed me off the porch, repeating my sentence as if it were a punch line.

Chapter Three

IT'S A CURIOUS THING ABOUT WOMEN, THE WAY THEY EXTEND themselves to each other for no particular reason. This is a behavior Buddy neglected to tell me about when we were boys. My wife, Diana, and Buddy's wife, years before they met, faithfully exchanged Christmas cards. Every December there came in the mail the studio photo of Buddy, Joelle, and the five children, not any of them looking the least bit sullen or inconvenienced in their church clothes, and all of them, according to the accompanying letter, noble citizens. The picture Diana sent of us was also studied, but we were outside, squinting into the camera, the missus and the doctor and the three daughters on a ski slope or a beach, somewhere far away, in expensive sunlight.

My wife has a dynasty of her own to occupy her, eight siblings, two parents, two sets of grandparents, all of whom live near us, as well as seventeen nieces and nephews and, farther afield, thirty-two first cousins. Over dinner one night a few years ago, when I was mulling over the phenomenon of the holiday communications, and especially those to strangers, Tessa, our middle child, explained that Christmas cards are the goods of the braggart. She had come home from college for winter break a day or two before, and still had her initial enthusiasm for us after the months of separation.

"The goods of the braggart," I repeated with fatherly pride.

"And also a way to mark territory, the single-spaced two-page letter exactly like a dog pissing on a hydrant."

There is not very often a wounded silence from Diana. It is even unusual for her to pause, as she did just then, for a fortifying breath, which is after all necessary for sustained speech. "You go," she said to Tessa, "and spend November at the printer. You take a picture that's good of everyone—Katie doesn't have her mouth open, Lyddie's not blinking, your head's not in a book, your father for a moment is not staring out at the Andromeda who-knows-what. I don't think you understand how demanding family is and how important. You have no idea."

Since we live on one long country road, every driveway for three-quarters of a mile an entry into property owned by one of Diana's brothers and their wives, I'd wager that Tessa does know a thing or two about the diplomacy required to keep the close family in a loving circle. Although the girls were at first astonished, it was no mystery to them why Diana once cut up the evil sister-in-law's cast-off Oriental rugs. She shredded the jewel-colored wool into strips with a box cutter and laid them down to make paths between the flower beds. As I heard tell, the rugs had been given to her in a great show of generosity, a blaze Diana interpreted as hostility. I'm quite sure that the Queen of England does not have such expensive mulch. Because there is no end of excitement in our neighborhood, when it came time for college Tessa chose a scruffy liberal-arts school in North Carolina, hundreds of miles from Wisconsin.

"Oh gosh, Mom!" Tessa said, hands to her head, the pads of her fingers hard into her skull. "Those Christmas cards must be so much work!" She had the right tone and pace, rushing in to comfort with a sincere mix of reverence, and exhaustion, too, at the very idea of letter writing. "It's fabulous you keep in touch with everyone, even people you don't really know. Someday it would be fantastic to have a huge reunion and meet all of Dad's relatives. I'd love that. And it would be easy, because you've connected with them, because you know so many of the addresses."

Tessa flashed a look across the table at me, eyes widening, lips firm together, an instant you can miss if you're not waiting. I don't admit to being gratified by that spark between us, but in truth little else that is so small makes me so glad. If I have had a long day listening to my patients' worries and my colleagues' complaints, and if at the end Tessa will reward me, then all is well in my speck of the world. I had missed her more than I'd imagined when she'd left for college in September. I almost never speak about my patients, but I was tempted to tell her about Mrs. Kosiba, a woman suffering from ulcerative colitis. She had been plagued that morning by the difficulty she was going to have juggling her first and second husbands in the hereafter. She'd liked the first mister far better than his replacement, but the second had left her with money. How to express gratitude to Number Two at the pearly gates without implying she wanted to spend time with him in heavenly recreation? I didn't mention to Tessa or Diana that for some persons the problems in the old bye-and-bye might actually be compounded, that it might do to save some energy for the tumult beyond the grave. My women went on to discuss their Christmas shopping, speaking in code, I gathered, about their secrets and surprises.

THE FOLLOWING SUMMER, on July 24, 2003, Buddy's son was killed in Baghdad. Nearly three months had passed since the war with Iraq had been declared over. We first found out about Sergeant Kyle Eastman from the list of the dead in the *New York Times*, a feature I always scan. As soon as I read the name out loud at the breakfast table Diana told me I must call my cousin or write a letter. Thirty-eight years had passed since I'd last seen him or spoken to him. His boy, a sergeant for the First Battalion, Thirty-fourth Regiment, had been struck by an improvised explosive device. What sounded like the kind of thing Buddy had tried to make on any number of occasions in his basement through the formative years. Before the idea of the boy's death had sunk in, the phone calls began to come from the Macivers scattered around the country, the network of cousins broadcasting the news. When I told Diana later in the day that I wasn't going to write the letter at the moment, thinking that anything I might say would sound fatuous, what did she do but sit herself down and toss off a note to Joelle, a woman she'd never met, expressing all of our condolences. My wife has stacks of thick beige card stock in the desk cubbyhole, DR. AND MRS. TIMOTHY MACIVER embossed in burgundy on the top, stationery that Tessa might say is also the goods of the braggart.

Shortly after the note incident, Diana began her work to try to get me to go to the funeral, which was being held near Fort Bragg. She started in slowly, saying how sad it was that we'd never taken the time to visit Buddy on our trips down to North Carolina. "Don't you think it's sad, Mac? I just think it's so sad!" I knew exactly what she was up to, my dainty Machiavelli, she whose narrative froth belies a stern taskmaster. One of the conversations on the funeral subject took place midmorning on a muggy Sunday, when our other daughters, Lyddie and Katie, had just shuffled in, their eyes not yet fully open, the two of them unable to move without bumping into the island stools as they toasted their strawberry Pop-Tarts. Next, what did my culinary philistines do but brew their coffee in the French press. Lyddie was wearing a T-shirt with a photograph of a western lowland gorilla on the front, and on the back a Virginia Woolf quote: "Women have served all these centuries as looking-glasses possessing the magic and delicious power of reflecting the figure of man at twice its natural size." Where exactly did the savage in my daughters end and the sophisticate begin? To tip the scale, there was something glaringly primitive, downright Biblical, about their odor. Whenever they entered a room, the place immediately steamed up, a blast of all the fruits of the Garden: mangoes in their shampoo, kiwis in their shaving cream, peaches in their lip gloss, pineapple in their deodorant. Cucumbers, the lone vegetable, graced their conditioner.

"Mac, sweetheart," Diana said, her voice rising a pitch or two, "this is what people do. They go to funerals."

"People," I replied into my coffee, "do all kinds of things." I had only the morning before seen a man who had managed to insert, or more probably have inserted, a hardball the size of a grapefruit into his rectum. Not a detail I would have brought up at the breakfast table, or at any time of day for that matter, but an argument, nonetheless.

"Why are you so stubborn?"

"Stubborn?"

She groaned softly—or, rather, she growled. When she does that she shakes her head, setting her dark curls atremble. She is the prettiest of her sisters, their features thick where hers are delicate, their eyes blue with light lashes, hers black, and one of them on a perpetual and ineffectual diet. Diana's springy tresses are her bane and my pride. She has never had any interest, none, in knowing that the wonder of her hair depends on the number of disulfide bonds between hair proteins in their shafts.

"He's not stubborn, Mom," Lyddie, the firstborn, said. "He just doesn't have pods of well-developed friendship the way we do."

"He's like the silent guy at the end of the block," Katie said, "the one you'd never suspect would go shoot all the kids in the library. Not that Dad would, but if he did you'd be totally surprised—and then sort of like, 'Oh! I get it.' "

They had the habit of speaking about me as if I were not present. Tessa, having entered quietly, stared at her sister. "Sometimes, Katie, I swear to God, you say the most imbecilic things."

"Kate's got a point," Lyddie said, she who was planning to study the law. She then launched into the story the girls seem never to tire of about the time I was watching a video of a new surgical procedure. It was a heart surgery, as I recall, angioplasty perhaps, and while I was watching I guess I was eating a stack of blueberry pancakes. They like to tell how the deep reddish-purple of the berries stained the plate and napkin and my teeth, as on the screen blood spattered the surgeon's gown.

Lyddie has my aunt Figgy's freckled skin, wavy hair, and the note-worthy bosom. Like Figgy, she is full of fun, capable and shrewd, dead serious when it comes to her goals. She intends to be a criminal law-yer and then a district attorney and eventually a judge. Katie is the youngest, plush and blond, enough bulk to be a good softball player, the Maciver among her sisters who has no enthusiasm for academics. She is a brave girl to have come in her brother's place. Tessa is straight and thin, small-boned like her mother, with a sharp chin and nose, the moodiest of the lot. She reads books quickly and compulsively, paper-back after paperback, as if she might drift away without the anchor of the printed page. Historically, until the older girls' college years, Lyddie mothered Katie. Tessa and Katie fought with their claws. And Lyddie and Tessa slew each other with words.

At one point, when Diana was still exhorting me to go to the fu-neral, Tessa leaned over the upstairs railing into our almost entirely open first floor, the great room a drafty three stories, and called, the-atrically, "Don't make him go, Mom! Buddy's what, a corporal or a major? How embarrassing for Dad."

Tessa has the gift—or foolishness—of finding clues where there may be none, of believing, as she noses around in her quarry's psyche, that even if she can't quite pinpoint the mystery, there is indeed *some-thing*. Buddy's son, not so much older than Tessa, was going to arrive in the U.S.A. in the customary coffin draped with Old Glory. He would be on the tarmac, one of the boxes in one of the rows. Had my mother been alive, I feel sure she would have had a momentary startle, grim satisfaction her involuntary response to this saddest of outcomes.

"You are president of the Youth Symphony Board," my wife re-minded me, "a library trustee, a founder of the homeless shelter, and, let's not forget, at the top of your profession. I'm sure you can face your cousin, honey, and be of comfort to him. You were so close!"

"Yeah, Dad," Lyddie said. "Get over yourself."

They all laughed. Tessa had gone beyond hearing range and was not there to defend me. It is a chronic amusement, to be surrounded on your own grounds by no one but women, including the dog, Nancy, the Rhodesian ridgeback, and at one time a girl hamster named Sammy. The holding is twelve acres, much of it landscaped, with a six-thousand-square-foot post-and-beam house, moderately efficient, and a three-car garage. The kitchen, which Diana calls Contemporary Country, reflects her rural upbringing and also her modern tastes. There is a gingham wallpaper design, tile inserts of farmyard animals here and there on the countertops, dried flowers hanging from the always freshly polished copper pots, but amid that rustication—boo!—an eight-burner Viking stove, a pantry with a thousand-bottle wine cellar, and a stainless-steel refrigerator the size of a tanker. Her cookbooks suggest that she has eaten at the restaurants of the great American chefs and that she believes in the slow-food movement. At the dinner hour there is no luckier man than I.

At the time the house was built, it was Diana's dream come true, along with the grape arbor, the apple orchard, and the bower of lilacs. Her latest wish to perfect that dream is a lap pool in a solarium. I have brought on the accounts and shown her our debt load, and I've reminded her how many times the house has already been in the Annual Hospital Tour of Homes, the doctors showing off their goods but of course for charity. Diana reads optimistic fiction in which, as far as I can tell, the heroine discovers her inner strength and lives out her life feeding off that rich core. In the end, both she and I know, she will get her way.

Nothing for the lone male to do but retreat into the paterfamilias silence, far away and yet close enough to hear, when they are home, the rushing murmur of the girls' endless chatter and internecine squabbles. To contain my love for them, I have a room far from the hub—"the cell," they call it—where I have amassed my books. It is there that I close my door and take up the histories of the ancient world, from 1999 backward.

* * *

IN CHILDHOOD, when a matter of a few months separated the men from the youths, Buddy was nearly two years my senior; I was the second oldest, and there were four boy cousins under me. There was, in addition, a much younger bunch we paid no attention to. The five of us, the elders, could not count ourselves in the same stratum as the master, and we gladly submitted to Buddy's command. It was we, I later thought, who trained him to be an officer, serving courageously in Vietnam, the recipient of ribbons and medals, including a Silver Star. After his initial tour as a guard, he re-enlisted, the second time with the First Logistical Command, working the supply lines from Da Nang. Through the years he made his way up the echelons, a career military man, until, as Tessa suggested, he was some kind of chieftain—a sergeant first class, last I'd heard.

How well he'd turned out, and against all the early predictions. In his school days he was no scholar, much to his mother's mortification. There was naturally talk in the family about the fluke, the genetic near impossibility, that Harvard and Radcliffe graduates, Figgy and Bill Eastman, had produced a boy who not only had average intelligence but was almost held back in the third grade. Had he been dropped on his head as an infant, or deprived of oxygen for a minute at birth? The relatives seemed not to consider that he didn't care enough about his studies to apply himself, that he had no academic interests, that he filled in the circles at random on standardized tests. There was fresh incredulity and some glee among the aunts when they'd managed to learn that he'd scored in the 20th percentile on his Iowa Basic Test of Skills in the eighth grade.

He made slightly above-average trouble as a teenager, before he was shipped off to a military academy, but on the whole it was trouble for its own sake. He wasn't angry or sullen, didn't hold a grudge against any particular person. His intentions, that is, were pure. Why not set a cornfield on fire at the lake—not just a corner flaring up, but the windy night sweeping the flames, one end to the other, five acres ravaged? That the barn and farmhouse hadn't been lost was a testament to the volunteer fire department. Even Buddy admitted it had gotten out of hand. There were other pyrotechnics no less exhilarating, tying M-80s to bricks and throwing them in the water to blow up the overgrown greasy carp. The fatsos of the fish world, he maintained, deserved to be obliterated. His need to rid the lake of aquatic ugliness seemed connected to our grandfather's wish to preserve the loveliness of the butterflies, and my father's trapping birds to immortalize their plumage. Buddy always managed to get hold of illegal fireworks, and up in the west pasture we were at least once a summer in the paradise of explosives. It probably goes without saying that there was nothing funnier in all the world than Buddy igniting his farts with a Bic lighter.

He went to jail only once, for taking an ambulance on a joy ride. That was something we only heard about. I was glad also to miss the shaving of the cat down to its whiskers, the animal staggering around the yard as if it had been blinded. Perhaps his most whimsical stunt took place after they moved to Washington, D.C., when he sneaked backstage in a high-school auditorium and inserted himself into the second act of *Brigadoon*, hamming it up in the dance line to amaze the leading lady. He'd had the foresight, the genius, to rent a kilt. Figgy had never been more embarrassed by her son, but only because the ingenue was the daughter of a member of President Kennedy's Cabinet, either Transportation or Agriculture. Shortly after that episode, Buddy was sent to the academy in West Virginia.

There was no end of Buddy stories, including the one about the girl who got pregnant, who had to go all the way to Tokyo to have her abortion and get over him. There were the stories, and there were the snapshots of his feats, water-skiing with theatricality and daring, playing tennis with panache, grace notes in his serve before the slam. His lips had that turned-inside-out puffiness, and yet the pillow of the upper lip was finely sculpted, the refinements people pay great sums of money for nowadays. The big joker mugged for the camera, that mouth puckered up, ready to kiss. Although I'd learned to expect it, he always managed to tackle me when I wasn't ready, even if I thought I was on guard. I'd find myself suddenly on the floor of the forest, Buddy yelling at me to fight him. "Stop being puny, Brains! Take me down, take me down!" I don't think he really meant me to, because he usually jumped me when the others were watching, to prove, I guess, that he was the stronger and also that there were limits to his ability to force my or anyone else's success. "How're you going to get out of this hold, huh? Huh? Stick your ass up, your wimpy little ass, come on, use your legs, use your legs, what are you made of?" And so forth.

At night, as I said, he gave us indispensable advice. His verbal skills were not exceptional, but he was a good mimic, and he was also an exhibitionist—and why not, since he was lean and muscular and immoderately well hung? We took it for granted that he was right to show off. Without his clothes on, and bouncing as best he could on the thin cot, he made sexual intercourse seem like an activity that was best performed on a trampoline, something that added to my anxiety about girls. Even in the guttering light his prowess was plain to see, and so we understood that any slight he received in school or on the playing field was an error, an injustice, a violation of the truth. He used to organize the five of us for pranks, and he was able to do this with great efficiency because he made it clear that he, and only he, knew our characters. He'd stand on the dock with his arms crossed over his bare chest, surveying the group, taking stock again of our strengths and weaknesses, our basic selves, which were so difficult to hide from him.

My grandmother owned the lake compound near Antigo, and she stayed all summer, making sure, she thought, that her grandchildren followed the rules. Boys past the age of six used the outhouse or the bushes, no matter the weather. Boys were never under any circumstances to come into the house to bathe, and only if they were near death could they sleep in the closet-sized room off the parlor. Boy creatures washed in lake water with lumps of scratchy white soap, did their business in the wild, and remained healthy. The girls, the young misses, were not allowed in our domain, in the upper boathouse, on pain of a punishment that would surely humiliate all of us. I imagined

our having to line up in the living room, my grandmother's demanding we speak about our misdeeds, her calling on us, displeased and
indeed violated by every word we said. When I thought of the inter-
rogation, of her disappointment and disgust—which we had brought
upon ourselves—I felt near to vomiting. Buddy always reassured us,
telling us that if we followed his directions we wouldn't get caught.
Thus was our path charted for us; thus was it our duty to cross the
unyielding line.

There were two or three plots we used to gain entrance to the
girls' quarters, in the long hours of the afternoon or the darkest night,
so that we could execute the time-honored violations, short-sheeting
the beds, tucking salamanders into neatly folded clothes, plunking tur-
tles in the toilets, and once, we stood sentry for Buddy while he spent
an hour with Cousin Mona. That evening we were sick with excitement and wonder, and never again could we look Mona in the eye.

It must be said that the four girls our age retaliated more or less in
kind. They TP-ed the inside of the boathouse every year, a trick that
always gratified them, rolls of toilet paper crisscrossing the open room
so densely it was impossible to move from one end to the other. They
managed to do half the job the year I was fourteen, while we slept.
Buddy was visiting for a weekend, the extent of his time with us that
summer, and it was he who woke and captured two of them. He told
Pammy to stay, and then he heaved Mona, the most comely, over his
shoulder, and walked with her down the stairs and out to the dock. No
doubt being thrown in the lake by Buddy was what she'd hoped for,
what she'd planned. He didn't push her but lowered her lovingly into
the glassy water, slipping in after her, moving quietly out to the raft.
They probably only took off some of their clothes at the ladder. The
rest of us, including the other hostage, sat around on the beds, rubbing
our eyes, unable to think what to do that might somehow match
Buddy's fun, or anyway the story he would tell when he was finished.

Although all of it seems innocent now, and harmless, what I remember is my terror of Grandmother, the idea of her wrath. In truth,

she was as mild a Victorian as they come, a woman who loved the thought of her family surrounding her even as she found it wearying. She did narrow her eyes down the table at us for an infraction as inevitable as belching; of course she did, because she was sure that if civility was taught to a child everything else of importance—schooling, profession, marriage—would fall into place. Her round face was weathered, and she wore her steel-colored hair in a loose bun. Even when she smiled fondly, I thought her severe. I suppose I dreaded what might come on the heels of her disapproving glances because Buddy claimed she'd once whipped him with a stick. That punishment, he explained sagely, had had the effect of making him her favorite. Outside of her stern word—"Hush!"—and her strict adherence to the rules of cards and parlor games, she never lived up to her tyrannical reputation; that is, she never found us out, she never had to exercise her dreadful power. Years later, I learned that one summer she'd demanded my mother join her in a raid of the boathouse, that Grandmother trembled at the thought of disciplining the younger boys, who she was certain had beer. Grandmother afraid of us! How dare she invert the world order and think us fearsome.

In those days I also quaked to think that Buddy would find out just how chickenhearted I was. He could see clearly that I was a weakling, but I hoped he didn't realize the depths of my cowardice. I was frightened of footsteps in the night, robbers in the kitchen, their climbing, climbing up the stairs to my room, wherein I would be smothered. I was afraid that a funnel cloud would sweep me away and set me down in a stranger's living room. What to say? Where would I sleep? Of course I feared the Russians, such cruelty in their thick accents and their bleak homeland. I was afraid of measles and meningitis, diseases that would blind me or kill me or, worse, reduce my brain to pulp. There was a man in the next block at home, Mikey O'Day, who it was said might have been the next Einstein if a fever hadn't turned him into a lunatic.

The only danger I loved, the only time I was thrilled being frightened, was in Buddy's company. We'd creep through the grass, Buddy either scouting out ahead of us or, more often, in the rear, watching the movement of his troops, making sure each boy played his role. He called me Brains in a jaunty, self-deprecating way, and I took him at his word: "You're the great mind here, so pipe up with your suggestions." I did have an educated knowledge of the grown-ups' patterns, because I had the habit of lingering at the supper table out on the cookhouse porch. It was often restful, sitting alone in the midst of the adults, unnoticed, listening and not listening to their arguments, waiting until the secret box of chocolates was taken from its hidden place and indiscriminately passed hand to hand. So it wasn't all dull, as the other boys thought. And sometimes the conversation, idling along, would flare up, the gibes tilting beyond good humor, the voices tuning higher, the summer heat rising.

The Macivers were fast eaters, gobbling their meat, swallowing in a hurry what they had not taken care to chew. Those indelicate manners must have come from the fur-trader line, from the ancestors who'd make a hasty rabbit stew over a small fire, eating quickly in case the enemy lurked. Therefore, the descendants with nothing to fear couldn't help savaging their sweet corn and swilling down the apple sauce. When the job was soon done, they'd sit for hours in front of their dirty plates, picking at the bones and drinking, the Roosevelt Democrats, the Adlai Stevenson zealots, some of them table bangers, versus those who were smugly in the Eisenhower camp. I could report to Buddy that the mothers were unpredictable in their movements, getting up now and again to check on the babies, and sometimes, according to my mother, dropping asleep on the nursery floor, finally, at odd hours, tiptoeing through the creaking house to their rightful beds. The fathers—how enlightened they were—often did the dishes, their talk drifting out the windows, carrying over the lake as our battalion prowled along the side of the fence. We could hear them when Petie shinnied up the trunk of the arborvitae onto the roof, when he threw down a ladder of dubious strength that we'd fashioned of rags in the afternoon.

We all went for the month of August in that golden age, my parents; my sister, Louise, who was two years younger than I; and of course Madeline. The 1950s and even the 1960s stretched on indefinitely, that everlasting period before my mother and Figgy had their break. Didn't they then miss each other, they who seemed to be opposites and yet were from much the same New England stock, both born and bred in the heartland? My mother hailed from a Quaker family of modest means, the Beeson parents treating their two children with respect and teaching them to do good works. The Macivers, with their old money and six children, had the same starch even if their philanthropy was showier. Figgy did carry herself as if the Boston bluebloods had been waiting for years for her to arrive in Harvard Square. She must have known, though, that she needed her own kind at Radcliffe, someone like my mother in her inner circle, a girl from home who could check her now and again. My mother, for her part, oppressed by the venerable institution, was often buoyed up by the antics of her saucy roommate.

I suppose the two of them had always had what you might call friendly arguments, long before the 1960 presidential campaign, and well before my mother left Radcliffe. After her junior year, Julia came home to Chicago to go to a Catholic women's college for her nursing degree. "Wait," Figgy said to her at the time, "wait just a minute. Listen to me. No one, no one drops out of Radcliffe and then enrolls in St. Anne's. And no one who was raised a Quaker, for Christ's sake, goes to St. Anne's. What the hell is the matter with you? You can't give this up just because your father is sick! A hair shirt, Julia, is not a garment that's particularly becoming, especially on someone with your frame."

Figgy was bronzed and busty, on the dock her cleavage glowing as far as the eye could see. She wore one-piece bathing suits that had sashes and sparkles and little skirts. What a contrast to my mother's standard-issue high-school swim-class tank, a suit made from a thick, dull cotton that never dried, with a panel across the front thighs, the V of the crotch never to be seen.

If you had seen my mother in her prim swimming costume, you wouldn't have suspected that she could keep up during happy hour, starting with scotch on the lawn and moving on to the gallon jugs of wine through dinner and afterward. The sky went rosy beyond the trees and then to black while she and Figgy's new husband, Arthur, the Yale man, bantered with a lively step, with a happiness that kept me at the table. I liked Arthur very much, not only because everyone said he was brilliant, because he was well on his way to becoming someone, but because of the interest he took in me and also the way he spoke to my mother. I knew it was possible he loved her, but of course in the proper brotherly manner. Certainly in the beginning, when Figgy brought Arthur to show him off, my mother was the favorite of his in-laws. He had wonderfully smooth skin for a man, a blush down his jaw, and sleek black hair that he combed away from his forehead, such health from the Ivory Tower. In the early days of Figgy's marriage, his enthusiasm for us seemed sincere. He listened with real thoughtfulness, as if nothing engaged him more than our ideas and hobbies. He wanted to know why my mother didn't trust the Kennedys, not the father, not the sons, and why she could make her pronouncements with careless verve.

"Kennedy's going to take us to war if he gets elected," she said over her plate heaped with corncobs. "Because, Art, because he's going to have to do something to prove he's as anticommunist as the big boys. The way he's been raving about Cuba, he makes Nixon sound like a dove."

Arthur had black-framed glasses tight to his face, and behind those lenses soft dark eyes, slightly thyroidal, bovine in their lashy sweetness. "Mrs. Maciver," he said soothingly, adjusting himself in his seat, coming close to the edge, readying himself for the night's work, "I suspect you haven't gotten over Stevenson's failure to beat Ike, two failed presidential races, such a shame. Still in mourning. But you don't strike me as an alarmist. Let's talk about the personalities in this race for a minute, aspects that have been troubling certain people." He ran his tongue over his top lip and then wiped the edges of his mouth with his thumb and index finger. "You don't mind at all about Jack Kennedy's Catholicism, for instance, but I'll bet Nixon's brand of evangelical Quakerism offends you."

Arthur could call Kennedy "Jack" because he was personally acquainted with him. My mother smiled broadly at her brother-in-law and batted her short eyelashes, something I'd never seen her do before. "I only want a president who's Episcopalian," she said. "I only vote for candidates who were once junior vestrymen and senior vestrymen and after that senior wardens."

That, apparently, was FDR's religious-education profile. Arthur nodded approvingly, not perhaps because of her love for Roosevelt but because of the particularity of her knowledge. In less than a year's time, he would go to work in the Kennedy administration, in the State Department, Arthur Fuller, part of the famous brain trust. The other aunts and uncles talked politics as most of us do, from our corners, without much historical context for our own thinking, and without an idea of the real personalities who affect the backroom discussions. Arthur, we all knew, spoke from an intimate understanding of the players, and a deep command and even experience of world affairs. If he was a frightening man, it was only because he grasped how dangerous other people were. On the occasions when he didn't offer an opinion, or the facts, it was out of discretion; it was because he was trustworthy.

While my mother and Arthur, and sometimes Figgy, too, were flirting with each other at the table, my father was off shining his flashlight at the bats up in the barn for the little boys, or in bed with one of the books of his childhood, *Penrod* or *Stalky and Company*. Arthur and Mrs. Maciver, in the meantime, were possibly the only people after dinner in Antigo, Wisconsin, that summer of 1960, who on several occasions discussed the fighting that was already going on in Southeast Asia. It was funny, I thought, how he called her Mrs. Maciver, as if she deserved that respect, or as if he, and only he, were allowed to mock her in that simple way.

"It's clear, Mrs. Maciver, that Laos is where the next crisis is going to take place. But let me ask you this. You really think North and South Vietnam would be fighting again if we'd used massive retaliation in '54, what Dulles was pushing for? You can't tell me that the postwar ambivalence hasn't been a disaster for Indochina."

"Art, Art, Art!" No one but my mother called him Art. "Dulles wanted to use nuclear weapons against the Vietminh. He recommended—"

"Yes, yes, he did. Quick and effective, as opposed to this bloody struggle that drags on and will continue to drag on. It's a complicated issue, isn't it, both sides with valid arguments. Do you bomb a hundred thousand civilians, women, children, to destroy Hitler's war machine? Let me take a wild guess where you come down. You'd like everyone at the United Nations to sit around a very large table and have a good long talk. The Reds and the Free World sharing Danishes, rice cakes, *pampushki,* orange juice, and vodka in the morning, another round of stimulating talks in the afternoon, and by cocktail hour everyone is holding hands and singing, 'Peace, I ask of thee old r-i-i-iver, peace, peace, peace.' " He had a light baritone, and everyone laughed at his lovely rendition of absurdity. "Do you think, Mrs. Maciver, that the fall of China was of any consequence?"

My mother always looked well when she was with Arthur on the porch, and sometimes, with a drink in one hand, she'd reach across the table for Figgy's cigarettes, all debauchery and merriment. "I think," she'd say, "what you fellows misjudge is the force of communism in Indochina, a force you believe transcends nationalism. Vietnam's interest in communism is trifling compared to their wish for self-rule."

He'd study her over his glasses for a minute, chin to chest, and then he'd want to know what she'd been reading, who she'd been talking to, how she'd arrived at her opinion. For a while they might review, harking back to the Han Dynasty, an ancient time when the Chinese had first overthrown the Kingdom of Nam Viet. My mother was perfectly able to interject and correct through the history before they returned to their initial positions—Arthur insisting that China was using Vietnam as its proxy to spread communism through the region, that substantial bombing would have settled the matter with fewer casualties than there'd already been; Mrs. Maciver holding firm about Vietnam's wanting little more than self-determination.

Julia's nonchalance about the dangers of communism on the other side of the world was considered a sign of perilous ignorance, but even so on those nights Arthur had the charity to seem both amused by her ideas and intrigued by her logic. At first she hadn't approved of Figgy's divorcing her Harvard man, Buddy's father, and running off when the baby was only four toward Arthur Fuller. But once Julia had met the replacement, she could hardly keep casting judgment. Figgy, after all, clearly had made a bad choice in Bill Eastman, had been charmed by his pedigree and his bucking of it. She had been sure his aspirations to be an artist would pass. For a time they'd lived the bohemian life on the Lower East Side, playing at being poor among those who were genuinely talented and poverty-stricken. It turned out, however, that Bill was able to lose money nearly as quickly as the trust fund was turned over to him, and he was also unreliable in every other respect. He died of alcohol poisoning when Buddy was seventeen. Arthur, in contrast, was not only wholesomely fun-loving, but a whippersnapper professor at Princeton, a think-tanker with important friends, piles of dough, a frugal nature, and an island off the coast of Maine. For example, whenever Figgy and Arthur came to Moose Lake they always had to stop in Chicago to have dinner with Leo Strauss.

The late night I remember in particular took place after the honeymoon with us was over for Arthur, or maybe everyone was exhausted from vacation, tired of sunburns and water sports and long afternoons, tired of there always being someone to talk to, tired of cooking for thirty, meal after meal. Possibly Arthur's grace period for us lasted only a few weeks rather than years, although it did seem to me then that they'd been discussing Kennedy's nomination for several seasons. The conversations I've recalled may have taken place all in one evening, or may have been spread out over many days, no way now to tell. In any case, around midnight I'd come back to the summer kitchen, hoping to find another slice of cake. My mother and Arthur were both speaking loudly, and I wondered if they'd drunk more than they'd meant to. "You cannot be serious, Mrs. Maciver!" His cigarette was burning to ash between his fingers. "To say that war is wrong is to say that existence is wrong. Don't interrupt me again, I know what point you—"

"We understand more than ever the cost of war, Arthur. That's what we're talking about here. I'm not saying private transformation—what is required to change society—won't take generations. But I believe, I do believe it is within our power to evolve as a species."

I knew enough to be embarrassed for my mother, talking about private transformation with Arthur. I understood in broad terms that he was a realist, his eye to our vital national interests and the balance of power, someone who could see all the rulers across the globe poised as they were about to make their incautious or evil moves.

Arthur yawned. "Private transformation, oh my, yes. To protect what we love, my dear—in fact, to love—is to have to fight against those who can't love. Every schoolboy knows this. Every babe in the woods who has lived through the last twenty years understands that we make war of course so that we may live in peace."

"Those who can't love," my mother repeated. "Those who can't love because the class system has relegated them to poverty, the class system has deprived them of education." Her voice was growing louder. "Schoolboys and schoolgirls know what injustice is on their first step on the playground, and the sensitive begin to realize the value of civil disobedience in the fight against injustice in junior high, when they read Thoreau—"

And then he said it, the line everyone would remember for years to come. "Oh, for Christ's sake, Julia!" He slammed the table with his fist. "To love," he cried, "to love means we must kill."

The two of them were speechless for a minute, she dumbfounded because he was in earnest now, the coquetry stripped back to reveal the self, and he startled that he'd said that truth in her company. "You listen to me," my mother said, rising from her seat.

He beat her to center stage, leaping onto his chair, raising his fist, and bellowing the usual war cry:

"Once more unto the breach, dear friends, once more;
Or close the wall up with our English dead.
In peace there's nothing so becomes a man
As modest stillness and humility:
But when the blast of war blows in our ears,
Then imitate the action of the tiger;
Stiffen the sinews, summon up the blood,
Disguise fair nature with hard-favour'd rage . . ."

I suspect Figgy loved Arthur best when he was dazzlingly goofy. She clapped, she swooped up and reached for his hand, as if he were a famous crooner on the stage. He bounced down and let her embrace him, and when that was over she dragged my mother from her seat, her arm around her old friend, no hard feelings. Most of the others got up, too, well on their way to their hangovers. Grandmother, on the far end of the house, would have been long asleep.

Still, my mother couldn't leave on the note of theatrics and poetry. As she cleared the last of the bottles from the table she said, "I have no doubt that you'll get to Washington, Art, that one way or another you're going to have a part to play. You've been well groomed for your role." Was there disdain in her voice? "What troubles me is the fact that you, your ilk, those of you who govern, see suffering as an abstraction. As has happened since time out of mind, you men make war without having to fight it."

Arthur had a bad back and had not gone overseas in World War II. But he had served for a few years, working in Washington, in Intelligence. My mother might have known that he would loom up over the table, one hand in a pool of spilled wine, the other in a smear of butter. "My ilk, Mrs. Maciver? My ilk?" He had tried to defuse the argument with Shakespeare, and there she was again, provoking him. "You think your guy, Stevenson, understands power and force, much less keeping the peace? You think so? He'd like nothing better than secretary of state under Kennedy, but he'll never get that appointment. This is a man who spends his morning deciding when he's going to take a shit. It's all fine, Julia, all very sweet to worry about hunger and poverty the world around. It's all very well to dedicate yourself with elegant turns of phrases to a fuzzy idea of morality as you search for world opinion——"

My mother put out her hand to stop his speech. Over his noise she said, "The fact remains, you will never be on the front lines! You will always now, if you get to Washington, when you get there, be one of those who draft policy, who will make orders that will kill our sons."

Arthur, I knew, would never do anything of the kind. He and I had gone out in the tin boat to fish, and all through the early-morning quiet he had talked about the physiology of invertebrates, about Wisconsin waterways and glaciers, about the Algonquian tribes; he'd told me how best to spear a beaver. There was no subject he didn't know about or want to understand, and I was sure he would do all he could under any circumstance to keep Buddy and me out of danger.

My mother must have at an earlier time admitted to Arthur that she was something of a lapsed Quaker. She must have explained that she no longer attended Meeting because three of the ladies who always spoke, who went on at length about the beauties of this world, distracted her from the inner light. She would have liked them to shut up. That night on the eating porch, Arthur put his arm around her and kissed her cheek, something she submitted to a little stiffly, I thought. "If you really think Kennedy is the hawk, Mrs. Maciver, then vote for your fellow Friend, Richard Milhaus. He may take you back to the faith."

Figgy was indulging me in the kitchen, scooping another lump of ice cream onto a second piece of cake. She called out, "You talk as if Kennedy has already been elected and declared war, Julia. What the hell is the matter with you? You seem to forget he's experienced combat. He's not going to be eager to stir up trouble. For once we have the chance to have a sexy president—come on, give in to his handsome mug. I know you're not going to vote for ugly old Nixon, so why haul yourself kicking and screaming into the future? Our man has a sense of destiny not only for himself but for the nation."

My mother had come to the sink with the empty bottles. "If he wins," she said, "it will be because his poppa buys the office for him, just as he bought the Senate seats for his boys."

Figgy flicked the lights. "It's late, love. It's later than it's ever been up here. It's bedtime. Kennedy for president! Good night."

My aunt's womanly intuition told her that her husband was going to Washington, that he was going to be important, and that she, Mrs. Arthur Fuller, would be invited to have tea with Mrs. Kennedy on several occasions. Also, they'd enroll Buddy in a private school along with other White House staff children. Finally, he'd start to make something of himself.

Chapter Four

THERE WERE A FEW STORIES MY AUNT LIKED TO TELL ABOUT
Madeline, but none gave her so much pleasure as "the Italian
episode," as she called it. Through the years, the Moose Lake
house, the broad front porch gave Figgy and me the opportunity
to talk about the family, to cloak those conversations, that
gossip, in the mantle of history. Because I was the closest of the
cousins in age to Buddy, because he and I were nearly brothers
for a time, she felt an affinity for me that she did not have with
the other boys. Although I've heard the Italian episode on
several occasions, I didn't understand her relish in it until fairly
recently. I thought she enjoyed it primarily because it was the
single complete story from Madeline's life before she was ours.
The big event, Figgy would say, in Miss Schiller's record as
herself.

"Did I ever tell you about the Italian episode?" she'd say.

"Remind me," I always said.

We might be in the dark on the Moose Lake porch, or in a
café in New York City. "Miss Schiller," she'd muse, as if she
could conjure the woman she'd known briefly. "Miss Schiller."
Wherever we were, the Italian episode began with Madeline's
high-school graduation, Mother Schiller watching the boys
parade across the stage as if they were auditioning for the role
of her daughter's husband. The day after the ceremony, Mrs.
Schiller took Madeline to Italy to shop for clothes, to look at
the famous paintings, and, most important, to send picture

postcards to the neighbors: *We stood in a swoon in the Bargello.* One afternoon in Florence, Madeline managed to escape the hotel, to take a
walk across the Piazza Santa Croce alone. She had grown tired of being forced to feel in front of the broken statues, all those lost arms and
blank eyes, and the unconvincing marble swirls of pubic hair. In that
free quarter-hour, Madeline at last was at liberty to develop her own
sensations. The Italian who provoked her had dark curls and, let's say,
the famous Florentine smile and the liquid eyes. Although Madeline
needed no special effects, it would be tempting to report that she
seemed to be lit from within, that the piazza around her, the pale gold
of the early-afternoon sun framing her, had made her seem other-
worldly. He came steaming to her from the other side on his bike, riding it scooter-style, pushing off, both feet on the same pedal. When he
got close he was unnerved and lost his balance. *Dio mio!* The only
person in all of the piazza and he comes at her as if he meant to run her
over. He had to drop the handlebar, falling into her, the two of them
clutching each other, trying to remain upright. As he got hold of himself he managed to say, "At this moment—I see in the piazza the angel." He reached out with just the right amount of hesitation, Buddy
might have said, and touched her cheek. "Are you—true?"

"So much of Madeline's fate involved the bicycle," Figgy always
said at that point.

Two days later, when Mrs. Schiller came into Madeline's room at
the pension in the morning and found the girl missing, she recalled the
handsome stranger in the lobby the night before, the same man—
wasn't he?—they'd seen behind the counter at the leather store. Before she phoned the police, she demanded that the desk clerk arrange
for two tickets on the earliest departing train to anywhere else. The
mother apparently had had previous experience combating her daughter's passions. When Madeline stole into her room before breakfast,
she found her bags packed. Mrs. Schiller, dressed in her gray traveling
suit and her hat with the plume, came briskly through the door to an-
nounce the waiting taxi.

There was no use protesting that the night had passed in chaste getting-to-know-you activities, the walk in the dark up to San Miniato, the church door magically open, the two of them sitting together, huddling, if the mother must know, in the chill, teaching each other to speak. An Italian lesson, that was all. Wasn't really the shopping, the Fendi handbag and the pink silk dress, for the purpose of becoming acquainted with just such a man—a man with a solid family business? There'd been the stroll in the dawn to his house, the parents' apartment, where they made hot chocolate. After that consoling drink he took her downstairs to knock on the window of the baker, begging him to let the *signorina* have a sweet pastry fritter. The mother would have none of it, and away they went, Madeline in that tragic pose, turned to look longingly through her tears out the back window of the taxi all the way to the train station.

For some time afterward, she had a secret correspondence with the Italian. She understood that he'd gotten married or killed when the letters came back to her unopened via the friend who'd served as the accomplice. She was inconsolable for months, so the story went, until my father rescued her from her grief. I like to believe that Madeline had gotten over Italy, that in the first year of her marriage the doe-eyed man careening across the piazza never intruded upon her fantasy of the future Maciver infants asleep in their cribs.

Although the Schillers had nothing to recommend themselves, Figgy couldn't help approving the story of the Italian. If there was anything she might love Miss Schiller for, let it be her pluck, for that single night shivering with the ghouls and the handsome leather salesman up in San Miniato. When I once asked Figgy why she liked that story, which was after all a fairly ordinary schoolgirl story, she looked at me with pity, as if she'd just realized I'd been too young to hear such a tale. And she was right, I was too young—but that was something it would take me years to know.

Chapter Five

THREE YEARS AFTER MADELINE'S ACCIDENT, MY PARENTS
married in a chapel up near Moose Lake. It was a brief
ceremony, and except for Figgy and Bill Eastman, none of the
170 people from the first Maciver wedding were invited. Figgy
and Bill in fact were the only witnesses. My mother's parents
were dead, and the one brother in California did not make the
trip. There was no mention in the Chicago paper of one Julia
Beeson marrying Aaron Maciver, no cascade of wedding gifts,
no rehearsal dinner or reception. You could say that they
practically eloped, or that they wanted their marriage to be a
secret, but I think, more reasonably, my father, unlike his sister
and his first wife, was glad for any ritual to be a quiet affair. In
the single photo of the day, my mother, overtaken in a silver
box of a suit that belonged to Figgy, has her mouth wide open
in a madcap grin. Figgy has used that picture against her,
making predictable comments to me about how Julia had gone
cuckoo in the moment of her conquest. My father is holding
steady, looking straight at the camera. I imagine he's just made
a wry comment, the trials of his previous marriage having
cultivated in him a darker humor. He is probably wondering in
disinterested tones if his sister should be smoothing the collar
of the Reverend Monder's robe, and in such a casual manner.

They were, I'm certain, as straightforward as they could
be with Madeline, and yet during the engagement how could

they not have betrayed some nervousness? It was an unusual situation, to be sure, no books to guide them through a potentially difficult transition, and it's doubtful that Reverend Monder was of much use. They were going on a short trip, they explained, and when they came back, when they returned to Chicago, they'd live together in the new house. My parents spoke into the silence, Madeline all the while looking slantwise at the floor. They talked about it bit by bit several months in advance, about the time when they'd be married. There were several visits to the house, to stake out Madeline's bedroom, to show her the place in the backyard for the flower beds, to discuss where they'd put the furniture and how they might eventually buy a piano. It's possible, however, that they were vague about the hour and day of the wedding; as I heard the story, it was when Madeline went down to the lake with Grandmother that they took their leave to the chapel.

I often wonder what slivers of memory Madeline allowed herself. My wife now and again tells me I'm unusually romantic for a doctor of internal medicine. And so poetic. "Deep down," she adds. She will say so in company, putting her arms around me from behind and kissing the top of my head, Diana taking pity on me or chiding me or having a wistful thought. What poetry is to her I do not know. I like to think she means I'm still open to the notion of mystery. For the most part, I hope that Madeline had successfully and permanently repressed her other life, her girlhood, her marriage erased. In the early days of my practice, I had considered talking to my parents about having her evaluated. We could easily have consulted together with a neurosurgeon, and somewhat easily have comforted Madeline through the noise and confinement of an MRI. We might have begun to understand what areas of her brain were still active, what centers had developed in the absence of those that were damaged.

It was peculiar, how difficult it was to broach the subject. When I asked—for it was something that never came up—the accident always seemed a thing that had happened so long before, the circumstances of little consequence past the great and unalterable consequence. They did not perhaps want to remember the length of time in the hospital, the day-to-day hopes and crushing disappointments, and their fatigue when the patient was discharged into her new life. That they never asked me to consider her records or solicited advice in relation to her injury is, I suppose, a result of logical thinking on their part, of believing that she was always going to be as she was, something really we all accepted as a matter of faith.

She was emotionally unstable, she had trouble with games and puzzles that were past a second-grade level, she spoke loudly, she showed on some occasions signs of disinhibition, the pathological lack of inhibition, although she was also capable of restraint. At first, as is common in the brain-injured, she had short-term-memory disorder, paranoia, and depression; she perseverated, she lashed out, she was probably dysarthric, her slurred speech something my mother may have helped her overcome. As I remember her in my childhood, she often looked blank. If I now and then considered her injury, I imagined it as a blow that had dulled her thinking, that hadn't so much severed the connections, synapse to synapse, as it made the circuits weak, the electrical flash, if we could see it, a stuttering yellow, a reluctant flare.

Through our growing up, my mother so often explained to Madeline that she'd had an accident, using the line if Madeline had a headache, a frustration, an upset. She did enjoy looking at magazines, and dressing dolls and herself, her interest in fashion undisturbed. I still hope that her forebrain is capable of synthesizing good dream material from the bombardment of impulses sent up from the brain stem, that her night life is full of silks and glitter, feather boas and high-heeled shoes, the glamorous strut down the runway. When I was a teenager, my secret maudlin streak was far more pronounced, and even though I knew Madeline could not recover, I half believed that Louise's music could captivate her beyond the usual power of song, that the aching beauty of Bach's Cello Suites could repair—for a split second and in exact proportion, beauty to area—the scar tissue in the white matter.

Louise was a serious girl with thin brown hair to her waist, a girl who always won the stare-down contests. She had my father's build, the long torso, the skinny legs, but my mother's large quick hands. So, when it came time to sign up for a string instrument in the fourth grade, it was the cello for Lu. She had the predictable burst of enthusiasm at the start, practicing ostentatiously, first very carefully putting the parts of the stand together, extending the trunk, another inch, easy does it, back a touch, until it was the exact height for her proportions. She opened her book to the lesson, arranged the chair, this way, that way, and set out the metal circle on the carpet that would hold the cello's stem. From the crushed green velvet of her case she removed her bow, and from the handy compartment up by the scroll, the bar of rosin. The sumptuous velvet and mysterious scarlet insignia embossed on the rosin box lent the whole enterprise an air of mysticism. She tightened the screw of the bow, again making subtle adjustments to the tension, and then she nursed the rosin along the horsehair with such thoroughness she became cloudy with dust.

Whether it was the music itself or her teacher, the dashing Mr. Blau, Louise's enthusiasm extended beyond the initial rental period. She became obsessed with her cello, worshipping Mr. Blau and Johann Sebastian Bach, always referring to the master with his three-part name. A few years later, she also gave her heart to the ill-fated Jacqueline du Pré. My mother believed that music was the most spiritual of the arts, and she was all for my sister's devotion. But even she on occasion worried. That Lu would rather spend three hours practicing scales than playing kick-the-can on a summer night, that she couldn't break for five minutes for a Black Cow, seemed a sign of monomania rather than of a disciplined nature. My mother feared she'd make herself sick, that she'd shrivel without sunlight and exercise, or, worse, she once joked, that with her tendency for rapture she'd grow into the kind of fanatical teen who'd give herself up to a cult leader. Louise's lank hair fell down around her cello, and so it appeared that she and it were joined, were outgrowths of each other, that it would take nothing short of a treacherous surgery to separate the two.

In her high-school days, her friend Stephen Lovrek came over several times a week to accompany her on the piano. As far as I could tell they were not romantic—or not in the usual sense. The two of them were concordantly under the spell of certain passages, having their spasms at the same crescendo, throwing themselves over their instruments, their eyes closed, both of them grimacing, their heads rolling forward, shaking slowly, and then the sudden lift, the gaze heavenward. If you didn't know better, you might have thought the beauty they were making was measure by measure killing them. Stephen also had a dramatic head of hair, a dense hedge that loosened when he sweat, curls breaking out from that dark mass. He was very pale, as if he, too, spent little time in natural light, both he and Louise candidates for rickets. They hardly spoke—no need, it seemed, for words. He'd come through the front door at the appointed hour without knocking, walk into the living room; she'd indicate the page of music on the stand with her bow, that ancillary finger; he'd nod, taking his part from his briefcase. He'd twirl the round piano stool in search for the acceptable height, up and down on its screw until it was right where it had been when he'd begun. They'd tune, their bodies alert to the wave of the perfect A.

I used to sit at my desk upstairs and listen to them. The music made me sadder than just about any mournful thing I'd yet encountered, but all the same it was a sadness a person welcomed. I was of the age and had enough privilege to entertain a general sorrow about life. There was in addition the matter of my musical ability, a deficiency I couldn't seem to overcome. When I was fifteen, the choral teacher at school, desperate for boys, asked me to try out for one of her singing groups. After my rendition of "White Coral Bells," after an amazed silence, Mrs. Yarmell said they wouldn't be needing me that time around. She thanked me for my interest. Louise, trying as she occasionally did to be comforting, said that my singing had the unfocused sound of an air-raid siren, but a soft one, a lulling one. That is to say, I loved music the way a person who has his mouth sewn shut longs for food. In the darkness of my room, it seemed to me that everyone in the family was swept up by the piano and the cello, the long line of a phrase carrying us inside our own selves, as close to our selves as we could get. It sometimes seemed possible in the moment to hold the turmoil of the Romantics, or the straight, clean order of Bach, on the verge of that single tender point. There was a weird forgetting that occasionally happened, too, arriving somewhere past the self, I'd guess, held in time by nothing but the music.

My mother often took her spot in the old wing chair opposite the piano, and if she sat down, Madeline, two inches taller, was sure to follow, first perching on her lap and after a while stretching along the length of my mother's body. "Great big girl," my mother would say, shifting her weight, trying to get comfortable. Madeline, in her blue shorts, blond fluff down her legs, a finger in her mouth, listened to the Francoeur sonata, played perhaps here more plaintively, there more ecstatically than the Baroque composer had dared to dream. The way Madeline rested her head on my mother's shoulder, staring at the far wall, might well have made Julia wonder if the original Mrs. Maciver was thinking sad thoughts that had brought her to a point of stillness, or if she had the blankness of peace. My mother might also have asked herself what curse was on my father, that they'd produced a child who could play the cello so soulfully—of all the heart-wrenching instruments. He'd sit at the dining-room table pretending to read, his hands cupped at his ears.

We lived in the house that Figgy and Bill Eastman had helped my parents buy just after their wedding. It was a fresh start in a new place, a village to the west of Chicago, away from the more conservative North Side, our town the Parnassus of suburbia, leafy, enlightened, and dry, dry! Not a drop of likker to be bought or sold. It was an oasis of taste without excessive wealth, where even the Mob was considerate, doing its business out of earshot, out of sight. Somehow or other, without a tavern, spirits still ran high in the parishes. There were racial quotas to spur integration in the 1970s and, later, an ordinance to welcome gays and lesbians to the community. At some charmed point it became a nuclear-free zone, a fact that Pakistan, Iran, and North Korea will surely be sensitive to when they are launching their missiles. My mother, I think, played a part in that whimsical piece of legislation.

To help out with the housekeeping in the new neighborhood, and as a wedding gift, Grandmother Maciver gave her old cook and cleaning lady, Russia, to my mother, to have all day once a week. It was in addition to the great-grandmother's silver tea service and the English china that had in the first round been given to Madeline. The dishes were whisked away, wrapped up, and presented again. Russia and her husband, Elroy, had lived with my grandmother in the old days, in the era when even ordinary middle-class whites had live-in colored help.

"Persons of color, Dad!" my daughter Lyddie would correct.

"Let him talk in the language of his ignorant and unfeeling time." So would say Tessa, my champion.

By the 1940s, my grandmother had raised her children, lost her husband, and moved to an apartment; therefore she didn't need Russia more than once a week herself. Russia always said that Miz Maciver had been her best friend, that Miz Maciver made the promise that Russia would never be without the care of our family. My grandmother was able to keep the vow by making Russia indispensable to us. Russia Crockerby was laced into our everyday life for much of my childhood, and yet I didn't know much about her beyond the fact that she'd come from Mississippi when she was seventeen, with Elroy. At breakfast once, Louise set down her spoon and stared at Russia. "When," Louise said solemnly, "is your birthday?"

"Can't tell you, honey." Russia stirred her muddy coffee and raised the cup to her lips.

"What?" we said. "Why not?"

"They was too busy to notice the day."

"Not know your birthday!" we asked, again and again.

"Don't know the year, either."

"Not know how old you are?"

We couldn't get our minds around that blank in your own history, how formless the years would be without the one day around which all the others spun. It didn't occur to us that nobody in her house, not the seven siblings or the parents, could read or write, that documenting the names and dates in the Bible might have been impossible. We were less impressed with the idea that her grandmother had been a slave, so far back, in that time too far away to have been true. It was curious that Russia's family would have been "darkies," because Russia was hardly black, so light, faintly yellow if anything; if all her people were like that, it would have been hard, I thought, to discriminate on the plantation between the master's family and her relatives.

My grandmother, for her part in the friendship, would say that Russia understood her place. There was grace in such an arrangement, she declared, real value in knowing where you fit. A girl who'd come up from hardscrabble Mississippi had found her life in a family of means. Grandmother didn't have to explain that within that abiding Maciver structure Russia grew to understand how to exercise her will. Certainly no one in the Maciver clan, no one, underestimated Russia's power.

Every Wednesday for nearly fifty years, and also many other days in between, Russia drove from the South Side, where she lived first with her husband and later with her sister, to clean for my mother. On the back porch she removed her plastic boots rimmed with fur, then tiptoed through the kitchen in her stocking feet, looking strange and large in her driving clothes, in her plaid wool skirt, a cashmere sweater, a string of pearls around her neck, all hand-me-downs from my grandmother. She had a wide, flat face with dark spots on her light skin, and soft black hair. In the bathroom she'd change into her white uniform and cushioned shoes. She wasn't really Russia to us until she put on that uniform. While my mother fixed breakfast, Russia went downstairs to throw a load in the wash and set the iron to heating. For forty years, until my mother's death, she served Russia two boiled eggs in the blue egg cups, two pieces of doughy white bread toasted just enough to firm them up, two strips of bacon dewy with grease, and coffee brewed to sludge. There was nothing difficult about the menu, and yet if there was any meal my mother fussed over as a housewife it was Russia's toast and coffee. If there was any morning when my mother felt ashamed of herself it was Wednesday, when she had not cleared off her dresser to Russia's specifications. It became a joke between them, my mother's squalor, her books and papers and powders, and Russia's stagy bright-eyed hope and disappointment, followed by hope-for-tomorrow.

Madeline always came in the kitchen and leaned against my mother at the table while they ate. "You look so pretty today, Miz Madeline," Russia would say. "Prettiest girl in the house, yes, ma'am. Ain't that right, Miz Julia?"

"Prettiest girl," my mother would agree.

I thought it funny then, that Russia called my sister Miss Madeline. She had a hard-and-fast system for the family: she addressed white people in my grandmother's generation with the ultimate respect—Miz Maciver—and those of my parents' age as Miss and Mr. with their first names—Miz Julia—but she had no titles for the children, even when we were grown. Later I realized that Russia had known Madeline before the accident, when she'd been a married woman. Russia was the only person who used my given name, who called me Timothy. It was Figgy who christened me Mac, a match, she probably thought, for her Buddy. Mac Maciver, a ridiculous stuttery name, and yet I have not been able to shake it.

In our block, all the houses had the same blueprint, all of them with long, narrow living rooms and built-in bookcases, leaded windows in the Prairie Style, and low radiators to sit on in the winter. The dining room had a chandelier dripping with prisms, and another set of built-in shelves to display the china. I suppose they were the tract houses of the 1920s, perhaps in their time a blight, the dream of an unctuous developer, the old clapboard houses giving way to what may have been considered the charmless new. Even if time and affection had not had their effect, they would surely now be to the dispassionate observer graceful and solid and deserving of historical preservation. There were four bedrooms upstairs and a porch, where I slept year-round, in winter with hat and mittens, insulated camping clothes, wool socks, and a heavy stack of old comforters. "Timothy," Russia would cackle, "he sleep like an Eskimo, he sleep like a whale in his blubber, he sleep like a poor old man who can't get a dog to be his friend." I was immobile but warm and safe in the midst of the swirling vacuum of the cosmos. In that era before yard lights, a boy could learn the constellations in the suburbs, and through the storm windows I watched the winter sky slowly glide to summer. The house seems small now, by our over-wrought standards, the bedrooms confining, the one full bath inade-quate. To us the dusty rooms with hissing radiators and dark trim were generous, large enough for escape and yet intimate enough to contain the air that seemed solely ours, rich with music and the promise of rump roast for supper.

We had the distinction of having a finished basement with a wet bar—something the fathers in the neighborhood admired, a feature that was wasted on my parents, since they didn't drink much and rarely entertained. The ground floor was laid out in a circle, so that the children must tear from the kitchen, through the dining room, the living room, the front hall, and back again—around and around we went, as the architects intended. When I was young, Madeline chased me on that route. She always pitched forward, from the waist up lean-ing hard into the race, her slow leg dragging behind. When I was older, she still loved that game, although it was I who pursued her. Russia didn't approve of roughhouse, especially when we were all larger, when our footfall shook the foundation. "Timothy!" she'd bark. "Miz Madeline! You stop that, now. No more of that mon-keyshines!"

When my parents moved in after their marriage, my mother prob-ably did not fully disclose the situation, did not go door to door announcing that she was caring for, or raising, her husband's first wife, that the separation had proceeded without incident, and that Madeline was so brain-damaged she had little idea just how she'd been displaced. Although, it must be said, the girl had strong feelings. But the new Mrs. Maciver did visit the neighbors to introduce herself and Madeline, perhaps the first woman to use the word "special" in just that way about the girl people supposed was a sister. Those neighbors who became so familiar, and yet were always unknown to us, came bearing their geraniums and casseroles. Mrs. Van Norman, Mrs. Kloskey, Mrs. Pindel, Mrs. Lemberger, Mrs. Rockard, Mrs. Stonewerth, Mrs. Pilska, Mrs. Gregory, they who soldiered forth from their back doors, the solid phalanx of them coming over the crest of a hill, blotting out the rising sun. That, anyway, that horror-movie scene, the mothers like enormous prehistoric insects, is how I once dreamed of them, waking on the icy upstairs porch in a sweat and with a racing heart. You'd stand before one of their front doors and ring the bell because you were selling candy bars or asking for a cup of sugar; you'd see into the hall, into the living room shaped just as yours was except it didn't look anything like yours, hazy with cigarette smoke and dog fur, or so bright and empty with plastic slipcovers and the glare of the polished coffee table. It was unsettling, that so much strangeness could be so near.

Because Russia later worked for the Pindels, the family across the alley, I have no doubt that in due course word spread about Madeline. It's possible that the neighborhood children understood the Maciver relationships long before Buddy told me at Moose Lake. My mother had come gradually into my father's daily life, and yet after the wedding there was nonetheless a period of adjustment for the Macivers. Madeline smelled a rat, she did, being left with my grandmother up at the lake while my parents spent thirty-six hours at a nearby resort, the only time I know of when they were alone. From the beginning of the marriage, Madeline regularly came into their room at night and stood by their bed. Miss Madeline, in her pink-rosebud nightie, blond hair falling loose around her shoulders, her two fists at her side, her feet planted. Surely, just then, she apprehended the whole chain of events. My mother opened the covers and told her to get in. My father's side of the bed was flush to the wall and made soliciting him cumbersome, or perhaps they situated themselves that way to protect him. I know they had this arrangement, because it went on for years, the bedroom door ajar in the mornings, my father holding my mother around the waist, his mouth against her shoulder, and my mother's arm hanging off Madeline's rib cage, the three of them fast asleep on the family Sealy Posturepedic. Not even the frilly canopy could keep Madeline in her own room, not with a new wife on deck. I suppose my mother's letting her in was the path of nonviolence, or at the least of nonresistance. Louise and I never slept with our parents, because there wasn't enough room with the trio cradled together. If there was a storm, we ran to each other's room and hid under the blankets.

Once, when Diana and I were up at Moose Lake, when we were first getting to know each other, prematurely in love, I happened to describe my father and my mother and Madeline, all in a row under the quilt. She and I were lying in the boathouse on the narrowest of cots, just the two of us on the property. We couldn't imagine that a bed could be too narrow for our delight, the closer we had to press together the better. There'd been romance right away, by candlelight pulling slivers out of her slender feet, shards that she'd gotten from walking on the crudely planed old floor. That made her, I said, an honorary Maciver cousin, if she'd like. She laughed and ardently said, "Yes!" Even though my grandmother had been dead for years, I was still nervous, afraid she might return to punish us. With the thrill of disobeying that most fundamental rule—a female in the boathouse—and feeling that at last I was catching up to Buddy in the women department—but, more important, with our intimacy growing in the chill of the dank room, I found myself telling Diana more of the Madeline story than I'd ever told anyone before. When I got to the sleeping part, Diana's lovely eyes grew round and she drew herself up, leaning on her elbow.

"What are you saying, Mac? I mean, do they—?" Her eyes somehow widened further. "Is it—?"

"Nothing like that! No, no," I quickly assured her.

"But . . . but . . . it's bizarre. It's kinky. You grew up with that? Wasn't it . . . ? How did you . . . ? It's—"

Even as I regretted telling her, I couldn't help laughing at her speechlessness. "They were just sleeping, Diana," I said, kissing her wonderful hair. She'd lived all her life in a Midwestern town of eight thousand, a place where the cheerleaders from junior high in short order become the society women, convention enforced from the seventh grade on, generation after generation. Her father was the big grocer, the wheeler-dealer; her mother dogged in her determination that each of the nine children make them proud. It wasn't that Diana had a cheap little provincial mind—those words came to me, and so I kissed her hair with greater fervor. I didn't want to think how a stranger would see my parents' marriage, didn't want to run the statistics, to find what number of freakish combinations you could spin from a threesome.

(Mother + Father) > Madeline

(Madeline + Father) > Mother

(Mother + Madeline) > Father

Madeline + Mother + Father = Three Bedfellows

(Madeline) + (Mother) + (Father) = Solitary Family Members

Maybe my mother in actuality had wedded my father's first wife, with him as their beard, standing by to protect the Boston marriage. Maybe they were swingers; maybe they invited the mailman in for lunchtime fun. And don't forget Russia! Imagine Buddy and Diana together, wolf to wolf, both of them gnawing on any bones they could dig up.

I wanted to tell Diana that I owed my life to Madeline's lack of skill in steering her Raleigh bicycle; I owed my sensibility, my own faith in goodness, to the texture of our family life, the warmth that my parents radiated to all of us and each other. I sat up on the rickety cot, confused by how much I loved her. "Is something the matter?" she said, tickling my back with her fingernails. How to try again to explain the twist of the story, how my father and mother were much better suited for the long years together than Madeline and my father were, the irony of their lives, the bitter part of my parents' happiness. It was I who was speechless then. How to make her see that my mother's tenderness for Madeline was a pure thing?

"Is something the matter?" my future wife had to ask once more. Her face in the candlelight and her concern distracted me from my equations. I lay back down, no more talking about my parents or Madeline or the old days.

Chapter Six

FIGGY FELT FREE TO BE ESPECIALLY FRANK WITH ME WHEN she'd had plenty to drink. And so she made a point to tank up if she was sure to say something unseemly. "Did I mention anything I shouldn't have?" she'd ask the morning after, all innocence. "Was I consistent, at the least?" In the last few years before she had a stroke, she couldn't seem to help bullying me with her idea of my mother's character. "The thing is," she'd say, "the thing is, it was subtle, the way Julia pulled off the martyr role." It's not always clear if a drunk is speaking her favorite truths or wallowing in melodrama; that is, I tried to give her the benefit of the doubt, hoping she was only being theatrical. When I remembered how much scotch she'd put away, I could for the most part forgive her.

Because I had once or twice asked her to tell me the story of my parents' early life together, she seemed to think that every time we had a chance she should repeat the parts wherein my mother's goodness irritated her. The more annoyed she became, the greater her pleasure seemed to be. "In the beginning," she'd declare roundly, "Madeline went berserk. The change in the patient was something the newlyweds weren't prepared for—all of a sudden the invalid alive and kicking. What a little brat she was! Your mother had the theory that Mrs. Maciver the First had been drugged in those years after the accident, to make caring for her easier. As if medication were a crime. Of course she was sedated! Who wouldn't sedate a woman who was in a fury? Later, when Madeline calmed down, when she started following Julia around like a goddamn puppy, that was worse. Julia encouraged the slavishness—she loved it, couldn't get enough. It was the most revolting thing you ever saw."

"Really," I always said. I was sure back then that Figgy's enthusiasm would keep her alive well into her hundreds.

"Along come you and Louise. It probably wasn't so terrific anymore, two real children plus the girl giant. Then wasn't Julia sorry she'd infantilized Madeline? Not that Madeline had ever had the capacity to be a brain surgeon, but they might have treated her like an adult instead of insisting she play the part of the child. What was she, nearly six feet at her tallest?"

"No," I tried, "not that—"

"There was no graceful way out for poor, poor Julia, no comfort but to be holier-than-thou, hauling that hulk around with her everywhere she went."

After my mother died, I thought that Figgy might become softer, perhaps even a little reverent. "There's nothing more tedious than a righteous woman," she blazed on. "I'm sure your father wanted to paddle their big tyke now and then. I'm sure he kept going on his expeditions for as long as he could to escape the—situation."

I'd refill her glass, wondering if she'd soon tire.

"To get as far away," she'd explain, "from the saint as he could."

In all the time since, most every imagining and remembrance I've had of my parents has been a remonstrance to Figgy. She is helpless now, having suffered a progressive stroke, multiple cerebral infarction. I find myself arguing with her still, although I haven't seen her in years. It is to her I owe a debt for the details, the small scenes she described that have made it possible to see some distance into the Macivers' marriage. But if I can on occasion muffle Figgy's rhetoric, I find that my parents after all are capable of moving around in their past without her.

It was, I think, on the whole true, what she told me about the first year: Madeline did howl and kick and throw things, staggering from upset to upset, her anger directed at Julia. This in an era when families were not as pharmaceutically girded for trouble, no reliable antidepressants for mother, no liquid nortriptyline administered in a glass of apple juice for daughter. It's likely, too, that Julia had disposed of the crude sedatives Grandmother had passed on to her for the patient. Though it sometimes seemed apparent what Madeline understood, it was impossible to predict what might provoke her, when she might fly into a rage. She would wake next to my mother, and she might scratch Julia through her nightgown or dig her nails into her cheek. "Good morning, lamb," my mother would say, carefully pulling away, climbing to the end of the bed to get out. On a better day, the *enfant terrible* whimpered and hid her head in the pillow. There was the long coaxing to the kitchen table. "Come, lamb, blueberry muffins for breakfast." But the morning in front of them was just as uncertain if Madeline opened her eyes, stretched, swung her feet to the floor, and padded in her uneven tread to the bathroom. The augur of a happy day? A few minutes later, by the time she got to the table, she might turn her bowl of cereal over and sit, her arms crossed, refusing to move.

"You'd want to smack her in the face," Figgy said.

In the evenings, when my father walked in the door from work, Madeline quit stirring the pudding or working at the sewing cards that occupied her, shoestrings in different colors threaded through cardboard pictures. She'd burst from the chair, the thick threads spilling, the stack of cards falling to the floor. She pitched herself at my father. "Hullo, Julia," he called to his wife through that assault. When he sat down to dinner, Madeline climbed into his lap, pulled at his face, pressed his cheeks together. She must not have liked her place at the side of the table, Mr. and Mrs. Maciver at the heads. "Talk to me," she said to my father. "Tell me about your day," she said in a mocking voice. "Talk to me. Tell me. Talk, talk." My mother was firm in her conviction that he should indulge her, that he should shove back in his chair and rock her for as long as she needed. As my mother saw it,

Madeline was just waking up to the fact that she'd been injured. Or, as Figgy might have said, "jilted."

"Keep rocking her," Julia instructed her husband. Madeline must have known she'd lost something. What was it that had once been so close and yet now was blurry in the distance? Not a dress or a dog, larger than that—a house, was it? A whole town, a lake, a thing you felt you were a part of but couldn't in any way hold? "This will pass," I imagine Julia assuring my father when they were alone in their bed, before the specter appeared from the other room.

"It took the accident to reveal the nature of his first wife to your father," Figgy told me. "I don't think he had ever admitted to himself that she was spoiled. It was the crash that brought her character to the fore, front and center, for him to see."

As all couples must do when they have children at home, my parents would have had to be hasty and quiet after the lights were out. Before Madeline made her entrance into the dark bedroom—and who could tell when she would open the door?—they might have their moment. I have turned over their love for each other any number of times in my mind. They were not either of them rudely self-interested, as Figgy insisted through the years. But I do wonder if my father at the start of the marriage harbored the sadness of having to be eternally grateful. My mother, knowing that she owned that gratitude, that she'd have it for the rest of her life, was able then to make light of her burden. I would guess that both of them cared for Madeline as devotedly as they did because it was she who had given them to each other. I'm certain this is a subject they never discussed, and yet she knew the facets of his feelings just as he might have understood something of hers, too. They'd begin to kiss out of all that gratitude, and quickly, quickly, like teenagers fearing discovery, they'd move together without completely removing their clothes, my father's boxers down to his ankles, my mother's nightgown up to her chin. Surely my father experienced some kind of religion in that hurry; surely it's possible that my mother's needs and talents were absorbing even as they were different from Madeline's.

There was an evening early on when Madeline bit Julia on the underside of her forearm. My mother had been wiping up a lump of mashed potatoes at Madeline's place, including the thin gravy that had run into the groove of the table. Madeline leaned forward to take the nip. There, in a snap, was the portrait of the new family: my father squinting at the women as if he didn't think he was seeing straight, my mother staring at her own arm, and Madeline unable to withdraw, although she seemed as startled as anyone, teeth to flesh. Julia finally put her other hand on Madeline's head and said, "Lamb, this is going to bleed. Why don't you come and help me wash it out." She spoke as if there had been a spill on a piece of linen, as if a swift application of cold water would remove the stain.

Off they went into the kitchen. My father, for encouragement, took himself to the bookshelf. When the poetry anthology, fifteen hundred pages, proved too unwieldy, the poems he kept hitting too fanciful—"Whenas in silks my Julia goes"—he settled on the life story of Helen Keller. Now, there was a monster child if ever there'd been one. He walked the long route to the kitchen, turning the pages and reading even as he came through the arch. "Where's Anne Sullivan when you need her?" He closed his eyes to feel for the countertop, not irreverently and not in mockery of the play, which hadn't been written yet, but to try to understand total blindness.

My mother burst out laughing.

He did open up to inspect the puncture Madeline's eyetooth had made. "You all right, Julia?"

She stroked Madeline's hair, her long fingers extending over the crown of the head, the slow pull down the length of it, past the shoulders. "You are our demon, aren't you?"

"No!" Madeline had her hangdog expression, the trembling mouth, chin down, misery mixed with contrition.

"You're our great big girl, of course you are," Julia said, taking her into her arms, careful of the bruise coming on.

While she went with Madeline to run her bath, my father sat down to read the manual on child care and training he'd bought, scientific advice for parents, a guide to conditioning that he thought might be useful for both Madeline and the future Macivers.

"They were sweet to her in a way that made you want to puke." So said Figgy. "They doted on her together, as if she were a pet, a chimp they'd befriended in the wild. It was your mother's doing. Your father was the yes man, making inane comments along the way, which I guess kept them laughing."

How lonely it must have been for Julia by day, cut off from her nursing work and her old college friends, surrounded by women in the neighborhood, most of them busy with their own households and normal children. She wiped up the cereal on the floor as Madeline thrashed and spewed. "This will pass," she must have kept telling herself, taking hope from that wish. She ate her dinner at the end of the table while my father rocked Madeline, hummed in her ear, patted her hands, waited for her to get tired of the game, his food growing cold. My mother dismissed the behaviorists Aaron was reading, those who believed not in the slow effect of love but in conditioned responses. She declined to act on Russia's advice—Russia, who, like Figgy, had no patience for sparing the rod. "She will come around," my mother promised. "In another year she won't be doing this."

She did want Madeline to be able to use what remained of her gifts, to sharpen them, if she could. When Russia wasn't in the house to worry about the mess, they covered the kitchen table with newsprint and painted on rolls of brown butcher paper. In summer, on the downstairs back porch there was always a card table with a beginner's paint-by-number project going, an assortment of horse, dog, and cat themes. My mother was not artistic herself, but she could see how engaged Madeline was, lining up her tubes of paint, setting out the brushes, how she'd go into a reverie even before she'd make a mark. Julia was interested in the care Madeline took with color and shape, how her feel for design was not entirely gone. Over the first winter they made a quilt, the dining-room table for months littered with rags and half-finished squares, the floor ankle-deep in scraps, straight pins glittering between the oak boards. It was an undertaking my mother later admitted almost killed her. When spring came, they knelt in the grass next to the flats of petunias and impatiens, Madeline determining the arrangement.

"Your nursing degree for this?" Figgy said to my mother, watching the taffy making in the kitchen. "I thought you were going to save all the poor people, the colored children of the South. Aren't you losing your mind? Can't you put her away?"

"Pull," my mother said, handing her a dull brown lump.

"Julia. There are places for people like her. Why can't I get that through your head? You don't have to live like this. She's never going to get better."

"She can learn, even if her capacity is limited. She can have enjoyment. She's very opinionated about what she likes. It's funny how she still has her eye. I should show you her paintings—"

Figgy, who had studied art history, said, "Spare me."

"She knows how to make a thing look nice. And she cares. Believe it or not, I'm learning from her. She has no idea that she's a teacher, but she's made me think about the self, about what we are without memory, without a sense of time."

My aunt stared at Julia. "Finally, getting the education you've always wanted. And taking style tips seriously. From a half-wit."

"Keep pulling," my mother said.

"Do you know what I think, Mrs. Maciver? I think she's childish on purpose. What is she now, my ex-sister-in-law, or is she my niece? I can't keep it straight. I think she only means to annoy with her tantrums. When she had—what was that tyrant nurse's name, the one who cared for her at first?—Nurse Kimball!—Madeline was a model patient for Nurse Kimball of the ugly face and big voice. What are you going to do, bring up baby until you drop dead? Have you thought of that?"

"Wait. Stop right now. Are the ridges starting to hold their shape? Is the taffy—wait, wait, what does it say—is it opaque, firm, and elastic?"

Although Figgy never paid Madeline much attention, she did

bring her extravagant gifts, dolls for grown-ups, she explained to me, not little girl bric-a-brac. After she presented Madeline with a Shanty Town Scarlett O'Hara doll, she said to Julia in singsong, "I'll get her something even nicer if you lock her up."

The first time she mentioned her fatigue with Bill Eastman and her idea of divorcing him, Julia turned to pet Madeline's hair, as if that action might demonstrate to Figgy one's duty to stay the course. Figgy got the gist. "I'm not like you, Julia." She felt strongly enough to repeat what was evident. "I'm not anything like you."

My father was gone all day, but even if he'd been home I think Madeline's affections would have changed. To battle the kindness of her caretaker for long would have taken real endurance, and it's not surprising that she eventually capitulated to my mother's program of industry and safekeeping. They walked down the alley hand in hand, Madeline drawing to Julia's side when they passed a barking dog behind a fence. They went to the community pool, both of them in their modest suits, Julia sitting on the edge while Madeline, towering above the waterline in the shallow end, held her nose and turned incomplete somersaults. She'd come spraying up, digging into her eye sockets with her fists, coughing. My father once remarked, watching her at Moose Lake, that Venus obviously had sputtered at her birth. Every Thursday afternoon Madeline stayed with Russia, so that Mrs. Maciver in her few free hours could do her work with the League of Women Voters, and once in a rare while Grandmother came out on a Saturday so the honeymooners could take their walk in the forest preserve.

At dinner, a few months before I was born, Madeline made her declaration to my father: "I don't like you anymore." She was sitting at her own place, pushing her mushrooms to the edge of her plate with a teaspoon. It was as if she were the one who was finally breaking up.

He nodded slowly. "I'm sorry to hear that."

"I like Julia better."

"Understandable."

Lifting her fine chin higher, she said, "There's going to be a baby in this house."

"Imagine that." He raised his eyebrows down the table at my mother.

At last, a baby for the couple, however you wanted to slice that pair. In the photos, Madeline is holding me, bent over, absorbed in my downy newborn face, my mother near her on the sofa. There's a picture of the four of us, Madeline and my mother standing side by side, both of them smiling at the photographer, my father slightly apart, peering over at the bundle in Julia's arms. It does for all the world look like the future, two mommies with the guest sperm donor. Not long after my arrival, my father found Madeline asleep on the floor by the crib. I don't think they worried that Madeline would hurt me purposefully but, rather, that her solicitude, her extravagant care, might make her headstrong. She didn't waver in her dedication to her self-appointed job as night and day nurse, always on hand with supplies my mother needed at the changing table, warm wet washcloths, fresh diapers, pins, rubber pants. My mother took pains to teach her how to hold me, protecting the soft spot and the neck, fearful of the inevitable, that day when she would find me gone, the buggy missing from its place on the back porch.

The first time it happened, Mrs. Van Norman brought back the abductress and the booty in the pram. My mother had fallen asleep on the sofa during my afternoon nap, had closed her eyes for a moment while Madeline cut out pictures from a magazine. Mrs. Van Norman was large-boned, with coarse blond hair that she raked into a ratty pile on top of her head. Even though she had twelve children of her own, she had energy to spare for the rest of us. It was Madeline's unusual speed crossing the street with the buggy, hurrying as if she already thought she was pursued, that had made Mrs. Van Norman wonder if the girl should be alone with the baby. When she had walked Madeline back home and stood on the front steps, she suggested that my mother employ any of the eight older Van Normans to help her with the one infant. "One infant!" she crowed, as if a single child in the home, and as if assistance for one child, were both outrageous jokes. Rather than scold Madeline or hire Stacey Van Norman, my mother vowed to keep herself awake, to be vigilant through the afternoons.

Ah, but Julia was so tired. The next time Madeline made off with me, she did not take into consideration her route, did not imagine that everywhere, everywhere there were spies. Russia was beating a rug on the front porch of Mrs. Blum's house, several blocks away, when Madeline came prancing up the street. Where were we going? I wonder. Were we about to hop the Soo Line, my first ride in a boxcar, and would we sleep in haystacks and rob a bank and steal a Chevrolet Cabriolet? I picture Madeline dressed for the event in an aqua-and-black polka-dot skirt, the type Louise called a twirly skirt, and black patent-leather heels, a matching pocketbook, and an aqua sweater, the sort that sheds, leaving behind her a trail of soft rabbity threads.

When Russia saw the fashion plate, she didn't waste her energy crying out. She threw the rug aside and tore down the sidewalk, going straight for the ponytail. Not just a yank or two, but a continuous pull as she shook. No one, not before the accident or after, had ever rattled Madeline Schiller's brains. No one had struck her. What satisfaction for Russia, finally, just like Miss Figgy said to do, giving the devil the business. Madeline's shrieks woke me, and I cried, too.

"You take this baby again, I'll steal you away, you hear? Russia's going to kidnap you for good, how you like that? Take you down to Black Irwin." Madeline screamed louder. "You think Russia don't know what you do? You think you can hide from Russia?" She gave a last tug. "Russia, she know everything."

Whether Madeline was most afraid of Russia or the idea of Russia's bogeyman, Black Irwin, she never took me out by herself again. Still, the hair pulling did not seem to affect her motherly pride. "Look at my baby," she'd say to strangers in the park. "My baby has a new tooth." Or, glancing into someone else's buggy, "My baby is bigger than your baby." Because my father was often gone, Madeline may have believed that I belonged far more to her than to the part-time husband.

He was away for collecting expeditions in Africa for three- and four-month stretches. When he reappeared, tan and stringy and with a reddish beard, he seemed for a time a stranger. He brought with him bolts of hand-printed fabric, and pottery, not all of it broken, and the animals of the ark carved from exotic woods, the elephants with ivory tusks, the dark-brown seals so smooth Louise abandoned her dear blanket and walked around holding them against her cheek. I remember my father embracing my mother in the kitchen after he'd been away, his face in her short, nappy hair for what seemed like half a day. He had given her presents to show her how much he'd missed her, a muumuu with green and gold swirls, and a necklace of velvety black seedpods, and still he seemed to feel it necessary to prove his love by clinging to her. Madeline watched them standing together, and when she got tired of looking she turned to me, trying to get me to hug her. I wriggled away, running into the hall in hopes she'd come after me. Around the circle of the downstairs we went, time after time passing our parents in their clasp.

STATISTICALLY, with eighty-five children on the block, there were bound to be some abnormalities, a chance for a Down's-syndrome baby, a case of spina bifida, a clubfoot, a cleft palate. Whether it was the sheer volume of prayer in the St. Rita's parish or lady luck, the Gregorys had nine unscathed specimens, the Lembergers fourteen, the Van Normans twelve, the Pilskas also an even dozen. The Rockards had eight, counting their ten-year-old who was killed on the El tracks the year I was fifteen. "God," Mrs. Van Norman said, "*and* the older brother failed to watch out for one curious boy."

Madeline, then, was the handicapped woman on the 400 block of Grove, and on the 300 block there was Mikey O'Day, neither of them, however, disabled by birth accidents or the roulette of genetics. The divide of the cross street was enough to keep us from Mikey's orbit when we were very young, his house far off, in a distant realm. But we'd heard the story and we knew what he was: birdbrain, screwball, goopus, dunce. His stupidity was a result, the older girls said, of meningitis. If it didn't kill you it would put your eyes out, an affliction, we'd thought, that was only likely to happen if you were running with a stick. Or your brains would shrivel, your skull like a gourd, nothing but dry bits rattling around, the seedy leftovers of intelligence. He'd had the sickness as a baby, Mary Beth Van Norman explained, so he didn't know he'd been born a genius. I used to lie awake thinking of Mikey, long before I met him, wondering if he would have liked to know that for fourteen months he'd had the potential to be famous and maybe rich. Even though Madeline's plight was similar, I didn't think about her in the same way, I suppose because she was always just Madeline, and because she often had tantrums over nothing at all. I could be pragmatic as well as soppy-hearted, and I thought that if she knew she'd once been smart she might never have stopped screaming.

The spring of 1963, when I was fifteen, Mikey began singing in the evenings at the ice-cream stand by the community pool. Despite the name, the Dari-Dip, it had always done a good business through the summer. No one could say what prompted Mikey, one night in May, to jump up from the picnic table as if he'd been stung. He began to belt out a Jerry Lee Lewis number, "Whole Lotta Shakin' Goin' On." There was probably even a recognizable rendition of the piano-and-guitar interlude. He'd been eating his cone one minute, and the next he was up by the trash can urging the world to shake it. "I said shake baby shake!"

The few people sitting on the benches were too stunned to laugh. Mr. O'Day was beyond being embarrassed by his son, or maybe he was worn out. He averted his eyes and stood by. Mikey wiggled his hips, his face to the moon, his eyes shut tight, his mouth wide open. There must have been enough applause, because he went right on with an instrumental, "Mau Mau," his lips pressed together for the trumpet embouchure, his cheeks puffed to the limit, his horn sound soft but always exuberant, always clear in his jazzy staccato. He found a stick for the metal trash-can lid and banged out, more or less, a regular beat. Irene and Stu, the owners, came from the kitchen, clapping and crying, "*Satchmo! Satchmo!*" There was another tune and another, and the next night he returned, and the night after, and the night after that, until Irene and Stu suggested he sing, when time allowed, two or three nights a week. For Mikey's sake and for the sake of his fans. If a singer kept such an unrelenting schedule, they explained, he might tire his voice. It might not be good for the long haul. So it was established that Mikey O'Day would be the Dari-Dip headliner for an hour on Saturday, Sunday, and Monday nights. The loyal customers might have avoided the drive-in after Mikey began his crooning, but instead for a time it was a hot spot. I like to think people stopped by not because they considered Mikey a freak show but because the local color was theirs.

His mother bought him a toy microphone, a prop that looked so real in his clutches you almost believed it made his voice louder. A reporter from the local newspaper showed up to do a feature, to write about Mikey's remarkable memory and repertory, from Tony Bennett to Peggy Lee, from Buddy Holly to Dionne Warwick. The article was also about the Dari-Dip's generous support of the retarded man. I remember my mother reading the *Journal* at the breakfast table. "Isn't that nice about Mikey O'Day," she said. "Isn't it interesting that he's developed an imaginary radio show, that he does traffic updates and weather reports in between his songs."

What was she thinking might happen when, on a Saturday night in June, she asked me to take Madeline to the Dari-Dip? Would I mind walking the few blocks with her to get a cone? *Would I mind?* It wasn't that I was humiliated by Madeline. I had realized much earlier that if I was going to be ashamed of her I'd have to be ashamed of the whole family. That not only seemed impractical but also required more energy, more vigilance than I could give to the project. I don't rule out the fact that because Madeline was attractive it was easier to shoulder the burden of a handicapped sibling.

Oh, but there was a price to be paid for that beauty. After it was established that we were walking to the Dari-Dip, we couldn't simply stroll out the front door, slap down the stairs in our sandals and along the sidewalk, buy our ice cream, and then turn toward home. No, no. Madeline must change her clothes to step out. "What's wrong," I said, "with your green shorts? And your shirt?" The small yellow-and-green flowered print was very ladylike. She looked fine enough to order a dessert as extravagant as a banana split, if she was to go that far.

She didn't dignify my question with a response. I could hear her up in her room, the hangers sliding along the pole in the closet, and she probably took out every single one of her shoe boxes and lined up her pairs of heels across the rug. As if for once she might be quick with her toilet, I waited for her in the hall downstairs, pacing and snapping my fingers. Little did I know that in a few days my impatience would be something I'd look back to fondly, an irritation so mild it would look like serenity in retrospect.

Twenty-seven minutes later, she tap-tapped down the stairs to the landing, where she stood, allowing me to admire her. Her head was high, turned to show off her noble profile. There's probably a name for the kind of dress she had on, the square neck, open to the cleavage, the short sleeves, the gathers along the breast, the lowered waist falling into a skirt flouncy with pleats. She might have gone to the opera in that satiny blue dress, and with the pearl necklace at her smooth girlish throat.

"We're going to the Dari-Dip, right?" I finally said.

"Ready," she breathed, as one dainty foot in a pair of white slingbacks—I believe that's the term—reached the bottom stair.

Had my mother told her about Mikey O'Day's entertainment, or was she outfitted for the public on general principle? Since she always dressed with care for any occasion, it was hard to say. She had a handbag, the color of her frock, large enough to hold a puppy. Inside, it's likely there was a stuffed dog, a few pennies, a comb, a shell, a spare necklace.

Mikey O'Day and Madeline were about the same age. She had seen him any number of times through the years, at the pool, at the library, from afar down the block, but I guess she hadn't really looked at him. I later wondered what he'd been so busy with, for decades, that he'd never strayed down our alley; I wondered if he'd had plenty of girlfriends who lived north or east or west of us. It's safe to say that if they'd both had normal intelligence Madeline would never have given him a second glance, but even so he was, as my mother testified, cute. A darling, she said. He had thick red hair that had a furry softness, and enormous shiny blue eyes that were magnified by his glasses. His mouth was red, noticeably bright, and unusually elastic, so that his funny faces were clownish and in fact did make us laugh. In the beginning Madeline often stared unabashedly at his lips. He was shorter than she was, and goofily, pleasantly plump. If he hadn't walked with his head to the sky, bobbing as if his neck were a spring, you wouldn't have known at first that there was anything wrong with him.

The Dari-Dip DJ always announced each number knowledgeably and with veneration. "This next one," Mikey would say, "is the Everly, the Everly Brothers, Don and Phil. They, they are brothers, they are very, they are very great, the greatest s-s-s-songwriting artists, songwriting artists ever, ever to be heard." Before he started, he screwed up his face, the skin of his nose bunching toward the bridge, his lips stretching to the ears, the effort of bliss. His brow was always rippling with wrinkles, and sometimes his eyes would pop open, out of amazement, probably, at what had come from his mouth.

That night, Madeline slowly and demurely licked her vanilla ice cream and nibbled at the cone, the tip of her tongue as enchanting as a kitten's, or so she must have imagined. Mikey stood fifteen feet from us, by the trash can, singing his sha-na-nas, the doo-doos and wah-wahs, as well as making the shimmer of a snare drum and the click-click of the maracas with his own fetching tongue and teeth. When he did his trumpet impression, Madeline couldn't help giggling into her hands, blowing her cover as prima donna. There were plenty of people sitting around us, but we were the only fans actually listening to Mikey. The crowd was usually respectful, looking up long enough to cheer when he was done with a song.

I remember him singing "Let It Be Me," how he did the violin part at the beginning, and the Hawaiian slide sound, too, and he worked at the beat with the trash-can lid and a real drumstick. His heart was in it; his heart was absolutely and completely in it. So it didn't matter if he couldn't quite hit the notes or he'd lose his place, or the beat would peter out and then come back with a vengeance, or if all of a sudden he was Frank Sinatra when he meant to be Don and Phil Everly. Even though he had serious trouble with intonation, his sturdy voice in those bright thumping early rock-and-roll songs had a sweetness that hit you in the pit of your stomach. There was nothing worse than Mikey, his eyeballs in the back of his head, singing, "Each time we meet, love, I find complete love," and other sentiments that seemed equally removed from his own experience.

Madeline, much to my horror, sat transfixed. She didn't seem to mind that her hand was sticky with ice cream, which is what happens if you take thirty minutes to eat a frozen confection. He went on to sing "Moon River"—so dreamily, with such volume—"Two drifters off to see the world." She sat up straighter, as if she were about to be called on. As unbelievable as it may seem, he sang "I Almost Lost My Mind." Also "Que Sera Sera," "Born to Be with You," and "The Way You Look Tonight." When Madeline put the last crumb of cone in her mouth, just as he was introducing "Are You Lonesome Tonight?," I said, "We need to go, Maddy."

"No!"

"Madeline."

"I said no!"

How was it that someone like Mikey, with his limited powers, had gained entrance to musical paradise? How could he have the knowledge that people like Louise and Stephen Lovrek had, he, a part of that secret society? "We have to get home," I said.

She stared straight ahead.

We sat through "Wake Up, Little Suzie" and "Short Fat Fannie": "She watch me like a hound dog everywhere I go." Without realizing I'd drawn blood on my leg from my own fingernails. I said, "If we leave after the next song, I'll bring you back tomorrow night."

She did turn to look at me.

"After the next song. If we leave, I will bring you back. If you stay, I'm never coming here again."

She considered her options. "Tomorrow night?" she said.

"Tomorrow night." I was sure that Sunday the place would be closed, and by Monday she would have forgotten.

"Tomorrow night you'll bring me."

"Tomorrow night."

On our way down the sidewalk, she had to stop every few feet and look back at him.

How deeply sorry I was to learn that the Dari-Dip never shut down in season. It was on the second night, then, that I sat, my veins heating once more, while Madeline ate another cone, again with excruciating slowness. I had been too embarrassed to mention the situation to my mother, and because she was gone all afternoon and into the evening, agitating for peace, she missed the violence stirring within Mrs. Maciver the First. Every five minutes Madeline would come into my room and ask me how many more minutes until eight o'clock, what time exactly were we leaving, when did the paper say Mikey started singing, where was the paper, why hadn't I read the article? Which one of us felt time moving more slowly, which one of us more acutely felt the up-and-coming minute tugging at the minute it was leaving behind, the pull to get to the next number?

It was on the second night that Mikey O'Day opened his eyes long enough to notice the single member of his public. We were under the fluorescent pole light that hung high over our table, Madeline bathed in the purity of that buzzing white glow. She was wearing another party dress, and she had a purple scarf tied under her chin, as a film star in a convertible might. Surely without the aid of electricity Mikey would finally have noticed Madeline's beam; surely he could not have avoided her determined gaze forever. It was during a self-imposed break, after he'd stood in line to get his complimentary sundae, that he at last made his move. He stood across the picnic table from her, his head tottering back and forth as if it might fall off his neck. "I'm Mikey, I'm Mikey O'Day, Mikey O'Day. I noticed, I noticed that you like, that you like my music."

"Mikey," she said into her lap.

"I'm good, I'm pretty good tonight, pretty good."

She nodded, the normal motion, up and down.

"We need to go, Madeline—"

"No!" The shy demoiselle turned to glare at me.

"M-Mad-Madeline," he said. "Madeline and M-Mikey, Mikey O'Day. Madeline and Mikey O'Day." He was firm in the final pronouncement.

She covered her face with her hands, something she did when she was excited. "You're, you're *not* my boyfriend!" she tittered through her fingers. She was starting to tremble, one of the first signs, I feared, of love.

"It sounds, it sounds good, the names, the names together, Madeline, Madeline and Mikey O—"

"Time to go!" I said, climbing out from the seat.

"No, Mac!"

Mikey took one large canine snap at his sundae before he rushed to the microphone that was resting on the trash-can lid. He began to sing another song, the type about loving you until the sun burns out and the oceans run dry, until the microbes, every last one of them, are exhausted. I suppose it was at that point that Madeline made up her mind. No reason to look any farther for romance. She was forty-four years old. The man knew the value of a love song. The hour had come.

Later there would be other suitors for Madeline, men she had to reject because they were disfigured or they couldn't make eye contact or they were obsessive, prone to reciting the phone book, or overly stimulated by fire trucks. Even in her own compromised state, she had to find a man who wasn't too unstable or compulsive or ugly, and I think it was also important that her beau have something besides pure craziness to distinguish him. She was still, in her way, choosy.

When he rang our bell the next afternoon, when I opened the door to his hard grin, and the dive for my hand so he could shake it and keep shaking it, I meant to tell him Madeline wasn't home. But it took him long enough to greet me, and he spoke loudly enough so that she came as fast as she could from her room, slowing as she neared the landing, her old feminine wiles, her native cunning, come back to her.

"I brought, I brought my records," he called over my shoulder. "My, my records." They had discussed this meeting on the previous night, in the few minutes they'd had alone by the pickup window, before I'd dragged Madeline home. Without the Dari-Dip, without his microphone and his trash-can lid, he was all nerves, stepping from foot to foot, breathing through his clenched teeth, his hands opening and closing, opening and closing. Behind him, indeed, were two blue metal boxes that held his 45s.

I had never had a girlfriend myself and believed I never would, but in that moment I felt as if I'd skipped ahead, as if I were a parent. Or at the least a maiden aunt who has been brought on board to watch the young people, to make certain there is no hanky-panky.

"You should go outside," I said to Madeline, sure that in the wide-open space of the yards, the long stretch of sidewalk, nothing could happen.

"We're listening to music," she snipped, pushing past me to let Mikey through.

The neighborhood children had always been welcome in our house, and yet it seemed wrong to let Mikey O'Day enter when my mother wasn't home. Down the basement, Madeline took the orange plastic record-player from the cupboard and set it on the carpet. I wasn't sure what to do with myself. There was no question that I was to watch over them, but where should I be? On the rug right next to her? In the laundry room with my ear cocked? I could busy myself at the bar fifteen feet away with my chemistry set; that was it. While I readied my lab for a titration, Madeline sat watching Mikey. She watched him decide what to play, watched him talking to himself about each record he considered. She watched the turntable spin while he danced. He danced to Joey Dee and the Starliters, he danced to "Love Me Do," and he danced to a song by the Cadillacs called "Speedo." These days, even now, if I stumble upon an oldie on the car radio, or if my daughters are playing music from my youth, it is always Mikey I see, always that stupendous head of his swaying.

That first afternoon, every time he tried to get Madeline to dance she'd turn away, smiling to herself. Good, I thought, don't rumba with him. After more of that than you'd think a fellow could stand, they went upstairs to get something to eat. I followed them as if I were their Secret Service detail. It was, predictably, in the kitchen that she felt free to exert a wifely attention. "Sit down," she ordered.

He swiveled in his chair to watch her reach up in the cabinet for his snack. She didn't ask what he wanted. At the counter she poured cornflakes into a bowl. She set it in front of him and then went to the drawer to fetch a spoon. "Now," she said, pointing at the small crock of sugar on the lazy Susan. When she turned her back to get the milk, he emptied the crock over his cereal. Did he think the mountain of sugar would escape her notice? She came with the pitcher to his place. She looked once, she looked twice. She frowned. He knew enough to explain. "I like sugar, I like it."

"That's why you're fat," she said, matter-of-factly.

"Hee-hee-hee-hee-hee-hee!" He punched his own stomach and then pursed his lips, made his cheeks big. "I like, I like being f-f-f-at."

She wasn't amused, not yet. "Why?" She poured the milk carefully, watching the crystals sink and melt.

"Because, because then I can eat, I can eat sugar!"

There was silence before they both exploded with laughter. She had to sit and put her head to the table. Every time Mikey dipped his spoon into his sucrose soup, they laughed some more. While they were consumed with mirth, I emptied the dishwasher. Louise came in and looked at them and at me. "What's he doing here?" she mouthed. Was it courtship, or what we now call a playdate? I no longer knew. I shrugged, and she went into the living room to tune her cello. As if the sawing of the open strings were a siren call, Mikey stopped chewing. Lu often warmed up with one of the simpler Bach suites instead of scales, and the instant she began to play, Mikey pushed back his chair. In a flash he was in the living room, kneeling at the cello's stem.

"What?" Lu said to him, as if he were a brother. "What do you want?"

In the beginning I was always thinking about what he'd have been like without his sickness. Whether or not he had had a genius IQ before whatever fabled illness struck, there did seem to be a touch of the savant mixed up in his childishness. The way music affected him, it seemed as if he might have been truly gifted.

"I have a radio show, I sing," he said. "I sing, I sing, on the radio. On the radio."

"I know," Louise said. "You're famous around here."

"I'm good, I'm pretty good."

"Me, too." She tightened a peg on the scroll, turning her head to listen to the string. "If, that is, I get a chance to practice."

Mikey stayed right where he was as she played the prelude of Suite No. 4. He closed his eyes, his lids fluttering, the seam of white flashing. He was as moved by Johann Sebastian Bach as he was by Perry Como.

When my mother came home from the store I said, "Mikey O'Day was here. He was here in this house."

"That's nice," she said.

"He likes Madeline. Likes her. He likes Madeline." I realized I was starting to talk just as he did.

She stopped unpacking the meat. "Mikey O'Day," she said, looking out the window. "Well, that is nice."

It didn't occur to me to be happy for my sister, even though I had lived long enough to see the pattern of Madeline's friendships. Every summer was always particularly trying, and I'd come to understand that her hardships were of a certain kind, that being more or less one age indefinitely meant a person had to keep facing the same sorrows, the sadness always fresh. I hadn't known if Buddy had actually meant for me to take advantage of Madeline when he'd told me about her, but, whatever his intent, I was sure I had become more protective of her, and also thoughtful about her capabilities. Although it perhaps seems strange that she played with the younger children, there was nothing more natural in those days than her going outside, as we all used to, standing around, watching a group in a sandbox or a couple of girls with a few bracelets and crowns, involved in a fantasy. Pretty soon, Madeline might be drawn in. There were always great numbers abroad, since the mothers sent their offspring out in the morning, barring them from home until lunchtime. I had seen how it worked for Madeline, how she shifted back and forth at the edge of a game, how she'd slowly move in closer, how by and by she'd be squatting on her haunches coloring on the sidewalk with Missy Lombardo's chalk.

Still, she could only go so far with them. The girls she'd played with when they were four, five, and six would outgrow her, and there'd come the year when she wasn't invited to birthday parties. There the crowd would be, next door or across the alley, in their pointed hats, the plank laid on two sawhorses, the paper tablecloth fluttering in the breeze, the penny carnival in place, the polka-dotted noisemakers and bags of favors, the fluted muffin cups filled with gum drops set above the plates. If my mother hadn't been alerted, if she hadn't taken Madeline away, and if Madeline noticed the big event, there was no help for her. She'd stand at the kitchen window for a minute before she banged up the stairs, down the hall to her room, slamming the door, the sound of her sobs coming from under the covers, the gathering of her breath, the hiccupping of those gasps before another round.

There were a few years in the cycle when the boys who had been her friends disregarded her, but there were some of them who, when they came into adolescence, might look at her again. As if she hadn't been living on the block all their lives, they'd one day encounter her sitting on a lounge chair at the pool. They didn't know what to call the confusion in her of naïveté and experience, but, whatever its name, she was smiling at them. I have through the decades wondered if the haziest memory of the Italian was with her, if on a rare day his words gently sounded in her ear as she woke. "At this moment—I see in the piazza the angel." She seemed especially emboldened at the pool, confident, even as she limped along the pavement past the diving boards, her ponytail swinging, her painted toenails shining, the rhinestones of her cat-eye sunglasses sparking. "Hi, Kevin!" she'd call. "Hi, Jerry."

She didn't look in her mid-forties poolside, in those glamorous shades, her figure so trim. I'd watch from my wet spot of cement and that old sadness would come over me, something I didn't know how to stave off. For a reason that baffled me, Miss Vanderbeak, my high-school English teacher, had made me memorize "She Dwelt Among the Untrodden Ways." I'd lie there dripping wet, those awful words looping through my head.

She dwelt among the untrodden ways
Beside the springs of Dove,
A Maid whom there were none to praise
And very few to love . . .

I knew what the boys were doing. I understood the liberties they took. They could easily stare as much as they pleased at Madeline, at the places they would have liked to touch on the girls their own age.

With my understanding of her predicament, then, I should have been glad that Mikey O'Day had come into Madeline's life; I might, anyway, not have minded so much that he'd barged into our lives. After he'd appeared at our door that first time, my mother, at dinner, said down the table to my father, "Madeline had a visitor this afternoon."

"A visitor, Maddy?"

She turned a terrible red, a blush that started below her clavicle.

"Mikey O'Day," Louise said grimly.

"The one who sings at the Dari-Dip? Who got written up in the *Journal?*"

A boyfriend, Father, for your old wife.

I remember how my parents looked at each other, a long wordless exchange, or so it seemed to me. It was my father's lopsided smile, an expression I didn't recognize, that made me think the wrong ideas were being relayed; out of misguided impulses, they might very well agree to something that couldn't be right for Madeline. It's nice, I could imagine my mother saying, that she has a friend, both of them in the same boat. It's nice, nice, nice; nice all around.

"He ate all the sugar," I said, the only charge I could bring against Mikey in the moment.

Madeline had just taken a drink, so that when she began to laugh, when she couldn't stop, the milk, in a most unprincesslike moment, came out of her nose.

After dinner, my parents usually sat downstairs, my mother in the wing chair with the weak light, and my father on the sofa under the brighter lamp. In that softly lit quietness they read. If we came downstairs in fear or sickness, they'd glance up at us as if they hardly knew where they were, as if they hardly knew us. That night, when they'd settled in, I went noisily to the shelf, searching for a book. I wanted to ask how it could be fine for that pair to—what were we supposed to call it?—date, go steady, rob each other's cradle? I don't think either one of them noticed me bumping around in the corner, blowing dust off the books, clapping my hands at a mosquito.

In those days my father referred to Mikey as "the Gentleman

Caller." He'd come in the house after work, kiss my mother at the stove, ask her about her life and times, and then wonder if the Gentleman Caller had shown up.

"After breakfast, before lunch, and all afternoon," my mother would say, looking at her husband fondly and perhaps helplessly.

We had in fact been invaded by Mikey O'Day and his endless colored metal boxes of LPs and 45s. Louise would go to her room to practice. She'd stuff a towel along the crack under her door to keep out the laughter and music that blasted up the two flights of stairs, the noise that was irrepressibly joyful, that could annihilate whatever melancholy piece she was working to perfect.

Chapter Seven

THAT SUMMER WAS A SEASON OF ONE ABSURD EPISODE AFTER THE
next, so that after a while I forgot to be astonished. Or perhaps
it is truer to say that I was conclusively stunned after one of
the boys down the block died; I settled into an unhappiness that
it would not have occurred to me to try to shake. It was the
summer Mikey O'Day got a Ludwig Accent Combo drum set
for his forty-second birthday, the summer Cody Rockard was
killed on the third rail, and throughout, rain and shine, it was the
star-bursting summer of Madeline's romance.

From the beginning I could see that my parents had resolved
to let Mikey O'Day in the house, into the basement, without
supervision; later, unfathomably, they allowed him to visit her in
the bedroom. This was well before teenagers, without blushing
or asking permission, bounded up to their boudoirs to watch
a movie and shake their bedsteads. I stayed on in my role of
sentinel just long enough to witness their first thrill, which I
wished I could have rewound and erased. Right after, I realized
that, on the one hand, I was invading their appalling privacy,
and, on the other, they didn't care if I was around. They were
going to come together even if I was wedged between them.

When at last they were ready for their moment, I was aptly
standing at the bar, mixing explosives in the name of chemistry.
There had been at least four long afternoons of record playing,
Mikey carefully removing a 45 from his metal box and then

from its sleeve, setting the holy object on the turntable and the needle into the groove. He danced with abandon, that terrific head a flower on its stalk, blowin' in the wind. He wasn't without grace, and there was always the beauty of his liberty. As far as I could tell, he never had as much as a flicker of self-consciousness, never doubted his word or deed. He'd get his arms jerking up and down in that rock-and-roll standard as if he'd been wound nearly to the breaking point.

Madeline sat cross-legged watching him, although you might have thought she was looking at her shoes. After he'd shown her how easy it was to breeze around the room, to twist and shake, he'd try to get her to be with him in the song. He'd take her hand and pull her up. She was as stiff and bashful as he was loose and carefree. When he yanked at her she'd shriek and giggle. If he was able to drag her nearly upright he'd stumble over air and fall down, taking her along with him. Right away she'd sit and smooth her dress and hair. He'd crawl around in time to the music, and after he'd get himself standing again, the whole routine would begin anew: there was the judicious choosing of the record, followed by the dance, the entreaty, the near success, the tumble. I had never known how much endurance it took to woo a girl. It was funny, I guess, how diffident she was even though she was at some point going to succumb. The big questions: How long would it take? How much more work was he going to have to do?

On the fourth or fifth afternoon, I'd gone out of the room to rummage around in the storage drawers by the laundry, and as I was coming back he managed to pull her toward him, close that time, and keep her. Finally, for whatever unknowable reason, she'd decided to let him. Her sleek body and his tubbiness in a slow dance. There was lounge music playing, Jim Reeves maybe, singing, "I love you for a hundred reasons but most of all I love you 'cause you're you." All at once she let her straight spine soften. She bent her knees and laid her head on his shoulder. His brows shot practically up to his scalp, his eyes were half open, no fluttering of the lids, the opalescent whites agleam. So that was how a person arrived at real ecstasy.

She seemed to be concentrating, her own brow furrowed. Or else she was about to cry. From happiness maybe, or from the strain of holding out for days, or from a sadness she couldn't understand? Or possibly from the magnificence of the feeling. It was awful to see. I knew the kiss was coming, nothing to do but drop the tray of empty baby-food jars on the cement portion of the floor. The whole package made a satisfying noise, the burst of metal and the breaking glass, all those jars, on the pitiless cement. Needless to say, the dancers busted apart as if they'd been shot in the chest. Without speaking, I picked up every shard. Their moment had passed, and my tenure as sentinel was over. There was very little of their future I wished to see.

Mikey's birthday was a few days after that, the unveiling of his parents' gift, the Ludwig Accent Combo drum set. There were two toms, a snare, a floor tom, and a bass drum, each in an elegant gray with a mother-of-pearl finish. Also, a ride symbol on its stand and a hi-hat, that pair of cymbals on a shorter stand, a single press to the foot pedal to make them clash. The set was fearsome with potential, a present you'd offer with trepidation to anyone who liked to make noise. Still, Mikey crashed and banged with so much enthusiasm you wanted to forgive him. He made it seem like it wasn't necessary to have any coordination in order to enjoy the instruments.

The O'Day parents had had six children, all of them gone off except Mikey, none of them any longer at the mercy of Mrs. O'Day's lavish care. I don't think I ever saw Mikey with a dirty face, with grass stains on his pants, or in socks that weren't sparkling white. Lu once said that he always looked like a baby who's just had his bath. Mrs. O'Day kept him in ironed blue jeans that turned up at the cuffs, and crisp plaid shirts, a fresh T-shirt underneath. He was well trained, always washing his stubby square hands before meals in the downstairs bathroom. His nails were clipped to the pads of his fingers, and I suppose his mother kept his toenails in that shape, too. Mr. O'Day did his part for his son, building Mikey a platform on their back porch for the drum set, so you could see from the alley the blur of his body and his sticks.

Ours was an age when very few people had air conditioning, when the windows were open all night long. At eight-thirty in the morning, Julia faithfully went around the house and slammed the sashes shut against the heat. But before breakfast, as the fathers were going to work, the spangle of the hi-hat, the direct cracks to the drumhead, and the tremor of the reverberations came to us from a full block away.

The set had come with a tutorial book, a play-along record that had a variety of songs in different styles. So there was also the matter of the stereo system, Mikey cranking up the volume in order to hear the guitars and leads over his own noise. That Mrs. O'Day let him practice at dawn should have tipped my mother off to the fundamental unreasonableness of her person. The racket must have driven the neighbors out of their minds, but no one had the heart, or maybe it was courage, to complain. Although in that era there was not yet a Bill of Rights for the handicapped, no Special Olympics or support groups for the parents, although it was a time when we could all use the colorful words for insanity without much guilt, there was of course the usual general wish that there be communal tenderness for the disadvantaged. Mrs. O'Day, at least, seemed to have depended on such a spirit. You might think that my parents and the O'Days would have commiserated about their common plight, but as far as I can tell my mother never spoke personally to anyone outside the family, never had a friend in for the purpose of private complaint. It was a matter, again, of dignity rather than repression, something I have tried to explain without success to my wife. Russia often said the good Lord couldn't make everyone perfect, a failure I wanted to question her about. Why, after all, suffer an imperfect God? "Bless his very own self," she often said when she saw Mikey coming up the walk.

That summer, I played tennis more than I'd planned and walked the streets, and when I was home I lay on my sweaty bed reading books I considered deep and philosophical—science fiction, on the whole. I felt a prisoner in my own house, forced into my cell by the couple downstairs. I'm sure my mother was around, but I don't remember her in those first days. Perhaps she had disappeared in order to let nature take its course, or maybe she, too, couldn't stand to watch the lover boy squeezing up against Madeline on the sofa, nibbling at his morsel. It was hard to say which was worse, who you wanted to look at less: Mikey at his worship, or Madeline, screeching like a schoolgirl, like a twit. It wasn't until I'd acquired the wisdom of the ages that I realized that, beyond her coyness, she was the one who had the real passion; although Mikey was always wooing her, she was the one more in love. Louise, as I said, had retreated to her own room with the cello, and so I didn't have the benefit of her playing freely downstairs. The Bach was muffled by the insulation she'd wadded around her door. She and I hardly knew what to say to each other, passing in the hall, glaring for the same reason.

Although I took it for granted that my parents loved each other without reservation, I naturally never thought about their sex life. Aside from Buddy's escapades at the lake, I'd never really witnessed anyone in love up close. But now, in my own house, even if I meant not to look, there was Mikey smooching away while Madeline half-heartedly pushed him off. Sometimes in the middle of the gaiety she'd suddenly get serious, a moment you'd hate to see. She'd seize his thick, ruddy neck with her white hands, or, before she kissed him, she'd pet his mouth with reverence, as if his lips were an adorable little animal. When she got like that, grave and full of industry, he'd open his eyes and bore into her with his magnified gaze. You felt like his soul was in his eyes—he was trying that hard to communicate. Without any shame, as if he didn't think anyone was watching, he'd put his hand to her breast, and she, on our sofa and in broad daylight—she'd arch her back. When that happened, I didn't break china or let a stack of books fall to the floor. The only thing I could think to do was bang out the front door, get out of the place that no longer felt like home.

Aside from our own hothouse, there were no signs that the sexual revolution was on its way. The Catholic girls in their plaid skirts and knee socks and loafers, their sprayed hair and black eye makeup, moved in an impenetrable herd on their way to school. None of the mothers could have been temptresses, none of them the type to have illicit sex leaning against laundry chutes or in commuter trains. No falling backward into swimming pools at a cocktail party for the squaws of 400 Grove. Our large, soft, graying mothers rang their bells and called one continuous name, KevinDorothyStacyPeterMichaeleenPatrickChrissySusan. It seemed to me that that was what most mothers lived for, to call and call, day after day. They'd sent their children out to play and wanted them back. They didn't seem to be reading *The Feminine Mystique* or *The Second Sex* out of curiosity as Julia Maciver was, weren't becoming enraged about their subjugation, raising their fists, and storming the streets like the women in New York City. They weren't inventing consciousness-raising, and they weren't either mending or cleaning or cooking. They were calling for us. Up and down the alley, they were so comfortably unattractive and worn that now, in my mind's eye, they have a sheen that is something like beauty.

Mikey's mother, Mrs. O'Day, was the ultimate Über-mother, a woman Mrs. Maciver came to oppose, cursing her, going as far as to wish ill upon her. At the time of the birthday drum set, she was still in Julia's good graces, a woman who had gotten her son a present so lovingly suited to his interest and desire, even if the neighbors were losing their wits. The wild crashing rhythms from the next block went on for a week and a half or so, until there came, one morning, a silence. Nothing but the birds to wake us along with the milkman, the song of his bad muffler a sweet old irritation. It shouldn't have been hard to guess why the quiet. After all, everyone wanted those drums, including those of us who had been abjured not to covet things. Why wouldn't an enterprising boy in the neighborhood find a way to make the Ludwig display his own? Jerry Pindel had long shiny black hair that was always in his eyes, a hunch when he walked, his rounded shoulders to his ears, his neck short and tight. When he was twelve, he'd shut his sister up in an old chest freezer in the basement—a murderous prank the mothers never forgot, proof of one of Julia's maxims: "For Reputation lost comes not again." His teenage misery, that bottled rage, concerned some of the mothers. By lunchtime, the news had spread in its pathogenic way from house to house: everyone knew that Mikey O'Day was going to be the backup drummer—the star backup drummer, that is—in Jerry's band. During rehearsals, if Mikey could get away from the Dari-Dip, he was going to be allowed to sit, to have an actual seat behind the real drummer. He would have the privilege of being in the Pindels' loft, above the garage, where the group, The Spellbinders, practiced. It seems almost shameful now, that the neighborhood gangsters had such a clean, hopeful name for their band.

On the morning when Mikey rushed in the kitchen to tell Madeline he was going to be in The Spellbinders, a negotiation that must have been completed the night before, he neglected, in his excitement, to kiss her.

"Jerry's band?" she sniffed.

"I'm the drummer, the backup, the backup drummer! The star, the star backup drummer for Jerry, for Jerry—"

"You're too noisy," she snapped.

Russia happened to be having her breakfast, and she said, "Sit down here, Mikey, sit yourself down. What are you talking about? What's this about Jerry?"

"I'm the d-d-drummer. I'm the drummer for Jerry, for Jerry's, for Jerry's band."

"I told you, you're noisy." Madeline crossed her arms on her chest and moved her chair away from him.

"You make sure you have time for your girl," Russia said. "Don't you go leave your girl behind for an old drum set."

Mikey, to his credit, stopped in his tracks. "Leave? Leave my girl?"

Madeline was starting to cry. Already a drum widow. No longer would she be able to sit at the Dari-Dip like the First Lady, prim and admiring. No longer would Mikey say, "This song goes out to my girl, goes out to my girl, my b-b-b-best girl." Never again would the regulars clap and call out, "Yay, Madeline!" She was sobbing into her eggs.

"No! No, no, no, no." He knelt at her chair, he tried to lift her head, tried to catch her hand. "I'll never, I'll never, never leave my girl." It went on, as this particular sequence always did, her tears, his pleading, more tears, his promises. Eventually, she'd turn to look at him, such a sad sight, her blotchy face, her runny nose. He'd hold her, rocking her, until he was forgiven. Pretty soon she'd tell him where and how to sit, what to eat, she'd lick her finger and try to flatten his cowlick. He'd close his eyes, throwing his head back, breathing easy, smiling with satisfaction, as if he'd just finished the long race. They were in love, all right.

It must be said that Mikey used every one of his fifty-two IQ points for all they were worth. He was clearly able to acquire practical knowledge, learning to read Madeline's humors and figuring out how to butter her up. In addition to his facility, his temperament seemed to be ideally suited to hers. I have always found the idea of the noble savage and the joyful idiot suspect. It's true, however, that one of Mikey's greatest assets was his inclination toward happiness. He seemed to have a neurological inability to be downcast for more than a minute or two.

"So you're going to be in Jerry's band," Russia said after the storm had passed. "You be sure Jerry's good to you, you hear me?"

"Jerry, Jerry's nice, he's nice to me."

"I like Jerry!" Madeline pronounced.

In the olden days, when we'd only had Madeline at table, she didn't speak up too much. Now that Mikey was around, she was either bossing him or expressing herself. She'd found her voice, which we are all supposed to strive for, but I missed the ancient times when I could better imagine, in her quietude, what she was thinking.

"I pray for Jerry," Russia said, "you know that? I pray he come to some use, just like I pray for our Buddy. Two bad boys who need the Lord. Two such bad boys."

That Buddy and Jerry should have an encounter two years later was right there foretold—the hoodlums on Russia's hit list, united by prayer. That Buddy would visit and beat Jerry up and all for good was a story Russia, even with her narrative gifts, couldn't at that stage have prefigured.

My mother had been on the telephone upstairs, and when she came into the kitchen Russia said, "You hear the news, Miz Julia?"

"What news?"

"I'm the drummer," Mikey cried. "Jerry, Jerry needs me for the drummer, in his band, in his band."

"Does he need your drums, too?" I was finally able to get a word in.

Russia cackled into her napkin. "They don't call you smart for nothing, Timothy."

"He's using my drums, using, using my drums, so I can be the star, the star backup drummer."

"Ah," my mother said.

"Uh-huh," Russia said, "uh-huh."

Louise had made her entrance at that point, and she said, "Those drums should be repossessed. Jerry Pindel is such a lousy little jerk."

"I like Jerry!"

"No, Maddy," was all I could think to say.

"Why?" Louise said with disgust in her voice. "Why do you like him?"

"He watches me walk," Madeline said.

We all turned to stare. Even Mikey looked momentarily startled.

She hung her head. "I like him!"

"Of course you do," my mother said. "He's a fine boy. He's going to turn out just fine."

Louise grabbed a piece of bread, tore it from its crusts, and made the dough into one meaty ball. "If Jerry comes around asking for my cello, you give it right to him, because he's a fine person." She popped the whole thing in her mouth and left the room.

Every Wednesday morning, Mrs. O'Day took Mikey to the record shop uptown so he could buy his one 45 of the week. He'd spend much of his energy for the next six days committing the songs, front and back, to memory, as well as anticipating his next purchase. It was what he called his work. Madeline was in on the routine, and shortly after Louise exited, the swain and his armpiece departed for their outing to Little's Music Shop.

"It ain't right," Russia said when they'd gone. "Jerry taking over those drums."

"Well," my mother said slowly, "I think there's a nuance, maybe, that we should consider."

"Nuance, Miz Julia? What do you mean?"

Miz Julia began by stating the problem: Jerry had in fact stolen Mikey's drums—yes, yes, he had. However. The fact that he'd invited Mikey to be part of the band should not be overlooked. We had all seen with our own eyes that Mikey was standing taller. He was proud and happy and excited—

"Mikey is always proud, happy, and excited," I said. "It's not possible for Mikey to be happier than he already is. Mikey has a continuous peaking point of happiness. In case you hadn't noticed." The morning's drama was making me feel satisfyingly high and mighty. "You know as well as I that Jerry is not going to let Mikey play his own drum set, his very own drums, in the band."

"I'm not sure that matters." My mother hacked away at her cold bacon with a knife instead of picking it up and eating it. "He's involved in making music with other people, even if he's standing by. He'll love that. He'll be thrilled. I think there's actually a nugget of generosity in Jerry—he's doing what he can to include Mikey."

"Generosity?" I said. "A nugget?" Even though Jerry cut through our yard every morning on his way to St. Rita's, we had never done more than grunt at each other. As little as I knew him, I was certain that if he in fact had some goodness within himself, it was far smaller than a nugget.

Russia agreed. "You are not of this world, Miz Julia. Not of this world."

"Aside from the flagrant injustice of it," I went on, "all of Grove Avenue will thank Jerry for grabbing the drum set. Now we only have to worry about The Spellbinders playing too late into the night, but that's probably better than Mikey splitting our heads open at sunrise. So, Mother, you can feel good about that. I'm sure most people will bow down before Jerry in thanks."

Russia laughed, wiping her eyes, shaking her head. "Ain't that the truth," she said.

It was my mother's practice to let a tangle work itself out, to be patient in conflict. Since there were remarkably few incidents through my childhood when she lost control, I remember them with a fair degree of clarity. You wondered, when you saw the eruptions, how she managed to comport herself with any serenity for months at a time. About the drums she remained true to her ideal. She did mean, eventually, to talk to Mrs. Pindel and Mrs. O'Day about the seizure of the instruments, but before she got around to it Cody Rockard was killed on the train tracks. The neighborhood went quiet. How was it that Cody couldn't take back the dare, playing up on the tracks, couldn't rectify the error of touching the third rail? *Wait, wait, didn't mean it!* We went to the wake to see the ten-year-old's powdered face in the white casket. Madeline and Mikey came along, too, leaning in to each other as if they'd been married for fifty years, as if they had only each other to depend on in a time of sorrow. Outside of the funeral home she cried into his neck, taking big sniffly breaths. It seemed to me that she was enjoying the tragedy, that having a padded shoulder—Mikey in a suit!—to weep on in public made the death worth her while. And her man, while subdued, managed to keep the sun shining through the bitter gloom: "Hi, Mrs. Van, Van Norman, hi, hi, Mr. Mr. Van Norman, hi, Mr. Rockard!"

We went on that summer behaving as if the old concerns were still important. We went on without speaking of Cody, but thinking of the boy we hadn't really known, carrying the implausible idea of his being dead, the idea that trumped everything else we knew. We went on as if we were preoccupied with the question—the pressing question—of whether or not Mikey O'Day was going to come with us to Moose Lake for all of August. Mrs. O'Day did not want to let him go for a month, and he probably, when it came down to it, didn't like the thought of missing the Dari-Dip in season. For the record, Joan O'Day never invited Madeline on any of their vacations. After several phone calls, it was decided that the O'Days would drive Mikey up and drop him off for a long weekend. Mrs. O'Day spoke about time alone with her husband as if it was a great inconvenience, as if there was nothing more disruptive to her schedule than having to pass seventy-two hours with him in a rental cottage in Door County. On our end, since Mikey was an unmarried male, a virtual boy, he'd have to sleep in the boathouse. My only consolation was that Buddy wouldn't be there, that I would not have to endure Mikey O'Day in the presence of my cousin. Buddy had been sent to a wilderness camp, another effort to whip him into shape.

It was an intolerable August for Madeline, the two-week wait for Mikey to visit, the unbearable excitement of his being with her, followed by the pining for him after he'd gone. I don't think the aunts could have stood any more necking in the water, Madeline in his arms like a baby. Or the hullabaloo of their splashing. Or his singing, morning, noon, and night, around the campfire, with or without a burning log.

By the time we were home from Moose Lake, school was about to start. Jerry's band was broken up for the moment, and the drums were returned to the O'Days' back porch. That seemed to be the end of it. Years later, I thought about how Mikey's drums had given him a certain cachet in the neighborhood. Madeline, too, had some prize possessions she could hold out as her drawing card. There was the Judy Garland Teen doll, a Cindy Kay, a Betsy Wetsy, also a Betsy McCall, a

Bare Bottom Baby, a Melody Baby Debbi, a TinyTeen, a Miss Deb-Teen, and a Twist and Turn Stacey. To name but a few. There was no one more electrified by the advent of the Cabbage Patch doll, and when Beanie Babies flooded the country, my father had to build yet another set of shelves for her room. Madeline, our fountain of youth. It was her collection that worked a charm on the Grove Avenue little girls, children too young and too dazzled by the display to worry over the fact that Madeline was taller than most of their mothers.

Julia was always firm in her insistence that the dolls belonged to Madeline, that she would not give them away. When Madeline still had us as her playmates, she and Lu and I would spread out the contents of the four trunks on the floor, emptying the drawers of the shoes and hats, stripping the metal hangers of their dresses. Naturally we always lifted the dolls' skirts to look underneath. Madeline would get angry if we were careless with the accessories, but she did like our inventions, the paces we put the characters through, their elaborate tragedies. Sometimes, though, we'd inadvertently tip her off into one of her legendary fits, if we put the wrong costume on a doll, or made a favorite into a silly figure. You couldn't always predict when or why she'd shriek and set off wailing through the house. We were used to the squalls, hardly noticing the turning point in the tantrum, when my mother could hold Madeline firm, rocking her until she was quiet. During the Mikey O'Day years, those outbursts, the hysteria for little reason, didn't occur nearly as often as they had. It was a good period for my parents.

There'd been an earlier time of relative peace, too, when Louise and I and Madeline were first roughly the same age, when we all started to play together. My parents were liberated into their own after-dinner conversation. It would have begun when I was four and Lu her precocious two. By day my mother could read the same book to us, Madeline in the crook of one arm, Lu and I in a heap on the other side, each absorbed in the adventures of Snip, Snap, and Snur. The three of us in my mother's circle, if given a chance just then, would have been happy not to grow even a minute older.

Chapter Eight

MIKEY O'DAY MUST HAVE COME TO OUR DOORSTEP IN 1963, A
few months before Kennedy's assassination. The Fullers, then,
had been on the East Coast for nearly three years. Figgy had
moved to Georgetown with Arthur when Kennedy was elected,
exactly as she'd envisioned. They'd dragged Buddy from the
Princeton High School, and not long after sent him to a military
academy in Fork Union, Virginia. You can pick out Figgy in
the clips of Kennedy's inaugural ball, Mrs. Fuller standing
right near Bette Davis in the few seconds when the stars were
shown processing into the hall. Arthur worked for the State
Department at first, was part of the Policy Planning Staff, an
arm of State that was supposed to provide independent analysis
and formulate long-term policies in relation to America's goals.
Later, in the Johnson administration, he became an aide to
the president. In 1960, it was essential to Figgy that Arthur get
his appointment before the inaugural ball, so she'd be able to
secure their invitation. Through his years in government, he
remained one of the few men among his colleagues who did
not have a real change of heart about the Vietnam conflict, as
they called it then, who believed that we must not let our
commitment to the South Vietnamese falter. There are black-
and-white stills from the Johnson days, twenty or so haggard
men around the table in their shirtsleeves, the sense that they've
been there for days, they are never going to leave, and no one,
but no one would think to make a wisecrack.

After their move to Washington, we might see Buddy and Figgy at Moose Lake for a weekend but they were no longer regular in their visits. Arthur usually didn't come along, because he was careening from crisis to crisis as his job required. But there was a memorable Christmas Eve party at our house in 1965, before Buddy enlisted, when they all showed up. The appearance must have been prompted by my grandmother's last illness, the Fullers alighting for twenty-four hours of their best attention. Our family holiday affairs were formal, the boys and men in suits and ties, the girls in red and green velvet dresses, the wives also in Christmas colors, except for Figgy that year, who wore black. Decades later, the aunts were still talking about that dress, which my father said surely had been cut off of Sophia Loren, Figgy snipping carefully around the wavy décolletage.

Russia arrived early in the morning to start her dinner rolls rising and to set us up at the kitchen table to polish the brass candlesticks and the silver. She covered Madeline with a tent of an apron and each year showed her how, pouring the pink clot of cleaner onto a rag, getting all of us to rub the utensils dutifully until our cloths bled black. Russia wore one uniform for the preparation, and before the party she changed into a second, identical uniform. In honor of the occasion, she added the pearl clip-on earrings Figgy had once given her, and a red ruffled apron that tied in a girlish bow at the back.

All morning Madeline would say, "Can I go upstairs now? Is it time yet?"

When the silver was done, Russia took her to the attic to retrieve the long green velvet dress from the garment bag. There was a matching headband, a tiara kind of thing with red silk roses on the top. Madeline was often at first shy in large groups, even among the relatives she knew, hanging back on the stairs, mysterious in her dreamy gown. Those were the moments when she looked like the Lady of Shalott, her eyes cast down, most of her in the shadows. Even though she'd come into her own with Mikey O'Day, if he wasn't with her, if she couldn't be with him in their bubble of love, she'd revert to her old tentative self. At Christmastime Mikey always went to Kansas with his parents to visit the rich sister who had seven children and two massive trees for all the presents. So Mikey told us with a great deal of rapturous stuttering.

At our party, my mother, issuing her orders and manning the stove, was usually a little rattled, a little dazed. When she was sure everything and every person was in place, she'd come to the head of the table, and you could see, as she closed her eyes, took a deep breath, and then looked to my father, that she had laid down her heavy load, that she had at last arrived at the gathering. She always forgot to take off her apron, so that she'd sit through dinner with meat stains up her front, her moss-green dress hidden from view. She was at her best in that hour, brightly flushed, the soft light shining through her ecstatic hair. Just when she was settled in her chair, she stood again, and we followed her lead, all eyes to the floor as we sang the Doxology, parents and children alike alarmed by the intimacy we'd been thrust into, raising our voices together.

There was an extra sparkle in the very air the night the celebrity family came to the party. I suppose I'd been looking forward to Buddy's visit. Everyone pointed out what a special occasion it was, to have the Fullers in town for Christmas. I remember how adult he seemed with the youngest cousins, how he stood in the hall with his dark coat on, pulling off his leather gloves, a finger at a time, expressing exaggerated shock at the boys' and girls' miraculous growth. It was as if he'd paid attention to them when they were four and five and six. Suddenly, somehow, he was in the category of fun uncle, and they behaved accordingly, piling on him. Buddy, crawling with children, had stepped across the divide and wasn't one of us anymore. He kissed Cousin Mona demurely on the cheek—and we cousins who knew, who *knew*, exchanged glances. Although he had been held back and had not yet graduated from high school, he shook her college boyfriend's hand and then gave him a fraternal slap to the arm.

The aunts and uncles of course were keen to know all the details of Figgy and Arthur's fascinating life. When Mrs. Kennedy had been restoring the White House, Figgy, brandishing her Radcliffe art-history degree, had finagled her way onto the committee that was researching paintings and locating period pieces. Those years had been a heady time for her, charging around the Executive Mansion examining paintings Dolley Madison had had commissioned, and going to New York, to auction houses, to have a look on the First Lady's behalf. It turned out Figgy had acumen as well as taste; one of her stock stories was about standing on a street corner on the Lower East Side in 1939 and becoming friends with de Kooning. Later she sent the impoverished artist checks, acquiring paintings for next to nothing. Also, she claimed to have picked out Pollock long before Mrs. Guggenheim took notice. After I graduated from college, she took me through the Metropolitan, stopping at her favorite paintings to clutch her heart, to tell me who was a homo, who had died cruelly of syphilis, who had gone mad. Over the years she developed an encyclopedic knowledge, something she curiously didn't often talk about or flash; her profession, perhaps, was where she practiced restraint. She traveled a great deal to Europe as a consultant, and eventually, well after her White House years, she was hired as the curator at the Phillips Collection. It was Mrs. Kennedy, she would say, who taught her much of what she knew, who gave her a start. Now that we understand so much about JFK's prodigious appetite, I wonder how or if Figgy escaped an encounter with him. Certainly there was no one who took Jack's death harder than my aunt.

That Christmas was the last time Figgy came to a holiday party at our house, although it was primarily Arthur and my mother who argued. The dining-room table had been split open at its center and the five leaves put in, so that twenty of the adults and the older teenagers could sit together. Madeline always took her place right next to my mother, the two of them squeezed at the head of the table. In the living room there were four card tables for the younger children, the group of ten-year-old girls managing the toddlers' spilled milk and excusing

them their vegetables. No amount of insisting could convince Russia
to eat with the elders. For a few minutes she'd lean on a stool in the
living room, her plate in her hands, before she set it down and again
made the rounds with her rolls.

My mother had simple ornaments, a blazing red tablecloth, greens
that she and Madeline had gathered in the yard before the meal was
served, the snow in a magical moment melting to glistening drops before the cloth was spotted with ordinary water stains. The brass candlesticks, gleaming after our labors, and with tall white tapers, gave
the room at once its warmth and a churchlike solemnity. At Christmas
I always had the sense that the neighbors fell away, that on the wide-
open plain there was our single house, golden with light, the windows
steamy with our breath, our life. My father's place was surrounded by
the platters, and one by one, as the ritual goes, he heaped the plates
with my mother's best efforts, adjusting for each person's taste, passing the wholesome turkey that had come from a family farm in Wisconsin, and the puffy damp stuffing, and steaming white potatoes from
that same good farm, and an array of buttery vegetables including the
detestable Brussels sprouts. There were the sweet things, too, fancy
Jell-O molds that looked like the neighborhood women's church hats,
and candied yams and cranberries popped open in their hot bath of
maple syrup. I was always hungry in those days, and the sight of the
turkey, its skin darkening and drawing taut and crisp over the breast as
it was basted through the afternoon hours, filled me with a fluttery excitement.

When at last everyone was served, my mother, ever the hostess,
asked the opening question, the most important inquiry, according to
manuals on manners, that should from the start draw the group into
spirited but congenial conversation. "So, Arthur," she said mildly,
"how much longer do you think the troops are going to be in Vietnam?"

The relatives turned down the table to my mother, cocking their
heads, as if they weren't sure they'd heard her. "You've got to love the
woman," Figgy said, looking at the ceiling. Her tone was insincere,

and I guessed that she was trying somehow to protect Arthur. He looked very tired, his lids at half-mast over his protruding eyes, as the vapors of his plate came up into his gray face.

The active combat had really only begun for American troops. There were mixed messages coming from the administration, the secretary of defense saying victory would take time while others predicted a swift fight to the finish. In November there had been the first major engagement between the regular U.S. and North Vietnamese forces. Arthur did take up Mrs. Maciver's question, speaking with a quiet pride about how the Third Brigade, First Cavalry Division, had defeated the NVA Thirty-second, Thirty-third, and Sixty-sixth Regiments in the La Drang Valley.

My mother, passing the cranberries, said quizzically, "The thing I've never understood is why Harry Truman didn't write Ho Chi Minh, back in, whenever that was, in 1945, it must have been, when Ho took over Hanoi. Have you ever read Ho's speech, the one he gave at the inauguration of the Democratic Republic of Vietnam?"

Arthur had been about to put a buttered turnip in his mouth. "It's Christmas, for God's sake, Julia," Figgy said. "The president is suspending bombing for the holiday, and I suggest you do the same." Warming just a bit, she said, "And you should take off that apron."

"Oh!" My mother reached behind her and undid the ties, bundled the thing in a ball, and pitched it through the arch that led to the kitchen. Maybe she couldn't help herself, her nerves unwinding up through her tongue after so many hours of cooking. She couldn't refrain from talking about how Roosevelt had waffled on Indochina through the years, how he and Churchill hadn't kept their pledge of self-government for the Vietnamese, and how Ho had lifted chunks from the Declaration of Independence for his speech, how he'd spoken about the pursuit of happiness.

"I'm aware of the speech," Arthur said simply. He watched the butter slide off the turnip into his pear Jell-O. He was no longer interested in my mother's ideas. It seemed possible that he no longer wanted to be in our company. I realized I had looked forward to his excited questions, the way he'd gaze at you and wonder what you'd been reading and why you thought as you did. I hated to think that the Fullers' being in Washington with important people had automatically rendered us dull. I hated to think that we were dull, and that he'd never like us again.

My father rarely interfered with his indefatigable wife, but at that moment he raised his glass to Winston Churchill, who had died the previous February. More gravely then, we toasted Grandmother, home in her bed, soon to join the prime minister in the hereafter. Some of the cousins were still watching Arthur to see if the expert, the man who was practically commander-in-chief, was going to say anything else. At last he set his turnip down, and, cutting through the few desultory conversations that had started up, he launched into his defense. He explained that President Johnson had made a generous offer in the spring in exchange for peace, some kind of development opportunity to generate electricity in the Mekong Delta, which apparently Ho Chi Minh had rejected. Although he became more animated as he spoke, he hardly glanced at my mother, fixing his eyes on Cousin Nick across the table. He said at least twice that Ho Chi Minh was no better than Joseph Stalin, that thousands of landlords had been murdered in Ho's land-reform campaign and thousands sent to gulags.

My mother was looking as beautiful as I'd ever seen her, the pinkness shining in her round face. I had once loved her thrill in the heat of the argument, but now I wished so much she wouldn't carry it on. "Oh, Art," she said, and she laughed a little, at her own folly, surely at her own foolishness. "All of that may be true, but can you really tell me that the United States is morally superior? You can't actually believe that, can you? We install and support Diem in Saigon, a tyrant who is every bit as brutal as those we anoint the Evil Ones—more gravy, Buddy?— and then we decide he's no good, and our men arrange for his assassination. *Viva* the democratic spirit. Now there's been coup after coup, mass chaos. It looks to me like we're the ones invading Vietnam—I know, I know, I don't have the whole picture. But I'll say it again. I've always had the impression that Ho Chi Minh is a nationalist at heart, rather than a dyed-in-the-wool communist, that first and foremost he's trying to liberate his country from colonists."

"The impression?" Arthur hissed.

"Wouldn't you, sweetie, with your bleeding sore heart, be such a breath of fresh air at our dinner parties!" Figgy said to my mother. "Shut up, both of you, I mean it, do you hear? Aaron"—she turned to my father—"help me out here. Stop talking to Nick about your dead old birds, and rescue this conversation from war talk so we can all part friends in honor of our Saviour. For one thing, I want to know what you kids have been doing this year. Mac, tell me about your plans for college."

One of the little boys, who had brought his meat to his father to be cut, shouted out, "Mac dissected a monkey on the bar in the basement!"

Before any of the others could express their disgust Madeline cried, "I helped him. I helped with the shark, too." She put her head down, shy again. "Poor monkey," she sniffed.

"So you still want to be a doctor," Figgy said to me. "That's good. Although sawing apart an animal on a bar has to be against a law of some kind. Your father, I assume, gets the specimens from the museum?"

"Leftovers," I said. Having the baboon in my possession hadn't exactly been illegal, but I wasn't supposed to advertise it. I'd been lucky to get it fresh from the local zoo about twenty-four hours after its death.

"There's monkeys uptown!" Madeline said in another burst. She meant the two rhesus monkeys that were kept in a large glass case in one of the smaller department stores on Main Street. My mother and Madeline always stopped in to look at them when they went shopping.

"How fascinating." Figgy smiled hard at Madeline without opening her mouth. "Honey," she added. I later realized that Figgy had been gone long enough to have missed the Mikey O'Day story, that she didn't know about Madeline's man. I wondered if she might have expressed more interest in her if she'd known. "Louise. What about your cello? You still on your way to Carnegie Hall?"

"Unlikely," Louise said, without looking up from her turkey. "But not impossible."

Figgy went on to interview the other teenagers, but before she'd gotten down the line Arthur couldn't help making a correction. My mother was talking with my uncle Fritz about the rumblings of the peace movement, the rumor that the second Tonkin Gulf Incident hadn't actually taken place. "Julia," Arthur called down the table, "we've established before that it's pointless to discuss these matters, you and I."

When? When had they stopped arguing for their own amusement? When had their interchanges become pointless?

"Not because you're not intelligent," he was saying, "but because you remain willfully misguided about a most complex situation. And yet perfectly happy to talk ad infinitum to anyone who will listen. You assume the administration is blithely ordering up troops, when in fact the discussions at every level are deeply somber. I shudder to think of your holding forth at the League of Women Voters, 'informing' your sisters. Again: do you tell them that Ho Chi Minh's pursuit of happiness involves the 'political struggle' he's authorized for the Vietcong, which means assassinations of village authorities and other government officials, which amounts to about four thousand people a year? Do you remind your listeners of those men and women who no longer have their unalienable rights?"

Madeline just then stood up and tapped my mother on the arm, expecting the usual in the absence of Mikey. Julia pushed back and drew her onto her lap. Arthur, who I guess had never seen Madeline reclining flat against the hostess at table, opened his mouth and gaped.

"I know," my mother said from behind Madeline's velvet shoulder, "I know it's heretical to say so, but I'm just not sure that if Vietnam went communist it would be the end of the world." She stroked

Madeline's hair, waiting for Arthur to pounce, giving him the chance. When he continued to stare she said, "Fewer people in the end will be dead. I'm not so certain that the rest of Asia and Europe will tumble to the Reds. We've already lost—what—something like six hundred or so of our troops? And our own boys—our own boys coming up to draft age. 'War,' " she quoted from the ancients, " 'loves to prey upon the young.' "

Although I'd eaten very little at that juncture, I stood and said, "May Buddy and I be excused?" I didn't know if Buddy wanted to leave, if he'd prefer to stay on since he'd been acting so adult. It was a relief to see the model guest gathering his plate and utensils to take to the kitchen. "Thanks, Aunt Julia," he said. "I can't remember when I've had a better dinner." He turned to me and, just as he used to, he snapped, "Let's go, Brains."

Our departure was the signal for the rest of the children to fly off to other parts of the house, to the basement to play Ping-Pong, or out in the yard to assess the snow that had just begun to fall. In my room, Buddy slumped in the desk chair, his legs spread wide apart. I sat on the bed hugging my knees. It was hard not to be shy with my cousin, with him who was suddenly polite and mature, the stepson of an impressive man, someone my mother should never have challenged. The summer before, I had also found new reason to admire Buddy, and I was still, after six months, suffering from that rekindled awe. There had been an incident in July, all of us gathered in the Pindels' garage to see Buddy display not only wisdom, not only physical prowess, but, I would have gone so far as to say, nobility. It was an episode that still shamed me, that I hadn't mentioned to anyone.

In the most casual way, sitting lazily in my chair, he announced that following his graduation at the end of May he figured he'd enlist in the army.

"Oh," I said, nodding.

He started to talk about his duty to his country, how his father had fought in World War II. Bill Eastman, according to Buddy, had always remarked that being in the army was one of the great experiences and had taught him important values. It was the first time Buddy had brought up his real father since his death a year before. Even though he'd rarely seen Bill, my cousin had lived through a tragedy I couldn't imagine, losing his parent, another thing that separated him from me. "And Arthur," Buddy said, "Arthur's been a good stepdad. He's never treated me like he thinks I'm a dumb-ass, you know that? I've screwed up however many times, and my parents have always bailed me out, always ready to give me another chance." He was speaking with a seriousness that was frightening in and of itself. "I guess I'm just ready to make them proud of me, and if I can protect democracy in the world at the same time—hey!—double whammy."

I was speechless in the face of his resolve, his bravery. In the moment, I couldn't think of any flaw in his argument. Even if I'd remembered that Bill Eastman had drunk himself to death—in spite of the important values he'd learned in World War II—I wouldn't have mentioned it.

"What about you?" he said. "You could enlist, too. With your brains they'd put you in Intelligence, send you to China to spy on the little people."

"Sure," I said, thinking that I'd have to, that it would be only right to follow in Buddy's footsteps. Vietnam seemed remote to me, on the whole, even though my mother spoke of it every day and was already part of the Chicago antiwar movement, the fledgling group made up of Quakers and clerics, women, and some students. She had assured me that I'd be able to attend the college of my choice, and that afterward, if the war was still going on, I could register as a conscientious objector. In my room, Buddy had spoken as many young men do who know very little about the war they are going off to fight. At the time, he seemed not only certain but knowledgeable. I wouldn't understand until years later that he couldn't figure out what else to do with himself. As if to remind me that the real Buddy was still inside his upright self, he told me that since he was enlisting I could be sure that he was living it up, that there were places not far from Fork Union to meet women—all of them sorry for the boys' hardships at the academy, and so helpful at easing their pain.

It's probably not unusual for civilians to be vague about the intricacies of the military, fuzzy about the differences between the First Battalion, Second Infantry, and the First Squadron, Fourth Cavalry; the organization, the distinctions difficult to absorb unless you're on the inside. Buddy's career path all over the globe has seemed labyrinthine to me, but for him it became a clear course. No one could believe it when the news came in 1970 that he was going to re-enlist for a second tour, staying on when so many veterans were embittered. I remember my father saying, "He's well suited to it," a truth that put an end to the conversation.

"I'm not afraid," he said that night in my room. "And besides, we're going to whip their yellow asses."

"I'll probably end up going, too," I said, suddenly imagining our sneaking through the wet grass side by side, a thrill up my spine, the joy of our fear.

Two of the small cousins barged in right then to tell us that the carolers had come, as if this were an excitement we'd been waiting for all year. We went downstairs to listen to the group assembled in the hall, the Van Norman family singers, including their relations, twenty-five of them packed in our entry. After a minute, Buddy squeezed past into the living room to talk to Mona, and I went into the kitchen to see if there were any more of Russia's rolls.

"The army will be good for him," Figgy was saying over the noise of the carolers to my mother. "He's done just fine at Fork Union. Buddy's a boy who needs a firm hand, you know that. It's taken him a while to reform, but he's shaping up nicely." She'd tied one apron around her neck and another around her waist, more of her covered than usual. If Mrs. Kennedy—or dead Jack—could see her now, wiping the dishes.

"You can't let him enlist," my mother said. She was at the sink, doing the washing.

"He's a long shot for Harvard, sweetheart. The conflict may be over before he's finished his training, and if it's not he'll be able to pick a job far from combat. I'm not sending him over there to be killed."

"Support positions can be dangerous, too. And there are other colleges besides Harvard." Arthur came into the kitchen carrying the last basket of rolls, and my mother right away went after him. "You can keep Buddy from enlisting, Art. You of all people know how desperate the fighting is, how savage. And how long it's going to go on." She had taken off her rubber gloves and was appealing to him with her outstretched hands.

I had a fleeting thought that Arthur might not have been willing to send his flesh-and-blood son, if he'd had one, to war. He set the basket on the counter and shot Figgy a look: *I don't know why I put up with your relations.* He must never have seen dishpan hands before, because he looked as if he might be ill at the sight of my mother's saturated skin, the puckery whiteness of her fingers.

"Buddy has been brought up to understand the responsibility of those of us who live in freedom." He paused to allow that idea to sink in, to let my mother reflect that some persons didn't raise their children to the highest standards. "And, as Dr. Johnson remarked, 'Every man thinks meanly of himself for not having been a soldier, or not having been at sea.' This would be particularly true of Buddy if he didn't serve."

"I know you served," my mother said, "but you were neither soldier nor sailor. And yet you aren't someone who thinks meanly of himself. We always come back to this notion, don't we? Those of you who didn't go to war will freely bring others to peril. What did Brutus say? 'The abuse of greatness is when it disjoins remorse from power.' "

Figgy just then cried out, *"Nel mezzo del cammin di nostra vita / Mi ritrovai per una selva oscura, / Che la diritta via era smarrita."* She stamped her foot. "There. I win. You dopes only quote in English."

Despite Arthur's fatigue, he was a gentleman, and he meant always to acquit himself well. He took my mother's ugly hands in his, a gesture that must have been a real effort, although he shook them more firmly perhaps than he should. "Thank you for the evening, and we will go now." Before he shot down the hall, he bowed to Russia. "You always win my heart anew with your rolls. Thank you, ma'am, and Merry Christmas."

"Mr. Fuller," Russia murmured, closing her eyes, her palm to her heart.

He was out of the room, pushing past the carolers, going fast into the cold to sit in the car. It was a long time before Figgy and Buddy could claim their wraps from the pile on the bed upstairs and say their goodbyes to all of us.

"Merry Christmas, goddamn you, Julia," Figgy said. "I think I'll probably get over it, but at the moment let me say I'm never coming to this house again. My husband will be frozen out there."

"I wanted to hear what he had to say." My mother kissed Figgy on the cheek.

"No, you didn't. You wanted to talk. You wanted to hear your own self-righteous voice." With Arthur's coat to her chest and her fur over her shoulders, she sailed out the door.

Buddy shook my hand and wished me luck in the rest of the school year. Russia had always spoken in the privacy of our kitchen as if she believed Buddy would never amount to anything. That night she put her arms around him. "You take care of yourself, you hear? I'm so proud of our boy. You tell your mother make sure and send me a picture of you in your uniform." Even stranger was the sight of Buddy chucking Madeline under the chin, avuncular again in the parting, saying, "You be good, now."

Chapter Nine

THERE WAS A PERIOD IN MY GIRLS' EARLY-TEEN YEARS WHEN they could not stand the sound of their mother's voice. The pitch of her nagging, her laughter on the telephone, the way she loved up the dog. "Do you have to breathe?" Tessa once snapped at her while they were watching TV. The sight of Diana's flesh also disturbed them. If they happened to catch her wrapped in a towel, the ends tucked into her cleavage, their eyes widened, their nostrils quivered, and they turned tail. Diana took their revulsion personally and once wept about it in her closet, her face pressed to a chiffon gown she'd worn to the breast-cancer ball. "They make me feel like the scene of an accident," she said through her sniffles.

"Aw," I said, trying to draw her to me.

"And after all the years of the aerobics classes, the yoga videos. And Jeffery!"

"Jeffery?"

"You know," she managed to whimper, "at the gym. The trainer."

I'd forgotten that phase of her body management. "You're in very good shape," I said. She'd always been slight, and although she might have gained ten pounds since I'd met her, that amount is like keeping up with inflation and in middle age signifies nothing. She still had her youthful prettiness, the thick black lashes against her blue eyes, the dash of freckles across her nose.

"And for what?" she cried. "For what?" She glared at me before she sank into her bank of dresses.

"Come on now, lamb," I found myself saying, "you're beautiful." She clutched the bar then and opened her mouth wide, a thin rattle coming from the back of her throat. I'd seen a patient that day with ALS, Lou Gehrig's disease, a brave man coping with the loss of speech, of movement, no longer able to swallow easily, and along with him his upbeat but realistic wife—and yet Diana's boundless misery in the moment seemed the greater tragedy. "Diana," I said, "Diana," but she would not be soothed.

She had told me when we first married that a career was really only a fancy name for a job, that she wanted to spend her life, the decades before her, educating our future children, five of them she wanted, and also making me fat. She has kept her word, driving the girls to the end of the county and back for ballet lessons, ceramics lessons, soccer teams, drama workshops, and she's done more than her share of good works, too, serving on the school board, hosting AFS students, running the local garden club, working at the literacy center, chaperoning proms and field trips, including one to France with Tessa. We were all proud of her when she was voted Woman of the Year 2000 by the local women's business association. As for her early goals, I have not grown fat only by virtue of the treadmill up in our bedroom alcove. There were some years that I regret, the undercurrent of acrimony running through the household, the era when I was working very long hours and Diana was frustrated by my absence. I sometimes thought she was deliberately subverting the girls' affection for me. If I promised to get home to put them to bed, she'd do it herself earlier than she should, so that when I arrived ready to roughhouse they were sound asleep. Once when I planned an afternoon off she, a model of organization, got the date wrong and had arranged an outing with her sisters and their children, an irresistible trip to a water park. My idea to take them fishing on the muddy Fox River did not win the hour. I now and then wonder if Diana would have been happier with a career, both of us flying in opposite directions in an ordained frenzy. I sometimes wonder, if she'd had a paying job that had absorbed her, whether she might have been more open to my ideas of real service, spending a year in Africa or other desperate continents, treating AIDS and malaria patients. As it was, I knew better than to bring up that fantasy.

"Your family, Mac! Your *family*!"

During the daughters' eye-rolling phase at their mother, they seemed to want more than anything to please me. When I came into their adolescent favor, when they turned their backs on Diana, I assumed in my closely held smugness that I'd always, from then on, be in their good graces. Even at that stage, however, I would never have had the nerve to ask which of them did love me most.

There was a bittersweet night a few years past when I realized that their allegiances had shifted yet again. Lyddie had just come home for Thanksgiving after her first stint away at the University of Michigan, and Diana was asking her about a boy we had met on campus. Trance, he was called. A name whose origin I didn't want to know. Diana has the habit of thinking that each girl's beau is going to be the one, and, if he is especially suitable, falling in love with him herself. I suspect that Lyddie behaves like a proper post-postmodern girl, that she believes in Mr. Right—or, rather, Mr. Perfect—but while she's waiting for him to materialize, for his brain to descend from the ether into his hunky body, she'll strap on her little high-heeled shoes, and come what may. Tessa is probably more discriminating, full of doubt that a mortal male will meet her requirements, even if for an evening. Katie, the sturdy catcher for the softball team back in her high-school days, has always had a pack of studly athletes around her, the lot of them in front of the TV like puppies on a blanket. In all their futures, I see children and houses and mountains of things, electronics, kitchen appliances, educational toys in hand-crafted baskets, hills of shoes, forests of earring trees, cashmere sweaters by the acre, along with the requisite storage units in room-sized closets. I am hopeful that one of the sons-in-law will be a computer whiz, that he'll install my software and make complaints on my behalf to the cable company.

It was the night before Thanksgiving, the five of us glad to be together before the crowd appeared the next day. For a few months, Lyddie, like many students her age, had been flirting with filmmaking. Diana was still bustling by the stove while the rest of us were at the table, listening to Lyddie's freshman-year adventures. "We were setting up a shoot on the railroad tracks? Oh, my God, it was ridiculously cold, and the tech guy was running back and forth for—"

"That reminds me, Lyddie," Diana said, coming to us with a platter of marinated lamb tidbits, an appetizer off the grill, a recipe that the cookbook author had appropriated from Italian shepherds. Diana, as often happens, had no idea that she was interrupting a conversation.

"Ahhhhh," I said, my face to the plate. "You've done it again." The marjoram and garlic, the earthy meat smell, always makes me want to grab a blanket and head outside to my flock.

"What are Trance's plans for Easter vacation?"

"Trance?" Lyddie said to her mother.

"Would he like to come to Vail with us? Does he ski?"

Lyddie blinked several times in my direction. It seemed she was appealing to me. A rare moment, the oldest Miss Maciver losing her self-possession. It took me a minute to realize that she was trying to remember who Trance was, that he was probably one of many boys she'd dated, or whatever it is young women call what they do. She'd introduced him to us at the Homecoming Weekend maybe because he was presentable, or perhaps because he happened to be standing nearby. He did in fact have an impressive vitae, and we'd met his mother, a dentist, and heard tell of his father, the attorney. It was possible that Lyddie had had one encounter with Trance, the night before at a frat party, or he was only called Trance on that occasion, or after the introductions all around she never saw him again. Diana had approved the boy's rough-hewn good looks and his strong white teeth, no doubt already picturing her hardy meat-eating grandsons. She had literally jumped up and down once we'd turned the corner and were out of sight of our daughter and her prospective mother-in-law.

It was Tessa who did the rescue at dinner, Tessa who said, "Wasn't Trance—wasn't he going to do Habitat for Humanity over spring break?"

I had never been aware of her coming to her sister's aid before. It was gratifying to see that the separation, the salve of distance, in that semester had for the first time in their lives made them allies.

"Great memory, Tess," Lyddie said, flashing her a smile. "Also, Mom, Trance is a total klutz. He'd probably kill himself on the slopes."

Katie, who was fourteen then, and not quite up to speed, said, "I like the other guy you were with when I visited, not the first time, not the blondie. The one with the dreads."

"Who's that?" Diana shrilled.

"The Dave person?" Tessa surmised. "Your Sherpa? The one who always carries your equipment?"

"Oh God, Dave! He's ridiculously smart." Lyddie leaned over until her head was at the edge of Diana's place mat and said liltingly, "He's just a friend, Mom."

That exaggerated gesture made the sisters laugh but was nonetheless a comfort to Diana; she could believe that Trance was still in the picture. I was struck by how careful the older girls had become of their mother, how they understood her aspirations for them, how they didn't want to disappoint her. And how they didn't need me in any of their machinations. They were going to go off into their lives, to have it their way, but for as long as possible they'd do their best to shield Diana, and me as well, from their unsavory interests and appetites.

One of my favorite of the many, many ridiculously clever mechanisms of the body, one with the thrill of a sporting event, occurs when an egg is being fertilized, when the most ambitious sperm penetrates the ovum shell. A chemical signal shoots off from the ovum's inner membrane to the wall, shutting the place down, keeping out all other seekers. Those gates slamming shut are the very beginning of the singular person, the *I-am.* No one can tell the younger generation how harrowing parenthood is in the face of that *I-am,* although the signs are everywhere for the attentive child. But who wants to face the pain of the mother, the matron, no matter how buff, sitting at the head of the table, who is wishing the age-old wish even at this late date, praying, with a heady brew of self-interest and selflessness, for her daughter to marry a good boy from a nice family.

Madeline Schiller had married a Ph.D. candidate, the future owner of a historic lake home, the scion of the Maciver glue dynasty. Figgy once told me that Madeline's parents, Nadine and Christopher Schiller, came to see their daughter now and again in the first few years after the tragedy. They stopped dropping in not long after my mother became the second Mrs. Aaron Maciver. There was an awkward visit, Madeline refusing to acknowledge the guests, hiding her face in my mother's lap. For some reason, whenever Diana starts talking about our daughters' marriages, I can only picture Madeline starting out on her bike with her new husband on a soft Sunday morning.

EXCEPT FOR MY EXCESSIVE HOUSE and the tropical vacations and a sporty car I once succumbed to—and it did drive like butter and it did purr like a kitten and it did make me feel a man—I labor under the impression that I am my mother's legitimate heir. My father would have been satisfied, suspending judgment, interested in our business no matter what profession Louise and I had chosen. My mother, despite her party line of live-and-let-live, would have been devastated if we'd become the usual bad guys, strip-mall developers, self-servingly born-again, lobbyists for the NRA. The best way, I've found, is to do good works behind the scenes, and if your beneficence is discovered, then there you are, exposed in your generosity. Nowhere, for example, on the plaques at the homeless shelter in my town, or in the new wing of the hospital, does my name appear. My mother would call that reticence humility; she would approve. But as for the secret life, the dream life, would she forgive me my indulgences? I've been taking piano lessons for a few years, my teacher a young woman who tells me I'm doing a Good Job! It has been my lifelong goal to play "Für Elise." Although I've plateaued at two-handed "Jingle Bells," I still hold out hope. If I allow myself a non-medicine-related fantasy when I'm on the treadmill, or in the seconds before I'm snoring, what I see is Timothy Maciver just about to step onstage for his debut—never in Carnegie Hall's history will there be as affecting a rendition of Beethoven's love song, not to mention as hearty a "Dashing through the snow." On alternate days, Chef Maciver is preparing peekytoe crabs in a puff pastry for his television audience. Chef Maciver has a glass of Romanée-Conti (1985) with his staff after the taping, and although few know it he grew the grapes himself in an undisclosed location. Off to sleep I go, into that life of many talents.

Buddy ended up making Figgy prouder than she might have imagined in that time when she was fighting tooth and nail to get him past the third grade. In the revised history of Buddy, the story goes that it was his F's in penmanship that tripped him up, a skill that by today's standards was absurdly overvalued. His handwriting still looks as if it's come from the clutch of a palsied schoolteacher.

It was the summer of 1965, the July before the notable Christmas party, when I began to believe again, in spite of myself, that Buddy was a person of real valor, that he was imbued with something like a high moral purpose. He'd come to Moose Lake on his own, and for a few days after seeing our grandmother he'd stayed with us in Illinois. His trip coincided with the visit of two teenagers from the slums, a boy and girl who were experiencing suburban life in our home as part of a program called Project Share.

Before we went to collect our Project Share brother and sister from their tenement on the West Side, I'd argued lightly with my mother, informing her that the concept was not only cockeyed but unconscionable. I didn't say that I hated the idea of strangers in our house for two weeks, but she probably understood the real thrust of my protest. Project Share, I said, was brilliant, very smart, giving a tour of middle-class wealth to the poverty-stricken. What good people we were to open our doors to the needy! Further, if they wounded us, stabbing us in the night, we would have the pleasure of martyrdom. Most probably Malzena and Cleveland Simonson, fifteen and sixteen, would go back to the ghetto and either fall into a profound depression or begin to hold up women on the El train, ladies in white gloves and spring coats who were going to the symphony. As for our heavenly reward, the big pay-off, we'd already absorbed Mikey O'Day into our lives. Wasn't that enough? Having to watch the eternally young go steady until the end of time?

"It's two short weeks," my mother said serenely. She was putting dishes away, moving around me while I stood in the center of the kitchen. "This is the one chance some children have to be exposed to culture and to the idea of possibility. It can be life-changing. Take them to the Field Museum and let them help you with your job. It's a privilege to go behind the scenes, and I'm sure they'll be fascinated by the specimens and your cataloguing tasks. It's not that difficult to ex-tend yourself." She looked me in the eye on her path to the dining-room silverware box. "They might be interesting people." She did not avert her gaze. "It's possible they'll have something to teach you."

For a good part of our Project Share weeks, Louise lugged her cello over to Stephen Lovrek's house, the two of them disappearing into their music. The work of the artist, apparently, was more impor-tant than giving alms to the poor. With her usual diplomatic sarcasm, Louise said, "You've got great brainstorms, Mom, no doubt about it. When I get older I hope I'm not still completely close-minded, but for now I don't have the energy to participate in your scheme."

My mother, as was her habit with Louise at that stage, wisely said very little. "Do what you can to help," she murmured.

Up in my room Louise said to me, "Isn't it great how Mom can have a slave and at the same time be full of concern for all peoples?"

"Slave?"

"Russia, Mac, Russia? The woman who comes to clean our toilets, who we say is family, our *relative* who lives in her shack on the South Side."

"It's more complicated than that," I said. "Do you think Russia would be happier if we let her go, if Mom told her the setup was rotten? I'm not sure she'd have such a good time working at Marshall Fields. I'm not sure she knows how to read."

"Don't tell me the bullshit lines—you don't have to repeat Grandmother's standard sales pitch about how there is mutual care and dependency between slave and owner, how lovely, really lovely it is that everyone knows his place." Louise all at once grew tired of the conversation. "Never mind," she said before her last word. "I hope both you and Mom feel absolved for the white man's sins." She went downstairs, picked up her cello case by the leather strap, and, carrying it like a pocketbook, walked out the door.

There was the trip to the tenement to fetch Malzena and Cleveland, the green paint flaking in the long dim hall, most of the light-bulbs smashed, bits of jagged glass still screwed into the sockets, the frightening smell from the one bathroom that six families shared. Madeline didn't seem to notice the gloom or the stench. She walked slowly, trailing behind, her eyes open just enough to see her feet. It would have been easy to forget her, the woman who was fading away, who was so listless she was hardly alive. In the car on the way home, she curled up against the window and stared at the door handle. Mikey O'Day was at Disneyland with his parents and one of the sisters. He was an uncle many times over, and every summer there was at least one trip to visit the grandchildren at a historic site. Two whole weeks without him, two weeks without song, without dance.

As my mother drove, she exhausted her store of questions for the guests, so that when we came up our street even she couldn't think of another thing to ask. After she had shown Malzena and Cleveland to their rooms—that is, my room and Lu's—she suggested, all cheery-

like, that I take them to the pool. I already knew that they had mute-
ness as their defense, that we could adequately blot each other out
with silence.

"Madeline would probably like to go, too," Mrs. Maciver said.

Maybe *you* should take them—everyone, the black, the white, the
lame, the old, the young. I did not, of course, say this out loud.

I didn't know who was lower in the Simonsons' estimation, the
first Mrs. Maciver or me. It was clever of my mother, as always, to
mask the order to take Madeline along by saying how much she
would enjoy the entertainment. Still, since the advent of Mikey
there'd been fewer demands on all of us. Louise and I took turns
walking to the Dari-Dip at nine-thirty at night to pick the perfect
couple up and to shadow them, making sure Mikey got home safely.
That was the extent of our summer duties. At the beginning of their
friendship, Mrs. O'Day had prescribed a routine to their week, a
schedule that they took for granted. Soon after the romance got off
the ground, Mikey began working on weekends at the uptown movie
theater for a few hours, taking tickets. He wore a cheap black suit and
a red bow tie. Madeline, in silk and jewels, spent her Saturday and
Sunday afternoons watching a double feature. It was one of Mikey's
perks that she got in free of charge. "The boss, the boss knows Madeline, knows Madeline is my girl." On the appointed summer evenings, there was the Dari-Dip. Wednesday mornings, they went to
Little's Music Shop. My mother took them in hand for cookie making
and apple peeling, and she paid Mikey small change to help her wash
windows or dig holes for shrubs or carry boxes up from the basement
for Goodwill. On their own, the couple went to the pool, and they lay
around necking, and they sat out on the front steps watching the little
girls play, those children who finally were beneath Madeline since
she'd gotten herself a boyfriend. They were inseparable except during the sacred dinner hour, when Mikey was called home to eat with
his parents. None of us looked forward to his vacations, those weeks
when she walked around the house as if she were newly blind, as

if she didn't know where anything was, as if nothing would ever interest her again.

Mikey was gone now as we struggled to the pool in formation, I leading the way, Malzena and Cleveland behind me on the pavement, and Madeline dragging along on the grass. I thought about the water, how the Simonsons would jump in and how then I wouldn't want to follow after them. I felt that way when Jerry Pindel in his red briefs stood at the side about to do his cannonballs, and when the sweaty Van Normans, who never showered, did their sloppy dives; even Mikey O'Day, clean and soapy-smelling, his hairy gut hanging over his suit, made me squeamish. You thought you were swimming in water that was automatically disinfected by the chlorine, but actually you were pawing your way through the neighbors' snot and spit and specks of shit they hadn't taken care to wipe away. The small white sun bore down on us as we walked along, as I said to myself, I'm not going in that pool. The only people I wanted to swim with were the Maciver cousins, and only in the glittering water of Moose Lake.

I suppose I had to talk to Cleveland in order to point out the lockers and give him the towel I'd been carrying for him, but whatever we said to each other didn't feel much like speech. We changed our clothes and went through the spray of the shower and out into the glare of the light-aqua water, which looked refreshing even though I knew it was a thick, greasy brine. My guest, a muscular six feet three inches, in very small briefs that were as black as his skin, met his little sister coming out of the girls' changing room, she in her pink two-piece, the bottom with a ruffled skirt, and matching pink plastic barrettes in her bouquet of braids. Together they—or that is, we—walked toward the diving boards. Madeline went her own way, to the shallow end, where she'd inch by inch lower herself down the steps until she was standing, the water up to her waist. Without Mikey to carry her around, she'd probably stay in one place, watching. The lifeguards in their towers, their whistles to their lips, turned to stare at the Simonsons. The pool was of Olympic dimensions, and around it there was a wide apron where the members baked in their slatted chairs or on the hot cement. The women looked up from their books and, without meaning to, squinted at the glossy blackness of my brother and my sister. But we were a progressive people in our town, and next they made a fuss of not looking. They rearranged their towels, they fiddled with the locker keys that were pinned to their suit straps, they flipped through their books to see how much longer. The neighbors who knew us were pugnacious in their enthusiasm. "Hello, Mac!" Mrs. Lombardo called. She waved both hands at the Simonsons. "Hello there! Hello, hello! Great day to be at the pool!"

Mrs. Lemberger shouted, "You'll love the water! Absolutely love it!"

Mrs. Gregory was up on the observation deck, fully dressed in skirt and blouse, heels and nylons, an alien in our midst. She waved, too, her smile, the dark lipstick, taking up her face.

Without his clothes on and after the speedy shower, there was still a cigarette smell mixed with hair tonic, that odor both clinging to Cleveland and radiating from him, as strong as his color. He managed to stroll down to the deep end without glancing left or right, his gaze narrow and sure, that self-containment also drawing us to him. Had my mother considered how the Simonsons would feel in the presence of the neighborhood women who wanted to think well of themselves? I matched Cleveland's stride, trying by that effort to let him know that, though the other pool members were show-offs in their nonchalance, their enlightened acceptance of ghetto youths, really I was so color blind I hadn't even considered that race or class divided us. I'd been raised by Madame Civil Rights, after all, our household heroes Ida Bell Wells-Barnett, Ella Fitzgerald, Scott Joplin, Sidney Poitier, Langston Hughes, Percy Julian, not to mention Porgy, not to mention Bess. You couldn't find a white boy who was blacker than Mac Maciver. We fair Anglo-Saxons, and the even more freakish Irish Catholics with their freckles and the blue veins pulsing under their translucent skin, were burning up and would someday succumb to hideous cancers. But not so the Simonsons, the both of them evolu-

tionary success stories, the melanin in their skin serving as a nifty bio-
logical shield against ultraviolet radiation. The sickle-cell-anemia
gene aside, Cleveland and Malzena had the upper hand, and maybe, if
I mentioned that, maybe he'd pound me on the shoulder good-
naturedly, something that I wouldn't like much but that would mean I
was all right in his book.

The pool was noisy with children bobbing up and down and chasing each other, their arms outstretched as they bounced along. The Simonsons, one after the next, climbed the stairs of the lower board and
took their dives, Malzena's yellowish soles together and pointed. They
weren't so poor they hadn't learned to swim. Cleveland's long, shad-
owy form moved near the bottom, and when he burst into the air he
whipped his head to one side, a shower from his modest Afro. They
made their way through the crush of swimmers and the spray of their
splashing to the shallow end. The children were children, staring if the
pair came close, looking over their shoulders, and then paddling on. I
guess I stood at the edge for quite a while, watching the members
warm to their own friendliness. They had passed the phase of fiddling
with their possessions and were trying to be welcoming, smiling hard,
with their hands at their brows out in the general direction of the
guests. I knew I was going to jump in the water although I didn't want
to, and also I was sure that I was never going to take the plunge into
that warm, mucousy slurry.

When I was pushed I did feel the hand, the nudge that tipped me
over. I didn't at first know it was Jerry Pindel I was on top of, both of
us tangled in each other, both sinking to the black line. When we
blasted up, Jerry's arm was around my neck. "You fuck!" he spat.

The lifeguard was standing on his platform, blowing his whistle as
if he were screaming into it. For an instant I was as startled by Jerry,
by his face, as I was by being in the water. His hair was slicked
back, so for once he was visible, a kid with enormous dark eyes, wide-
set, his skin brown and clear, his mouth, two peaks at the upper lip, the
slight downturn of the full lower lip, the feature that probably drove
the girls crazy.

"Sorry," I said to Jerry. "Someone pushed me."

"Nigger." He splashed me with both palms, the bitter wave going down my throat.

It was after I got out and lay on the cement that I began to feel the heat of the broad hand that had been on my back. Had it been an ordinary shove? It wasn't that it had been unusually forceful but that there had been keen feeling behind it, a reason beyond playfulness or even regular old retribution. I had been dunked and launched against my will into the water hundreds of times, but I came to know slowly that the push had been different. There had been malice in it, I was sure; the hand had burned.

When the Simonsons climbed out, they settled several yards from me, lying on their stomachs, shivering, their arms tucked under themselves. If I closed my eyes halfway, my wet lashes served as a curtain, veiling the guests in my field of vision even as I looked at them. Cleveland had known what I'd been thinking as I'd hesitated at the water's edge, and what better way to serve me right than to make me drink his bath, to choke on it. While we were still wet, the lifeguards blew their whistles for rest period. The mothers put on their white rubber caps, buckled the straps by their ears, and began their languid crawls down the placid lanes, fifteen minutes for their exercise. Cleveland sat up and cocked his head slightly, once, twice, so that at first I thought he had a nervous tic. When he did it again with irritation, I understood it was time to go. He was annoyed that I had to take a moment to talk to Madeline, to tell her we were leaving, to remind her to look both ways crossing the two streets between the park and home. It wasn't often that she went past our block by herself, but she was capable of it, at the curb turning this way, that way, checking again, the hard gaze along the empty street. When she was sure there were no cars in sight, she ran as fast as she could.

The Simonsons and I had been quiet before, but after we left the pool our silence thickened. We moved around each other as if none of us were there, as if we believed that if we could shut our mouths a little tighter and stare harder straight ahead we would gratefully find ourselves alone. My mother expected me to show them the town, and we began an aimless walk. She must have thought I'd suddenly become like a middle-aged docent, explaining the salient features of the Prairie Style architecture: the leaded windows, the low roofs—isn't it interesting, and they all leak! Remember the great Frank Lloyd Wright's idea of organic architecture, you know the concept, boys and girls, integrating the site and the structure, just as the fellow surely did who built your cold-water firetrap in the city.

The Simonsons did not glance up on the block where there were several famous examples, including Wright's home and studio—heads to the pavement, all of us walking as if we were shackled together but five feet apart. We went on to the monkeys in their sawdusty cages at the department store, and because the air was still and heavy upon us we drifted into the library, down the cool dim hall to the drinking fountain. And out again into the scorching sun. That was as much fun as I could provide for the underprivileged. In a moment of willful charity I supposed that they had as much interest in staying with the Macivers as I had in being their host; I was sorry for the three of us. When we got back to the house, Uncle Harv, the mailman, was stuffing our letters into the slot on the porch. He reacted just as the women at the pool had, turning, gaping, and then, when he'd gathered himself, becoming hearty in his tolerance—nay, his affection, his abiding love—for the Negro. "Greetings!" he cried, a stiff grin on his face.

"Uhh," one of them said.

Cleveland went up to my room and shut the door, and I went down the basement to sit on the beige-and-brown-speckled linoleum behind the bar. Why had my mother sicced the Simonsons on us, on the neighborhood, on Uncle Harv? Why? If she so dearly wanted to do grandiose deeds, why hadn't she been swimming in the piss water with the poor children? Why hadn't she taken the burn of that push? She was the worst of the suburban do-gooders—Louise was right about her hypocrisy. When she called me for dinner I didn't come, not until they were all finished, and I didn't go along with them to the park to hear the Kiwanis playing patriotic music in the gazebo. I didn't feel well, I said, unable to look at her, unable to look at any of them.

Cleveland and I were supposed to share my room and the sleeping porch, but I chose instead to lie awake on the basement floor wrapped in an old army blanket. My mother had demanded I move my snakes downstairs, so why not sleep with the bedfellows to which I was accustomed? Let the Africans and the Anglos alike roast in their sheets upstairs, let them dream of their cultural experiences, let my mother stew in her own virtue, let the flame of her purity turn her black.

In her own way there was probably no one more racist than Russia. She was leery of the project and kept her distance from the guests. Even though there were a handful of middle-class minority families in town, Russia didn't like to see the coloreds on our streets, in a place she felt they didn't belong. I remember more than once walking with her to the grocery store and her saying under her breath, "What's that spook doing here? Where's he think he's going?"

On the third day of Project Share, Buddy arrived. My cousin strolled through the door, took one look at Cleveland slumped on the sofa staring at nothing, and said, "Hey." There was the short flurry of hellos for the rest of us, and then Buddy, harking to the sound of the dribbling ball, suggested they go out into the alley. So obvious, so simple. He had been on a bus for ten hours, and had no wish to sit in the living room answering my mother's questions. The neighborhood boys with their St. Christopher medals around their hot necks opened out and drew Buddy and his friend into their heat. "Great to see you," Buddy said, as if he'd known them all for a long time. He peeled off his shirt and threw it on the trash can, his summer skin the color of a glazed ham. The game began.

That was the year my parents were trying to remodel the kitchen. As if it weren't enough trouble having visitors, the downstairs was torn apart, the laths and studs exposed, the sink standing alone without countertops, the stove and refrigerator on the back porch. I never had the sense that money was tight; in fact, I never thought very much about how my parents managed. It wasn't something they talked about in front of us, but they were careful, I later realized, planning for the things we needed, saving for our college, and they had a stash for Madeline, too, if the time came when they couldn't care for her. There was starter money from the Schillers, but my father was dutiful about adding to it. As part of their remodeling economy, he brought home a discarded countertop from the museum with cabinets that had been used in a hands-on exhibit about Turkey. No one had bothered to clean any of it out, and so you'd open the cupboards or a drawer to find a replica of a pitcher, a stone shovel, or a jar of beans, what the Hittites might have had for supper, a slab of dried fish from the Bosporus, a vessel filled with fossilized lamb meat. A shame to waste the perfectly good pine cupboards and the long red Formica, the dream kitchen of the ancients.

Once Buddy was around, the days with the Simonsons fell into a sluggish order. There were some mandatory educational trips that my mother planned for all of us, excursions to the zoo and the arboretum, but when we weren't on those forced marches, Buddy was out in the alley with Cleveland or exploring the town with Malzena in tow, buying lunch at a joint called The Beef, and going to movies. Buddy and Cleveland took over my room, their underwear and socks and wet towels and comics on the rug, the desk, the beds, the closet floor. I remained in the basement. I had a job three mornings a week at the Field Museum and a regimen of tennis practice, but even when I was around, the dynamic threesome seemed to forget I was living in the house. It didn't matter. I didn't care. I had a freshly dead male baboon to work on, and in the long afternoons I'd take him from his plastic bag that filled the basement refrigerator and disassemble him bit by bit on the bar.

The first time Malzena saw him, I was slicing open the abdominal cavity, and the intestines, which I'd nicked, were predictably foul-smelling, the stench rising into the room. She narrowed her eyes, plugged her nose, swore, told me I was sick in the head, and retreated into the TV corner. At that point in the visit, she'd gotten bored with the array of Madeline's dolls, which had held her interest, as old as she was, for a day or two. After she'd exhausted that entertainment, and after Buddy arrived and the boys were outside in the alley, she often came downstairs and turned on the TV, an activity we were ordinarily not allowed before nightfall. The few Maciver rules were breaking for the wretched of the earth: dessert before dinner, and also after; chewing gum in the art museum; candy in the bedrooms; TV by day. I examined my baboon to the flickering light of *The Many Loves of Dobie Gillis*.

Because Mikey was gone, Madeline stood by during the dissections. She was just as surprised as I that the stomach smelled like a salady mix of leaves and fruit. She wasn't exactly interested, but she wasn't repulsed, either. It was something to do, sit at the bar as I worked. While I was at it I'd talk, explaining the systems both to her and to myself. I'd make an incision and draw back the layers of skin and muscle, and she'd bend forward to see, dutifully saying, "What's that for?" She asked the same questions on most days, which helped me refine my explanations. Every now and then she'd remember the animal—"Poor monkey," she'd say in a pouty voice—but on the whole her pity was perfunctory.

There was one day early on in the visit when Buddy came downstairs, I suppose because he knew he hadn't talked to me much. "Why don't you play ball with the alley gang?" he said.

"I never got in the habit," I said, truthfully, the Pindels and the Lembergers and the Van Normans so feral and loud, they'd scared me when I was little. I glanced down at my mother's faded blue smock, which I always wore for dissections, wishing that for once I hadn't put it on.

Madeline was sitting at the bar kicking a foot against her stool. "How you doing?" Buddy asked her, both of us, I guess, his charity cases.

When she didn't say anything, I answered for her. "Madeline's friend is on vacation."

"My boyfriend!" she clarified, suddenly enlivened.

I knew Buddy was looking at me for verification, but I kept my eye on the glory of the liver, so darkly purple.

"Where is he?" Buddy asked, a question that could only make Madeline go off to cry for the rest of the afternoon.

Chapter Ten

THERE CAME, ON ONE OF THOSE SUFFOCATING JULY NIGHTS
during the Simonsons' visit, an upset, a cruelty that I suppose
I should have been prepared for, that Buddy, ironically, had
made me think possible. The house had been closed all day
against the heat, and at last, in the early evening, it had become
warmer inside than out. The doors and windows were opened,
the sodden air beginning the slow drift through the downstairs.
My father had grilled hamburgers on the patio, and we were
all sitting at the dining-room table, beaded up with sweat as
if we'd been digging trenches in the noonday sun.

Louise, fresh from Stephen's air-conditioned bungalow,
happened by, bringing along her musical soulmate. "Good
of you," I said to her, "to stop in." She had been coming home
late every night, sleeping on Madeline's floor, and was usually
gone by breakfast.

Time held that meal in a single everlasting moment, the
nine of us plastered into the leather seats of my grandmother's
chairs, the nine of us spearing our pickles and coaxing the
ketchup along the glass neck and blasting the mustard from
the plastic bottle, the rectal spurts making Buddy & Co. plus
Madeline laugh uproariously. The hilarity seemed to take their
minds off the heat. Cleveland had three burgers spilling off
his plate, and one full bag of potato chips from the Jay's box in
his lap. There was no one like my cousin, as always, to make

the forest, the black night, or the dinner table a good time. He told his stirring anecdotes about schoolboy Buddy at the military academy, the beleaguered lad who must outsmart his captors. Cleveland nodded with great appreciation, as if Buddy were merely giving voice to his own experience. Whether I was sitting across from Cleveland or next to him or passing him in the kitchen, I felt the pressure of his hand on my back, the hot palm between my shoulder blades.

When Buddy paused to take a bite my mother said, "Louise, I'll bet Malzena and Cleveland would like to hear you and Stephen play after dinner. I don't think they've heard your music yet."

Louise thrust her knife into the center of her bun. For a few seconds she glowered at her sculpture as if it were a voodoo cello, as if she couldn't wait to slash up her instrument. She did remember something of her manners, and at last looked up to smile wanly at Malzena. I was beginning to see why my mother had wanted the Simonsons on our block, in our house, in our rooms, in our beds. She had said portentously, "It's possible they'll have something to teach you." She knew how I'd feel about the superficial cheerfulness of the neighbors, and she was sure it would do me good to watch the Simonsons bear the burden of our kindness. She also knew how I'd feel standing on the lip of the swimming pool fighting my base instinct, my revulsion at the water. Mid-course, I could see that Project Share wasn't for the Simonsons' education—no, not any of it. Project Share was for Louise and me, for the Maciver brats, to show us the world, to introduce us to our real feelings. Project Share would make us examine our limited viewpoint; Project Share would make us understand the shallow nature of any tolerance we might think we had. We would come to despise ourselves, and through that self-hatred rise up against all injustice, not with swords but with our sharpened pens and ancestral plowshares. Oh, what a skillful leader Mrs. Maciver was!

Cleveland and Buddy had moved on to recapitulate the stunning plays of the afternoon pickup game. "Your dunk shot, Bud," Cleveland was saying.

Bud?

"Your number-A specialty. You slams into me, I steals the ball—"

"You popped it in, Cleve, score for the team." Good old Cleve could stand at the hoop, catch the ball spinning on his thumb, and set it in the basket.

With the kind of savage indignation you might reserve for condemning tyrants, Malzena announced that I was sick in the head to be taking apart a monkey.

My father looked up from his coleslaw. "Have you ever done a dissection in a science class?" he asked her.

Before the Simonsons could tell us about their sad, awful school with the broken windows, the textbooks gnawed by rats, Buddy managed to unglue himself from his seat and stand. He pushed up the imaginary sleeves of his lab coat, and primly fitted the safety glasses over his ears. The Buddy Show! My father had unwittingly opened a new vein for his nephew, a subject rich in comic possibility, the mad scientist mixing yet another series of volatile compounds over his Bunsen burner. Not since the silent-screen comedians had we seen anything so funny, so very, very funny, nothing funnier than Buddy, all innocent curiosity, measuring poison into his beaker. Such an actor, such a mime, the acid foaming over onto his hands, he rubbing his nose, his chest, and, out of sight, his privates. Ha-ha-ha-ha-ha-ha! His mouth was a long oval; his eyes were first shut tight and then, in wild surprise, they snapped open. Malzena laughed so hard she tipped over in her chair. Madeline put her napkin to her face, beyond the giggles to joy. If Mikey O'Day had been with us, he would have screamed. My mother, my own mother sang out, "Oh, Buddy!" before laughter overtook her.

And so—another aspect of her plot revealed. She had arranged for Buddy to visit us alongside the Simonsons; she'd meant for Buddy to demonstrate how to be an unaffected host to those less fortunate than the Macivers. Somehow she'd known what he was capable of, that he'd save the Simonsons and thereby us. I pushed back and began clearing the table. Louise did the same, both of us scraping and stacking and clattering, the high-quality staff of 422 Grove Avenue. When it hit her that she was either going to have to do serious cleanup or else play for her Project Share siblings, she and Stephen retired to the living room to tune. The prodigies were working on a Chopin polonaise, a tempestuous march that was beyond their reach, that did not show off their talents to best effect. They played it too fast, roaring down the scale together, the perspiration spinning off of Stephen's brow. My sister, having acquired a new habit, the sign of true genius, was grunting. Malzena came to the edge of the room and, either amazed or disgusted, stared, her mouth wide open. Cleveland sat on the hall steps, elbows bent on his knees, chin in his hands, the posture of acute boredom. The instant Buddy came from the bathroom, the two of them were slamming the front door and down the walk, shouting for Malzena to get a move on. They were going to the pool to have a swim before the place closed.

I couldn't in fact help but wonder at Buddy's surprising ability to speak our guests' language, to treat them as if they'd always been at our house, as if they were there for his pleasure. Off they went down the street, bumping into each other, sniggering, and poking, Buddy at one point doing a handspring. I suspect he took them into the bosky part of the park to smoke dope every night, before or after the swimming. He'd never spent much time with us in Illinois, and I'm sure I seemed painfully priggish in my own town. It must have been a relief to him, to have someone on hand who could share his hobbies. I realized that I'd never had an interest in repeating at home any of the derelict behavior Buddy taught me at the lake; that kind of thing was only entertaining if we were alone in the boathouse, Buddy showing me how. I always came back from my grandmother's seemingly uncorrupted and went straight to school with my intentions and seriousness intact.

Although the children in our neighborhood played outside all day long, when twilight overtook the yards they came into their finest hour—like birds they were, twittering up a storm as the sun went down. That night Madeline wandered over to the Pilskas', where several girls, hard into the horse phase, were running around jumping over boxes and whinnying. Every now and then it struck me that Madeline had a knack for her station in life, that she must have given herself a talking-to: *I guess this is what I am, and so I might as well embrace it*. I had felt that acceptance especially when I watched her with whoever was horse crazy in the moment, Madeline with her wonky gait effectively doing hurtles. Once she had Mikey, she didn't, as I said, join in as much, but she probably stood by patting the Pilskas' terrier and watching the girls canter and jump, or balk at a fence, Roxy Pilska whipping her own rump with a stick.

"You should be with Buddy," my mother had the gall to say to me in the kitchen. There were drill bits and nails, a crowbar on the counter next to stacks of dirty plates and the condiments and the bowls of leftovers. "He seems to be having a good time, but I'm not sure he should be doing the part of host when he's the guest."

I closed up the nail boxes severely. "Someone's going to swallow a screw with their raisin bran," I muttered. I started down the basement without saying anything more. Although the baboon had been refrigerated, it was beginning to smell in that putrefying way, and I wanted to keep working, to finish my dissection while I could still stand it.

"I'll have you know that Buddy has risen in my estimation," she chirped after me. "I won't think ill of him again."

I paused at the landing. The one weekend I'd seen him, the summer before, he'd coaxed me through the trials of learning to get good and stoned. He'd been patient with my coughing, very encouraging. We had laughed ourselves silly and eaten contraband Dolley Madisons. I could have told my mother that I had no interest in getting high with the inner-city teens, that the single poker game I'd played was as far as I was willing to go toward depravity during vacation. Nor did I mention that Buddy had won thirty dollars from Cleveland, robbing the pauper of his last shekels.

Before I could speak, my father appeared. "Leave the mess, Julia. Let's take a walk before it's dark."

I didn't know how to frame what I wanted to say to my mother, but now there was time to think of just the thing. I went down the rest of the stairs to my baboon, imagining my parents walking out into the town; perhaps they'd keep pushing on, the waning light drawing them forward. I liked the idea of them strolling toward the setting sun, a Sisyphean exercise, walking without end. For some time while I was downstairs, Stephen and Louise played a gigue or a gavotte, a cheerful dance from the days when no races mixed in the drawing room. If my mother returned I would tell her that once Lu and I were released from the bondage of our childhoods we were going to join the Klan. In addition to burning crosses on lawns, we would fight right back up to the Supreme Court for segregation.

I remember carefully slicing the duodenum from the stomach, my heart beating with the excitement of my precision. I was just about to take out the pearly heap of the small intestines, having the idea to lay the jejunum and ileum along the bar to measure them. All the while, I was telling myself I was glad, very glad to be in the basement, my hands in the cool, slippery, decaying baboon insides, much better than swimming with Buddy on a sweltering night. I might have been speaking out loud when I felt the movement. I looked once to see if the cat had come down. It was a speck in my eye, I thought, not Tiffers. I might have gone on with the dissection if the floater hadn't coughed.

"Stephen!" I cried, nearly throwing the guts in the air. "I didn't see you."

He was standing at the foot of the stairs, staring at the child-sized corpse laid out on the counter. "Where's Buddy?" he said.

"Buddy?" I wiped my filmy hands on my sissy-boy smock. "He's at the pool, I think. It closes at nine, so he'll probably be home soon."

"Okay." He was his pale self, but he seemed more uncomfortable than usual, clutching his ribs.

"Is something the matter?"

"I'm not sure. I don't know—if Madeline is all right." He jerked around to look up the stairs. "Wait," he said. "I hear them."

I laid the plastic over the baboon and followed after him, asking what he meant. By then I could hear Buddy in the kitchen with Louise. At the first I thought, What does Stephen know about Buddy? Why does he need Buddy? He had only just met my cousin at dinner. At the top of the stairs I saw the star guest striding out the door even as Louise was trying to tell him something. He'd made the motion to Cleveland, the universal cocking of the head that meant Come. Before I could ask what was going on, the rest of them were down the back-porch steps, Stephen and Louise and Malzena, all walking purposefully to the alley.

For a minute there seemed to be nothing in that night but insect noise, the crickets belting out relief after the heat of the sun. For a flash there wasn't even us. I had been in that strangeness before as the hum of the teeming world came up into the air, and I was glad that the street lights right then slowly began to burn on, that illumination the beacon to bed. In the distance the mothers started their calling. Some of them stood on their porches and rang old cow bells rescued from the family farmsteads, and others opened their doors to sing out the names. All at once I was so homesick for my mother, for her old self, my old self, her calling me in for my bath. Where had we gone, she and I? Where were we? The younger children were tearing from their games, blowing through the yards to their houses.

The Pindels' garage, across the alley, was built like a barn, the lower part for cars and an upper loft that Jerry had claimed for his private, No Trespassing pad. Two years had passed since the

Ludwig-drum incident, The Spellbinders getting along with the drummer's own battered instruments. When Mikey had lost interest in his birthday toy, Mr. O'Day stashed the set in the attic where, safely quiet, it gathered dust. The Pindels' lower garage was always open, the red station wagon at the ready. In front of the Ford, Buddy said to us, "Stay here. I'll take a look-see."

"What's happening?" I asked for the fourth time. *"Bud."*

"Let's go, Cleve," Buddy said. The two of them began to climb the ladder to the trapdoor; the others, their fearful faces turned, watched the ascent. I was damned if I was going to stay downstairs, damned if I, Brains, was going to be kept from the look-see, kept from rescuing Madeline, if that's what the matter was.

With expert slowness Buddy pushed the trapdoor open and tiptoed into the short hallway. "Quiet," he said in a thread of a whisper, although we hadn't made any noise outside of breathing. I feel certain that Cleveland, too, stopped respiring at Buddy's order. Maybe Buddy had assumed I'd come along; of course, that was it. He knew I'd fall into place as the second-in-command, no discussion necessary. There was canned music coming from the loft room, guitars twining sweetly up the scale, and in the dark the faintest smudge of light under the inner door. I hadn't been in the loft for years, not since it was used as an attic, the storage place for broken fans and steamer trunks from the grandfathers. Buddy turned the knob. Maybe because I was with Buddy, I had the sense that whatever was going to happen, large or small, would matter, that even if behind that door the scene was insignificant, we would more or less remember it. And so we pressed together, trying to see through the crack, Cleveland, against the prohibition, murmuring, "Motherfuck!"

"Down," Buddy said, and we crouched.

What a wall it was! Across the room, the painted pink flowers pulsed from their stamens and pistils, the green toucans were about to squawk, the orange umbrellas opened so fully, so gladly. The paisley pants kicked up their heels, the yellow forks chasing after. I'd had art education under the supervision of my mother, but in the reverent galleries of the Art Institute I'd never seen anything like the mural in Jerry's loft.

"Faggot," Buddy muttered, as if only a homosexual would think to use fluorescent paints with a black light.

The radio was blaring, but the music was lacy, violins joining the guitar, the tremolo of a mandolin, the singer starting to get choked up with longing. At Buddy's signal, we one by one squeezed through the door and crawled to the blanket chest just inside. Was that Mikey O'Day's big head, Mikey O'Day with his back to us, sitting on the sofa in the middle of the room? No one had a head quite like Mikey's; no one had a ten-pound bubble like his, floating above the neck in musical delirium. Why was he home from his vacation? Had Madeline seen him yet? What was he doing sitting by himself in the dark? I thought then, Everything is fine. There is no problem if Mikey is around, he who is a patrol of innocence. I should tell Buddy Russia's line about how the good Lord couldn't make everyone perfect. Funny, to think of God saying to Himself, Whoops! I should tell Buddy that Mikey was the man, Madeline's sugar-eating sugar daddy.

Before we were settled, the three of us like snipers behind that chest, Madeline came from what must have been a closet in the far corner. Jerry was there, too, his arm around her, loosely, casually, the way you would hold a steady girlfriend, someone you are proud to take for granted. He was standing straight, far taller without his usual hunch. Madeline had that particular tilt of the head, her crown toward his face, her eyes, no doubt, cast up at him in her worshipful gaze. I couldn't see exactly, not only because of the darkness but because there seemed to be a shadow over her. Still, I was sure she was looking at him just as she stared at certain men if they paid her any attention— the construction workers in our kitchen, the Fuller Brush hero, or the boy who delivered groceries. As she and Jerry walked to the sofa, the black light shining down upon them, her yellow dress brightened.

"What!" I said, at a volume beyond a whisper, I guess, because Buddy elbowed me hard in the ribs.

"You, you, you're my girl," Mikey called out.

Madeline turned on him. "You're not supposed," she hissed, "to talk during the fashion show!"

Fashion show? The dress was misshapen, a garment she would never have chosen for herself. The shirt-type thing, a full skirt, buttons all the way down, had probably belonged to Mrs. Pindel, the rag too broad in the shoulders for Madeline, too big in the hips, and too short. At one time it had been molded to a dumpy body, and because it was missing the belt there was no possible way for it even to begin to fit my sister. Why had she allowed herself to put it on, and how? Had she changed her clothes in the closet? Had Jerry been in there with her, or had he waited outside? Had she put it on willingly?

Jerry began to talk, a strangeness in and of itself. "Isn't she lovely?" He spoke in a loud voice over the radio but in sincere tones, the word "lovely" so odd coming from his mouth and in that freakishly lit room, the dark center, the glowing edges.

"Madeline, Madeline's my-my girl."

"Wait," Jerry said, yanking at the hem. "Let's see if we can fix the droop." He gave another tug, as if that single motion could make the costume fit. "Okay, turn around, Suzy Q, so we can see."

"My name isn't Suzy Q!" Madeline said through her giggles. Her heels were too small, and she was having trouble walking.

"My, my girl, my girl is always, she's always b-b-b-beautiful."

"Don't you know it, bowzer." Jerry followed Madeline back and forth in front of the sofa, pulling at the skirt once more. "We want this to fit you like a dream."

Right then I did reach out, as if from that distance, as if I, weeny Brains, could smash Jerry's face. Buddy's reaction was immediate, his viselike grip on my arm: *Don't move until I say.* He was as alert to the possibility of my making a blunder as he was to the drama in front of him, the old order, general and soldier, ineluctably in our every movement.

"You could be a model, you know," Jerry was saying. "Easy. *Life*-magazine spreads."

"She, she, she's b-b-beauti—"

Madeline turned on Mikey again. "I said quiet! I'm with Jerry, you, you big fat dodo!"

There was snickering from the wall by the sofa, or I finally noticed it in a still spot of music, the peanut gallery assembled.

"No, Maddy," I whispered.

She was rotating slowly, pausing as models do to give a full view to everyone in her audience. The shadow over her head was a hat with a veil, what the mothers wore to mass.

"You could catch a man, a husband, in this outfit, Suzy Q. You could walk out into the alley and knock a bruiser—"

"I'm her, I'm her husband!" Mikey called softly. "I'm, I'm the—"

"Oh, right, I forgot about Mr. Music here, the breadwinner. Your wife, then, Mr. Music, with her looks, she could have a lover man." Jerry was taking an old fur from a box and draping it over her shoulders. "On a cold night, Suzy, when you're sneaking away from your husband to meet your lover man, a cold, cold night, this will protect you. Brr! Brr, button up, doll, it's freezing."

It was the dusty, thick heat of the room, the fact that all of us were drenched, and the way Madeline eagerly clutched the coat around her throat that made the boys on the floor, from the sound of it, roll sideways. They were probably holding their stomachs, mouths wide open. The gentleness of Jerry's instruction made them laugh, too, the exaggerated kindness, the fatherly affect. Kenny Lemberger lurched into view, the white squares of his plaid shirt catching the light. There were six or seven boys, a few Lombardos and Van Normans, a Pilska, a Gregory. "What about this?" Kenny said, taking from the box what looked like a girl's gym suit from our mothers' era, the one-piece monstrosity, the knee-length uniform with starchy bloomers.

Jerry nodded thoughtfully, holding it up. "This, this prize, is what Miss America is going to wear next year for her swimsuit competition. I'll bet there's a crown somewhere out there for you, Suzy Q."

The boys whistled when Madeline, as any seasoned model would do, dropped the coat to the floor. "What do you say, Miss Illinois?" Jerry was still showing off the gym suit. "Isn't it great? Isn't it you?"

"I like it," she said.

"No, no," I moaned under my breath. "Buddy—"

He put his fist to my mouth. "Not yet," he growled.

From the box Jerry pulled out a pair of saddle shoes. "How about—? Hold it!" He handed her one white go-go boot. "What do you think? How much do you love these boots? How much?"

Madeline had her hands at her face as she nodded. Those most fashionable boots, what must have been mistakenly relegated to the old clothes box, were, even from my vantage point, items from a girl's fantasy. "I want them," she said. She threw her head back and laughed. "I want them!"

I suppose Buddy knew that at some inevitable point we would see Mikey O'Day's penis, the last statement in the fashion show. Buddy had to know that Jerry would opt for the ordinary cruelty a person expects from the neighborhood bad boy. Even though we were behind the sofa and would not have been able to see Mikey's lap, in my memory I am suddenly in front, witness to the radiant sprout, as dazzling as the birds and flowers, as if it, too, had been slathered in fluorescent paint. Mikey had been away for two weeks, and maybe it was general longing coupled with the idea of Madeline in those bloomers that popped his tool through his open zipper.

One of the boys noticed, calling out, "Miss Illinois gave her *husband* a boner."

"Well!" Jerry said. "Well, well, well." He took Madeline by the hand. "You'll want to say hi to the happy fellow. I'll bet you've seen this happy fellow before—'course you have." He knelt down with her in front of Mikey. "Don't laugh like that," Jerry said to him. "You don't have to get hysterical. She's not going to hurt you. She knows how much your willy likes a sloppy kiss—come on, Suzy Q—"

Although at that stage I didn't idolize Buddy, or not much, still he did appear to fly down upon them, alighting by the sofa soundlessly, as if on a wave constructed for his own travel. Surely that was how the others saw it, and if they told anyone later, if they felt compelled to dress Buddy for the story in cape and codpiece and tights, I would not have blamed them. He grabbed Madeline by the elbow and in the same motion kicked the radio; the thing went dead. "Nothing to worry about, honey," he said. "Go on downstairs. Go with Mac." He turned to Mikey. "You get home, too."

Mikey was scrambling up off the sofa, trying to zip up his jeans and tuck his shirt in, neatnik that he was, and leave, all at once. He was babbling again about Madeline being his girl. "The party's over, pal," Buddy said, nudging him toward the door. Without needing to, as the neighborhood gang was slipping away, he added, "You assholes-in-training might want to get out of here, pronto."

By then Louise and the others had climbed the stairs and were hovering in the anteroom. Madeline was blubbering and trying to shake me off. "Let go, let go!" With some effort I handed her into the arms of Lu, with Stephen to steady them, and Mikey close behind, squealing he was talking so fast. When I came back into the room, Buddy had Jerry by the blanket chest. He was holding the unfortunate ringleader by the shoulders, speaking to him with a quietness that was menacing. I wondered if Buddy's teachers at the academy talked to him like that, or if Arthur had ever used such a tone. Buddy was older than Jerry by two years, as good as a man. My cousin alone would have been impressive, but add to the glory the fact that Cleveland was standing by.

"You think Madeline is like that queer?" Buddy was saying to Jerry, his voice going higher. "That what you think? She's a retard, too?" He shoved Jerry against the wall so hard his head banged against the stud.

Mikey, a queer, a retard? I hadn't thought of him in those words for a long time. It was startling to hear them.

"What kind of pervert are you, anyway?" There was the dull thud of Jerry's head again. "You get thrills from watching a beautiful woman blow a goof? A woman more beautiful than any little twat you'll ever hope to screw."

What did "blow a goof" mean? Jerry was whimpering, maybe because he didn't know what Buddy was talking about, or maybe because he understood that it was useless to struggle. Next Buddy would surely clobber Jerry for the fashion show: he'd say so, naming it, one satisfying wallop that would serve him right. We'd go home, justice dispensed.

"What does that do for you?" Buddy was saying. Another thud. "Was she going to perform the favors all around, or were you saving some of the boys for yourself?" He paused, standing back, so that Jerry thought the punishment was over. As if they were seasoned gangsters, a bank-robbing duo, as if they had choreographed the move, Cleveland reached out, hooked Jerry by the elbow, and passed him to Buddy.

"Jerry's got the message," I said. I may not have figured out what was going on exactly, but I knew enough to think of concussion, of hematoma. "You should stop. It's time to——"

"Shut up." Buddy whacked Jerry's head to the stud once more. "If you ever. If you ever try to pair Madeline up with that yo-yo, I'll punch your brains out."

"They go," Jerry croaked, "they go together."

"My ass they do." And then Buddy socked Jerry in the nose with such force my hand went straight to my own face in sympathy. "That knucklehead will seem like a rocket scientist compared to you. The dogs won't even let you fuck them."

There was one last good crack before Buddy and Cleveland sauntered past me. I did start to follow them. I was halfway down the ladder before I wondered if Jerry might be hurt enough to have trouble getting out of the garage and into his house. He could die in the loft, choking on his own blood. He could pass out, and Mrs. Pindel, with all her children, might not miss him for a few days.

"You all right?" I said, when I got back up to him. He was on his stomach, his head in his arms. I could barely hear his muffled "Fuck off."

I hadn't, as I said, understood what Jerry had expected Madeline to do for Mikey O'Day. His idea for Mikey was a pleasure I had never considered; I didn't know that such a thing had been imagined by anyone, that it existed in the world. I had thought of Madeline as mine while I'd watched her in the hands of Jerry, but in the moment, it was he, Jerry Pindel, blood streaming from his nose, who seemed to belong to me. That is, we were left over to be with each other. Since I had failed to fly to Madeline's rescue, this was the place where I could be heroic, even if my ministrations were something only I would ever know about. I remember being that self-conscious about my good deed. I remember thinking, too, that when I became a doctor I would have to heal people I hated.

"You're bleeding," I said, kneeling next to him.

"Genius." He had the wherewithal to say so snidely.

"Sit up, why don't you?" I pulled a little, on his arm. Although I was unsure if making him move was sound medicine, it was the only action I could think to take.

"Fuck," he said again. If I hadn't heard him speak at such length moments before, I wouldn't have known he was capable of saying much of anything but that one word. I wouldn't have known that in his own way he had what might be called, in today's parlance, "leadership skills." As the fashion show MC he'd been both relaxed and animated, as if he'd been onstage, an actor removed from his usual self. I rested my hand on his back. It felt like a mature gesture, a placement that might make us able to understand each other. I didn't have any idea who Jerry was, but I wondered, not only if his secret talents would be part of the future Jerry Pindel—the painting, the public speaking—but if everyone had hidden strengths, artistry it was best to keep private.

"Put—put your arm around me," I said. "If you stand up I can help you get out of here." I think he knew that he had to, that if he didn't he might really be in danger. The blood started to gush from his nose, and he must have thought, as I did, that you could die from a leak like that. I spotted him in a coachlike way, arms out in front of him as he got himself, half sliding, half stepping, down the ladder. It was frightening, how weak, how floppy he was. When we were on firm ground, I leaned him against the rungs. "I'm going to get a rag over there by your dad's workbench." I handed him the oily cloth, asking as casually as I could if his parents were home.

"Fuck you." He pressed the old T-shirt to his face and weaved out the door into the yard.

I watched from the garage window, standing by until his mother came onto the porch. "What's the matter with you?" she yelled, thinking, no doubt, that he was drunk.

When I got back, Buddy was in the kitchen throwing open the museum cupboards, one after the next. He'd changed his shirt, whereas mine, I realized, was spattered with blood. For the first time since his arrival, he was noticing the labels on the drawers: "Look inside!" "A Hittite lunch." "Spoils from a lost city." "Discovery from a river bed." All of our food was in boxes on the back porch, so it wasn't nourishment he was after. He reached for a clay jar with a stony bit of meat rattling around on the inside, a dried-up onion, a red curd of what may once have been a fresh tomato. It was as if nothing unusual had happened, as if his heart weren't still beating wildly.

"That," I managed, pointing at the jar, "is the precursor to the shish kabob." Jerry Pindel, my first patient!

Buddy seemed to think I was breathless because of the artifact. "What the hell kind of place is this anyway?" He spoke with real contempt.

"Freaky sons of bitches," Cleveland muttered.

Our liege started to laugh, pulling open drawer after drawer, yanking out the pottery tablets, the pebbles, the postcards of Istanbul, the archeologists' tools, the plastic magnifying glasses, the sand-sifters and scrapers—each item funnier than the last.

"All of it is from a museum exhibit," I began. "It was supposed to show how the Hittites—"

"Sure, Brains," Buddy said, through his chuckles. "Yep. And upstairs it's the Pharaoh's can, built to hold a great big golden turd."

"No, really—"

"It's okay, pal." He nodded to himself. "Go down the basement. Get back to your important experiment cutting up our furry friends. Something to do while Madeline sucks the dick of the neighborhood moron. Let the village idiots line up for a knobber. Go on, go down there. The men in the white coats understand." I guess I was standing still, staring at him. "Brains!" he shouted, clapping his hands. "You're going to start drooling if you don't blink."

My parents walked in just then. Buddy turned to close the drawer, and at the same time said with what sounded like real interest, "How was your walk?"

No one mentioned the incident. I later learned that Stephen Lovrek had been in the bathroom, that he'd happened to look out the window, that it was he who had seen Jerry taking Madeline from the Pilskas' yard into the Pindel garage. Whether Jerry had meant to involve Mikey, or if Mikey had just happened along the alley to see Madeline after his trip, I don't know.

"It's a beautiful night," my mother said to Buddy. To me she said, "Why aren't you wearing your smock? You're covered in blood!"

Louise and Stephen were in the living room, taking another stab at Chopin. Cleveland and Malzena were out on the front porch, eating the candy they'd bought with money the church had given them for their educational experience. Louise had probably told Mikey to go home, or maybe he had needed no prompting, running off down the alley. Madeline was in her room bawling. The dress! Where was that dress? Had she taken it off, and would she hide it?

My mother listened up the back stairs. "What's wrong with her?"

I had never lied to Julia, or not much anyway, and I did not on that occasion begin. "She's mad at Buddy," I said. Poor Madeline, ripped from Jerry's arms, deprived of his manly attention.

"Now, why would anyone be mad at you?" my mother said to Buddy. "Great big girl—you'll have to excuse her. She'll be fine in a few minutes. Actually, she'll be right as rain by noon tomorrow, when Mikey gets back. She doesn't know what to do with herself when her sweetheart is away."

I was slow to come to it, but I suddenly realized that Buddy hadn't figured out who Mikey was; he thought the man on the sofa was a nobody, a generic neighborhood misfit. And why would he have known Mikey was the sweetheart when Madeline had degraded him so? "You, you big fat dodo!" Not to mention the fact that we were geared for Mikey's arrival home the next day, all of us unprepared to see him early. "The one you called the moron?" I murmured to Buddy. "That's him, the boyfriend."

I went down the basement as my cousin had directed, to be in the company of the baboon. I didn't know which shock to consider first. How could Madeline be so fickle? How could she lose her senses over Jerry when she loved Mikey? Happy Mikey, hurrying to see her! Joyful Mikey, caught in Jerry's snare. Because this was long ago, before teenagers knew so much—because this was years and years ago—I thought, How could . . . ? How could a woman put her mouth—there?

Overhead came the rushing sound, all those feet steaming to the kitchen, the sign that Mrs. Maciver was serving ice cream. It was no surprise to me that Buddy had done the job in Jerry's loft that should have been mine to do; how could it have been otherwise? I understood that I'd been watching Madeline for a few years without knowing what to look for, a gap Buddy would not have tolerated in himself. Of all the things to grieve for, though, of all the things that made it impossible to go upstairs for a sundae, was the humiliation Madeline had suffered in Mrs. Pindel's hideous dress—what she would have been crying about if she'd known better.

Chapter Eleven

IT MUST HAVE BEEN A WHILE AFTER THE CHRISTMAS PARTY,
after we learned that Buddy was going to enlist, that my
mother came knocking at my door. I was half asleep when I
heard the timid tap-tap, what sounded like a nervous girl at
the headmaster's study. The last time she had tucked me in
had been—when? Between her tap and my response, I woke
completely. How could I have no memory of that important
ritual's ending or even petering out? I couldn't think why I
had let the vespers go, or if, in fact, it had been she who had
stopped reading to me.

"Come in?" I said.

"Good," she said in the light of the hall, "you're not on
the porch tonight. It's twenty below." She went straight to the
end of the bed, and as she had in the old days, she kicked off
her Hush Puppies and pushed herself to the back of the wall,
her legs stretched out in front of her. She wore a skirt and a
blouse always, with stockings and a girdle. I had on occasion
caught a glimpse of her dressing and had seen the contortions
she had to make in order to get herself into that foundation.
She hoisted the contraption up to her thighs and then gyrated
as she pulled it over her hips and buttocks, stuffing the last
bit of the tum into those panels that were advertised to hold
you tight for eighteen hours. This, for a woman who was
not fashion-conscious; this, without question, from her who

rabble-roused for half a dozen radical causes. Her eyes bulged, her whole head distended on her pulsing neck. When I was small, that moment in her bedroom was the only time I felt afraid of her or maybe for her: what might happen if she accidentally left the girdle on into the nineteenth hour, if it all of a sudden failed? I don't think Madeline, with her natural slimness, the grace of her long limbs, had ever thought to wear a girdle. She watched my mother's daily exercise with interest, and often she'd open the top drawer and pull out a string of pearls, an accessory to gussy up Julia's skirt and sweater, a trinket to make all that effort somehow worthwhile. "Not this morning, lamb," my mother usually said. "Let's save those for an important event."

Most of the mothers on the block dressed for homemaking, many of them probably squeezing into their girdles just as Julia did, and some of them surely in later life enduring back pain or even prolapsed uteruses as a result of weakened abdominal muscles.

"How we suffered," Figgy would say.

In my room, my mother was settling on the bed, in no apparent danger of bursting from her threads. I had the vestigial sensation that because she was there I could turn over and sleep without fear of robbers or the commies. We had, months before, more or less recovered from the Simonsons' visit. I had pretty much put it aside, and maybe even forgiven her for inflicting the guests on us, for trying to educate us. She and I had once talked, without going into the details, about how some of the neighbors had blamed Cleveland for Jerry Pindel's broken nose. She admitted that the racists in our midst had shocked her, and that he had been in a difficult situation. Louise had probably told her in vague terms what had happened in the Pindels' garage, enough of the story anyway to make my mother keep a stricter hold on Madeline and Mikey.

"Are you still awake?" she whispered as an afterthought. I already knew she hadn't come in to see if I was warm enough.

Along the wall closest to her, my new acquisition, a demure orange corn snake, lay coiled in its terrarium. The magnificent and vain python and the retiring king snake were in their tanks, too. Farther down the shelf were the four cages of white mice to feed them. I don't know that my mother had been in my room for months, and I silently gave her credit for not mentioning the fragrance. Or the climate I had made equatorial with the aid of a space heater. I had started keeping snakes when I was twelve, and it did occur to me as I watched her in the dark that the air quality of my room might have something to do with her staying away.

She asked me right off, without any more pleasantries, how I'd been thinking about the Vietnam conflict, and what Buddy had said about wanting to join the army.

"Not much," I said, answering both questions. I didn't want to dwell on Vietnam in the night. Also, I was surrounded every day not only by my mother's talk but by the impermeable membrane of her convictions; I knew about the situation without even knowing that I knew. If I'd been held at gunpoint I could have recited facts and figures, could have told my assailant that Henry Cabot Lodge had succeeded Maxwell Taylor as ambassador to South Vietnam, that something like 180,000 military personnel were in the country, and that four million civilians had fled to the cities. Further, I understood that my mother's asking me what I thought was bound to lead to her own disquisition.

She said that she wanted to give me a little background, that of course I was free to make up my own mind about world events, but that she didn't wish me to end up like Buddy, outfitted in a uniform, filled with the passions of his military-school demagogues, with no real idea what he was getting into.

"Why would I end up like Buddy?" I'm sure I sounded as peevish as I felt. Stephen Lovrek's question still thrummed in my ear from months before: Stephen coming down the basement stairs on that hot July night, seeing me at the bar, knowing Madeline was being toyed with out in the alley, and saying, "Where's Buddy?" Stephen hadn't known Buddy for more than two hours, but it was clear to him whom he should call for help.

Still, my mother swept through the thousand years of the Chinese, Japanese, and French occupations of Vietnam. She lingered at the Geneva Convention, 1954, and a 1950 speech of Eisenhower's in which he made a commitment to maintain South Vietnam as a separate country. There was a sidebar about Kennedy's handling of the Cuban Missile Crisis, the scare that had made her finally embrace her president. Even as she spoke to me on that night in 1966 it was clear that she was losing her heart to Bobby Kennedy. She veered farther from Vietnam to talk about Bobby's trip to the Mississippi Delta, and how he, much more than his brother, had taken on civil rights as a moral issue. She forgave him his various sins, including all the photo ops, parading around with the multitudes of little Kennedys, a nation unto themselves. Back to the war, she feared that Johnson was only going to get us deeper into the quagmire from which we would not be able to withdraw, not until thousands, perhaps hundreds of thousands of people were killed. The Vietnamese, she said, were fighting against us with a ferocity we weren't prepared for.

"Got it," I said, clutching my pillow.

"And there's Arthur," she went on, "with his charts, his incredible memory for the tonnage of bombs dropped, the numbers, the casualties from each battle—the abstraction of the conflict. Well, you know the kind of man Arthur is."

"Yep," I said. Actually, I didn't know anyone else like Arthur. I knew only Arthur. As far as I could see, he was the single person who was most likely to understand the situation—how could he not, when his job afforded him access to the president, the generals, and to classified documents?

"There is evidence," she was saying, "in an interview Kennedy gave just before he was shot, that he was going to withdraw the advisers from Vietnam, that he was going to leave the country to determine its own fate. I do think he knew that we had to pull away, that the hour had come, that he would have taken our nation in another direction." She paused before she said, "I hate to think of Buddy going over there."

All at once I thought of the images I'd seen in magazines and on TV, the villages in flames, the children burned and running, the bandaged soldiers, the bloodied water of the rice paddies. The North Vietnamese, the pitiless and cunning enemy, would have no trouble finding soldiers to butcher who weren't necessarily on the front lines. I sat up and almost said out loud that I didn't want Buddy to go. My mother was right on that score; they shouldn't let him. He could find a job, or be stupid and get into trouble, the police hauling him to prison, to safety. So what if it was a worthy cause, as Arthur believed. Worthy enough to give Buddy to it? In order not to embarrass myself, I slid back under the covers and put the pillow over my head.

"Good night, Mac," my mother said, thinking she'd been dismissed. She patted the form of my leg under the blanket. "One of these days it would be good to let Russia in here to clean. She's itching to get her hands on the place." She patted my leg again. "I'll find her a surgical mask so she's not asphyxiated." I think she kissed the pillow, for want of my hair. "Darling Mac," she murmured.

She had no idea that her talk of war would prevent me from sleeping, not just on that occasion but for weeks after. If she had tucked me in routinely, it most certainly would have killed me. She couldn't know that her history lesson had imparted nothing to me but anguish. Or, rather, at first I thought that she was innocent, that she had no notion of her effect. Later, I wondered if she understood full well what she was doing. It's possible, it's likely that she meant to lead me to sorrow in order to distract me from my admiration of Private Eastman.

IN THE YEARS THAT HAVE PASSED, I've read quite a bit about the war. I've watched the documentaries, not only out of interest, and out of dismay at my own willful ignorance at the time, but also out of a sense of obligation to Buddy. Whenever I see anything about the period or read about it, I can't keep from inserting Buddy into the scene. It's Buddy rounding up a group of Vietcong, holding an M-16 to their backs; Buddy smoking a reefer in camp; Buddy giving directions to his men over a shortwave radio; Buddy going into a madam's hooch with a slim Vietnamese teenager. It's the best I can do for him, to have tried to imagine his life. Including his being decorated by President Nixon and returning home to people who spat on him and finding himself a good wife. Those are among the forces that compelled him to remain in the military, to train young men in the armed forces for future conflicts.

"Where's Buddy?" So said Stephen Lovrek in the crisis moment.

Right after Buddy's son was killed in Iraq, Diana threw herself into the task of persuading me to go to the funeral. As I said, she was skillful, restating her arguments in each round but also throwing a surprise punch now and again. First she usually talked about how sad it was that we'd never visited Buddy, that she'd never met the man who had meant so much to me as a boy. Next, she'd speak about family responsibility, about the importance of my representing the Aaron Maciver branch of the clan. She'd bring up the idea—which proved to be fanciful—that all the cousins were going to the funeral: I would be the only one missing. "Your absence will serve, as usual," she'd say, "to draw attention to yourself."

This is something she has said to me before in other appeals. I'm not sure if she is being ironical—my husband, the show-off—if in that one complaint she is proving herself capable of irony. It is true, however, that I had not gone to Buddy's wedding, not gone to any of the family reunions that have been thrown over the years, and I'd avoided Moose Lake on the few occasions he'd visited. He had never had ownership in the property, because Figgy had sold her shares to my father in 1970, going for a killing. She didn't need the Wisconsin place when Arthur had the island in Maine. In order to buy out his sister at full market value, my father dipped into Madeline's retirement fund and spent his inheritance from his mother.

I have found it difficult under any circumstances to leave my office on short notice, inconveniencing my patients and colleagues. "Mac, sweetheart," Diana said in round four or five, "I know you have an old score to settle with your cousin, I know you do, but it's—"

"Diana." How she enjoyed stirring up drama, something you'd think she'd tire of with so much family around her, the sisters-in-law always either building toward a tizzy or in the whirlwind of one.

"You know you're holding a grudge, you know you are!"

"Men don't hold grudges," I pointed out. "It said so in the paper recently." Women, according to the study, nurture along their hurt feelings for years, backstab, gossip, don't forgive. Men are more likely to blow up or beat the shit out of each other and move on. "At my stage of life," I explained, "there is no reason to be acquainted with Buddy except for a sentimental notion we may have had about each other. There is no tragedy when time and distance have easily done their work."

"Mac," my wife said sorrowfully, her hands to my shoulders, "I just can't understand you. I try, and I cannot."

In fact, Diana understands plenty. She knows I mean to protect my dignity by being quiet, a tactic she does not approve of. Risk being a fool, she has instructed through the years. If I drink too much and, a rare occurrence, end up dancing in my socks in Mikey O'Day fashion, or singing a tone-deaf selection, she becomes very excited, as if she has found herself a new man. When she demands I pipe up, she often goes at it strenuously, a beagle baying to my fox in the hole. Nonetheless, if I were fond of aggravating her, I would say so. She is in many ways on the opposite end of the scale in temperament and personality from Sophia Cooper, the girl I earnestly loved in college, and yet she is a far better wife than Sophia would have made. Not that I am to speak or think, not ever, about wives in terms of good, better, best, or for that matter conjure the valiant beagle in the same breath as a woman, on pain of death from my daughters. But there is no doubt that Diana in her role of wife has allowed me my life's work as well as the joys of a family. I try to honor her for that feat, not only with thanks in every day but with a shower of gifts which she has circled in the catalogues before the major and minor holidays. Let me never forget Sweetest Day, which falls somewhere between Mother's Day and Valentine's Day, a tricky, no-man's-land observance.

Before Diana, when I was at Oberlin College, I fell in love with Sophia, a long-brown-haired violinist. She was not a beauty by conventional standards, something my roommate pointed out. The first time I saw her, she was onstage in rehearsal, bow poised on the strings, waiting to make her entrance in a Schumann quintet. From the beginning, she was set apart from the usual zealots, those students who called themselves musicians, who read their scores in the dining hall over their veal Parmesan. Sophia had a narrow jaw and an overbite that made her mouth jut forward—please let me say with impunity—in a weaselish way, but a nice weasel, a soft, bright-eyed weasel, a rare *Mustela* you'd want to trust. Her overbite was one of her features that drove me wild with love. I suppose it was in part the temporomandibular dysfunction that made her look so eager and focused. I didn't expect her, then, to play as if the music was revealing itself to her, as if she was continuously surprised at the turns it was taking. It wasn't so much that she was playing her violin, she said, but that the music came through her. She was able to argue for hours about intonation and phrasing, as all her peers did, but also to lapse into a learned forgetting, so that the music could spin itself into the requisite gold. There were probably others on campus who had that Zen approach to their art, but she was the one, I thought, who really lived it. Other appealing features: her hair went past her waist, her enormous glasses came down nearly to the maxilla, so much of her oversized on her small self or askew or a little bit bestial.

Louise ended up going to Oberlin, too, because of the conservatory that was part of the college, and for a few years we were there together. Stephen Lovrek, incidentally, came along also, a person I studiously avoided whenever I saw him in the library or the cafeteria. He dropped into the jazz warp, and Louise hardly ever saw him at school. On vacations at home, they resumed their classical music as if nothing as large as an aesthetic had separated them. For a while, Louise and Sophia and a trombonist friend of Lu's and I were a foursome. There was competition between my sister and my girlfriend:

claims of possession on Sophia's part, and superior knowledge of my habits on Louise's.

"I think it's interesting," Sophia would say, "that Mac always listens to everyone else's opinion before he'll comment. You don't know if he's looking upon you with benevolence, or if he thinks you're an idiot."

"Benevolence!" I'd insist.

She'd turn to look me up and down. "Or he'll say one quiet thing that you realize after a minute is funny."

"The only person Mac has ever strenuously argued with is my mother," Louise would counter loftily. "Which is perverse of him, since my mother is probably the only person he agrees with wholeheartedly on just about any subject. If he was married to her he'd be—what's the word?—uxorious. And of course," she'd add, "of course he's funny."

"Do you think," Sophia might forge ahead with some deference, "he's going to be one of those doctors who always speak in Latin, who assume that the lay person knows what the *flexor pollicis longus* is?"

"He'll talk that way until one of our cousins shoots him." Louise was gratified by laughter all around.

When Sophia announced that we were going to join the vegetarian eating co-op Louise said, "Are you kidding? Mac, a vegetarian?" Without as much as the hint of a smile she said flatly, "Hilarious." She turned to me. "I'll make sure to put a weenie in your mailbox every few days so you don't croak."

They'd start talking about music and forget about me, but I remained happy in the glow of their initial rivalry. Sophia had the creamy skin, if English literature is reliable on the subject, of a milkmaid. There were no pores across the sweep of her faintly pink cheek. When I mentioned the miracle of her epidermis, she snorted and said it was insane to think that a subjugated worker's skin could resemble the liquid that came from a dirty cow's udder. I called her Lass or Miss Cooper, both of which she tolerated despite her feminist tendencies.

She was dramatic and moody and very deep. In order to keep company with Sophia Cooper, I was ordered to read Jane Austen and George Eliot and Virginia Woolf and Henry James. No one should have to endure James, not even for love. She insisted that I spend my spare time in the music library, sitting before the turntable, listening to all of the Beethoven string quartets. I had no requirements of her other than that she make demands of me. I could have dropped out of Oberlin and still received a liberal-arts education merely by attending to the syllabus of Miss Cooper.

I had a dream once that I was her violin, that I was the wood, the varnish, the cunning bridge, the pegs and their holes, the strings, the ungainly chin-rest. Sophia took me out of the crimson velvet sepulcher of the case and swooned. I woke as if from a nightmare, soaking wet, understanding that I would have gladly dissolved to a note on the page if it was the note that Sophia cherished. My sister said she had never seen me in such a state, and it's probably true that I was never in love that way, before or after. None of Buddy's advice about women served me, no comfort in the idea that there were girls around me for the taking if the one didn't work out.

Miss Cooper made it plain that I was not the end of the line for her, that her goal was to travel the world as a member of a string quartet. The labor and intimacy of the group would consume her energy. Even if she wasn't so lucky, she had no interest in settling down, and less in being a doctor's wife, being woken at three in the morning, watching me stagger into my pants to go deliver a baby. "No thank you," she said politely. "There I'd be stuck at home raising the family, nursing along the colds and earaches with no help from the resident expert. I've seen how it goes, Mac, seen my uncle working seven days a week while my aunt, on the verge of collapse, manages the kids, the house, the relatives, the holidays, the PTA meetings." In a firmer tone she said, "No."

I don't think I actually believed that she was as ahead of her time as she seemed, that she wouldn't come around to my idea of marriage and fulfilling domesticity. Aside from her crushing view of my wife's future, we fumbled along—joyfully, I thought—learning the ropes together in the college beds that kept us conglutinated, one to the other, beds designed for the students to learn intensively about sexual relations. Sophia taught me anatomy in a most thorough, satisfying, and profound way, an educational method not possible from dissection or observation—should that have been practical. I don't mean to sound clinical or unfeeling, because the experience was as far from being cold and intellectual as it could be. She had very few inhibitions, which is something I knew even then to be rare. She would demand that I put my fingers inside her so I could feel the intensity of her orgasm, so I could know where it originated, which muscles were triggered. This instruction, she said, was for the benefit of my future patients, information she was sure I could put to use in some way. She was not very practiced, if she is to be trusted, outside of one former boyfriend and her deliberate exploration of her own body, but she did have a gift for anticipating a person's need, and also no hesitation in claiming what she must have, making me think she would perish if I couldn't help. When we remembered, we offered up thanks that the dorm hours for women were abolished before we met. Finally, I understood the gratification Jerry Pindel had wanted Madeline to render unto Mikey O'Day. I wondered briefly and slantwise now and again, did Madeline take Mikey O'Day into her mouth? As much as I didn't dwell on the idea, it occurred to me that Mikey's capacity for rapture might have its limits, that his head might have exploded with that particular stimulation. And what of Madeline? For Sophia that service seemed to be as interesting and involving to her as it was ecstatic to me.

I noted that she was most grateful to me in our lulls, that it was as we rested, my arms around her, that she seemed to say, Yes, I am with you. It was in those interludes that she admired my coarse thick hair, my brown eyes, that she traced my mouth, kissing the top lip before she dedicated herself to the fuller bottom lip. She would become positively soppy with approbation and, even better, ownership. "My love," she said, holding me fast. This evident binding of her to me made jungle sense, the female sealing herself as best she can to the male for protection while she carries her child to term, an idea I would never have dared mention. During her devotions after the urgency, I could do little but submit as she sang my praises. In those moments I knew that she'd stay with me, that with such strength of feeling, and biology on my side, she wouldn't have the heart to break it off.

Before our senior year, we spent two weeks at her family's cabin in New Hampshire, just the two of us in a pine forest in the White Mountains. It was a stretch of time when I had a happiness I knew couldn't last, and yet I also believed that it would, that it must, that it couldn't help itself. It rained for three days, and we stayed in bed. Beyond the pattering on the roof there was silence. When the sun shone we did mean to get up. On the occasions when we tossed aside the sheets, she practiced the violin and I studied, preparing for the fall term. Together we cooked simple meals. Veiny soft French cheeses with pears, sourdough bread that we made with starter from a long, venerable, yeasty line. Soup that she conjured out of lentils and a few vegetables. We were living on the cool mountain air and love, love! And the spindly sprigs of parsley that grew in pots on the porch. I managed to keep up my strength without so much as a morsel of animal flesh, without sneaking out of the house to get a gyros sandwich, as I used to do when we were part of the vegetarian co-op. We took walks and washed each other in the pond with biodegradable soap. She read Edith Wharton to me and sometimes let me win at Scrabble. As always, I declared my love to her before and during the peak moment, and she returned the favor afterward. There seemed to be no end to our subjects, her music, her books, my science, the Eastern gods, American politics—even if we didn't always discuss them out loud. What was on the verge of being said was understood between us as much as those things we articulated. Or so I thought. Curiously, I didn't ever tell her, not really, about Madeline. My story for her went like this: Madeline was my older sister, compromised in a sickness that occurred before I was born. I didn't explain the first marriage, the accident, Buddy's revelation at Moose Lake, Mikey O'Day, all those things that had nothing to do with Sophia Cooper or my life with her. They were omissions I later regretted.

When we locked up the cabin to go back to school, we stopped talking. We didn't say a word until we reached the interstate, as if we were in a limbo, no longer the pair we'd been in the cabin and not yet Mac and Sophia, strangers by those names who moved through the public world. We both probably knew we'd never have another time like that again.

On May 4, my senior year, the four students at Kent State were killed by the National Guardsmen. After that day, no one went to classes. I had been struggling with physical chemistry, but there were no more tests and no final exams. Everyone passed, the living set free. There had also been the matter of my modern-dance class, something Sophia thought would broaden my horizons and possibly loosen me up. I had yet to begin choreographing my solo piece, an assignment that had had the unfortunate effect of paralyzing both brain and limb. My girl said I looked extremely cute in my tights and T-shirt, a remark that did not make it any easier to think purely of movement.

The day of the shootings, a student group took over the administration building, although, as I recall, they were always, that year, taking over Peters Hall. Later in the afternoon, there was an assembly in Finney Chapel, and it was then, by mutual agreement between the student government and the faculty, that school was declared over. I would not have to stumble around the parquet floor in my tights in front of twenty girls in the name of dance! I remember putting my head down, trying to purge my thoughts of all things that weren't dark and sad, and how Sophia put her strong hand to my back. They encouraged us to stay on campus, to take on a project that would contribute to the peace effort. I suppose they didn't say anything as overtly political as "the peace effort," but instead used the words "to further understanding in the world." We knew what they meant. For two weeks I worked in the library, researching and writing about Agent Orange.

The night of the shootings, most of the school gathered on Tappan Square, many of us weeping from rage. There were speeches and singing and the promise of a vigil. Sophia had stayed for a respectable three hours, holding her candle, but around ten o'clock she'd blown out her little light and slunk off to practice. I leaned against a lamppost on the square, suddenly longing to be with my mother, to be comforted by whatever call to action she would suggest, to be taken up by both her energy and her calm. It was too late to call home, so I walked aimlessly trying to find Lu, and when she didn't turn up I went down the halls of the conservatory, listening in at the few practice rooms that were occupied, hoping that either she or Sophia would come forth. I knew enough not to interrupt, not to disturb the arpeggios even if F-4 and A-6 bombers were flying straight toward Ohio, even if I could see the whites of the pilots' eyes. After poking my head in at Lu's usual haunts, I found my sister in her dorm, tunneling in her dirty laundry for a sweater. She intended to go back out to the square, to be her mother's daughter and stay the night on the hard ground. We hadn't seen each other all day, and we sat on the bed, admitting that we were afraid.

She was scared to death for me, she said. It was one thing to be worried about the draft myself, but to see my sister in tears over the dangers before me only intensified my sense of doom. I brought up the subject of our father, about how he had escaped serving in World War II because of his eyesight, and how funny it was that he broke his foot in three places in the munitions parking lot—how the officials must have thought him hopeless, how they were probably glad to give him his marching orders. "You're not as puny-chested as he is," Louise said, "but you do have the clod factor. You might be able to do something really ungraceful and hurt yourself just enough. Without trying, you could do that."

One subject about the family led to the next, and after a while it seemed as good an opportunity as I might ever have to tell her what Buddy had mentioned to me those years before at Moose Lake. Even though outside, in Tappan Square, history was in the making, it was consoling to be with Louise, to be away from the collective anger, just to be us for an hour or two. "For a long time," I began solemnly, "I've been trying to figure out how Madeline fits into the family." I told her about Buddy, and about how I had found a box in the attic with Madeline's leftover wedding invitations. The font was medieval and severe, *Mr. and Mrs. Christopher Schiller request the pleasure of your company.* It was as if I'd been meant to find the yellowed card stock at just that point, after Buddy's revelation.

She let me go on for a minute before she said, "But Mac! You knew about Madeline." She went on to explain that we'd always known, that Julia had taken pains to show us the photographs when we were small, that there'd always been full disclosure.

As I said, I felt ridiculous there on her bed, having held our parents' secret so carefully for so many years. It had not seemed to me a dirty secret, not something shameful to keep private, but, rather, as if I were privy to their real identities, as if, unbeknownst to everyone but me— and also Buddy—they were in the Witness Protection Program. And now to find out that there was no reason for my heroic effort, shielding Louise from the details, holding up the façade of the Macivers. I did go on to tell her that I'd spent one night at Moose Lake before my freshman year talking to Figgy until three in the morning, that it was Figgy who had told me most specifically about Madeline's history.

"Figgy?" said Louise, screwing up her nose.

It had been the summer of 1966, just after Buddy had enlisted. I'd ducked onto the porch around midnight, looking for a book I'd left behind in the afternoon. My aunt was sitting on the swing by herself. I wouldn't have known she was there if the ember of her cigarette hadn't given her away. "Come over here, Mac," she said, patting a place next to her. "But wait. Before you get comfortable, pour yourself a drink—see, on the table? I'm certain Buddy has taught you how."

I felt very important drinking expensive whiskey with my aunt.

She seemed unfocused or else sad, I couldn't tell. Maybe she was thinking about Buddy, about the possibility that he'd get killed. Or maybe it was then that she began to consider selling her Moose Lake shares. My grandmother had died in the spring, and surely Figgy felt how much the old spirit of the place was gone. Already she was weary of the arguments about upkeep and the future drain on her finances, and after all she did have Arthur's island, the cold, windy hunk of rock off the coast of Maine. After a few small sips of whiskey, with that smooth burn in my throat, I asked her if she'd been at my father and Madeline's wedding. It seemed fairly easy to ask, and it seemed like a good deed, too, a topic to distract her from her troubling thoughts.

She began with Madeline's going to Italy, falling for the stranger, and disobeying her mother. At the time I thought it odd that for Figgy the story started there, but I realize now she was telling me everything she knew; she was providing as full an account of Madeline's life as she could, passing on the family narrative to the next generation. She told each part slowly, with a long lead to the wedding, and she drew out the day of the accident—that is, describing her own life in New York and how my father called her, and her guilt at not being at the bedside. Because it was the first occasion when she spoke to me about my parents, she was careful and generous, in spite of the whiskey. "I admire your father and your mother," she said, "for taking on the burden of Madeline with never a complaint. They're good as gold, I'm sure. I would have stuck her in the state hospital and run off to lead my life. That's the kind of woman your aunt is, kid. I wouldn't have given her a second thought." Figgy was not quite to the point of slurring her words, but she was close. "I've got one big gripe with them, though, more than a quibble. It's a beef, a bone to pick, a—"

"What gripe?" I said.

She took hold of the chain of the swing. "If I'd kept her," she said, "I wouldn't have pushed her back into little-girlhood. I've got to tell you, they handled that part all wrong. They made her into a freak! Madeline's a grown woman, and even if she's mentally compromised she could probably do some kind of work. She could put candies in boxes, or cotton in aspirin bottles, or water plants in a greenhouse—something!"

Madeline a freak? Madeline with a job?

"It was wrong," she said again.

"She helps her friend Mikey take tickets at the movie theater," I offered weakly. "And she still likes to do art projects."

"Oh boy," Figgy said, laughing, "art! Your mother thinks she's a prodigy—is there some kind of word for an old-lady wunderkind? Now, you, you're the real McCoy, National Merit Scholar, valedictorian, a bona fide smarty-pants, all right. You're a person every single family member can take pride in. You're going to do great things, mister. I can't hate you for being so smart because you're such a goddamn decent person, you punk, you. Don't think I haven't watched you being good to your, your ex-stepmother, taking her by the hand down to the lake to pick up stones, giving her boat rides, playing checkers with her. Don't think no one's noticed your kindness."

"I wouldn't be here," I blurted, "if Madeline hadn't had her accident." I didn't actually realize that truth until I'd said it.

"Yeah, well, there's that." She sat straight, shaking her head and rubbing her eyes. With that small effort at composure, she did seem to sober up. "It's funny how fate plays its tricks, how things are taken away and given. I'm in a very sentimental mood tonight, so I'm going to say this." She gripped my shoulders to make her point, and also to keep herself upright. "We all make sacrifices along the way, and you will, too. I think if Madeline could know that she'd sacrificed to make you, she'd crash into that stone wall again." Figgy put her arms fully around me and started to tremble. "She would, I know she would. You're wonderful, you're so wonderful." I was more thrilled than alarmed to be in my aunt's boozy embrace, and certainly I had no impulse to cry. "I'm going to bed now," she said, sniffing into my neck, "before I regret this evening, or morning, or whatever it is." As she pushed off from the swing she muttered, "Don't mention our chat to your mother, will you? She worries, I'm sure, that Buddy and I, my entire family, such as it is, has corrupted you." She turned to me, asking wistfully, "I haven't, have I?"

I assured her that she had not, or if she had I was the better for it. She kissed me full on the lips before she shuffled off to bed.

I told some of that story to Louise, omitting the last part, Figgy's pride in me and the large wet kiss. We got talking about our parents again, remembering scenes from our childhood, as if everything had happened long ago. From Lu's shelf I pulled down a cloth doll with an open face, two stitches for eyes, another for a mouth—the present Madeline had given her when she'd left home for college. Louise had been a good sister to Madeline until she was about nine, until she took up her cello to the exclusion of everything else. She didn't apologize for being remote, because there could not have been any other way for her, but she did note it. We remembered together the nights when she and Stephen played music in the living room, how Madeline lay over our mother in the wing chair. I told her how I'd sit at my desk and listen, how much I looked forward to it, something she had never realized before. "And Father used to bawl," I told her. "You probably thought he was doing nothing more than his accounts at the dining-room table, but when you played the Bach Suites he was a wreck."

We got to crying over our father's tears. Lu pulled me to her in the bed just as she used to when we were small, when she came to get me in a storm. We were going to weep for every sadness we could think of, starting with our nascent adult understanding of how difficult it must be for our parents, carrying Madeline along for the rest of their lives. "And now this thing, now this thing, this thing with Mikey," Louise said between her tears. From the start we'd had the habit of talking like him when we were talking about him.

"This thing with Mikey?" My mother had recently sent me a letter, but what had it said? Where had I put it? "What thing?" I must have been in a hurry at the post office and slipped the letter in my pocket; I must never have opened it.

"This is the real problem we have to cry about," Louise said, bursting into fresh sobs. I later thought how unusual it was, to have seen Louise crying. She'd been a stoic little girl, filled with the courage I lacked. In the moment, after the day's events and the abrupt ending of school, we had very little self-consciousness.

Madeline and Mikey had gotten together the summer of 1963. They'd been a couple for nearly seven years, a hard fact that had its peculiar aspects. It seemed, for one, that Mikey had always been in our house, more or less ruining my life, although you couldn't help in theory liking his sunny self. When people asked them how long they'd been going out he'd say, "Do you, do you mean how long has, how long has Madeline been my girlfriend, or do you, do you mean, how long we've been, how long we've been *engaged*?"

It was probably a year or so after they'd met that Madeline began to talk about getting married. Like any couple, they'd sit at the kitchen table while she planned the wedding. She'd cut out dresses from magazines and paste them into an enormous scrapbook my mother had bought for her. Every page had its subject, its devotion. There were the bride's pages, the bridesmaids' pages, the flower girls' pages, as well as whole chapters for cakes, ring pillows, bouquets, garlands for the pews, and the getaway car, cans and ribbons trailing behind, the Just Married sign in the back window. Page after thick gluey page with the dream wedding of the season, winter, spring, summer, and fall, and then the year would turn, and again, winter, spring, summer, fall. Every now and then you might spot a groom in the background. Madeline did allow that Mikey was the groom, and in addition he was the entertainment. He'd sit at the table tapping his feet and hands, singing through his repertory of wedding songs, including, without irony, "The Impossible Dream."

My mother was all for the marriage, although as time went on she worried that Madeline had spent so many years fantasizing about it that the real ceremony would be a terrible disappointment. She was in favor of a small wedding at the Congregational church, punch and cookies at the backyard reception, and some kind of semi-chaperoned weekend trip, activities by day and adjoining but separate rooms in a hotel by night. Afterward, their companionship would go on as it always had, each in his own family, Mikey running off home for supper, Madeline working on her general fashion scrapbook while Mikey memorized a new song, Mikey visiting for a few days of the Moose Lake vacation. My mother couldn't say whether it was Mrs. O'Day's Catholicism or the fact that she was a generation older than the Macivers, or whether it was her ecumenical stubborn and righteous selfishness that made her obstruct the couple's happiness.

Joan O'Day was small, her wrists and ankles thin as a child's, her feet charmingly narrow and delicate even in Keds. She was so short and little but otherwise unremarkable that the hard-looking ball of her potbelly was always a surprise. When she shouted at my mother, you imagined that downstairs was a robust, bosomy matron who could sing. I was away for nearly all the big scenes, but I recall that her voice in anger had a vibrato. She'd come over on weekend afternoons, when the betrotheds were at the movie theater; she did, at least, show that consideration. In the front hall, so my mother's stories went, Mrs. O'Day would shout: "Mikey is not going to marry Madeline! Do you understand? You have no business, no business encouraging them to get married. Married! Mikey can't boil an egg without setting the stove on fire."

She'd bellow equally about every aspect of the bad idea. Mikey had plenty of people to care for him, and there was no reason to introduce someone else into the family who needed looking after! The Macivers might dream they could pawn Madeline off on the O'Days, but they should think again!

When my mother tried to explain that the wedding was a ceremony to honor the couple's love rather than the beginning of a domestic arrangement, Mrs. O'Day would start in after Madeline. Madeline had wrung the engagement ring out of Mikey, wrung it out of Jack O'Day, too, the husband who couldn't say no to anyone. She'd demanded a ring that was far too expensive, draining Mikey's savings account for a real diamond. A real diamond! "You think the wedding is going to be the end of Madeline's extortions, do you? Once they're married she'll want an apartment, and then she'll go after a house, and next you know she'll be signing an agreement on a summer home! The wedding is the tip of the iceberg. It will never end, Julia Maciver, and I say it is never going to begin!" Out the door she'd go with a hearty slam, blazing back home to iron Mikey's undershirts and bake his macaroni and cheese.

Madeline's fervor about the marriage waxed and waned, but apparently that spring of 1970 she'd been pushing for it with greater urgency. There was very little else she could think of or talk about. What my mother's letter told me, Louise explained, was that the crisis had come to a head.

"What do you mean?" I said.

"The O'Days are retiring to Florida."

"Retiring?"

"They are taking Mikey and moving away." Before I could register the news she cried, "What'll she do without him?" She folded into my side, moaning, "What'll she do?"

"They can't do that," I said. "They won't." It was bad enough when Mikey went on vacation, when Madeline had no one to hound, no one who was willing to sit by her side all through the day. They couldn't do it to their own son; I was sure they would not. Mikey and Madeline went to the grocery store together, they went to each other's dentist appointments, they held hands in front of the pet-shop window watching the guinea pigs. They were as good as married; they were better than married. For all Mikey's silliness and his tendency to be self-centered, he was courtly, holding Madeline's elbow when they crossed the street, running around her to open the door, and once I saw him so carefully and lovingly move a strand of hair out of her eyes. Despite their height difference, when they were spooned together on the sofa watching television, his arms around her, they had a physical comfort that was enviable.

"Mom won't let it happen," I said. "She'll find a way to keep them together."

"She has to," Louise wailed.

Somewhere in the middle of our flood, Louise reached into her desk drawer, drew out two handkerchiefs, and handed me a wad of linen. I smoothed the wrinkles as best I could, down to the corner where "LMM" had been embroidered years before by our grandmother. Louise Margaret Maciver. I had my own set of twelve, with my initials. One of the things Madeline loved to do at home was iron the handkerchiefs, a job she'd work at in the basement while Russia folded clothes. Without Madeline our handkerchiefs were shriveled slabs that looked like enormous dried fruits. I turned on my back, drawing Lu to my chest, stroking her hair the way girls like, the way my mother had always done. We started remembering Mikey, as if we were gathering material for his eulogy. "Do you remember him," Louise said against my heart, "the night Madeline got taken prisoner up in the Pindels' loft, and how Buddy came to the rescue?"

"Buddy didn't realize Mikey and Madeline were a couple," I said. "I wanted to beat Jerry up for making Madeline parade around in that ugly dress. But Buddy thrashed him because he thought Jerry was forcing Madeline to pair up with a stranger. It was all confused."

"That dress," Lu ruminated. "I tried to find that thing the next day, but I couldn't. She must have crumpled it up and stashed it deep down in her trunk or in the back of her closet. A prize possession, I guess. I just wanted to get rid of it."

"Was the fashion show a game she'd been playing for years with Jerry, do you think? Or a one-shot deal?"

Louise shook her head. "She was always so gaga over Jerry."

"Poor Mikey," I said.

"That was the only time I ever really saw him run—when he took off down the alley. He looked as scared and disturbed as we all felt."

We remembered the stir the following day, after the seriousness of Jerry's injuries was broadcast. He'd had to be hospitalized with his broken nose and a concussion. My mother had come slowly up the back steps from the yard that morning, the color drained from her face, her jaw tight. I was intently reading the cereal box, thinking that I might, even at my age, send for a magic rock garden or a handful of sea horses. "What happened to Jerry last night?" Julia said.

"What's the matter with him?"

"Was it Cleveland who broke his nose?"

"You'd have to ask him." I wasn't going to tattle, not on anyone. My duty was to watch out for Madeline, and Mikey, too, to make sure his girl didn't wander off with the grocery boy.

"That's what they're saying, Mac, that Cleveland beat Jerry senseless."

"You should have thought of that," I said, "before you got involved with Project Share." So I got to shoot my arrow into my already stricken mother.

She went with a heavy tread to wake Clark Kent and the Negro suspect. I had thought Buddy could not rise any higher in my mother's esteem, but, no, he proved to her that he was not done, that there were greater heights to be climbed to the peak of her affection. Down he came to the kitchen, yanking his T-shirt over his head and zipping up the fly of his shorts. He was barefoot, but at the threshold he must have thought better of it; he realized he'd be more respectable if he was wearing shoes and socks. Around the block he went, ringing the doorbells, telling the neighbors with no fanfare that it was he who had hurt Jerry Pindel, that he had his reasons, that he was sorry, but that under no circumstances did the blame go to Cleveland Simonson. Cleveland had not touched Jerry. There were witnesses if they'd like. The Pindels could arrest him, Buddy Eastman, take him to court, make him do time. He shook his blond head and said mournfully that he was sorry, but even so it had happened and he couldn't take it back. "I'll be with my aunt and uncle for another few days, in case the authorities want to come and get me."

We had all been mum the night before, but Buddy said enough of

the truth to keep the story contained. I don't underestimate his bravery. It was civil rights in action—Buddy, the future Atticus Finch. Up
and down the alley, the mothers were impressed, even if some of them
didn't believe him. According to the legend, he also had a conversation with Mr. Pindel—Jerry's father concluding with "Boys will be
boys" and a handshake. We were all in the kitchen after Buddy had
gone door to door, and I remember my mother praising him for his
honesty and then saying plaintively, "But why did you do it? What
reason did you have?"

Looking at me, he said, "It was a question of honor."

"Honor?" she said, without comprehension, as if she'd never
heard the word.

"If you don't mind, Aunt Julia, I'd rather not talk about it."

Too humble to blow his own horn, our Buddy. He had taken care
of the business, and nothing more need be said. He would go to prison
if he had to, rather than recount a lurid scene and his own heroism.

As Louise and I lay in her dorm bed, sniffling and coughing and
blowing our noses, she remembered again how furious Madeline had
been. "It took both Stephen and me to haul her away from the loft."

I marveled at Madeline's admiration for Jerry, strong enough to
cast her fashion judgment to the wind. Even though she'd been terrible to Mikey, I'm sure the next day they went on as if nothing had happened. The times I had slept in the boathouse with him, he'd always
literally jumped out of bed at dawn, running to the window to see if
the sun was going to come up. A clean slate every morning, the awful
words "big fat dodo" wiped away.

"They won't take him to Florida," I assured Louise again. "They
can't." I'm afraid that set us off once more, another teary bout for
those two people who had enough sense to know they weren't normal,
who had had the astonishing luck to find each other. It was when Lu
was locked in my arms, groaning, that Sophia pushed open the door.
She'd knocked, I guess, but we hadn't heard. It probably took us a
minute to realize that she was there, but finally we did notice, and

slowly we lifted our heads. I felt as if I were trying to see through a heavy rain, as if I were driving through a storm.

"Sophia?" I rooted around on the bed for my miserable soaked piece of linen.

Louise had a more finely tuned sense of disaster, and after the initial hesitation she popped out of bed. "Mac and I," she explained, "are in the middle of a nervous breakdown." When Sophia didn't move, didn't come in or back away, Louise tried again. "It's not what it looks like—although I'm not sure what it looks like. I don't know, we were talking about old times, about family problems."

Sophia blinked rapidly. "You're talking about family, your family? When the entire world is burning?"

"One thing," I said, "led to the next."

"Ah," Sophia said. "I see. Like it always does."

I was up and going to her. "We were talking about the killings and—"

"I would never want to interrupt family togetherness," she said before she bolted.

Although she had a head start, I was able to catch her by bounding, a half-flight in one leap. On the second-floor landing I managed to pin her to the railing. "Get your hands off me!" she cried.

"Sophia, don't be crazy. Don't be insane! We—"

"I am *not* insane!" She was off again, down the next flight. When I'd leapt once more and barred the door to the lobby, I tried to tell her in a rush about Madeline, the real story, as fully detailed as I could make it in a few sentences.

"You know my sister? No, no, not Lu, but Madeline, she's not really my sister, she was married to my father, but then, one day, she hit a stone wall, bam, on her bike, no one saw it, it ruined her, oxygen deprivation, brain damage—and then my mother cared for her, she was a nurse, she wasn't my mother yet, not yet, and later she married my father, there was an annulment or a divorce, nothing sneaky, it was legal . . ." It sounded so nutty, so melodramatic, I started to laugh.

"Not that it's funny"—I was only laughing harder—"it's not at all, as a matter of fact, Lu and I, we were talking . . ." And, as if to make it worse, a stream of snot coming from my nose, I began to cry again. "They're taking Mikey O'Day to Florida." I looked through my tears at Sophia. "They can't do that! She'll die." I started to cough. "Of loneliness." I repeated, choking, "Of loneliness."

Sophia was staring at me in amazement. "What," she said at last, "in the fuck are you talking about?" When I couldn't begin anew, or take up in the middle, or even end the story, she said, "I don't know why you never told me whatever you're trying to explain before. But that's just you, I guess. Strong and silent, the current running too deep for me. Way too deep."

It was no doubt just the scene she needed to be able to go off with a clear conscience, to pursue her career as the second violinist in a quartet that did achieve some fame. Because there were no more classes, she left the campus the next day and didn't come back until graduation. I saw her after the ceremony, in the distance. She was looking over at us, at my parents and Madeline. I waved through the crowd, the only chance I got to say goodbye to her.

Chapter Twelve

A FEW DAYS BEFORE BUDDY'S SON'S FUNERAL, TESSA GRACED
us with her presence at the supper table. She was working as
an intern at the local newspaper, the lone daughter at home for
the entire summer. Diana stood at the sink, running water into
a kettle, speaking to me in her voice that was high and clear
over the tap. "Your inability to extend yourself is more than
plain bad manners, really Mac, but it's that, too. It's rude. How
would you like it—" She stopped, realizing perhaps that it was
tempting fate to consider the deaths of your own children, even
for educational purposes.

As she ran the water, and with dinner on the way, I had
enough hope to think almost cheerfully of marriage as a
mortification not of the flesh but of the soul. Just the soul,
that's all. I'd had a trying day in my kingdom, the fortress with
peaked skylights, the bright veneer of germlessness, the homey
touches of flowered wallpaper borders, and at regular intervals
large framed still-lifes of ribboned hats among plates of fruit.
There were TV monitors, too, in every corner, attractive men
and women dispensing information about menopause, sexual
dysfunction, osteoporosis, high blood pressure, and the benefits
of the dread colonoscopy. To devote oneself to wellness at the
clinic is to sprint from exam room to exam room, trying both
to fulfill and to ignore the dictates from the new corporate
headquarters, the efficiency guidelines, ten minutes per patient.

It's the American way, and although we old fogies are not resigned, although we subvert as best we can, we know that without revolution from all quarters we are powerless in the face of the business gurus at the central office and, beyond, at the insurance companies. The big joke, how stressed and bitter the doctors are as they try to promote health in others.

That afternoon my nurse, Gretchen, had twisted her ankle, leaving me in the trembling hands of a shy student on the second day of her internship. I have tried through the years to become a better listener, something the women doctors tend to do well, tilting their heads and appearing to give the patients time to tell their stories. I had made a point to be attentive to Mrs. Ozanick, an eighty-two-year-old widow who has had chronic migrating pain for the twenty years I've known her. For fourteen minutes, I had followed her solid wall of talk concerning her cell-phone plan, her nephew's phone arrangement, and the paucity of calls she received, on land or otherwise, from her children. I have not been able to find a real remedy for her discomfort, aside from the solace she seems to take from my interest. Since she pays out of pocket, she can visit me as often as Gretchen will schedule her. When she left the office, her stomach pain was in fact gone, I was edified about the merits of her carrier, and the miracle of medicine had proved itself once more to be a vapory thing. I was twenty-five minutes behind, and in the next appointment had to tell a thirty-seven-year-old mother of four, a woman who had come in with fever and anemia, that there had been primitive leukemia cells in her blood leukocyte count, an indication of acute granulocytic leukemia. Remissions, I did not tell her, saving that piece for the oncologist, are usually partial or brief. After that, now fifty-four minutes behind, there was a case of poison ivy, a man who, incidentally, had a tattoo on his back of Georges Seurat's *A Sunday Afternoon on the Island of La Grande Jatte*—his wife's favorite painting. It had been done over a five-year period, spreading out the torment and expense. The rash, much to his relief, was on his legs, and did not interfere with the artwork. As I was walking out of the clinic, around the corner from the hospital, an ambulance was just pulling in at Emergency. A twenty-year-old boy had been struck by a train on a back road and was dead on arrival.

"Comfort me with apples," I said in Diana's direction at the sink, "for I am sick of love." There was too much genuine suffering in the world to be anything but filled with happiness on the home front, an idea, when I've voiced it, that makes Diana go fearsomely hard and cold. Diana is a model of decorum—her anger, which of course is rightfully hers, clean and bright, blossom of snow. But I was not going to Kyle Eastman's funeral merely as a corrective to my character.

"Do you need therapy, Dad?" Tessa wondered softly. "Would that help? Sometimes it seems like you married—well—not your own mother, not Grandma Julia, but someone's mother. The mother-brides were switched at the wedding. It's a mistake of karma!"

Where, from what realm, do our monstrous children come? And when did children blithely start to analyze their parents at the dinner table? What television show taught them this?

"Mom obviously can't stop gnawing on the old bone of your reconnecting with Cousin Buddy. So—what's the deal?"

"What did you say, Tessie?" Diana at last turned off the water. "I didn't hear."

"I was telling Dad that it would be interesting to meet the cousins. Buddy has five kids, right?"

"Four now," Diana said. "Living, I mean. They'll always have five, always. Kyle—bless his soul—Robert, Mallory, Vanessa, Brittany."

Tessa reached across the table to grasp my hand. "Why don't you take me to the funeral? I'll be the ice-breaker."

An apt role for Tessa in any situation. When she looks at you, it is best to clear your mind of insincerity. She does not listen with womanly sympathy, no cocking of the head, no steady warmth, no encouraging nods. Tessa is a predator when she listens, the girl taking your full measure.

"Buddy's family has great faith," I muttered. "He doesn't need any of us to witness his grief." My cousin, as far as I knew, had not gotten religion, but perhaps a little of his wife's zeal had rubbed off on him.

Just then one of the newer sisters-in-law entered, Nan from across the road, the pediatrician among us. Diana's younger brother had taken her to be his second wife a few years before, after the first one ran off from the family compound. I was pleased when Jim married Nan, because she reads, she is curious about any subject, she votes as I do, she has never said a single word about her emotional state, and also she seems to understand how the family operates and still she appears to like us.

"Mac won't go to his cousin's son's funeral," Diana said, by way of greeting Nan. "The boy died in Iraq." She brought a wide bowl of greens in all the salad hues to the table, from purple lettuces to the glowing jade of chard to the blue of young kale. She had managed to grow lettuce through the heat, her garden a weedless wonder of verdure and nourishment.

"How beautiful!" Nan said, with genuine awe. Her Nordic good looks, towering height, and straight blond hair make her seem chronically wholesome and vigorous. "I'm sorry to hear about your cousin," she said to me. "That's awful." After she'd inquired about Kyle's age and the circumstances of his death—questions that Diana answered—she again turned to me, to praise and to say thank you. I had seen a patient of hers that morning, a boy with a rash, swollen glands, fever, peeling skin. It's quite difficult to diagnose an illness if you haven't encountered it at least once. I'd been able to tell her that Stevie Tolbertson had Kawasaki disease, something that isn't very common in Anglo-Saxons, and in addition is apt to show up in winter and spring. Stevie was Nordic himself, and it was fully summer. "I'm so grateful," she was saying. "I think you should give a talk to the staff about Kawasaki, the way you did about tetanus last year." To Diana she said, "He told you about that, didn't he?"

"My husband, speak?"

"It's just that he's modest," Nan explained. "A reluctant hero. But let me tell you. He was walking through the ER, there was a woman with muscle spasms, Dr. Prentiss didn't have any idea what was wrong with her, Mac took one look and said, 'Tetanus.' The fact that Mac just happened to be walking past saved the woman's life."

Her story was not true to the letter: it had taken me more than one look to make the diagnosis. Again, I was able to do so only because I'd had the privilege of seeing tetanus, in D.C. it was, a man half dead from a puncture wound.

"Anyway," Nan said, "I'm sorry to barge in here, but I wanted to thank you."

While she'd been talking, Diana had come behind my chair and put her hands on my shoulders, as she often does when she is feeling sorry or left out. It had done me no harm to have Nan say in her presence that she was indebted to me. Nan paused, looking at Diana and looking at me. She said, "We might be able to spare you for a day or two, Mac, for your funeral. We probably could get along."

Diana pressed closer and said in my ear, "I understand you're busy, I do."

Nan thanked me again as she got up from the table, and I thanked her—for what she did not know, for her kindness, her diplomacy, her excessive compliments. A reluctant hero! I was always much improved after seeing her. The minute she was out the back door, Tessa leaned forward in her so-called shirt, an orange scrap with one string each side, and the secondary purple straps of her brassiere. "Tell me," she said, "about the last time you saw Buddy." She was a sophomore at her eco-friendly, vegetarian, composting-toilet college in North Carolina, a student of history and journalism. She was practicing her trade, just as a dental student pulls the wisdom teeth of all her family members. The small rectangular emerald-green frames of her new glasses added to the serious and yet hip investigative-reporter effect. I had no doubt that she would go far, not only because of her intelligence and wit but because of her other, equally important attributes:

the wardrobe, the velvety skin—so much of it to see—and her persistence.

"The discussion of human relations is overrated," I said to her. "When I was a boy we talked politics. We discussed the world around us, science, art, music. We didn't spend our lives picking apart—what do you call them?—relationships."

"You didn't have to pick yours apart," Diana said wearily. "Your family tore itself to pieces over current events. You all argued and argued until you didn't speak anymore." Despite her fatigue, she made that most generous of motions, sweeping up the linguine from the bowl with two wooden forks, swinging the mass of it onto my plate.

"Thank you," I said.

"The last time your father saw Buddy was the summer of 1975, in Washington, D.C.," Diana began.

Tessa raised what serve as her brows, those tiny pencil lines above her eyes. "True?"

I put my head down, nose to the tomato sauce that Diana had made with her own jeweled hands.

"I love that Mom knows this stuff and you hardly remember! That's so symbiotic. Did you have a major argument about the Vietnam War with Buddy? Since you wimped out and didn't serve—right?"

"Right," I said.

"What I mean, Dad, is that no matter how justified you were in avoiding a ridiculous war, the fact that he went and you didn't had to be this *thing* between you, the elephant in the room, the—"

"Do you want some cheese, Tessie?" Diana said, passing the cutting board.

Tessa grated the mail-order parmigiano over her pasta, grimacing with her effort. When she finished she said, "What did Buddy do over there, anyway?"

"As I understand it," I said, "he was in support organizations, first as a guard, and when he re-enlisted he went through another training program for a unit that manned the supply lines."

"There's that picture of him being decorated by President Nixon on the Moose Lake mantel, so that must have been a big deal." She was speaking at her plate, as if she were working the details out to herself. "Even if the president was an asshole, still, it's the president, and there were probably people in the family who thought it was exciting." She looked up at me. "When you met in 1975, the war was over and you were finally hashing it out? If I'm going to meet my cousins, I want to know about your brawl."

"Diana," I murmured. That very afternoon, she had put up a bushel of the San Marzano paste tomatoes, nine sparkling pint jars on the counter. She was still wearing her charming smock, spattered with juice and pulp, and further, her curly hair, the gray dyed to brown, was covered with a blue bandana. She was in that moment my Antonía, the love of my life. Surely it has never been more dangerous to love than in our time; the feminazis would undoubtedly lynch me for warming so to Diana in her farm-wife costume, the ensemble—such a vision—that made me want to jump up and polka with her out to the hayloft. "Diana," I said again. "This is the most delicious thing I have ever tasted." I had to close my eyes, to hold the trace of basil, the rumor of garlic in my mouth. "I feel like I'm back in my native Italy."

"Seriously, Dad! What happened?"

I opened up to look at Tessa. "Happened?"

"You're being obtuse on purpose! Don't be stupid."

"Usually nothing much actually happens." I was still in the trance of the pasta and also the Bryant Family Cabernet, 1996. "I'm not sure you're aware of that. It sounds unexciting, but as you get older you're grateful every time nothing at all occurs." I can count on one hand the incidents through my years that have spurred concrete change, starting with Madeline's bicycle accident, an essential marker in my life, as important as conception. To my daughter, in a vain attempt to make a joke, I said, "We put on diapers, Buddy and I, and we wrestled."

Diana exhaled theatrically, as if to say to Tessa, See? See how impossible my life is?

Tessa spoke quietly. "I'd really like to know. I'd like to know your history." In her voice there was disappointment—*You are letting me down, Father*—and also tones of determination: *I will get the story from you.*

"You want to know," Diana said to Tessa with exquisite patience. "You want to know how it was between your father and Buddy. They were like brothers, that's what Louise says. Inseparable. When the families split it was like . . . what's-their-names, in *Romeo and Juliet*—"

"The Montagues and the Capulets."

"Those boys on either side of the fence."

"Except no double suicide," I said, my mouth full of noodles. " 'She's dead, deceas'd, she's dead; alack the day!' "

"Your father had a summer job at the VA hospital in D.C. I stayed behind in Madison, working at a day camp, such wonderful, sweet girls, ages eight to ten, lots of fun. Buddy was just home from Vietnam. There was a dinner at Aunt Figgy's house, and that's when some of the animosities about the war came out. The family, like I was saying, was always arguing about it."

"There wasn't any animosity between Buddy and me over the war," I said, clearly, having swallowed.

"Excuse me?" Diana said. "I beg your pardon?"

The dog came up and put her nose between my legs, looking at me dolefully, as if there were nothing to say about my predicament, nothing to be done about my women, whose great subject is the emotional landscape, their own and the hazy terrain of their loved ones'. It is a tottery position for them, trying to acquire self-knowledge without going overboard, without becoming stridently self-indulgent.

"And there wasn't a dinner at Figgy's," I said.

I do, however, remember meeting Buddy for a drink at a hotel near Union Station in Washington, and no doubt Diana is correct, that the year was 1975. It's also probably true that there was a story to tell, one that could well satisfy the women. My cousin was passing through the city, on his way to Maine to visit his parents. From the window where I was sitting in the bar, I could see him coming along the street, walking swiftly, chin up, eyes straight ahead, as he must have had to do in training, and in drills overseas. He was tan as always, with that particular Buddy sheen, as if he'd been lightly washed in gold. His skin tone was an ornament, an essential accessory to the man, the sun-studded soldier.

I came outside and we shook hands heartily, and then, in that way veterans have, he threw his arms around me and hugged me hard, swaying back and forth. He was twenty-nine. There were faint lines under his eyes, his face was leaner, the angles were pronounced: he was fit, and also he'd suffered. I knew very little about Buddy's time in Vietnam, but we'd all learned about the Silver Star he'd received for showing uncommon bravery through the Tet Offensive. He had been a guard, and so he hadn't at first been in combat, standing sentry at his base somewhere, I think, near Nha Trang. His mother had thought he'd have a desk job, but Buddy had decided to be as close to the infantry as he could without actually fighting. During Tet, he'd come under fire and, using his old general's authority, that gift he'd honed at Moose Lake, he'd repelled the enemy and also protected most of those he'd been working with. Although Cousin Nick once said that Arthur Fuller pulled strings, that no one who had fought in a little skirmish like that would have earned such an honor, I had liked to think Buddy deserved the decoration.

Once we were inside the bar and sitting he said, "How is every-one? Your mom, your dad, Madeline?"

"Madeline?" After all those years, after having been away, he found it important to ask after her, to make sure that she was fine, that the neighbor boys weren't abusing her. The thought of Buddy proba-bly still made Jerry Pindel's blood run cold. "She's doing all right," I said. She was fifty-six, her blond hair in her updated coif streaked with white, the shine gone. The thin fall of her hair to her shoulders and the bangs made her actually look younger than she had with her ribbons and rubber bands. Five years had passed since Mikey O'Day had moved to Lantana, Florida. She still refused to go to the movie theater, and my mother always drove out of her way to avoid the Dari-Dip. Julia had managed to get Madeline a job at a beauty salon uptown, gainful employment, what Figgy had envisioned from the start. A few afternoons a week, she did shampoos and swept the clippings from the floor. She was proud of her work and excited to have her own money. The first thing she had shown me on my last visit was her passbook from the bank.

We figured, Buddy and I, that it had been ten years since we'd last seen each other. During much of that time he'd been out of the country. He'd found his place in the army, he'd gotten engaged to Joelle, a woman who'd been in the Miss America Pageant. Before her state title she'd been Miss Alamogordo, an accomplishment that sounded even more exotic than Miss New Mexico. Buddy hadn't been to Washington since he'd been decorated by Nixon in 1969. "An amazing moment." He shook his head as if he still couldn't believe it.

I had read accounts of soldiers who had not felt the same way, who had not attended their ceremonies, but Buddy was in earnest about his awe. "Watergate blew everything," he said. "It blew the Peace Accords, it blew our ability to stand behind the treaty, to protect Vietnam. It blew Congress's will to finish off the war honorably."

I agreed with him that the break-in had been unfortunate.

"There's always foul play in elections," he said. "The country acts like Nixon's the first guy to tamper with the process!"

"And to tape himself at the same time," I noted.

"When I got off the plane at Dulles, after my first tour, people spat on me. You folks out there"—he waved his hand to indicate the Midwest—"don't believe it, but it's true. I was spat on in our capital because I'd served my country." He frowned into the polish of the bar. "What could they know?" he muttered.

That kind of ingratitude, I said, was unforgivable, and I was sorry he'd had to endure it.

"Especially for enlistees, the guys who signed up because we believe in our country."

"Do you remember," I said, "how startled everyone was when you joined?" I suppose what I meant was how frightened I'd been for him.

"Are you kidding, Brains? There was no big secret there. It was a hell of a lot easier to go into the army than not get into college and not win the girl of my dreams. Don't get me wrong, I was prepared to do the job. But I did practically flunk out of the academy, something my mom probably kept to herself. I'm not just saying I almost flunked out a little. Arthur, I'm sure, had to talk sweet or pay up so I could graduate."

It was the first time we were talking as fully fledged adults, the first occasion when we could look back on our youth with some kind of perspective. I was suddenly very glad that he'd made the effort to meet. It had been common knowledge that he'd had to stay back a grade in high school, but Figgy had always made it sound as if they had opted to have Buddy experience certain subjects again so that he would be strong academically, as if they'd had a choice, as if repeating was like taking megavitamins. I could imagine that, rather than doing his homework, he'd been teaching his friends indispensable lessons for their real lives.

"I'm wired for the army anyway—my dad, my grandfather," he was saying. "I come from a long line of warriors." He stretched his arms their full span, as if to tell me there had been legions before him, all the way back to Achilles. "How else was I supposed to figure out manhood?"

"Manhood." The image of Jerry Pindel rose before me, blood streaming from his nose. "I was always impressed by your courage," I said, "well before you joined the army." "Courage," I thought, wasn't exactly the word. How much of Buddy's force was actually bravado? "There was that night—you might not recall it—the night in the neighbor's garage the summer you visited us, the year before you enlisted." That small scuffle, that violence would be nothing compared with the tedium and heroics of years at war.

"That fucking made me crazy!" he cried. "Yeah, I remember. The scumbag operator—what was his name? The bunwad, trying to make Madeline blow that idiot on the sofa! I wanted to blast that asshole's brains to smithereens."

I couldn't help laughing at his indignation. "It was a fashion show at first," I reminded him. "I'm not sure Jerry planned for anything beyond dressing Madeline in the Goodwill clothes and having some hilarity at her expense."

"You're out of your mind, Brains! He had the retard on the sofa so Madeline could dickie-lick him. You are still out to lunch, aren't you, pal? Head in the clouds. I did want to kill that kid for mixing Madeline up with the half-breed."

"Her boyfriend," I said. "Mikey, that 'half-breed,' was her boyfriend. She was engaged to him."

He squinted to think. "Yeah, oh yeah, I knew that, that's right. What are you saying, though? You saying it was okay for the butt-wipe to—"

"Of course not. I'm only saying that Mikey wasn't a stranger to Madeline, and also I wouldn't call him a half-breed." I probably sounded not only sanctimonious but dramatic when I said, "He was the best thing that ever happened to her."

"Sure, sure, I can see that. She was a very pretty lady, and she was dying for it. I was a babe in the woods, and I knew that much. My mom said she was like a bitch in heat, always rubbing up against the back fence, mooning around the yard. You did want the poor girl to have some relief." He felt it necessary to add, "But not up in that attic with all those dumb-ass kids watching."

He trolled in the communal snack-mix bowl for the peanuts, and I drank my beer. I remembered that hot afternoon when Mikey and Madeline for the first time disappeared alone into her bedroom. I'd been reading an enormous Hermann Hesse novel that I took for the last word on the meaning, among other things, of rivers, the profound flow, the taking, the giving, the changing, the sameness. It was with a weighty seriousness that I rolled off my sticky bed to go to the bathroom. As I was at the toilet, I realized that the two of them were upstairs, in Madeline's room, together in her room. I could hear her light laughter and his guffaws, which were unusually throaty. Back in the hall I listened some more, the voices behind the closed door as changeable as the river, but also ever the same. Mikey was making noises the way he did if my mother presented him with a dish of ice cream or a juicy hamburger, yum-yum sounds. I went straight downstairs to see if Julia was home, and so she was, in the kitchen chopping carrots, without a care in the world. I stood staring at her.

"Hello," she said.

"What do you mean, 'Hello'?"

She continued chopping. "Everyone," she said, "deserves their privacy."

"Their privacy."

I had not yet learned that Madeline had had a hysterectomy, and I wondered if I should give my mother a lecture, edify her about the consequences of irresponsible sexual behavior. Or was she advocating free love for each member of the family? Were there going to be bundles of retarded joy at nine-month intervals from here on out? I supposed genetically they'd have normal children, but who would care for the pint-sized geniuses when the parents had trouble figuring out how to set an alarm clock? I was going to seize my book from my own bed and leave for the farthest reaches of town. Only to see, on my way back upstairs, that their door had popped open, a two-or-so-inch aperture. There was Mikey standing stark naked in profile, there his tight little butt, his Buddha belly, his magnificent—and long!—glistening, ready, and willing tumescence. If I called it that to myself, it was because I'd been reading great literature. And Madeline, or anyway her legs on the bed, Madeline, herself waiting and ready. I walked down the stairs, out of the house, thinking of the few couples who, it was rumored at school, were having sexual intercourse. I'd invite them over so they could fuck on the dining-room table as my mother was trying to serve dinner; they could fuck on the kitchen floor, in the tub, on the piano while Louise practiced; they could fuck in my parents' bed, on top of them while they slept.

So Madeline, to use Buddy's phrase, had gotten some relief. "It's funny," I said to him, "but it seemed to me that you were beating up Jerry for the wrong reason. Not that it matters, but the fashion show was the greater cruelty, far more ugly, meaner, than the generalized humiliation of the sexual favor. The evil tease of the runway was perfectly tuned to Madeline's vulnerability." I'd wanted to tell him that for a long time. "Your outrage at Mikey's being a moron—"

"You know, Brains?" He shook his head, the slow back-and-forth of amazement. "Isn't Brains a fucking cute little scientist, dissecting a monkey in the basement!" He managed to say that with almost no rancor. "Here comes Brains with a bucket of dead fish, the scholar"—he let out a cackle—"with his head up his ass."

I had once wanted to set him on fire, almost sure in the moment that I was capable of it. We were again coming close to the tender, murderous point at the center of our fraternal affection. "It was good of you," I went on, "to prevent the neighborhood from erupting, to go door to door and absolve Cleveland of guilt in the beating. It turned out there was racial hatred on the block. Although not everyone believed you—some of those women held it against us for a long time, that we'd sheltered the Negroes. I don't think Mrs. Pindel ever spoke to my mother again.

"That asswipe," Buddy spat, still referring, I guessed, to Jerry. "The little faggot."

A clarifying moment, in the smoky bar, the glass to my lips. Buddy perhaps had clocked Jerry most of all because of the whiff in the loft of our neighbor's homosexuality. Maybe the thrashing had had nothing to do with Madeline: Brains, at last understanding the deeper impulse of his strong and courageous cousin, the hero, and champion of certain minorities.

"So," I said after a decent interval, "you're going to make a life of it. A career military man."

Buddy was signed up for the Drill Sergeant Program, a future that had amused the cousins with its rightness. He explained at some length what was required of him, how he'd gone through security clearance before and passed various tests, and also proved that he had no speech impediment, an important detail in the drill-sergeant profession. He was hopeful that with his experience he'd advance quickly. He'd been in the army long enough to assume that I knew what he was talking about, that I was familiar with the chain of command and the military acronyms, that they were all household terms. Even if I didn't understand the finer points, I could see that his service in Vietnam had somehow not diminished his enthusiasm for being a soldier, that if anything his commitment had intensified through the years. When I wondered out loud if that was true he said, "Someone has to do this job. It's up to those of us left to rebuild the reputation of the military, to keep our great country strong. I ask myself, if I don't do it, who will?"

When I didn't say anything he repeated, "Who will?"

The aim was admirable, I said.

"You think so, Brains?" He turned his body on the stool so that he faced me, so that he could look at me squarely.

"Sure," I said, "yes. Absolutely."

"Yeah, well, I'd like to pass down some of what I've learned in the field and contribute to our nation being strong. You better believe it. I'd like to combat all the shit that's been heaped on the good men who fought hard."

I had the unfamiliar sensation then that although he was staring, it wasn't for the purpose of seeing me. For a minute he went still. He was no longer present, just like that, gone. It was as if he'd been cut away from himself. Even though I couldn't have imagined what hell he'd been through, I thought I understood how going to war would separate you not only from your old friends but from the civilian you'd once been, how you might not be able to reclaim much of your old character. That such a thing would happen to Buddy, that he'd lose his essential Buddyness—I'd rather have had him insulting me or being furious for a wrongheaded reason than going so quiet. "Aren't you," he said, finally blinking, taking a handful of the pretzels, "aren't you going to ask if I believed in the war, since your mother isn't here to grill me?"

At the ready to be obedient, I said, "Did you believe in the war?"

He threw the snack mix in his mouth, chewing, chewing and reflecting, as if he hadn't solicited the question, as if he didn't know the answer. After a while he said, "I hate to say this in present company, but whether you believe in it or not is beside the point. Tell that to Aunt Julia. You've over there, you have a job to do, it's a job. You're bored off your ass half the time, you hope nobody in the detachment goes too nuts, you hope you don't go nuts, you hope your superiors aren't sadists, you hope no one gets so drunk they start shooting you, you hope the guy who got blown up screwing a fourteen-year-old gook—you hope his mother doesn't write to you to ask about his noble death in battle." He put his hand back in the feed bowl. "It's a job, like I said."

I was relieved when he changed the subject, when he said, "So— you're going to be a doc. Make the big bucks."

"I'll be working in a small-town hospital, I hope." The fucking cute little scientist tells his dream to the drill sergeant. "Internal medicine."

"You always were a whore for guts, weren't you, pal?"

"A real whore," I agreed.

"That's great, Brains. I'll make sure to get to your doorstep before I have my heart attack. Which might happen soon, since I'm about to be a married man." He did liven up then, telling me about Joelle, the beauty queen, a kindergarten teacher, the sister of an academy friend. I assumed he'd been careful not to catch anything overseas, or, if he had, to get it treated. Surely everything unsavory that happened stayed within the group, the exploits collectively blacked out when the troops touched down on American soil.

Soon after, when we were parting, he said, "I forgive you—you know that, right? Don't you?"

"What?"

He gripped my hand. "For not serving." He held on to me, unwilling to let go. It seemed, it did seem that he meant what he'd said. He was chewing gum, his mouth the only part of him in motion. If Tessa had been born and grown and present, she would have whipped up a story about our meeting in no time. She might have noted his urgency, his nervousness. She might have said he wanted *me* to forgive *him,* but for what exactly I didn't know.

Chapter Thirteen

WHEN RUSSIA'S HUSBAND WAS SHOT DEAD OUTSIDE OF THE pharmacy on the South Side, it was Buddy, out of all the absent Macivers, whom the widow missed the most. That killing in the spring of 1968 was sandwiched between Martin Luther King's and Bobby Kennedy's assassinations, but, then, everyone in that year seemed to have personal claims of violence that went along with the public tragedies. Elroy was ours. My mother phoned Louise and me at college, saying that we must come back for the funeral, that, no matter Louise's part in her friend's senior recital or an exam I had to study for in genetics, Russia was family. Our presence at the service was required.

"Family?" Louise said to me. "I hate it when she says that. I've never even met Elroy Crockerby."

"Never met Elroy?" I didn't say that I had seen him only once, although the ten-minute sighting had made an impression and I had not forgotten him. For the first time it occurred to me that Russia had always had to work on Christmas Eve. Where was Elroy while his wife was baking rolls at the Macivers'? Maybe Russia would rather have stayed home, gone to church, and cooked exclusively for her man. My father always drove down to pick her up before breakfast and took her back after the last dish was washed, around midnight. I wondered if Elroy had routinely worked on the holiday, at the Michigan Avenue Hotel, where he was a doorman.

To Louise I said, "Why didn't Elroy ever come to Christmas Eve?"

"Because slaves leave their families when the master says. They have to abandon their husbands to serve dinner up at the plantation house."

Louise's trombonist had recently jilted her, running off with a dippy flutist—a modifier she used, she explained, even though it was redundant. She'd had a disappointing audition for a summer program she was desperate to attend, and she was on edge about that outcome. There was no point arguing with her when she was already scrappy. "I'm not going to the funeral to satisfy Mom's idea of our racially balanced family," she said. "I'm sorry, but I'm not going."

We both did fly to Chicago for the morning service, and were back in Ohio with an hour to spare for Louise's recital. The tickets cost my parents a fortune, but they insisted it was money well spent. Lu and I had never been to Russia's neighborhood, let alone her church or her house. Over the phone my mother said she was thankful a white person hadn't killed Elroy. "If there is anything to be thankful for in this situation," she amended. The murderer had been caught five minutes after the shooting, with Elroy's wallet in his pocket, including the kingly sum of $12.42.

I remembered my mother's words as I took my place in the front pew of the Pathway to Victory Baptist Church. Russia had gathered my aunts, uncles, first cousins, second cousins, and great-aunt around her in the vestibule. This was well before the O'Days moved to Florida, and Mikey and Madeline were there, too. Since Russia had always been fond of Mikey, Mrs. O'Day, after hemming and hawing, gave permission for her son to go to the dangerous South Side, with the stipulation that he be home before dark. Russia had drawn me to her chest, her long spidery arms flapping at my back. "Timothy," she cried, "my boy, my own child." Her voice had gone thin and wavery. We processed up the aisle, all of us in a clump behind the casket, all of us ahead of the Crockerby retinue, the sixty or so family members who were shedding their tears. My mother was right: how much more terrible it would have been to be on display and in the prized seats if one of us had killed Elroy.

Every Saturday afternoon, Russia cleaned the church with two teenage boys in tow. The curved oak beams across the ceiling gleamed as if they'd been rubbed hard by a brave crew outfitted with chamois cloths and furniture polish. There was no ladder that could have reached those high places, and I imagined the boys swinging from beam to beam as if they alone knew the purpose of the design. "No more of that monkeyshines!" Russia would shout at them. Whatever building she cleaned was a place she felt was hers, and at the funeral her head was high, not only as star mourner but with that air of ownership. She was wearing a black slippery-looking dress that stuck a little to her stockings, and a deep-purple sweater with gems embedded and twinkling along the button row. The tragedy had already made her scrawny; she later told me she'd sobbed her flesh away.

At the altar there was an enormous china vase, big as a washtub, filled with gladiolas, sent by Figgy. So of course we felt she was with us. Two steps away from that floral monument, the eighteen Macivers in our drab good clothes were in a line, squeezed into the pew. Behind us, the sea of dark faces, the shine of their mourning black. Russia sat next to her beloved Mr. Aaron, holding my father's hand in her lap through the service.

The casket had been parked next to Figgy's bouquet, and so we had continuous viewing without having to stand up or crane our necks. I had briefly seen the neighbor boy Cody Rockard when he'd been laid out, but I had not ever had the occasion to study a dead person for the length of a Baptist funeral. It must have been something of a job to put together a man who had been shot in the head and the chest, to make him not only presentable but recognizable. The one time I'd met Elroy, I'd been walking around downtown with my father and we'd stopped at the hotel to greet him. In the casket, resting on the cream-colored satin, he seemed all bones in his beige suit, no substance to his body, and I doubted that his eyelashes had curled in real life, and it seemed unlikely that his nose had lain so flat to his face or that his hair was normally dyed a blackish purple. They'd put a cap on him to cover the cavity the bullet had made, and it was set at a rakish angle—Elroy Crockerby, the life of the party, a regular boulevardier on his way to the pharmacy.

When I'd met him, he'd had rheumy eyes and he'd seemed to be a man of few words; at least, when my father and I had stood with him under the hotel's canopy, he'd said very little. He'd nodded as my father spoke, and smiled warmly at me. Through the years he'd probably heard quite a bit about us, and I hoped that he was able to reduce Russia's epics to the basic elements, that after his years with her he understood how little of her news was based on fact. He did search my face as if it took him a while to square the Timothy of Russia's stories with the boy in front of him. The hotel made him dress in doorman livery, a bright-green coat with tails and brass buttons and yellow epaulets and a top hat with a gold band. It didn't seem to bother him, having to wear that clownish costume, complete with yellow-and-green spats. While we were talking, he'd opened the door for a woman in sable, and he'd tilted his head slightly, making the gesture to lift his hat even as he kept it firmly in place. He managed to make the servitude seem like something he was only too happy to be doing, as if it were an honor. I wanted to tell my father I was sorry for Elroy, but I didn't speak to him about such things. And anyway it wasn't true that I was sorry only for Elroy. I was sorry, in my habit of grief, that the world accommodated the haughty woman in her coat, and the fence across the way with litter washed up against it, and a grown-up like Elroy forced to wear frippery.

When it came time to pass formally in front of the casket, Lu had as much trouble moving forward as I did. My father took Russia to Elroy first, and they spoke quietly together above the head of the dead man. We knew we were supposed to pause before him, as if finally we were getting a chance to be acquainted, and also we were to pray for his time in the afterlife. Mikey in his church suit, and Madeline came next, hand in hand, both standing with their heads bowed. Russia watched all of us as we paid our respects. I must have performed all right, because on my way back to my seat she reached weakly for my arm and held on while she dabbed her handkerchief to her nose. I had to stay in front of her as she wiped all the moisture from her wet face. It seemed to do her good to keep me in her clutches, and when at last she let go she croaked out, "Precious." I knew nothing about her or Elroy, and yet she needed to show me off to her people. Had she not had children because, more than with any other families she worked for, or her own husband, her loyalties and even her love lay with us? At the end of the service, as we filed down the aisle, the congregation pressed toward the center, the better to see the Macivers.

Afterward, in Russia's apartment, the relatives packed into the small rooms until there was hardly space to open the kitchen door. Osella, Russia's sister, said, "I'm so proud of you, Timothy." I had never met her before, but, as Elroy had done, she, too, seemed to know me well. She was unsteady on her feet, and she grabbed my arms as if I were always on hand to hold her up. "Look at those straight teeth," she demanded, something of course I couldn't do myself in the moment. "So handsome, just like Russia always say."

"Thank you."

"You're the favorite, you know that?"

"It's, it's something—I hope for."

She threw her head back and laughed. "Don't you worry, don't you worry one little minute. She always tell us about your smart brains."

The kitchen was narrow; the counter and the pink Formica table were empty and cleaned to a dull gloss, one lone African violet on the windowsill. In the living room, the same clean nothingness, a yellow sofa with scratchy cushions, the first television my grandmother had owned, a thing as large as a stove, and the two card tables for food, the ten folding chairs from the church. The door of the bedroom was ajar, no space for anything but a dresser and the bed covered in a brown blanket. There were no shelves, no reading material outside of the *Time* magazine on the coffee table, and no paintings or pictures on the wall. On the small end table by the sofa there was a faded photograph of Russia's mother, and another of the Maciver family at Christmas, the year Buddy visited. Russia is with us, standing next to Arthur. There was also a studio portrait of Mikey and Madeline, the gift my mother had given them for Christmas one year. In lieu of a wedding. They'd gotten all dressed up, they'd been driven to Sears, they'd sat very close on a carpet-covered bench, and they'd smiled handsomely at the camera. The eight-by-ten photograph with its cherry frame was the fanciest thing in Russia's living room. I wondered if the apartment was bare because she and Elroy didn't have enough money to furnish it, or because they didn't have any interests.

Each time the kitchen door opened, it seemed impossible that more people would squeeze in, and we all jostled farther along, as if we were on a subway car. Although we had hours to go, I said to my mother that probably we should get to the airport sooner rather than later. She must have wanted to flee, too, because she nodded heartily.

If only we would leave, the party could begin; everyone, both black and white, knew we Macivers were holding the Crockerby spirit down. If we could as fast as possible put away the feast that had some-how materialized from the spotless counter—if we could chug the corn pudding, the chitlins and maw, the fried cabbage and bacon, the string beans with ham, the short ribs and gravy, the fried chicken—if we could quickly, quickly clean our plates, we could get out of their hair and they could shout, they could weep, they could talk, they could sing. As it was, the polite Macivers took up the chairs and the sofa, agreeing with the relatives who stood by that the service had been beautiful and Elroy indeed had looked well. We accepted the compliment that Figgy's flowers were remarkable, that Figgy herself was a woman of uncommon generosity and artistry and perseverance, as if my aunt had dug around in the earth with her own paws to grow seeds and then arranged the blossoms just so and slipped in during the night to set the vase center stage.

Russia sat on the sofa between my parents—still holding my father's hand—and said, "I wish Mr. Buddy was here. Mr. Buddy would be such a gentleman, and he'd make us laugh, now, wouldn't he?" Ever since Buddy had enlisted in the army, Russia had broken her rule; he was the first and only person in my generation she would confer the "Mr." upon. "I say Timothy is my favorite, I say so, but Mr. Buddy, oh, Mr. Buddy." She wiped yet another tear from her cheek. "Mr. Buddy, he's flying right into the storm to deliver us."

Louise was at the card table getting her food. She set down her plate, which had nickel-sized servings of each dish, something the relatives would want to comment on later. "Mac's going to be a doctor," she said to the group on the sofa. "He's going to save lives, not murder people."

"Elroy got murdered," Madeline sang from her place next to my mother.

"That's right, darlin'," Russia said. "The good Lord took Elroy. The good Lord said it was Elroy's time. We all got our time, child. We all come to the Kingdom."

Louise said, more loudly this time, "Mac's going to save lives."

Russia looked across at my sister as if she was only then seeing her. "You come here to Russia, Louise. Russia has something to tell you."

"What?" Louise advanced a few feet to the sofa.

"You come closer."

Louise took a baby step and another.

"Mr. Buddy, he went down the street to say the news. You understand me? He said the word about our brother Cleveland to Miz Pindel. Timothy, he's a good boy, but Mr. Buddy—he walks with the Lord."

My mother was fixed on Louise, willing her to be quiet.

"You go on now, and eat your dinner," Russia said. "You keep still and eat."

Although Elroy had just passed, Russia couldn't keep from launching into the story of the summer evening in the Pindels' loft, not only as if it had been a highlight of the Maciver history, but as if she herself had witnessed the near fellating of Mikey O'Day. A perfect postfuneral entertainment for all ages. Louise, abandoning her plate, elbowed her way into the kitchen and stood by the door with her arms crossed.

"Mr. Buddy's the one to heal the wounds," Russia began. "Russia say so all his life, ain't that right, Miz Julia—Mr. Buddy's the one to heal the wounds."

"He's a very thoughtful young man," my mother murmured.

"Our child here"—without turning her head, Russia moved her eyes to the right, in Madeline's direction—"was in danger, you know how I mean. Locked up and held tight, held tight and locked up. But Mr. Buddy that night, he run through the storm, he run in the wind, and he run in the rain and the thunder and the lightning. Mr. Buddy, he climb hand over hand, all wet and cold, to help the children. Didn't Mr. Buddy set you free, Mikey, didn't he set you free? It was that night you two kneeled before Mr. Buddy and you said, 'Mr. Buddy, we going to get married someday.' You said, 'Mr. Buddy, you saved us so we could come down the aisle to get the Lord's blessing.' A man and a woman, they should cleave together, like it says in the Good Book. It don't matter if you don't read the Gospel, it don't matter if you can't spell the Word, a man and a woman, they cleave, they got to cleave together. Mr. Buddy, he showed you the way. Mr. Buddy, he took you to the light."

As benediction to that astonishing revision, that poem, Osella quavered, "A-men. A-men."

Madeline was concentrating on cutting the pretty pink frosting roses on her cake in the least violent way, and Mikey's head was bobbing as it did when he listened to music. To my mother I said, "I think we better go." After we'd cleared our plates, after the Crockerby women embraced us again and the men shook our hands, we hurried down the five flights of stairs and came out blinking into the mild spring light. How relieved we were to find ourselves back in our own story! My mother made a point to praise Louise for her civility, and she said once more that our being at the service meant the world to Russia.

Who cared? We were out of there, we had escaped!

Madeline sat up front in the station wagon, the three adults in a row. My father and I filled the car with talk about a breeding experiment I was working on with my biology professor, a project that required mice and the hemoglobin of their unborn.

Louise was somehow able not to say a word until we were in our seats on the airplane, strapped in and waiting to take off. She had bought herself an extra-long hot dog in the terminal and eaten it ravenously over a magazine. "Every single minute of that nightmare," she suddenly cried, "is Mom's fault."

"What—"

"For having a slave in the first place!" She was yelling over the noise of the propellers.

"You can't blame—"

"Where do I start? Where? Can you believe Russia holding Father's hand through the funeral like he's her new boyfriend, like she's bragging about her guy? The Macivers have done that to her. The Macivers—we—are responsible. Don't tell me having a slave is complicated, because it isn't. It is not! It's simple oppression. What's Mom been doing all these years anyway? What'd she need a servant for?"

"Do you have to talk so loud?" I managed to say.

"And what is that utter bullshit about Jerry Pindel and Buddy? Buddy breaks the kid's nose and knocks him out, he almost croaks? Mom, the almighty pacifist, should have reported Buddy to the police. They should have incarcerated him! And it was not raining that night, and it was not thundering, and it was not cold. There was one-hundred-percent humidity."

I had to laugh at the way Russia had set the story in a thunderstorm, the preferred weather for melodrama. If you'd listened to her enough over the years, you came to think that nothing important had ever happened without her somehow looking on, and certainly no story had its real meaning until she told it. That idea made me laugh harder.

"It's not funny! Goddamn you!" My little sister was beating me on the arm. "Russia turns Buddy into a pastor? Some kind of superhero minister who flies into Jerry Pindel's loft to anoint Mikey and Madeline so that their fucking up in the bedroom is somehow legitimate? That's her main concern here, sex out of wedlock—to make herself feel better about that sin, she invents Reverend Jesus Buddy Christ. I can't stand it!" She yelled even louder. "I can't stand it!"

"Is all of that Mom's fault?" I had the nerve to ask.

It was convenient to blame my mother for every ill, and for Buddy's misdeeds, too, such as they actually were. I wanted to remind Louise of our parents' seriousness, of their moral life, even if they weren't perfect. In my head I ticked off my mother's volunteer work at Hull House, tutoring adults, her part-time job at West Suburban Hospital, on the night shift, to help pay for our college, the eternal playschool for Madeline, the 1967 bus trip with Madeline to march on the Pentagon, the fact that, Madeline aside, my mother was stranded for twenty years because we came home from school for lunch, the cheese sandwiches lined up on the counter about to be grilled, the apple slurry coming through the sieve, the pudding stirred to the satin stage. The roast for dinner was also on the counter, the meat in its net thawing in a pool of blood, the potatoes and carrots scrubbed and in the Dutch oven. *What's Mom been doing all these years?*

"Don't start talking to me," Louise said, pressing her head to the window. "You've probably memorized a seminal Sophia Cooper feminist manifesto about the bondage of suburban women. Well, guess what? I don't want to hear it. Go back to school and butcher your pregnant mice."

Below us as we lifted off lay the flat grid of the gray city, the desolation of the urban landscape. We were leaving it behind as we'd done before, but this time was different; this time the entire scrim had been pulled away from the home front, and we could see the outer world that all along had been part of us. I would have liked to return to our cozy, selfish ignorance, but that seemed no longer possible; from now on we'd walk hand in hand with our entitlements, nursing them along, feeding them up. In the brief years of childhood, I had cried more than a boy should, shaken with sorrow if I saw a person in a wheelchair or a blind woman trying to cross the street. The deaf son of the grocer nearly killed me. My mother had identified our distinctive gifts—my sensitivity, she called it, and Louise's music. Maybe the sound of the cello had been the only important, the only productive thing that had happened in our house. I wished for a minute that the older Lu weren't sitting next to me, that the Louise of Oberlin College could take herself back to our living room and sit herself down to her three-quarter-sized cello.

Before we landed, just to irritate her, I said in my best Russia voice, "Timothy is my favorite, but Mr. Buddy, he's flying right into the storm to save us."

MY MOTHER COULDN'T STOP POOR BOYS, minority boys, or foolish boys from fighting the war, but she was not going to let the government have me for fodder. For her, in the matter of the Vietnam War, all young men were not equal. The summer after college, when I was living at home and working again at the museum, in Fishes, my number for the draft came up, just as we'd feared. The antiwar movement had by then seized the country, and it's hard to imagine even the most freedom-loving person thinking that Southeast Asia would be a worthwhile place to die. Nixon had been pulling out troops for some time, and I had no interest in being the last to be killed for any reason, not least for a cause the administration appeared to think futile. There was one terrible dinner at Moose Lake with Figgy and Arthur, right before I pleaded my case as a conscientious objector at the county courthouse, citing my Quaker heritage and my upbringing as a pacifist. After that night, my aunt and my mother never really spoke again. Buddy had enlisted for a second tour and was back in Vietnam, part of the First Logistical Command, the organization that supervised a number of depots, support groups, ammunition supplies, and mortuaries. For a while the word went around that he was driving trucks to the front lines, but as I said there were different reports through the years. Cousin Petie, who seemed to have his own reason for disliking Buddy, maintained that Sergeant Eastman was well behind the scenes and in no real danger. After Nixon's election, Arthur was going back and forth to Princeton to teach, and Figgy was staying in D.C. for her work at the Phillips Collection.

I remember that the Fullers left Moose Lake before their scheduled departure, and that Figgy took me aside as the car was idling, saying she would hold me in her prayers.

You pray? I wanted to ask.

She said I must always know that she admired me even if she didn't agree with my family's politics.

They had argued while they ate sliced turkey and boiled new potatoes. Arthur had become owlish in his delivery, staring at his adversary longer than was comfortable for any of us and then blinking slowly as he spoke. With severe forbearance he explained to my mother that the North Vietnamese were gaining power because of the American peace movement. The antiwar protesters had created a schism so deep in the country, he said, that it had destroyed the war effort; they had made it impossible for the military to call up the men that were needed and for Congress to allocate the moneys for victory. It must have required courage on Arthur's part, to have been one of the last holdouts on Johnson's staff to insist it was within reach to beat the enemy. In the election of 1968, Figgy and Arthur went Republican, voting for Nixon because they felt he would proceed with the conflict until it was finished honorably. It was unclear to some of us what precisely that meant, if it required all-out winning or somehow gaining enough leverage to broker a settlement. My mother was fond of saying that Figgy was the vocal part of Nixon's Silent Majority.

Because Julia couldn't forgive the Fullers for defecting to the GOP, she did her best to avoid seeing them. Whether the meeting at Moose Lake in 1970 was planned or accidental, I don't know. Since she was forced to eat dinner with them that night, she as always threw her own research in Arthur's face: 80 percent of the armed services addicted to drugs, and privates attacking their superiors, wounding or killing their captains. If Arthur hadn't raised his voice to speak over her, you might have thought, looking at him, that he was unruffled. His lids slowly closed over the bulge of his eyes; his lids slowly lifted. He said again that the antiwar propaganda had demoralized the troops, had turned the army upside down.

"They are demoralized, Arthur, because all along they've been lied to! They are demoralized because they're being slaughtered senselessly!"

"It is difficult to keep the large picture in mind, certainly," he said. There was, I noticed then, a steady tic in his lower jaw. "Without American intervention, communist hegemony will likely spread through South Asia, East Asia, Thailand, India. Without our intervention, the Soviet Union might well take it upon themselves to secure oil-producing nations in the Middle East."

Arthur's relative calm was more than my mother could abide. "Forty thousand troops have been killed," she cried. "The South Vietnamese have been denied elections, they have been murdered, they have been polluted by our chemicals and all of our garbage they can get on the black market. Corruption is running—"

It was at that moment, I believe, when the argument fell to pieces, when Figgy entered the fray, shouting, "Don't tell us what it's like. Buddy has served for four years. Arthur has been there several times. You—you've not ever been to Southeast Asia!"

"That has nothing to do with what we're talking about, Figgy, and you know it. I have not been to Vietnam, I have not been to Timbuktu, but there have been reports from trustworthy writers—"

"Trustworthy writers!"

"Mac will not be killed because Johnson's men and now Nixon's men have made the most tragic mistakes of this century!"

It was the same argument they'd been having for years, only just then I realized that all along what they'd actually been fighting about was their sons. Each of them as a parent had committed his child to a certain path, and each needed to insist time and again that his way, and the boy's willingness to follow, was right. Whereas, in the early days, their volleys had had the feel of sport, now their dislike was bitter and personal, the stakes high because we were both draft age.

"Mac," my mother was close to screeching, "will not die because you, people like you, refuse to face the terrible truth. The policies you have supported have killed thousands of men in a war that was not winnable from the start. You, you are responsible! You have made all of us in this country murderers. *Murderers.*"

She left the room, and did not come downstairs in the early morning when her old friends left.

FOR TWO YEARS AS A CONSCIENTIOUS OBJECTOR, I ran blood samples in a lab in Trenton, New Jersey. I spent the twenty-four months working, and also mourning Sophia Cooper. In the evenings I reread Miss Cooper's books, those weighty assignments, in my studio apartment, as if that application might one day help me win her back. It was a lonely period, and although I suspected it would end, I did not really believe that the slow time would ever pass. I did remember now and then to think of Madeline, to remember that without Mikey O'Day she might well be as wretched as I. The summer before my stint as a CO, when I'd been at home, I was so distracted by my own troubles that I paid her no attention. My mother had gotten her a job, there was that. She probably so accurately mirrored my misery I didn't want to look at her.

In New Jersey I sometimes thought I should send her a postcard or a package, a little thing to cheer her up, but I don't know that I ever did. On the weekends I took the train to New York and wandered the streets and museums, wondering if I'd bump into my former vegetarian–co-op housemate. And planning my moves if I happened to see her. So casually I might say, "I never dreamed I'd run into you here." I'd explain that, instead of being gunned down in a rice paddy, I was available to have a cup of coffee. The alumni magazine had said she was in the city studying with a violin guru who only took students bound for glory. I understood that a person who has been spared his death in the jungle, who has been spared from killing, should not admit to suffering from a loneliness so keen it seemed a physical affliction. I knew I should be grateful to have a heart and stomach, arms and legs, and empty hands with which to register that loneliness. Later, in my married days, when I closed the door to my study, I was after that old ache. I'd grown nostalgic for it. I'd listen to symphonies and read, drowning in the wisdom of Beethoven and the virtue of Lincoln. But if I fell asleep on my study sofa, and if I woke as dawn was coming on, I was sure for a horrifying moment that I was back in Trenton, that the rest of my life was only a dream, and that I'd remained in New Jersey. I'd throw off the thin blanket and hurry up to the bedroom, where Diana would instantly wake to scold me. What a relief to climb in next to her while she listed all the reasons it was thoughtless and also unhealthy to sleep on my sagging old couch.

In my conscientious-objector years, every now and then, I'd meet Figgy in New York. She'd take me to the Metropolitan, or we'd walk through the East Village so she could point out where she'd lived with Bill Eastman, where they had gathered in bars and cafés with those hard-drinking, womanizing painters who were on their way to inventing Abstract Expressionism. She talked about herself in that period with some vagueness, as politicians now do about their druggy days in college. She was kind enough to speak to me about the artists and their work, to avoid the subjects that had separated the families. She never asked about my conscientious-objector status, and she didn't have much curiosity about my life in New Jersey. We were always glad to see each other, and I think we both felt the pleasure of doing something slightly illicit. The Capulet and Montague cousins having a drink outside of Verona.

When at last I did leave New Jersey for medical school in Madison, Wisconsin, I couldn't believe my fortune, to have classmates again, to have my cadaver, to study the body down to the molecular level so as to come someday to that simple act, both hands to a sufferer's throat, a cool touch to the hot forehead. Although I imagined myself in a clean, well-lit office with state-of-the-art equipment at my disposal, a fleet perhaps of nurses, beyond those trappings I still hoped to end up like old Doc Riley at Moose Lake, the dignified hoary man for whom the little children had parted the way. In my third week at school I met Diana, the girl down the hall. On our first date she spread out her napkin, drew small squares to represent each apartment in our building, and not only wrote the names of the inhabitants but described their persons, their problems, their liaisons with other residents, and also she told me their pets' names. She had done her research thoroughly, but she seemed to enjoy the fact that I found her work so amusing. "I'm serious!" she protested when I doubted there was a woman one floor up who actually weighed four hundred pounds, kept seven cats illegally, and had reported a UFO landing on Lake Mendota the winter before. She was charmingly petulant. She didn't need anyone to jump-start her for talking, and when I was with her I entered a state of deep relaxation. Her energetic generosity, her sparkly happiness were pacifying to me, but I could see how her zest could be inspiring, too. I had no doubt that she was going to be a fine grade-school teacher. It's usual, I suppose, to believe that our beloved is more of a certain something than anyone else, that she has more beauty or wit or enthusiasm or determination. Sophia had had an enlightened musical sensibility, great powers of concentration, and unusual physical ease. Diana, for all her distinguishing virtues and joys, seemed a standout because she loved me more than I deserved. We were both eager for the future and soon were sure of our choices.

I remember my panic when I'd counted out the money for the ring, and, even so, how her eyes welled up in the moment of presentation. How could I have known that she wanted the one with the two small stones either side of the diamond? "No, I like it, I do, I really do!" she cried into my chest. "I'm just all emotional, I've waited for this for about a million years, for you to come into my life."

I was sorry that I'd guessed wrong in the jewelry store, and as we walked downtown the next morning—she huddled against me, still weepy—I very much wanted to make the scene right for her. The ring was exchanged, an upgrade made possible by another loan from my father. She wept again, from delight and gratitude, and thus the anecdote of our engagement, of my ineptitude as a shopper, was sealed.

We have never been unfaithful, not I, and Diana—no, I feel sure that she has not. About fifteen years ago, when I was at a meeting in New York, I went to a concert of an up-and-coming string quartet at Avery Fisher Hall. I don't know what I hoped for, or what I supposed would happen. They were playing some of the early Beethoven quartets. Did Sophia Cooper steal the show because she was the only woman onstage, or because in her black strapless gown she'd come into the kind of beauty everyone would recognize? Gone was the long hair, gone were the glasses falling down her nose, gone her college pudginess. Her overbite, her gorgeous malocclusion, was accentuated in her lean face. Even if she'd had a shaved head, and if her vertical overlap had been surgically corrected, I would have known her as she began to play, as she sat on the edge of her chair waiting for the music to take her to the surprise destination. That was the Sophia Cooper I remembered. Afterward, I waited like a schoolboy outside the stage door with a small spray of roses.

She saw me as the door opened. "Mac?" She came two steps toward me. "Mac Maciver? Is that you?" She set her violin down—her half-million-dollar instrument, right there on the pavement—and threw her arms around me. She no longer smelled of the co-op, no longer drenched in the odors of dark sesame oil and boiled kale. She was a woman who wore expensive perfume, who ate not only meat but brains, who used makeup that had been tested on animals. "Mac—oh, Mac!"

I would have been glad to leave her after that embrace, satisfied with the outcome. But she had time for a drink—plenty of time, in fact, for dinner. Her husband would have gone to bed hours before, falling asleep with the baby.

The baby!

"Gabrielle," she said, returning to her violin. "Five months old yesterday. Oh, but you're here! This is wonderful, this is perfect, this is glorious."

"Glorious," I repeated. The music, I remembered to say, had been transcendent, her playing bewitching.

"We four were in accord tonight," she said, slipping her arm through mine. "More or less."

I recall little about the walk to the restaurant, or the food, outside of the *cervelle* that she ate. It was almost as if we were back in New Hampshire, as if all the years had fallen away and we were again those two young people strolling through the woods down the path to the pond. We'd believed then that we'd been sprung from our families into our own lives. Although the evening is a gleamy blur, I know we did not explicitly discuss the terminal night our senior year, when Louise and I had been rolling around in the dorm bed, squalling like infants. She did ask after my sister, and was pleased to learn that she had a place in the Cleveland Orchestra. It was the mention of Louise that led gracefully into her apology for leaving me abruptly before graduation. She said that she'd always wanted to write to me, to search me out, to conclude respectfully what had been so important to her.

Those years in New Jersey rose before me, day after day, night after night, the miasma of that time, the mute suffering as I'd tried to heal from her. When I couldn't speak, when I only nodded, she said,

"You were such an odd mix, Mac Maciver, of seriousness and exuberance. You were the only uptight hedonist I think I've ever known." With her long fingers she dipped whatever we were eating—oysters, for starters, maybe—into the spicy sauce, and then put the fleshy mass into her mouth.

"You were serious, too," I managed.

"I was only serious about my playing, but you—you were quiet and intense about everything, about each of your classes, about baking bread, about buying a pair of shoes, about being learned, about . . . making love. But then you'd sometimes bust out of yourself . . ."

In the interest of moving the conversation along, I told her that I had been rereading some of her assigned books—not *The Ambassadors,* no, but *Middlemarch* again. And she asked did I relate to the character Lydgate, the young ambitious doctor? I wondered if she was actually asking if I, like Lydgate, was trapped by marriage in a backwater with small-minded people. I replied that some of Lydgate's challenges in a provincial hospital were similar to those I encountered, and that the book had much more meaning to me than it had in college. She had set me on my path, and since then, without once communicating, we had read many of the same books. It is well known that there is no greater aphrodisiac, none, than the realization that you and your acquaintance have been reading the same treasured lines at roughly the same time.

Out on the pavement, she asked me where I was staying. I drew her to me, and in that firm hold, that minute, another, and a little longer, she somehow understood that I couldn't invite her back. "You are beautifully old-fashioned," she said to me as I opened the cab door for her. She kissed me in that unrestrained way I remembered so well. "I do love you still," she murmured, and then the door slammed and she was off.

It was one o'clock in the morning, and I was walking along Columbus Circle. Madeline appeared before me, Madeline in her mourning over Mikey O'Day. When Mikey had left for Florida, the two of them had understood that they would be able to visit each other. But Mikey was far more a creature of the moment than Madeline. They couldn't very well carry on much of a friendship by phone, so little to say without the actual presence of the other and their old routines. The communication trailed off, and before Mikey could come back the next summer, he'd found another place to sing and, according to Mrs. O'Day, another girl. No matter that girl. In my slightly sad but still exhilarated drunkenness, I would have traded that evening to Mikey and Madeline if such a thing were possible. I would have given them the chance to walk ahead of me to the hotel, where they could, just once, have renewed their old bond.

WHEN LOUISE AND I WERE BOTH IN COLLEGE, those late summer days when we were packing, my mother would always say to Madeline, "You're going to be my only girl left at home." She said it again before Louise's wedding, and again, nonsensically, when I married Diana. Buddy was up in Alaska then, and could not get to the ceremony. It was in 1978, during the Carter years, the president my mother rejoiced in and Figgy and Arthur loathed. They abhorred what they called the president's phony homespun graciousness, the undermining of our sense of national identity, the hoax of the energy crisis, and the pussy-foot approach to rescuing the hostages. We all knew the arguments they would have had if they'd been in each other's company. Diana thought my mother intelligent and fascinating. She liked to tell her relatives about that, how smart Mrs. Maciver was. Julia had enjoyed Sophia Cooper the two times she had visited me at college, but I think, despite her progressive thinking, she had the good-wife approach: she knew that in many ways Diana would make a better home for me. She saw how much we were in love, how smitten I was, and trusted that I knew best. If she worried, she didn't let on. She didn't change her tune in our company, continuing to talk as if we all had the same interests, as if we'd listened to the State of the Union Address and were concerned about gas consumption and had run to the library to check out the Pulitzer Prize–winning novel. She and Diana discussed the new math, ability grouping, and children's literature, even though my fiancée was going to quit teaching second grade when we moved back to her hometown. The future Mrs. Maciver was going to try to get pregnant directly after the wedding. She had been told by the family doctor that she might have trouble conceiving because of her irregular periods and her tipped uterus, and she was anxious to get to work on our project.

"Be good to each other," Julia said to us when we announced our engagement.

How could we do otherwise? I had studied—so I thought—my parents' marriage. I believed that marital felicity came from lively conversation over a well-prepared dinner, children, reading at night, bed, and, in the morning, work. Marriage should contain those things, and if a person had his health none of it should be too difficult. And what did Diana think? She was thrilled by the idea of being Dr. and Mrs. Maciver, excited by our plans to move to her hometown so we could surround ourselves, on all sides and beyond the sides, by her large and close-knit family, the five brothers and their broods, the three sisters and their children, the parents and grandparents.

In the heat of anger once, Diana said to me that my parents could not be as happy as I thought they were. I had invented their happiness—as always, I had blinders on, *blinders,* and couldn't see what my mother and father were.

"What are they?" I said, thinking of myself as a tired old horse plodding down the street with patches close up to my drooping eyelids.

"They are—they are—"

"I know it sounds unlikely, their contentment," I tried to say without whinnying. "I know it sounds impossible to you."

The handful of Macivers sat up front on the groom's side of the church, as custom dictates: my parents, Russia, Madeline, Louise and her husband, Dale, and their two daughters. Three of the cousins came with their wives, but no Figgy, no Arthur, no Buddy. As Diana came floating down the aisle, blue-eyed and pink, her ringlets on top of her head, I knew there was little to regret. Still, for a minute I was certain I was in cardiac arrest. Just as Buddy had said might happen to him when he married. How good it would be to look out and see him there, the drill sergeant reassuring me that my heart would continue to beat. The mass of Hartleys on Diana's side, all of them having given their approval, smiled upon us in our hour of fulfillment. I had learned their rituals, enough of them to know what teams to root for, what meat, what cuts to grill for the gatherings, what kind of jokes would play. I had done my studying, and I might just as well have made a dive into them, mosh pit style, so they could carry me to their home.

Chapter Fourteen

IT WAS JUNE 1993, JUNE 11, WHEN MY FATHER CALLED TO tell me my mother had died in her sleep. I thought that he must be mistaken, that he had misread the event he was about to narrate. "I don't believe what I'm saying to you," he began, "but it appears that Mom died sometime in the night." He spoke as if he were relating an everyday occurrence, as if he were telling me about old Mrs. Lombardo walking her schipperke dog past the house.

"Sometime in the night? What—where is she?"

"In her sleep."

He's gone mad, I thought. Or else she was having a dream so deep, lying so still in the hush of her fantasy, that the attentive husband was crying, Wolf, wolf! We'd all laugh about his overzealous care later. My mother couldn't be in any mood to die, and in her sleep, too, a squandering of an experience, one she'd like to have while awake.

"Where is she?" I asked again.

"Right here in bed. I haven't moved her."

She was seventy-one, her outrage and interest as sharp as ever, her hair a salt-and-peppery tumble, her face a little rounder than it used to be, her laugh a little looser. She had enough padding to keep that future old-lady osteoporotic hunch at bay, and she was in fine shape, walking two or three miles a morning. It was not possible for her to be dead. All the same, I barked my orders. "I'm going to hang up. I want you to call 911. When you've done that, Father, call me back." She might have suffered a stroke, a cerebral embolism that had paralyzed her, that had rendered her unconscious.

"Mac," my father said gently, "she was cool when I woke. I've felt for her pulse, I've listened for her heart. There is no life in her."

When he'd gone through the motions of checking her vital signs for my benefit, he said, "If you can come now, soon, I'll wait to make the call. So you can see her as she is."

Louise got on the next flight, and I drove down, both of us going home without our families. Diana was already riding a bus to the children's museum with Katie's class and would be away for most of the day. According to the calendar, she had her usual breakneck schedule, dentist appointments for all the girls after school, Lyddie's piano lesson, and the regular Friday-night dinner for her parents. Followed by cribbage club with the sisters and the in-laws. I was grateful not to have to face her: she would absorb the fact immediately, her empathy forcing me to the quick. I put myself in the car, squarely in the seat, in the void of no time, of not yet knowing, not yet, not yet. I would drive on. Although I have no memory of taking care of any work detail, I must have called the office before I left. A death in the family, I might have said, without elaborating.

I had always imagined her going with a short illness at an advanced age—aging for Julia that would take place without the side effects of senescence. She'd wake one morning with a wildly disseminated cancer, an invasion that had occurred without her notice, with no pain. It was the way to go—diagnosed on Tuesday, dead by Friday. There she'd be, set up in a bank of pillows, her hair spun to an airy white, giving last-minute instructions, and also making a pronouncement that would elevate the past to legend and illuminate our futures. Everything that one wants from the dying.

Although I didn't yet understand that she was gone, I did know that once the medics came she would be taken from the house. That was the evil I could think to prevent. If I had my way, if we could buck the law, I'd insist she be laid out in the parlor for a week, so we could begin to adjust to the idea of her leaving. How I missed the days long before my birth! At the hospital morgue or a funeral-home viewing, she could not very well be herself. For a second I imagined standing with Russia next to the casket, hand in hand, talking quietly about Miz Julia. But that was absurd, too, just as ridiculous as my mother being laid out anywhere or being cremated, cooked down to a paltry heap of dust. According to her wishes, that fistful would be buried in front of the headstone that was already in place at the Moose Lake cemetery.

To see the body in her own bed was the best I could want in my state of not knowing, the intimacy of her things around her, Julia at the center in her nightgown with the rips in the armpits and the tattered sleeves. If she had to be dead, I reasoned, then she should stay in her room. I could also at least hope for a sense of the ineffable close by. Even those who are not afflicted with religious conviction so often plan in the last moment of their loved one's life, at the last gasp, to see the glimmering of the spirit as it rises up and passes out the window or through the ductwork. I had never felt that breeze or seen the vapor, as some have reported, but I was sure that with Julia, even hours past her death, there had to be—there would be something of her remaining in the air. That is to say, I had the optimism of a person in shock.

Along the interstate I thought almost nothing of her. It was 1993, after all, the year the Chicago Bulls were playing the Phoenix Suns in the NBA Finals, unarguably the most dazzling games of the century. There happened to be a call-in show on that subject for most of the eighty-mile trip, and yet even at the closing there seemed to be a great deal more to say about the players, their spectacular baskets—so lavishly remembered—the brilliance and stupidity of the coaches through the ages, the salaries, the trades, the tussles on the court. I was sure that Jerry Pindel and the old alley gang, in whatever states they lived, were following the games blow by blow, eager for the inevitable victory.

Jerry had turned out well by the world's standards, running a high-class resort in Tucson, a job that probably required him to be a showman on occasion. When I drove up the street, I didn't more than glance at the Lemburgers' house, the Rockards', the Van Normans', nor did I look at ours, the new coat of gray paint with the white trim, the evergreens in front gone tall and bushy. There was no need to look, when it was so clearly in mind. My father was at the door, in a crisp blue shirt and chinos, his summer work uniform. His hair was wet from the shower, his wrinkled face rosy from his scrub. How peculiar that he had bathed while his wife lay in bed, that he'd taken even ten minutes away from her when there was so little time left.

"Madeline's upstairs," he said, embracing me lightly, as if my sister would be my first concern.

"All right," I said.

In their room, the spindle bed, the counterpane, the geraniums in their pots, old as trees, the library books stacked on the floor, the white curtains luffing against the screen—everything was in its place. Madeline was lying next to my mother, petting her shoulder. I went to her side and kissed her damp cheek, but she hardly noticed. My mother was on her back, the quilt up to her breasts, her eyes closed, her mouth slack, Julia Maciver with the still, smooth face of death. An arrhythmia, an embolism, phlebitis? "You can't," I murmured, peeling back the sheet to touch her stiff hand. The blood had begun to pool there, the skin darkening, no stopping, no turning back that lividity. She must have been gone for six or seven hours. "You can't," I said again.

My father pulled up another chair for me, and we sat watching her, in that watching waiting for our own understanding to come. Madeline was making a low drone, a continuous hum, what sounded like a machine in the far distance, an ominous hulk on its way. The noise was a comfort, someone among us knowing what to do. I'm sure my father and I talked about the cause of death and what needed to be done, but I only remember trying to converse with Julia. I admonished her, asking within myself, Why have you done this thing? What are you thinking, to leave us when we're not ready, when we haven't had enough?

I had been planning on there being entire decades before us when I'd agitate with my mother for her heart's desire. Decades when I wasn't in the thick of child-rearing responsibilities, when I wasn't working long hours seeing patients, decades when the dictates of the Hartleys' holiday regime would somehow have relaxed. Then—oh, then—my mother and I would march on the Capitol for whatever she said, for gay marriage, the family farm, medical marijuana, and, why not, universal health care. When all the battles had been waged, after my father and Madeline were in the grave, she'd come to live with us, spending her remaining strength trying to convert the Hartleys to her party. How the sisters-in-law would look back to their petty rivalries with fondness!

Louise arrived at the house, pale and dry-eyed, and we continued to sit watching the bed. She was another female who in adulthood had chopped off her long hair, who looked more girlish with a pixie cut. In middle age Louise still had a serious, determined air, no sign yet of mellowing. We talked again about what had killed Julia, a topic that distracted us from her death. My father recalled that the week before she'd had palpitations during her morning exercise, but she hadn't mentioned any distress on the following days. I gave an oration on arrhythmias—the prime suspect as far as I could tell—waxing upon tachycardias, bradycardias, flutters, fibrillations, conduction disorders.

"I wonder," Louise said, before I was quite finished, "if she chose to make her exit without interference from the medical profession."

I still had my hand in a fist, the crude model of the heart, about to explain what happens when the myocardium fails to contract as a whole. "What?" I said.

"She might have been fully aware that palpitations are a sign of heart disease, or whatever it is, and decided not to go to the doctor."

My father nodded twice, considering. "That seems unlikely," I said, as dispassionately as I could. "There's a large family of drugs on the market that suppress ventricular tachycardias. Mom would have known that it was unnecessary to die because she had an irregularity. Implanting a pacemaker, even, is relatively simple. It takes about an hour and is routine—"

"But maybe she had some deeper knowledge."

Louise and I had turned to each other, away from Julia. "I don't think Mom was ready to go," I said, "if that's what you mean. I don't think someone as vital as Mom would all of a sudden, because of a few palpitations, decide to give up the ghost. The problem with arrhythmia in our case is that it might not show up in postmortem, but, whatever the cause, we shouldn't jump to the conclusion that Mom was negligent about her health, or that she had an awareness of her own mortality."

"I'm not saying she was negligent. I'm saying she might have felt there was something wrong with her—maybe palpitations were just the tip of the iceberg—and she believed that her illness should take its course without anyone fiddling. There's great dignity in that approach—"

"Fiddling? An exam at an office, a prescription? Lu, that's hardly—"

"Children!" my father called out gaily, as if our squabble brought back the days of our youth, as if nothing could make him happier than our regression. "She may not have been ready," he said, "but how many times through the years has she wished for a swift departure?" Lu and I shifted in our chairs, looking at her again, as if that time she might answer. "Probably," he went on, "she would have returned her library books if she thought she was about to go west. She would have left a casserole or two. But you know as well as I that she didn't want to be strapped to a high chair outfitted with a drool bucket. She was often reminding me that I was to pull the plug without a moment's hesitation. I don't think there's anyone more enthusiastic about euthanasia than your mother."

Though that might be true, it had nothing to do with the matter at hand. When I looked at her, I could do little to keep my bewilderment at bay. How could she, of all people, have such a sudden lack of consideration? Why hadn't she called me? What good was having gone to medical school if I couldn't be of use to her? This death was avoidable, and Louise and my father were wrong to comfort themselves with the idea of a secret wish on Julia's part. That we should be happy for her was absurd; to imagine that her premature passing was a blessing against imaginary illnesses down the road was to disregard wantonly her relish for life. I began to mutter. "I'm sorry for us," I said. "Maybe someday, Father, I can be glad for her, but not now. Not now. She's seventy-one. She's young! None of us are ready for her to go."

He put his hands to his face. Madeline's hum grew louder. Louise knelt by him, softly saying, "Father. Father."

When you looked at her, at Julia Beeson Maciver, really studied her, you could see that she'd never been more at peace. Although the body was already at work breaking down, lactic acid flooding the muscles, the wrinkles were gone from her brow, and she did look serene. The skin on her arms seemed paper-thin, a covering that might flutter away with the slightest breeze, as if it couldn't have stood much more wear. Tessa had seen an Indian saint in a Sheraton Hotel in Illinois, and she'd reported that the woman's skin was giving way from hugging hundreds of people, day after day. And that seemed to have happened to Julia, too, all those years holding Madeline, sleeping against her, tucking her in, smoothing her hair, rocking her through a tantrum. Nevertheless, it couldn't be true that she'd grown tired of this world, that she wanted out.

When the medics came to take the body away, we thought ourselves ready. We'd gotten hungry and had stopped looking at her. It was not as difficult as we anticipated, to pry Madeline from the bed. Her yellow T-shirt was moist, and she was sweetly warm when she buried her face in my neck, that rumbling still going in her throat. When the men were set to move the bag that held Julia through the front door, I found myself gripping the gurney at her feet. They paused as if they had their own reasons for stopping, the need to shift the weight, and one of them scratched his cheek. After a minute, they lifted their load a little higher over the threshold, the signal that they were about to take her from us. When they were gone, I went down the basement and, like the child I'd reverted to, I sank to my old knees behind the bar, that place of refuge. Mother. Beloved. Don't go.

IT DIDN'T TAKE LONG for word to get out, and by evening we wanted for nothing in the Maciver kitchen. We sat at the table keeping up our strength with butternut-squash risotto, grilled vegetable pinwheels, orecchiete with broccoli rabe, tofu dengaku, slivers of Kobe beef raised in the foothills of Mount Haleakala, and twice-baked potatoes as long as my shoes. There was chocolate cake draped with a ganache that could put out our lights with a mere thimbleful. This was not the standard lasagna and banana bread that circulated in my part of the world in time of trouble. Most of the old neighbors had moved on, and the new couples seemed to have taken up cooking, or at least shopping at high-class delicatessens, rather than rearing squadrons of children. Gardening was the other activity that had replaced wholesale procreation, and they brought flowers from the raised beds in their yards. There was a strange festivity as we ate and the neighbors came and we oohed and aahed over their offerings; and when they left, we reviewed the visit, and through the conversation and the food the telephone kept ringing, and one of us leapt up, taking the phone to the dining room, trailing the ten-foot cord to tell the particulars again to another shocked relative.

It might have made sense to ask my father about the early days of his marriage to Julia, but he was so intent on his meal, moving slowly from beef to potato, chewing carefully, as if eating might now take up all of his time. For years I had wanted to hear the family history from him, but I realized, watching his knobby fingers work his knife and fork, and as he made his affectionate comments about the Grove

Avenue families of our time, that the story had always been visible, that my parents had lived it fully in our presence, no need to hear him frame it in words. I believe that I have never idealized the marriage, that what I saw was its truth. Her voluble yang to his steady, quiet yin; her calm, knowing yin to his abstracted yang. There was no person he wanted to talk to more than my mother, no greater pleasure than his homecoming to her, night after night. That was what Louise and I had understood through our childhood, that they'd celebrated each other in everyday life, and that their love was the sort that radiated outward. For a while in the 1980s, we'd tried to get our parents to find a group home for Madeline, but to no avail. "This is her group home," my mother had said. My father asked, "Move Madeline so we can do what? Go on a cruise, maybe get to sit at the captain's table? Drive cross-country in an RV? Smoke pot freely now that the children are gone?"

At some point in the far-off future, they planned to sign up for a retirement community, the three of them, or, if they didn't manage to clean out the house before they fell apart, a nursing facility. When Mikey O'Day left town, my mother had made it a point to keep Madeline busy. Miss Madeline still went to a morning program for the handicapped, and many afternoons she worked for Shelly, the neighbor who ran the beauty salon. Shelly had a cadre of senior citizens who were used to Madeline, who favored her gentle fingers moving through their wet hair before they got their weekly permanents. My mother had reminded us that there were more services for the disabled than there had been when we were growing up. Although none of us said so, I'm certain we'd all thought how Mikey O'Day had been the greatest service, occupying Madeline with his music and his ticket-taking for hours at a time. In her old age, Madeline was a favorite member of the Sunshine Club, an organization that went on trips to the zoo and sponsored holiday parties and dances. It was an ecumenical group—young, elderly, physically handicapped, mentally challenged. Through the years there'd been a few suitors, quiet, odd men who called Madeline on the phone. She seemed to tolerate their entreaties, and she might deign to sit next to this one or another on a trip. That was the extent of the liberties she allowed.

The day before the service, Louise and Diana, with help from Madeline, went through the photographs and assembled the obligatory picture boards of Mother's life for the church viewing. They sat in the dining room all afternoon, sorting through the piles on the table, the years and subjects all mixed up. There was a book from my first few months of life, but otherwise my mother had not found a moment to arrange the photos into albums. "She had no organizational skills!" Diana exclaimed in amazement. There were quite a few pictures from the Mikey O'Day years, Mikey on the boat at Moose Lake, Mikey at the Dari-Dip, Mikey and Madeline sitting on the front porch, Mikey at our kitchen table, Mikey sitting in a kiddie pool in the Van Normans' yard, taking up the whole thing, with, as they say, a shit-eating grin on his face.

"He was fun, wasn't he?" Diana said to Madeline. "I've heard about how much fun he was."

Madeline nodded without glancing away.

"Shall we have some of Mikey?" Louise asked. "This one, with Mom, at your birthday party? And here, look, you and Mikey toasting marshmallows."

Madeline ran her fingers over the three photos Louise had chosen. It was as if she hated to let them go, hated to hand them over, even though she wanted them on the board.

There was a large turnout for the memorial service at the Congregational church, the community my mother had finally settled on while she waited for that day when she'd return to Quaker Meeting. The Reverend Hollister, a jackpot minister, half black, half Asian, and lesbian, had taken to the streets with Julia to try to defeat an Illinois judge who was in favor of capital punishment, to elect Bill Clinton, and to oust a school-board member, the anti-taxation zealot who wanted to cut the music program. The old friends and neighbors came to church, the relatives, the fellow volunteers and activists, my father's colleagues from the museum, a handful of Diana's people, classmates of Louise's and mine from high school, most of whom we hadn't spoken to since graduation. The Sunshine Club brought in a busload, and they sat together, dignified in their lopsided ways.

Russia, who was ninety as well as we could figure, took her place between Madeline and my father, holding tight to them. She'd still been coming to the house every Wednesday. One of the Pathway to Victory Baptist Church boys brought her—Charles, who did what she said even while he regarded her with suppressed amusement. She'd settle herself in the chair in the kitchen and start her commands. "Do the sinks first, you hear?" My mother always offered him breakfast, and he always declined. "The boss, she don't let me," he'd say, shaking his head with exaggerated woe. For two hours the boss sat over her meal, taking her time with each bite, commenting on the neighbors, although there wasn't nearly the activity there had once been, the women off to work, the children at preschool. "What'd you stop that vacuum for?" she'd cry, leaning out of her chair to try to see around the corner to the living room, to Charles looping up the chord.

"I'm all finished, ma'am, unless you tell me I'm not."

"You go over it once more, one more time."

After she'd scraped the last crumb of toast, the last bit of hard cold yolk from her plate, Charles helped her into her coat. My mother slipped him an extra few dollars, went to her bed, and took up her book; there she fell asleep, her duty done, no more Russia to tend for a few hours, until she phoned with a complaint about Osella or her hip or her new glasses or her achy tooth. When my father told Russia about Julia, she could only say, "Bless her heart, bless her heart," about as close to being speechless as she could come.

At the service, just before the minister came to the pulpit for the invocation, who should sweep into the church but the voodoo economics Republican, the mortal enemy? Down the side aisle she flew, sliding into the front pew, her lipstick fresh, her perfume wafting to us even on the far end. Russia saw or sniffed her first and leaned over to poke me. "Miz Figgy," she said, her eyes widening.

There was a collective gasp from the family, and those close to her reached out to touch the hem of her jacket. She and my mother hadn't seen each other in years and didn't really speak. On the occasions she called, Julia would ask a cursory question or two before she handed over the phone to my father. There was no pretense of friendship in that civility. Figgy had gone further right as the years passed, a staunch Reaganite, an acquaintance, naturally, of the Gipper and Nancy. My mother voted for the mainstream Democrats, but she cried foul if they crossed the line, if they became too moderate. Despite her faith in acts of generosity and exculpation, despite her ability to reason, she half believed that Figgy was personally responsible for the rise of conservatism—that if Figgy had gone down that road, there was no hope. And so it was Figgy who was going to bring debt, environmental ruin, and general cultural barbarism down upon us all.

I did not pay strict attention through the service. I thought about how Diana had once said that my parents hadn't had a real marriage because they didn't fight. That meant that I didn't know to fight, having had no role model for battle, a significant deficit in a husband. I suppose it was quite a bit to live up to, the Macivers' union. Through the poems and readings we had chosen for Reverend Hollister, I tried to count the arguments I'd witnessed between Julia and Aaron, those conversations that were different from heated discussions. I could recall one spat that had been personal; I would go so far as to say it was violent. I remember it because my mother swore. Over coffee after dinner, Julia had been complaining about Mrs. O'Day's opposition to Madeline and Mikey's wedding. My father listened as he usually did, nodding and making standard guttural noises to indicate he was paying attention. When he remarked that Joan O'Day had made a life of caring for Mikey and that it wasn't such an easy thing to give up, Julia said, "Nothing is going to change! That's what is ridiculous about her protest. Nothing is going to change."

"They'll be married," my father pointed out.

"Are you saying you think the wedding is a bad idea?"

"I can understand why she'd be against it."

"Goddamn her."

"Julia."

"I said goddamn her."

"A wedding, a marriage, is a weighty action. It's not just a party. We can't really know what it would mean for Madeline, how she would understand it."

"Then we'll have a party, a tent in the backyard, a band. We'll have a party to honor them."

"That could be confusing to her. She wants a wedding."

"It's you who don't want a celebration!"

"I think it's more complicated than you're acknowledging, Julia. I don't think you've thought it through."

My mother appeared to consider as she sipped her coffee. "You and Joan are taking it too seriously," she said after a minute. "Madeline wants to dress up and be a bride. She wants to have photos to look at."

"There's only one thing for you to do," my father said, trying as he spoke not to smile at his forthcoming joke.

"What's that?"

"You and Mikey and Madeline will just have to elope."

"Goddamn Joan," Julia said, getting up from her chair. Downgrading her curse on her husband, she said, "And damn you, too." She stormed into the kitchen like a wife well versed in the rules of combat.

AFTER THE SERVICE, Madeline stood with me in the church parlor to greet the friends and neighbors. Louise had helped her choose an ensemble, a light-pink sweater and a long gray skirt, low-heeled pumps, and silver earrings. It was her new stylish hairdo, very short, that made her look like an ultra-cultured, with-it, liberal old lady. When one of the longtime neighbors, Mrs. Gregory, came through the line, she stopped in front of the easel right next to us, zeroing in on a picture of Julia setting a cake at Madeline's place for her birthday. It's a great photo of Mikey, his big face level with the confection, the rims of his glasses glancing the frosting. Mrs. Gregory tilted her head back, wrinkled her nose, let her mouth fall open, her upper lip lifting toward her nostrils, in the effort to study the picture through her bifocals. "That's you!" she said to Madeline. "And he, he must be your boyfriend."

Madeline stepped close to see who Mrs. Gregory meant.

"Where's your boyfriend? Everyone should have a boyfriend, eh? Go find your boyfriend!"

Madeline turned around, as if he might be right there waiting for her after all the years. She was tired and confused enough without Mrs. Gregory's excitement.

"Mrs. Gregory, hello," I said, taking our demented neighbor's hand. Her daughter was with her, also keen to push her through the line. Madeline right then wandered away from us. She sat on the sofa, rocking back and forth, done with the greeting. I don't know if Figgy had witnessed that moment with Mrs. Gregory, but she, too, went and sat down. "Come here, darlin'," she said to Madeline in Russia-ese. She put her arm around her and kissed her cheek, going so far as to try to nuzzle her. "You *are* a great big girl, aren't you?"

It was awful to watch, a performance that wanted to be heartfelt but didn't quite achieve the mark. And yet it seemed enough of a gesture. I forgave Figgy on behalf of my mother, for all the slights through the years as well as the brazen remarks. It was good of her to pay Madeline a bit of attention, to consider that Madeline was perhaps the most bereft of us. For several minutes they sat quietly together, Madeline holding her arms around her ribs and rocking, Figgy drinking her coffee. Some compensation, then, for losing Julia: having Figgy back in our midst. Later, at the house, she blew in the door, threw off her heels, and yanked her quarter-sized pearl earrings from her lobes, tossing them on the chest in the hall before she collapsed in the wing chair. I'd forgotten how much she could eat, and how beautifully loud she was, calling out across the room to Tessa, making her come and give a report on her life to date, ordering Lyddie to play the piano, demanding that Diana put on a few pounds.

Much later, long after my father and Madeline had gone to bed, and Diana and the girls had driven to Wisconsin, and Lu's family had retired to the hotel, I sat in the kitchen talking to my aunt. She didn't seem tired, and in fact it wasn't until two in the morning that she took herself to the sofa and, like a teenager, curled up there with a blanket. She had a room at the downtown Hilton, she said, but she didn't feel like getting a cab and checking in at such an hour. She refused in no uncertain terms to take my boyhood bed, saying that one of her few talents was being able to drop into a profound sleep in any circumstance. Louise's room had been turned into my mother's office and was piled high with newspaper clippings and books, and underneath the mess, somewhere, the Olivetti manual typewriter she'd always used. Through the evening, Figgy had told me the news: how Buddy had trained a support unit that had performed well in Desert Storm, Arthur was writing a book about how liberalism had been unraveling as the Great Society was being made, and as for herself, she was doing consulting work for museums and spending as much time as she could with her grandchildren. A model grandmother, Figgy. "Buddy's children," she said, "are masterpieces, each one."

I couldn't help myself, couldn't keep from asking the question just as my mother would have. I asked knowing the answer; I asked only out of a sense of ritual. "What's the general feeling in Washington about Operation Desert Storm now?" I said. "Among those in the know?" The first Gulf War had been over in 1991; it had seemed, in the few months it took to secure victory, a nearly bloodless enterprise. I was sure that Figgy would have nothing but respect for General Schwarzkopf and for her president, George Herbert Walker Bush, a foreign-policy realist in the tradition of Nixon and Kissinger. I was sure she wouldn't mention the dismay among some Washington pols that the war had left Saddam Hussein in power.

She was going to oblige, but first she had to refresh her drink. She had requested brandy, and when the dark-golden liquid was full to the brim she said, "Over all there is still the sense that Desert Storm was a success. I don't think that's going to go away. Certainly, as President Bush said, 'We've licked the Vietnam syndrome once and for all.' We've shown that America still has the power and the brains to achieve our goals militarily. And we defanged Saddam Hussein, no mistaking that. Saddam as a threat to peace in the Middle East is finished. Not that we still don't have to keep eternal vigilance over him, but he's not going to be a threat in the same way he was before the war. We accomplished what we meant to do with minimal losses of life on our side."

Although Diana had gone home, she would, if she were present, send me signals across the table to let the dull old arguments go. Especially at this hour. So I said, "That's great, Figgy." And I said—without thinking, without knowing if it was true—I said, "I've always felt safer knowing that Buddy is on our side."

Figgy raised her glass to me, in honor of her son, and we drank to the lees. "I do have to give your mother credit," she said, wiping her mouth with the back of her hand, "where credit is due."

"Oh?"

"All that quarreling we did in the old days about the war. She was right to see the Vietnamese struggle as one of nationalism. Very few people at the start understood it that way, but of course she's proved herself right. It was a complicated situation, and I'm not sure, ideologically, that we were wrong to give aid, but she was right about that particular point. Pour me a little more of that, and let's drink to her."

We clinked glasses once more. *Julia, Julia, a small thing maybe, but do you hear what Figgy just admitted?* "Isn't it ironic," my aunt said, "or fitting, that here we are back to the original Mr. and Mrs. Maciver? Just the two of them, both, in a way, widowed?"

I had been thinking of my father in the role of parent, left with Madeline, the grieving child. I laughed out loud at the weirdness of her idea, the Macivers restored to one another. Since the service, I'd been mulling over the remark the minister had made about Madeline. We had left the eulogy in the Reverend Hollister's hands, and she'd struck the right tone, telling the tried-and-true anecdotes about Julia's irreverence, her stubbornness, her optimism. "It has been said that nothing is simple," the Reverend declared near the end, "that if you look into any relationship its complexity is revealed. But I think the life that Aaron and Julia had with their children, and with Madeline, their commitment to family, was simple, that there is sometimes nothing elaborate in the living out of *caritas*—of charity. Charity, devotion—those gifts that cannot be explained, those gifts from God, that are part of His grace."

I had on occasion wondered past the simplicity of my parents' goodness, wondered how much or if any of their dedication to Madeline had to do with the fact that they owed her their life together. Was their care a kind of payment? Would they have taken any handicapped young woman into their home, into their arms? I would have liked to know how much impurity goodness can have and still be considered goodness. "What," I said to Figgy, "did you think of the eulogy?"

My aged aunt clattered a fork inside her empty glass and sighed. "Lovely, very nice." She sighed again, her signature bosom rising and falling heavily. "I'm just sorry her *caritas* didn't extend to me. Your mother tried to believe that we all need each other, the dummy and the scholar, the king and the serf, the left and the right, but she couldn't really pull it off. Those of us who were wrong—wrong!—made her so angry. Maybe the afterlife will even her out. Maybe death is like taking a hit of Prozac."

Surely it was safe to say that Julia Maciver in the box in the closet was about as evened out as a person could get.

"Oh well," Figgy said, closing that subject. "Do you think we can talk your father into setting Madeline up in some kind of place? I'm sure he doesn't have a clue how much your mother took care of Miss Schiller. He still works every day, doesn't he?"

I had no idea how he was going to cope. Although he had retired, he continued to drive to the museum several times a week for his research on migrating populations through Chicago. Every morning for twenty years, spring and fall, he or one of his workers had picked up the dead birds that smacked into the glass structure of McCormick Place, cataloguing them, charting the species on the move across that part of Lake Michigan. Since my mother's death, we hadn't had time to discuss Madeline's future in any detail. She had cried herself to sleep most nights, and in the mornings she'd come to any of us who were near for consolation, sitting beside us, her large blue eyes beseeching, as if she thought we might somehow help, as if we might be able to stitch our mother back into herself merely because Madeline was sad. Her grief was unalloyed with regret, pure in her every gesture.

Over the years she had grown to like my father well enough, to accept him fully as part of the family. On the day after the service, Lu and I again tried halfheartedly to talk him into placing Madeline into assisted living. "We'll assist each other's living!" he said. "We'll manage. We've always managed."

We knew better than to remind him that it was Julia who had taken care of the home front. We didn't press him to sell the house, to pack up all the relics of our childhood that were still in the attic and our rooms, to sell everything that wouldn't fit in a five-hundred-square-foot condominium. "Madeline and I," he said, "will be fine."

FOR SOME TIME AFTER JULIA'S DEATH, Louise and I were braced for a domestic disaster in the old household, one of them falling or having a stroke, or growing too lonely to carry on. It was Russia who helped Madeline find a new place for herself. On her first Wednesday after the service, after she'd set Charles in motion with the mop and pail, after she had dismissed my father, telling him what to buy at the grocery store, she laid out what Madeline must do in order to deserve her rest at night. Over the weeks she helped her refine her egg-poaching techniques and made her mistress of the coffeemaker. In short order Madeline mastered the art of heating Lean Cuisine to perfection in the microwave, and she learned to sort colors and measure out soap for the laundry. She took wifely pride in her decorations—a pitcher of marigolds on the table, an arrangement of seashell soaps in the powder room. But it was on that first morning that the ground rules were put in place. "Charles, come here," Russia snapped, just after she'd ordered him away. She dictated a schedule to him, leaning over to see that his careful printing was neat enough, and then she affixed the list of seven theses to the refrigerator. "Monday: Dust. Tuesday: Change Sheets. Wednesday: Make Russia Breakfast. Thursday: Wash Clothes. Friday: Clean Sinks. Saturday: Buy Fruit. Sunday: Praise."

This list, which surely includes all things, which my father read out every morning for his own amusement, seemed to bring the day into focus for Madeline. It made it possible for her to rise in the morning with purpose. She combed her short hair, put on the clothes that she'd laid neatly on the floor the night before, and descended to the kitchen to start the coffee. On Saturdays they went early to the farmers' market in the high-school parking lot, smelling the tips of the melons before they purchased them, and carefully picking out apples from the bins, for Madeline did not like marks or bruises. On Sundays they went to Reverend Hollister's church for praise, and also to feel closer to my mother, as if she might linger there, as if they could be alert to her presence more naturally in that sanctuary. On the weekdays they sat at the breakfast table, Madeline watching the *Today Show* on the little TV my father had bought, and he reading the paper. It was what retired couples did the world over.

Chapter Fifteen

THERE WERE NO CRUISES OR ELDER HOSTELS FOR THE
reinstated Mr. and Mrs. Maciver, although they sometimes
came to Moose Lake in the summer, when we were all there.
They had a routine. A short walk in the morning, breakfast,
and sitting on the porch, my father reading, Madeline looking
at magazines. They often both had a nap in the afternoon.
Madeline stayed in the south bedroom, in the iron bed where,
long before, she had been so sick. Diana did what she could
to try to fill in for my mother, inviting Madeline to the store,
giving her tasks in the kitchen, and they gardened together, the
two of them in straw hats out in the overgrown flower beds. In
brief spurts Madeline seemed to enjoy digging holes for the
flats of annuals and pulling weeds. She had a white cushion she
knelt on, and she patted the earth around her plants with real
conviction.

For several years we'd owned Moose Lake with three
other Maciver families, running it as a time-share proposition,
each of us with two weeks in the summer, and months on end,
if anyone wanted, in the winter. Although we could have used
the place with Louise, her children were quite a bit older than
ours, and they were usually busy with their instruments or at
camp. Without cousins for the girls, and without the rule of my
grandmother, the estate, even when it was all ours for a stretch,
was diminished. I had wanted to carry on the Victorian rules,

but somehow that ironclad tradition didn't take. I suppose it was no fun to have rules to break if there was not a band of girls and boys to scheme with. Copulation, I'm sure, did take place in the boathouse, my daughters with their high-school and college beaux. They didn't know what they were missing, didn't know that their pleasure was hardly worth the trouble without the threat of punishment.

I wondered if for Madeline there was the lingering sense of the romantic days when there had been twenty children, when at dinner there were two long tables on the porch, and the lineup of babies in their high chairs, always someone for her to mother. When my daughters were teenagers, they didn't love the lake and couldn't be persuaded to come without their friends. They complained that there was nothing to do. One of my younger cousins had for a time lobbied for a TV on the premises, including a satellite dish and a gaming apparatus, but we elders won the day, much to the girls' disappointment. Tessa was the only child who knew to take up a book. In our weeks, they put on their little suits and tanned on the dock, waiting for me to take them water-skiing. Madeline, in her sleeveless blue cover-up dress that came to her knees, holding her hat to her head, was always the watcher, calling to me from the back of the boat when a girl went down. My daughters were polite with her and formal. Madeline was after all a lady in her seventies, the innocence or impassivity in her wrinkled face a strangeness to them. She'd sit on the end of the dock watching them wrestle each other on the raft, those small, muscly, near-naked Amazons. They were part boy, part woman, part beast— hard to say what Madeline thought as she looked on. In the new era, the trunk of Lincoln Logs was dusty in the corner of the living room, and the sheet over the dollhouse never came off.

There was a bright afternoon when I came upon her at the fire pit. She was squatting, bending over her long haunches, marking in the ashes with a stick. "Miss Madeline," I said, "what are you making?"

"Don't know." She put her chin to her knee and kept scratching. Nothing to do but make an occasion of it, setting fire to the paper trash already assembled—the two of us, poking at the glowing embers.

* * *

I'VE HAD A FEW real lapses in my adulthood, at least that I can identify. One was the blankness on the day that started with my father's phone call at breakfast, when he announced that my mother had died some-time in the night. I had registered very little through those hours, until suddenly I found myself on my knees behind the bar in the basement. There was another incident like that in Italy, an hour or so when I re-fused to see the world as it was, stubborn in my unwillingness to take into account what I knew. That time was not a blank, however. If any-thing, the afternoon was too full of emotion—rich, you might say, with operatic feeling.

It was 1998, five years past Julia's death. Louise's daughter Isabel was marrying a boy she'd met during a college program in Rome. Marty Raffin was a solid citizen of the Northwest, a boy who had climbed Mount Rainier several times, pickax in hand up the broad gla-cier. Not someone you'd immediately think to insert as bridegroom into the cobbled piazza of a dinky medieval town in Tuscany. The couple was going to be married outside of Fiesole, in the garden of a professor they'd befriended in their charmed semester a few years be-fore. It was a small gathering—Louise's family and ours, the groom's parents, and the three friends who had been able to afford the trip. I'd been surprised when my father, nearly eighty, had said that he and Madeline would come along. In all his collecting expeditions, he'd never been to any of the European cities except to pass through the airports. Before he died, he said, he'd like to add an Italian bird or two to his list—an *orchetto*, a *garҳetta*, a *mignattaio*—and also to see if the sparrows and wrens, those species that had been brought to the New World, sang differently in the presence of the pervasive smell of gar-lic. "Not to mention the pleasure of seeing my granddaughter get married," he said. He noted that he still had his own teeth and he could walk and he was not yet incontinent. "Real readiness," he de-clared, "for travel of any kind."

We were sitting at a long table in a low-ceilinged peasant cottage of a restaurant in Fiesole, on the night before the wedding, having eaten a meal of such tenderness and simplicity that everyone's present seemed sublime and the future destined to be happy. There had been fettuccine with cream-and-butter sauce, delicately garnished with shaved white truffles, and veal chops cooked with sage and white wine, and asparagus from a northern spring, neither too fat nor too thin, bundled up with prosciutto that had been aged a year and a half, the fine balance of savory and sweet, moist and firm. A bowl of fruit, each glossy strawberry more perfectly ripe than the last. While everyone else had drifted out to the street, into the evening, my father and I sat, two men submitting to Italian-style digestion, grappa as our aid. As we lingered there, I wondered out loud if Madeline had any memory of her European trip, over sixty years earlier, when she'd met the suitor, when her mother had swept her away from Florence. The question was theoretical at that point, something to consider lazily, whimsically, on a full stomach. It was poignant, I said to my father, wasn't it, that Madeline had returned here at this stage of her life?

He untucked his napkin from his shirt and dabbed at his mouth, one side and then the other. "What's this, now?"

I reminded him that Mrs. Schiller, the first mother-in-law, had taken Madeline to Italy before the marriage.

"What marriage?"

"She must have been in high school. Before you and she got married. Your wedding was in 1943, so probably their Italy trip was '37 or so. Before the war."

I'd never seen him looking confused as an old person will, the brow sharply furrowing, the eyes going vacant even as they narrowed. He was still usually so quick that his befuddlement startled me. "Nineteen thirty-seven?" It took me a minute to realize that his difficulty didn't stem from memory loss, not really. Time had done its work to absorb Madeline fully into our family; it was as if for him she had always been a Maciver, as if there had never been any Schillers.

"I don't recall that," he said, giving up the search, the frown for the most part easing from his face. "It beats me."

Madeline was outside, standing by the fountain with the bride.

They must have been talking about the wedding dress. Isabel appeared to be conjuring it with her fingers, first floating them over her breasts and then her arms widening in the promise of a full skirt. Madeline put her hands to her mouth and laughed, out of sheer delight at how beautiful it was going to be.

AFTER THE WEDDING, after the sun-drenched day as advertised, and the dark-haired bride sealing her vows in her ivory lace, and another meal that filled our hearts with gladness, after that we spent three days in Florence. My girls—twelve, fourteen, and sixteen—shared a long white room with a close-up view of one small section of the Duomo's intricate marble walls, the jewel box of gargantuan proportions. Every morning they threw open the shutters to the ringing of the bells, and although they'd been woken early they were awestruck instead of annoyed. I liked to think of the three of them and Madeline lying in the starched sheets of their dormitory, waiting for the bells to peal across the city, as close as they'd ever come to being novitiates. They knew better than to ask Madeline to braid their hair, because if it didn't go well, if Madeline got frustrated, it would spoil her morning. But she did some of their preening, one after the next waiting for the in-house beautician to brush and comb and make their ponytails. You could see that she was nervous and excited, taking on the responsibility of hairdresser to the princesses.

It didn't take long for the girls to figure out the lay of the land, and then they were off, charging across the Ponte Vecchio, to the Boboli Gardens, ducking in here and there to a church or, at the least, a gift shop. Tessa would come back to the hotel with stacks of postcards, Katie with medals of the saints, and Lyddie once with a gutted bird tied at the feet for my father. She'd picked it out from a line of them hanging on a string at a butcher's, and with her head turned away and her arm outstretched she'd handed it to him. He was so pleased, and keen to find a stove and a frying pan, to see how a Florentine sparrow tasted.

The adults took turns with Madeline, morning and afternoon shifts. She was spry, and for short periods she enjoyed walking, looking at the shopwindows, the tourists, the paintings and sculptures. Over the years she had developed real stoicism, or perhaps it was resignation, an animal patience, waiting, waiting for time to pass. She could sit peaceably at the dinner table while the others talked, for many minutes turning a salt shaker around and around, or rocking, her upper body moving in slow back-and-forths. In our forays into museums and churches, she was drawn to the Baby Jesuses and the Madonnas, if the Virgin didn't look too somber, and she stared unabashedly, her mouth open at the sometimes larger-than-life penises of the statuary. In the Uffizi, she was as transfixed as I by the Botticellis. She couldn't believe how long Venus' hair was, and I think it amazed her the way the tresses so conveniently covered the genitals. She stepped as close as she could to look at the golden locks obscuring the place. When she'd gotten over that part of the painting, she pointed at the feet, at how well Venus was balancing on the lip of the seashell. We'd spend forty-five minutes or so walking slowly through a few of the galleries, sitting for a while to watch the crowds, and then we'd take a break in a café so she could have a gelato and I a coffee spiked with Benedictine.

At one point I found myself walking with her across the Piazza Santa Croce. It was the spot, if I remembered correctly, where, according to Figgy, Madeline had met her swain on his bicycle. That is, one afternoon, after drinking a bottle of Chianti at lunch, I deliberately strolled in that direction with Madeline, arm in arm, just as a mother and son might do on a fine summer day. How Figgy knew about the location of the love moment is hard to say. I can only assume that, once upon a time, Madeline had confided in her, that they had a luncheon, sister-in-law to sister-in-law. Because I had read my Baedeker thoroughly, I knew that geniuses such as Michelangelo, Machiavelli, Galileo, and Rossini had graced the Franciscan church with their bones, that there were splendid tabernacles and sepulchers for their glorious dust. I talked to Madeline about St. Francis as we walked, about his love for animals and the poor. She was the only one in the family who was willing to listen to my lectures. Standing at the edge of the piazza, I explained how the people had lived huddled on top of each other in their crammed quarters in the Middle Ages. It was the monks who came up with the idea of the large squares, space for people to gather, for games and conversation. "Just like the alley," I said, "the way it used to be, the boys playing basketball, the mothers discussing their children."

"Room to play horses," she observed.

As far as I knew, she hadn't had a horse friend in years, the younger generation on the block no longer building jumps in mud-packed backyards. In the present-day era, there were preassembled play structures pounded into the thick grassy ground, and no one ever in sight. "You remember that, do you?" I said. "Cantering around with the Van Norman girls, whinnying and clicking your tongue?" It was unusual now to hear a basketball thumping in the alley, that noise as constant as a clock ticking the seconds when I was a boy.

The pigeons were bullying and bobbing for crumbs, and the tourists with their baseball caps and fanny packs jostling us made it difficult to feel much of any kind of past. And yet my heart was racing, to be crossing the piazza with her. She was wearing a light pink dress, sleeveless and straight, feminine and even flattering on her eighty-year-old frame. There was that stillness in her face, her mouth open slightly, the eyes cast down as she dutifully waited for the minutes to pass, waiting for nothing much to happen. Alcohol destroys brain cells in the left hemisphere especially, the seat of language, of logic. Perhaps I was drunk; perhaps the nerve membrane in my frontal lobe had become structurally unstable from years of drinking through dinner. How to account for the suddenness of my feeling, my wish for Madeline to have happiness, to have a jolt of life. I gripped her shoulder as if somehow I could prod her to it. "Madeline," I said. In a time when my brain was probably failing me, I had hope for hers. I can offer little explanation for that hope, that she have access to a scene that had once thrilled her, except to say that after my lunch I was overcome in the shadow of Santa Croce. *For just a minute, darling Madeline, become yourself.* "Madeline," I said once more.

"I'm okay," she said reflexively.

I wondered if she'd gone into the church on that day, when she was a teenager, or if the imposing building had served only as a back-drop to the Italian as he rushed to her on his bike. I suggested we go inside, thinking that the nave might somehow be familiar to her. After the conflagration, bike and man and girl, maybe they had gone to-gether into the church and stood looking up at the terrible height of the ceiling, an architectural impossibility. I had often thought about how Madeline's recovery would have been significantly different if she'd been a young bride in the year 2000, if her frontal-lobe syn-drome could have been partially treated with neuropharmacology, neuropsychiatrists, and continued rehabilitation. It is conceivable that she might have overcome some of her deficits.

In the enormous cavern of the basilica, we both did grow solemn. Our footsteps echoed, and although the other tourists were trying to be quiet and respectful, even their whispers seemed to ring out into the gloom. I could see that Madeline was spooked, that she didn't want to hear her sandals on the stone, didn't want to move for fear of mak-ing noise. It wasn't going to be worth trying to see the Giottos in the side chapels, or the Donatello Crucifix, or the tombs of the great men, and in any case just then I didn't care about the masterpieces. "Should we light a votive candle before we go," I said, "and make a wish?"

Yes, she would like that. With a mission, with her goal the tiers of guttering candles in their glasses on the far side, she didn't so much care about clacking across the floor. As I dug in my pockets for coins, to make our plea legitimate, she asked the age-old question: "Does it have to be a secret when you wish?"

"No!" I said. "Absolutely not. I'll tell you what I'm going to wish. Let's see—I might wish that the bride and groom have a long future." My heart quickened again. "Is that too dull?"

She bit her lip as she thought. "No," she pronounced.

It had always been impossible to know if the scar tissue had disrupted the network between her hippocampus, the temporal lobes, and their connection to other midline structures, those memory components that must be linked together as a whole for a person to retrieve comprehensible chunks of the past. Still, I had grown certain that Madeline's long-term memory must be intact, that she had gaps in her history only because neither she nor anyone in her household told the stories of her girlhood. As far as I could figure from Figgy's sketchy anecdotes, Madeline had had post-traumatic amnesia after the accident, her short-term memory, as usually happens to the brain-injured, coming back slowly, within a month or two. If she had merely repressed her early years, then perhaps being in the piazza, in the church would trigger the moment with the Italian, just as the famous madeleines had given Proust his flood of recollections. All that had been lacking in Madeline's life up to this point was a simple trip to Italy! It wasn't a moment too soon for an old lady who might be suffering from standard forgetfulness. If there was magic to be had in all the world, wouldn't it take place in a country where saints still performed miracles from the grave, where St. Januarius' blood, for example, dried and preserved, turned into a liquid when it was brought near a certain holy statue? Not only did it liquefy, not only did it froth, it *bubbled*. Therefore, I said, "I've changed my mind. I think I'll wish that you, Miss Madeline, that you remember something that once brought you joy. Long ago, so long ago you might not ordinarily remember. How about that?"

Did I feel foolish saying so? Not at all, not then. I handed her the taper, and she touched it to her wick. Perhaps now, midway through the first decade of the new century, we have to be too alert to entertain mystical experiences, but in Santa Croce, before the millennium, I very much wanted one. She had a faraway look I thought might possibly mean something. "I wish," she pronounced with great seriousness, and also, it must be said, genuine altruism, "that the bride looks like an angel. Forever and ever."

"Angel?" I whispered. What was it that the Italian had said to her when he'd nearly run over her on his bike? "At this moment—I see in the piazza the angel." Was it a coincidence that Madeline was speaking of angels, or did she in fact remember? Her saying so couldn't have been prompted by the angels everywhere in Florence, the cherubim and seraphim in the churches, the museums, on postcards, on the walls of the restaurants, on packets of tissue, on the wrappers of chocolate. How many hundreds of annunciations had we seen? She was surrounded by lovely winged women of great purity, but I was certain in the moment that none of those images had superficially affected her. She remembered. I knew she remembered.

I lit my candle, restating my desire. "I wish that Madeline remembers something forgotten, something that once brought her a great happiness." Let her basal forebrain bloom with acetylcholine-producing neurons, those that are essential for memory. And then what? Let her remember, and let that happiness remain within her, neither fading nor becoming sour; let there be that miracle, too, that the joy remain fresh.

We both stared at the slender white flame for a minute, both of us, maybe, expecting a scene to appear out of the small bit of fire. When that didn't happen I said, "Let's go out and sit on the steps a minute. Let's go see what we see."

"See what we see," she echoed.

Once we were on the shady end of the stone steps, when we were sitting, looking out into the square, I asked, "Have you ever been here before?"

"Yeah." She said so dully, the way she often did when she didn't know the answer.

I wondered if the man, let us call him Giorgio, was still alive. He would also have been in his eighties, and perhaps he still lived in Florence, above the leather shop that his sons now managed. Maybe he was one of the elegant elderly gentlemen sitting outside in front of a café, having his coffee, his cane resting against the table. If he looked up at Madeline, would he have a jolt? Would he see that essential divinity in her still? In order to help her get back to 1937 I had to try to find out where her memory easily started. She had access to Mikey O'Day and the horse-jumping era, and so maybe I could nudge her backward. "Do you remember when Lu and I were little, when you chased us around the circle downstairs?"

"Russia made me take a nap!" She pouted. "I was too old for a nap."

"Of course you were. But you had to, because everyone did what Russia said."

"She was mean to me."

"She was bossy, that's true. But she always said you were the prettiest girl. Do you remember that?"

"Prettiest girl," she repeated, brightening.

"Do you remember a long time ago, a very long time ago, when you were in high school, when you went to Evanston Township High School?"

"Yeah," she said again.

What question could I ask for the miracle? Did you use to like to ride a bicycle? Did you ever meet a man who was riding a bike? Do you remember the severe woman who wore the ostrich plume in her hat? Not the person you called Mother who died five years ago, but that other mother, Mrs. Schiller? When, incidentally, did you begin to call Julia Maciver Mother? I put my arm around her and kissed the cheek that was covered with fine down, and then I drew away and said it right out. I said, "At this moment—I see in the piazza the angel."

She sat idly scratching her leg, squinting up at the sun as it started to come across us.

"Tessa caught Isabel's bouquet," she said. "I wanted to, but Tessa got it before me."

"And then Tessa divided the flowers so you could have some of them. Lyddie, Katie, and you all got roses." It had been wonderful of Tessa to realize that Madeline was hoping for the bouquet.

She wrinkled her nose as if a bad smell had come her way. "But I wanted to catch it."

"I did, too," I said.

She bent over her lap. It took me a minute to realize she was laughing. "They—they don't—don't let . . . *boys* catch the bouquet!" She lifted her head to stare at me, and then she laughed again, the sound starting down in her throat and hitching upward. "That's funny! B-boys don't catch the bouquet."

I stretched out my legs and let the sun shine full on my face. Perhaps there were going to be no miracles for Miss Madeline, at least not today. The magic of winter to spring was no doubt less intricate than Madeline's finding one small memory from her youth. Maybe it was in an effort to redeem myself that I began to talk, or maybe even before I started I knew that it was up to me to give her what she couldn't make on her own. "Long ago," I said, "there was a girl walking in the hot afternoon, by herself, across this piazza. Coming from over there—do you see?—from the Borgo dei Greci, a boy was running an errand for his father, on his bike. The piazza was empty because most of the people in Florence were taking their siesta. But he came riding across and he saw the girl. They were the only two people awake in the city." It was important to outfit the heroine, and I said with absolute confidence, "She was wearing a white dress with a full skirt, and a straw hat with a blue ribbon that went down her back. It was fluttering a little, in the breeze. She had left her mother in the hotel and was glad to be by herself, just this once, to walk along the streets looking at everything without someone explaining the details, this dead saint, that dead saint, such-and-such who was a famous artist, what's-his-name who was burned at the stake. She was tired of history. When the boy saw her, he stopped his bike. He had to put his feet down on the pavement so he could stare at her without falling over."

"Why?" Madeline said.

"Because"—I looked at her; I gazed upon her—"because she was beautiful. She was more beautiful than anyone he'd ever seen. The beauty," I added for moral purposes, "came from deep within her. But she was walking, walking, and if he didn't ride to her she'd be across the piazza and down a side street and he'd never see her again. He rode as fast as he could, faster than he needed. He was so worried he'd lose her he couldn't stop, he had to leap off his bike and catch her—otherwise he would have slammed right into her. 'Signorina! Signorina!' He didn't know much English, and it sounded strange to her, funny, the way he talked as he helped her up. 'Sorry! Oh, sorry—I feel more sorry, I—you, tell it to me that you are are all smooth—that you are no hurt. Tell it to me that you are joy.' She studied his face for a minute, the dark brown of his eyes, his mouth, as finely cut as the sculptures she'd seen. She found she couldn't speak. She was looking at him and she couldn't—not right away—tell him, 'I *am* joy.' "

Madeline was staring out into the center of the piazza. "Did they get married?"

"Yes. Her mother could see that they were in love, and so she gave her permission. They had their wedding—"

"Was her dress like Isabel's?"

"Exactly like it."

"Oh," she said, scratching her leg again. "That's good." She nodded. "That's good."

After a while we made our way toward the Piazza della Signoria. For the first time I understood why Figgy had considered Madeline's Italian episode fit for an adult listener, and also why she delighted in telling it. "You can live other lives in stories," I tried to explain to Madeline as we walked. "For a minute you can go back to a beginning. You can . . ." What I meant beyond that dribble, what Figgy had shown me through the years, was the pleasure of lingering in a single moment of possibility. Instead of bringing up that idea to Madeline, or introducing her to the theory that all time is happening in every moment, I said, "There are always so many what-ifs. If the girl hadn't escaped from her mother. If the girl had decided to walk up to San Miniato instead of across the piazza. If the girl hadn't been wearing that white dress. If the boy on the bike hadn't had to run an errand at that moment for his father."

"The boy on the bike," she repeated. And then, in a remarkable, a stunning flash of insight, she said, "Was the mother mad?"

I stumbled and had to clutch her. *Madeline, oh, Madeline, yes, yes!*

The mother was furious, she was enraged. "Was she angry?" I asked, slowly, slowly. "Maybe at first. Probably. It might have taken her a while to come around. In the end she was sorry to give her daughter up but she was thrilled for her, too. She knew she had to let her go, let her go off into her own life."

When we came from the narrow street into the open, I spotted Lyddie, Tessa, and Katie, the three of them in their summer dresses standing by the Fountain of Neptune. Three long-haired blond girls, flushed from the heat, with change in their purses. I grabbed Madeline's hand again. It was involuntary, my crying, "Look! There they are!"

At that moment I would have been so glad for each of my girls to meet her own Florentine young man, each in his turn the most handsome. Lyddie, Tessa, and Katie swept up by Guido, Fabrizio, and Carlo right before us at the fountain. I would go back to the hotel and tell Diana that the marriages had taken place, that the girls were set, that before them lay years of golden sunshine and olive harvests and dark-eyed babies.

Chapter Sixteen

BUDDY'S SON KYLE WAS BORN IN 1982 AND DIED IN 2003, SO
mused Tessa one night at the kitchen island before we went
south. "He lived from the Apple IIe to the iPod. Isn't that
incroyable?"

Chef Maciver was serving a cheap but not terrible South
African Sauvignon Blanc, a wine that had a rich, bouncy
finish. Since my underage daughter weighed 105 pounds,
she'd gotten tipsy in no time.

"He lived from AIDS to Ebola! From indie rock to hip-
hop and teen pop. From *Dynasty* to *Six Feet Un*— Oh, my
God!" She clapped her hand to her mouth. "*Six Feet Under!*"
The fountain of cultural history remained plugged for a
moment.

Kyle had been twenty-one years old for a few months,
glad at last to be legal.

Tessa took another swallow and then rattled on happily.
"It would be interesting to meet someone who's part of the
army. I don't have any idea what that's about. Not to mention
seeing my gene stock. Are all the Eastmans going to join the
military, every single one of Buddy's kids? Do you think?
What if they all get blown up? There were families in the
Civil War that lost all their sons, entire towns that were—"

"Tessa," I said firmly, about to remind her that a slightly
drunk girl should be able to show respect.

"Something else you don't realize," Diana called, coming through the swinging doors of the pantry, the one feature of our kitchen that makes me feel as if I'm in a Western, as if Diana might draw her pistols out of her holsters. "Don't you understand? Buddy would be honored for you to be there."

"Fort Bragg is the base where four men killed their wives during a six-month period," my daughter went on in her instruction. "Did you hear about it? I wonder what your cousin has to say about that scandal?"

"Were they convicted?" I asked.

"Now you get intrigued by Fort Bragg," Diana said, as if murder, as if uxoricide, had always been my primary interest.

And so, another funeral. Though it's true that in adulthood there has been little reason for Buddy and me to stay in touch, and that, further, in middle age a person begins to scale back, conserving energy for pastimes that matter most, I admit that seeing him in North Carolina, the mere sight of him, and in his dress uniform, too, gave me a shock. It was a pleasure I would never have anticipated. He was standing in the parking lot at the back of the church when we drove in, next to the hearse. The sergeant first class was wearing his navy-blue coat with gold buttons and roping, his insignias and decorations on the lapels and at the breast. His cap had a gold emblem that even from a distance stirred a person to think of lionhearted conquerors and the ceremony of their homecoming.

From the comfort of our cool, clean rental car, it was Diana who said, "There's Buddy!" She who had never met him.

"Which one?" Tessa loomed between the front seats. She might have been about to go to a cocktail party in her sleeveless short black dress and the heels that would surely make her a long-term patient of a podiatrist. Her vanilla-flavored perfume had required me to crack the window.

The pallbearers were gathered around, and he had his hands on two of them, on their shoulders, as he dispensed directions or consolation or thanks. "Buddy's the one in charge," I said, gesturing in his direction. My own kind, despite the fact that we had no interests, no aesthetic, no values in common. My littermate, a member of the tribe. I might have liked to stand next to him, stand, that's all, breathing in, breathing out. How unexpected affinity is! From twenty yards away, his compact athletic form brought on that old frisson of both danger and safety. Because hadn't he always protected us? Even as he led us toward peril, we always knew that Buddy would shield us from trouble.

The church was one of those modern white barnlike structures with cushioned pews, enough space to seat two thousand. Figgy had once told me that it was Joelle who was the Holy Roller in the family. Buddy went along with her for the holidays but apparently was independent enough not to have become born again. I am still unclear of the denomination; I don't know what warehouse-proportion generic evangelical is called, and with a touch possibly of Pentecostalism, a tolerance for but not wholesale encouragement of glossolalia. Inside the building there was no gloom, no hush, and no sense of an age-old story. The few stained-glass windows were abstract, decorative rather than instructional. There was so much light and space, all an emptiness, that I wouldn't have been surprised to see a drive-through window for the quick-fix, for a gobble of pastoral intimacy. I tried to imagine what Buddy would think about on his forced marches to church, if he ever reflected in that arena upon his sins or the grace of salvation. Was he, I wondered, ever tempted?

We were early and able to watch the place fill from the spot I chose, I insisted upon, in the back. As is my habit, I counted the crowd, eight hundred or so mourners by the start of the service, a staggering number of people to know. Joelle's prayer circle, *Moms in Touch,* were up front, in a space reserved for them; they had networked with other chapters of *Moms in Touch* across the country to pray for Kyle and the Eastmans. Buddy, Joelle, and the four children appeared in the foyer, readying themselves to walk behind the casket. Joelle looked just as she had for years on the Christmas cards, stately enough to do a swimsuit competition but also sweetly pretty, a blond puff framing her face, her diamond earrings twinkling through, all as befits a kindergarten teacher. Any self-respecting five-year-old would fall in love with her at first sight. She had her arms around the two younger daughters while Buddy, from behind, whispered into her hair. The oldest daughter rested her head on her brother's shoulder. That private family moment shut out those of us who were looking on, made us turn back in our seats to face the pulpit. I assumed that, the formal rules for a military funeral notwithstanding, Buddy could have elected to be a pallbearer, and that he had opted to walk instead with his family, to be one of them, to offer them his comfort.

Or perhaps it was he who needed them. When I happened to glance around once more, he was looking at me. My cousin, I now saw, was no longer bronzed. He had let himself go pale like the rest of us, his face flat without the old color. Of course his hair was thinner, of course, and what was left was faded.

Buddy!

He was staring at me, motionless, his eyes glazed. And then he put his cap back on and smiled, one corner of his mouth spreading upward, such a rueful expression I wondered if I'd been mistaken, if that man was actually my childhood playfellow.

I raised my hand, and although he couldn't hear I did say his name. He nodded as if he'd understood my meaning before he turned back to his group. He had kept us safe in the time of our quaint dereliction at Moose Lake, but he had failed his son: Buddy, it came full upon me, had lost his boy.

At the appointed hour, the soldiers carried the coffin down the aisle—no wheels for those warriors. They also wore navy-blue dress uniforms, with white gloves and dark caps. They must all have only that morning had the same barber shave them to exact specifications, so that in their line from the rear you saw the square of those nearly bald heads and their clean ears and the caps sitting high on their crowns. Tessa's mouth fell open, in awe of that precision. That their solemnity seemed permanent was probably meant to be a solace.

Figgy was alive but no longer herself, in a nursing home in Washington, D.C., a place, Buddy would tell me, providing the finest care money could buy. A few years before, she'd suffered a stroke, losing both speech and motor control. She no longer seemed to recognize Buddy when he visited. Arthur had gone quickly, of pancreatic cancer, in 1999. During the funeral, I imagined that my mother had returned. As Diana did, she, too, would feel the pressure to be present at the family event, no matter the obstacles or the length of the journey. Especially in view of the fact that after all the talk none of the other cousins had made the trip, and because she had always had a soft spot for Buddy. Diana, I knew—as I suppose I had from the start—had been right to urge me to come, to be part of the ritual that renews our dedication to the past.

If Julia had been with us, it's possible she might have gotten the idea, a flash for a second or two, sitting through "Sheep May Safely Graze," and then an electrifying rendition of "Amazing Grace" by a mere girl, and from the minister's eulogy, that Kyle Eastman had made a substantial contribution, a valuable contribution to the Republic. Even if you didn't believe in war on general principle, even if you didn't believe in the war at hand—even if you had little use for nation-states. You were nonetheless in the presence of a tradition, the pomp, those somber soldiers parading up the aisle carrying the draped box, we wretches assembled, the ceremony, yes, tugging at your heart, making you feel something that lay hidden within yourself. There it was beating in your blood, a sense of nobility in service, and a love for your imperfect country. We were as the Trojans gathering Hector's white bones from the funeral pyre, the warm tears streaming down our cheeks as we put the remains in a golden chest and shrouded it round and round in soft purple cloths. We were burying the beautiful warrior, the brave hero, who had been sent to war by the machinations of the gods. Why not call it that? If you closed your eyes, if you let yourself fall into the collective sadness, you might start to believe that Kyle had not died in vain, that his sacrifice had meant a great deal; you might think it possible that he was meeting his Maker. You might, if you hadn't slept much and were feeling dizzy, you might imagine the streets of Baghdad, the pavement glittering, the mosques rising up white and holy, the American servicemen and -women flowing into the city in their armored Humvees to liberate—

Diana poked my leg. "What are you doing?"

I opened my eyes, astonished for a second by the light.

"You were swaying," she whispered.

"Is he okay?" Tessa asked.

There was the reading by the energetic young pastor of the last letter, Kyle's just-in-case letter. Kyle had written that he would always be with his family and they with him. He'd addressed each sibling. Little Squirt. Tippy. Gongo. Pep. "Little Squirt, keep your eye on the ball. You're going to get past eighth grade, and believe me life is going to look up. Tippy, dance like no one's looking. You know the drill. Love like you've never been hurt. Gongo, mess up your room sometimes, it won't kill you. I hear you playing the piano in my dreams. Pep, Pepper, don't ever lose your spice. Remember, there's no basement in the Alamo!" To Joelle, "You're the kindest, most beautiful, the greatest mother in the world. Where do I start? From the smallest things like doing the coloring on my school projects to the bigger ones, sticking up for me in Principal Borg's office. You are my angel, looking down on me." For Buddy there was this: "Dad, you've always been there for me, always shown me the way, always got me to do my best. You've never let me down, something I know now is pretty impossible to pull off. Whether I live or die I can never thank you enough."

In the front pew, Buddy must have had his head in his hands, feet apart, elbows on his thighs. The only visible part of him was the hunch of his upper back. The minister waited a decent interval before he went on. "How many young men," he then cried out, "how many young men are prepared to make the ultimate sacrifice, as our Kyle was? A young man who knew the price of liberty, who believed that others should know the glory of freedom, the goodness of great love—and this work, this work, my friends, when it is done, when it is finally done, will be a magnificent thing, a creation of freedom and Godliness, a mosaic that will have as its part the bright, shining colors of Kyle Eastman."

When he was finished, Buddy's seventeen-year-old daughter, Vanessa, aka Gongo, marched to the grand piano at the side of the altar, sat herself down, and played Schumann's "Arabesque." She reminded me of a young Louise at her cello. How had Buddy produced a girl with Louise's focus when two of my daughters had complained bitterly up through "Hot Cross Buns" on their tonettes? Lyddie, the most advanced, used to play tinkly Disney songs on the piano, the kind of music that adheres to the skin, that causes moles to change.

Before the benediction, the long notes of "Taps" filled the white space of the sanctuary. The bugler stood near us in the back, his horn tilted upward, his eyes fixed yonder. There was again the sense that we were part of no ordinary tragedy but one infused with majesty. It is not often that a person encounters majesty outside of scenic views—the mountain peaks in the distance or enormous animals in the wild. On that day those simple intervals, the bugler holding the notes longer than seemed humanly possible, made all of us sit straighter even as tears welled in our eyes.

When the service was over, just after the casket came back up the aisle, Diana took me in hand. Without waiting for all the other rows to process out of the sanctuary, front to back, she followed behind the Eastmans so that we might be among the first to greet our relations.

"We have virtually cut in line," I remarked.

"We've come from far away and we're family," she explained. "We should have been sitting up there with them instead of being stuck a million miles from the pulpit." Down a ramp we went, into a spacious parlor that could have been a motel lobby or a clinic waiting room. Home away from home with the ficus plants, the blond wood, the paintings of fruit, the muted colors of the upholstery, hues for quiet suffering. The cross hanging above the bank of windows was the only ecclesiastical touch. Against the stretch of glass and light, the Eastmans were waiting for the assault. "Joelle," Diana said, moving toward Mrs. Eastman with open arms. "I'm Diana Maciver, and this is Mac."

"Diana!" Joelle cried. "Where were you? My gosh, I didn't know you were here! You should have been sitting with us!"

"We're just so glad to be with you," Diana murmured, sure to catch my eye before she embraced the grieving mother. The way the women looked long at one another, and embraced again, made me wonder if they'd been having reunions on the sly, get-togethers through the years without the stick-in-the-mud husband. Familial adultery, sneaking off to be with your in-laws, the cousins you profess not to know.

"I'd recognize you anywhere, Mac," Joelle said, smiling with radiant sincerity. "It is a blessing to see you."

We had to greet Joelle's parents and her sisters before we reached Buddy. "Put her there," he called out, plowing into me.

"Put her there!" I echoed. We had never said such a thing to each other before. "Put her there" had been an expression our fathers used. No matter; I knew he was Buddy because he still smelled of Old Spice, a loyal servant to his brand, a fragrance possibly worth fighting for. How sweet the air.

"Thanks a million, Brains," he said, when we'd separated. "I can't tell you how good it is to see you. It means so much, your coming down—whoa! Who's here? Which Maciver is this beautiful, beautiful girl?"

"I'm Tessa." She offered her hand to him. "I'm extremely sorry for your loss. I'm also very pleased to meet you."

"Thank you, honey." He bent to kiss her cheek. "You are gorgeous. I can see that, inside and out."

There were raucous introductions all around of the second cousins, Vanessa rushing at Tessa as if they, too, had participated in the clandestine reunions. Because Diana had been talking to one of Joelle's sisters, she was late to our love-in. "And here's Mrs. Maciver!" Buddy said to Diana. "The woman Mac has kept me from all these years." Hug, hug, hug. "We meet at last."

"At last," she breathed.

Surely after that was done, after we had performed our parts so well, we could be excused, we could shuffle out the door and go home. "Come," my wife said to me, "have a brownie." There were bite-sized cakes with white frosting and yellow crosses, and also larger chocolate squares with meticulously frosted American flags, each one requiring a baker's dexterity and patience. I didn't feel that I should eat either a religious dessert or a patriotic one, and I could see that Tessa was faced with the same dilemma. Diana had sped to the coffee urn and was unavailable for guidance. "How hungry are you?" I asked my daughter.

"This seems worse than eating the head off the chocolate bunny at Easter," she whispered. "But I'm starving! We have to have enough nourishment to make it through the burial, right? This whole thing is the weirdest experience I've ever had. It's so unbelievably sad and also it's—"

"You'd better eat."

She bent low to inspect the offerings. "I wouldn't want to offend Jesus in case he actually is the deity, but, on the other hand, maybe this place has cameras on us, and the administration is watching to see who will commit a crime against our flag. There will be shock and awe right here in Fort Bragg."

I decided to play it safe, taking a teaspoon of cashews and a teaspoon of mints on my saucer. She was still deliberating, asking, "Am I more frightened of God or my country? God or country?"

"Not so loud," I muttered.

She reached for a white cake with a cross. "My country," she said out loud. "Far more scared of my country."

* * *

IT HAD RAINED the night before, a downpour in a season of heavy rains, and the earth was still soggy, the air steamy; the puddles shone on the pavement between the rows of graves. There had been drought for a few years, but even so to some the mess seemed an insult, a heartless additional trouble. The procession to the cemetery had been slow, the line of cars extending for well over a mile. There were 205 people in a deep circle around the hole that had been readied for Kyle. When it came time to fold the flag, Joelle began to sob, the final moment, the last keepsake in its intricate turning, this way, that way, the handing over of what remained. Buddy, with the flag pressed to his chest, took his wife's hand and placed it over his own at the center of the bundle. There was then the ear-shattering and heart-stopping twenty-one-gun salute. It was a tradition, I later learned, that had begun as the signal to halt the fighting in order that the dead could be shoveled from the battlefield. Three volleys indicated that all was clear underfoot so the fighting could resume. From his formal army portrait on the easel in the church, in cap and uniform, Kyle looked to have been a youth with a clear face and a thick neck. I hadn't been able to glean much more than that from the photo. He had had his mother's jaw and mouth, his father's green eyes. The coffin was lowered into the ground, inside it whatever parts of him his unit had been able to retrieve from the blast. The torso, connected to the partial skull by a thread of muscle, perhaps, a shattered leg, the humerus that had been found a block away. That night, Buddy would say that serving in the army had been Kyle's dream from the time he was two years old.

They lived in a large house off the base, in an old neighborhood of Fayetteville. Diana admired the walnut trim and the fireplaces, the mail-order Persian rugs, the many tiered prisms of the dining-room chandelier, the generous pantry with the glassed-in cupboards, and a long counter for the juicer, the espresso machine, the six-slot toaster, ditto that number of spaces in the egg poacher, and down the line the waffle iron and panini press. By the looks of the equipment, the Eastman family was fed well and variously. The dark wood and red cast of the fireplace bricks were reminiscent of the Moose Lake house. I had never talked with Buddy about the lake, never asked if he had minded being cut out of the property when Figgy sold her shares. The Maine island had been sold, too, nothing left for him but cold cash, nothing to do but rent a cottage year after year on the Outer Banks, a place that would not feature our grandfather's butterfly collection, the moth-eaten buffalo skin in the parlor, the photographs of the Macivers from the present back to the 1880s.

Joelle excused herself from the gathering to give us a tour of the house, including the refinished attic where Robert, the thirteen-year-old, was playing a computer game called *Battlefield Vietnam*. He hadn't lost his baby fat, or maybe his soft round face, his pudginess, was the result of inactivity. With an exercise regiment he would come to look like his father, complete with the matinee-idol lips. Although I am sometimes still incredulous, I know I was of sound mind in the room with leather couches and a white ropy carpet, a large-screen TV, and a blue exercise ball: I was not hallucinating. I asked what the game was called, and one of the friends sitting nearby told me. I asked him a second time, to be sure. The women went on with the tour, and I stayed to watch Robert maneuver a swift boat through enemy waters, ducking the fire coming at him from a team in cyberspace.

"Well done," I said.

He did glance away, did look up at me to accept the praise. "Thank you."

"Your dad was in Vietnam."

"First Logistical Command," Robert said, turning back to the screen. When he hit his target he cried, "Sweet!" As if he had anticipated my next question, he said, "Dad gets a kick out of this game."

It was out of long habit that I continued to remember things to tell my mother, and I noted that detail for her as I went down the narrow stairway. Maybe Robert was in shock from his brother's death, and the computer a place to hide, to rest. That is, I was trying to think of ways to justify the game to Julia. Was a computer war game any different from our old evening ritual in the neighborhood, running around with cap guns in our holsters shooting at each other? Those of us who were not allowed toy guns made do with sticks. Like Robert, we got what may have been an important thrill from the terror of capture and our capacity for killing; maybe we were learning to connect with the story of humankind. *To love, Julia, to love means we must kill!*

On the second floor, in the master suite, Diana was again holding Joelle in her arms, both of them teary. I wondered if Joelle felt unequivocal about Kyle's sacrifice, if she was as sure as her pastor of its worth. When I came back from the bathroom, the women were wiping their eyes, so glad to find that they owned some of the same brands of clothing, in one room had the same valances, and did the same yoga video in the morning, their guru an Oriental man, shirtless on TV, with enviable pectorals and a black braid to his waist. I had never known, until that day, what a valance was, that we had several on our windows, and that Diana followed a guru. Was it Buddy's wisdom and advice from years past that had made me marry a woman who was similar to my cousin's wife? He himself later said, "We married clones, Brains, how do you like that? Look how they're jabbering at each other." They did seem to be furiously trying to make up for lost time. "Don't you," Buddy said heartily, "don't you just love 'em?"

He and I sat in the backyard as night fell, drinking my gift of Leinenkugel, the Wisconsin beer he had started me on so long ago. He had changed from his uniform into civilian clothes, into a new sports coat that was slightly less stiff than his army jacket. Kyle's old friends moved in and out of our conversation, many of them giving testimonials to their classmate, telling us how Kyle never lost his courage, never failed in his resolve to serve his country, never lost his idealism. One of his oldest playmates, a boy who'd flown in from Texas, spoke about how Kyle understood the responsibility of freedom. "He felt it here," he said, striking his palm to his heart. "He knew there had to be those who are willing to fight. He knew there are so many who won't make the ultimate sacrifice."

I was surprised by how little Buddy said. The standard lines seemed to hold no interest for him. He was eating a pile of barbecued chicken wings and drinking his beer, nodding on occasion. I'm not sure he was really listening. Out of habit, it seemed, the friends tore into Bill Clinton, bandying around the details as if they were still fresh, the cigar, the girl, the stain on the dress, as if their hatred was an important part of our history. At one point Buddy did hold forth, giving a short oration about how difficult it was going to be to bring democracy to the Muslim nations, and how those people yearned for freedom. For an instant he spoke with an evangelist's fervor, breathing into the word "yearn," drawing it out. He talked about freedom as if it were a material thing, an item to own, an object that, if you could just put your hands on it, you'd have. "Once they get it," he said, shaking his head, "once they get it, they'll see."

He seemed to have spent what energy he'd had left after the service on that brief speech. He finished his seventh or eighth beer, and, nudging me, he said, "Let's get out of here, Brains." He tipped the bottle back to get the last drop. "Excuse us, boys. Help yourself to the Leinenkugel, all the way from Wisconsin, in the cooler there. It's a very special brew, very special." As we were going out the gate he said to me, "Quick, before the dogs see." The two St. Bernards, Saint and Sinner, did not like their master to stray far.

Through the neighborhood we went, past the solid stucco and clapboard three-story houses, houses that graced old suburbs the country over, houses that surely always must shelter children who play musical instruments, and parents who read books. There were halos around the street lights, the air was thick with the smell of the wet August vegetation, the heavy balls of hydrangeas drooped over the lawns, the phloxes and coneflowers and lilies were dashed by the rain. I stepped carefully around the puddles while Buddy sloshed through without seeming to notice. He asked desultory questions about the cousins, the condition of the Moose Lake house, and my work. He was neither nervous nor engaged, but he listened well enough to comment. "Corporate America. It's going down. Down the tubes."

"Seems like it," I said.

When I remarked that he had interesting, talented, and caring children, he muttered absently, "Yep, yep, aren't they great? They're great." Out of relation to anything we'd been talking about, he said, "You know why I re-enlisted, don't you?"

"Re-enlisted?"

"Why I re-enlisted."

"No, not really. That always seemed something of a mystery. I do remember my father saying you were well suited to the job."

"Well suited. That's a good one."

"Why did you?" I asked.

"I was lucky to be in support positions, basically a desk job the second time around. I'm not saying I didn't work hard. I'm not saying I wasn't important to the effort. You do end up having some guilt about being in safe spots, though. You can end up thinking you're chicken shit."

"Chicken shit?"

"You're probably going to tell me that I served, that I'm still serving, I shouldn't have any cause for psycho-bullshit. Sure, I'll buy that. The army then, the army now, it's as fucked up as any organization. It was a screwy time, all those guys at the base, some of them losing their marbles. That energy, the waiting around, it just about kills you." He crossed the street without looking to see if a car was coming, as if we were on a continuous path that wouldn't have any obstructions. "The thing is, you're decked out as a soldier, but you're the one guarding a collection of shitty hooches pretty much out of earshot of the fighting. You're the one sending the grunts canned beans for what could be their last meal. It seemed the least I could do, turn around and sign up again, pay my pound of flesh in time."

"You were decorated," I pointed out.

"Yeah, I had a moment. During Tet. We almost got our heads blown off, a bunch of us. No one expected it—on a holiday, for Christ's sake, the lunar fucking new year. It was the kind of thing, it happens, you don't even remember much of it. You're going on instinct, working blind. I figured I was going to die, so I'd better make my mother proud."

"You knew what to do and you had courage." I had told him that kind of platitude before, and usually with the hope that it didn't sound patronizing. I didn't mean it to now, in any case.

"Tet gave me a good taste of combat. I fucking proved myself. So—fine. Bully for me. Stuff happens, the wailing of a woman, of a kid—I'm not going into it. Because you can't really tell someone about it, know what I mean? Don't worry, I'm not about to be all sensitive on you, I'm not going to have a movie-quality Vietnam-vet breakdown. You probably kill people every other day, right, Brains? A few too many aspirin in the IV drip?"

We haw-hawed.

"The thing is," he said again, "you've got everybody's idea of yourself as a soldier to uphold. That Silver Star made my mother wet her pants. Why come back Stateside to be a fuckup?"

"You weren't a f—"

"But Kyle, see, Kyle was different. He had real guts, my boy did. He put himself in situations—" We'd turned a corner, and without looking he said, "Nice houses, huh? Nice place to live."

"Very nice," I said.

"That kid was committed, that kid. Never seen anything like it. After the Twin Towers, he says to me, he says, 'Dad, I'm going to fight for what I know is right. I love this country.' My kid says that to me, how are you going to argue? There's nothing you can tell him. I'm trying to talk him out of enlisting, I'm thinking, What the fuck can I say? I felt like your mother, felt like Aunt Julia. 'Don't sign up, Kyle, don't go through officer training, don't love your fucking country, wait a few years, go to college, get yourself an education, then go in as a medic, a doctor, a nurse, who the fuck cares?' And he says to me, 'We gotta fight this war now, Dad. We gotta get the terrorists now.'"

When I didn't speak he said, "Yeah, I know, what's there to say?" He was brave as hell, my kid.

I would have liked to know Kyle. I wondered what, beyond the thin just-in-case letter, would show me the real boy. Were there other letters, or a drunken friend who might say more than the bromides, a girl who'd listened to Kyle's doubts? Buddy's sadness was in his tread, it was in the way his arms fell to his sides, the slope of his shoulders, the way he looked down at the pavement; it was in the squelch of his soaked shoes.

I could imagine talking and not talking, walking together through Fayetteville, maybe hooking into Sherman's trek, going all the way to Savannah and to the sea. I felt that long-ago pride to be with him, and possibly to be of some use as we walked. Maybe he understood that, because he said, "Thanks again, Brains, for coming. It's been too many years, way too many years." We'd reached another corner, a large dark house on a double lot. I remember thinking the place looked like a fortress, and noting the single green light up on the second floor, a computer terminal's watchful eye. "Let's cut across," Buddy said, veering into the wet grass.

I wondered, Cut across to where?

In the middle of the yard—and why should I have been surprised?—he hooked his arm around my neck, pausing behind me to enjoy the capture.

"Uhh," from my mouth.

He collapsed my knees, falling along with me.

"Oof!"

He pushed my face into the grass. *How you going to get out of this hold, huh? Stick your ass up, your wimpy little ass, come on, use your legs, use your legs, what are you made of?* He wrenched my arm across my spine. We boys of summer! I heard myself laugh. My cousin expertly torqued my shoulder, the acromioclavicular joint—"Christ!"—separating from the scapula.

"What's that?"

"Bastard!" Even as he pulled harder, the familiarity of the routine was a happiness. Tears smarted in my eyes, and I believe I said, to quote Jerry Pindel, "Fuck!"

"That's right."

It was like the repetition in a piece of music, the reprise that brings with it a deeper understanding of a thing you can't begin to name. I was suffocating from his weight and the grass up my nose. If I had been able to breathe, I would have laughed some more. If I wasn't about to suffer from either an AC separation or an anterior dislocation—I couldn't quite tell which one would come to pass—I would have laughed yet again at his ability to unravel the years, at the kindness of his gift. He held me for as long as he knew I could stand it, of that I am sure, his old instinct for precision serving him. When he let go it was slow, first releasing my arm bit by bit, and then rolling off me. He must have lain on his back for a minute, looking up at the few stars shining beyond the watery sky. It must have been a little while, my acromion settling back into position, the green computer light twinkling. As if nothing had occurred, we managed to get ourselves standing and dusted off. My glasses were bent and would need some adjusting back in real time. Without any more conversation, we walked the few miles to the Eastman yard where the Japanese lights, the colored globes, swiveled in the breeze.

JOELLE WAS AT THE PATIO TABLE, clearing the chicken bones and the bottles, when we appeared. The enormous dogs barked their throaty wuf-wufs and leapt to their favorite. Once Buddy was in his chair, he started to laugh. In short order he became convulsed. I took myself to the far reaches of the yard, gathering plates and glasses from the few guests who remained. Joelle glanced at her husband, shook her head, and said, "Don't tell me. I don't want to know."

"Mac?" Diana cried, coming from the house. "Where have you

been? Why—why are there grass stains on your shirt? Your face is all—"

"Go clean up in the basement," Joelle said to her husband. "Calm down. Calm down! Get hold of yourself."

"That's, that's," Buddy heaved, tears running down his face, "where we, where we, wash the, the dogs."

Not too long after we'd recovered ourselves, doing the best we could to wipe the dirt from our clothes, after I'd bent my glasses to their original shape, we began the round of farewells, including the promise of many future meetings, vacations together, Club Med! Hilton Head! Orlando! A reunion of all the cousins, perhaps, at Moose Lake. Years ahead of communion, the men disappearing into their bacchanalian rites, thrown back into their adolescence, the women tidying and commiserating. It was past midnight when Tessa and Diana and I finally drove away from that house, where violence and salvation met so companionably.

"What, may I ask," Diana said on the way to the hotel, "were you doing with Buddy?"

Were there any words from literature that I could use to explain? *In the middle of the journey of our life I came to myself in a dark wood where the straight way was lost.* No, it wasn't that. *So we beat on, boats against the current, borne back ceaselessly into the past.* Diana had never warmed to *The Great Gatsby,* the book ruined by her high-school English teacher. *Blow, winds, and crack your cheeks.* I wasn't as far gone as Lear, not yet. Without God and with fractured love through the years, without much insight, I had relied on poetry and what I thought was kindness as my guide. Now, however, I could not come up with a line that would satisfy both my wife and me.

She said, "I was so embarrassed, you with your grass stains and dirty face."

Maybe I'd had a real mystical experience, a genuine revelation of eternity there with Buddy, nearly suffocated by his own hand on a stranger's ChemLawn. A person didn't have certainty and happiness on that order just every day. "Lamb?" I said.

"What."

"It was good we made this trip. Especially since Russia and my parents and Louise couldn't. Thank you for pestering me."

It must have been the praise, the acknowledgment that I'd been stubborn, that made my wife burst into tears, showing more emotion in the car than she had for Kyle in the church. She opened her purse and retrieved one, two, three, four, five fresh tissues.

"It's too bad," I went on, ignoring her display, "that Russia couldn't have been here. The funeral would have been the high point of her life. She would have had such pride in Kyle's sacrifice."

Russia had died in 1997 in a nursing home near her youngest brother, in Mississippi. She fought him every day during the years of his faithful visits, she was miserable to all her guests, she drove the staff to distraction. The last time I saw her there, she beseeched me to take her away. "I'll come and live with you, Timothy, won't give you a minute of bother, not one single minute."

"Of course you wouldn't."

"I'm not making my crossing from this place, you hear me? You tell Mr. Buddy to help me, you tell him Russia needs him to get to the Promised Land."

"I'll tell him."

Without either my or Buddy's assistance, she made her transition after a short bout with pneumonia.

WHEN WE ARRIVED at O'Hare from North Carolina, the day after the service, it was late afternoon, and at my request we drove to my father's house, not far away, to tell him about the relatives. He would appreciate the news, and also he would understand, in a way no other person could, the confusion of the ritual. We found him sitting out on the new deck with Madeline, the two of them having happy hour, he with his bottle of Schloss Saarstein Riesling and she with a glass of something fizzy. There was a dish of salty peanuts, a plate of Wheat Thins, and, with a nod to urban sophistication, one tomato bruschetta each. Although Russia had not included happy hour in the daily cate-chism, my father had become religious about this habit after Julia's death.

He had made a small garden plot in the backyard so he could grow tomatoes and basil for that happy hour, as well as flowers for the woman of the house. Because he no longer went to the museum, there were four bird-feeders, two on poles and two hanging from the pear tree: the Grove Avenue oasis for the lesser birds, grackles and star-lings, and whatever high-class songbirds might stop by. The Merry Maids had been for their biweekly appointment that day, sweeping through the house in thirty minutes, four of them in checked uniforms fanning out to clean; even on the deck there was still the whiff of the air freshener they sprayed inside as their last act.

Once we got talking about the trip, Diana was good enough to marshal Tessa and Madeline into the kitchen, to assemble the dinner we'd brought. I was glad to have a chance to describe the visit with no others adding or correcting. "All that talk of valor and service and the Kingdom of Heaven," I said. "It was wonderfully primitive and per-suasive."

"Your mother would have croaked."

"Tessa, I'm sorry to say, did her grandmother proud, reducing an old friend of Kyle's to tears with her antiwar screed."

"Did she?" He perked up.

"What's remarkable, though, is that Buddy told me he'd tried to talk Kyle out of enlisting. He said he'd felt Mom's presence when he was making his arguments."

My father lifted his eyes to the heights of the pear tree. "There's nobody left in the family for your mother to spar with. She only picks on the ignorant people with advanced degrees, those who theoreti-cally should know better." He, too, considered her in the present. He took off his glasses and cleaned them on his shirt, and when they were back on his face he pressed close to examine me. "You don't look so great."

"Can't hold my liquor," I said. "I temporarily forgot that I'm old." I was moving my arm only by virtue of the Percadan I'd found in my bag.

"Old," my father repeated.

"Buddy's old now, too."

"Devastated, I'd expect."

"I almost didn't recognize him."

"I assume the military does something to prepare the boys for death. Maybe there's no better training in this life than that."

Was my aged father properly trained? I wondered. Was he ready?

"I got sad news a few days ago," he said, "news that Mikey O'Day died."

"Mikey!"

"His sister called, the younger sister, the one in Georgia he'd gone to live with when the mother passed away. Congestive heart failure, pretty quick, I guess. The sister seemed to think he knew he was going."

That was something people often mentioned. He knew, he recognized me in the end, he wasn't afraid, and so forth. To my father I said, "Did you tell her?"

"I don't think I will. I've been pondering, but I don't see any reason."

We were quiet for a while. And then I told him about Robert playing *Battlefield Vietnam*. We talked in our usual and not altogether uncheerful way about how the world was going to hell. When Diana and the girls came out with a tray of sandwiches, my father said to Madeline, "There you are."

"I'm always here," she said, smoothing her short hair as she sat next to him.

He put his hand between her shoulder blades and drew circles for a minute. She hardly noticed, and I realized it was probably a gesture he made several times a day, without thinking. When he was done he rested his fingers at the nape of her neck. "This spread is beautiful, isn't it, Maddy?" He gave her a quick pat before he helped himself to an indeterminate kind of sandwich, turkey or ham or egg salad, whatever was most oozing mayonnaise.

"Diana." I reached for her sleeve. How did a person keep the devotion running pure? With or without God's grace. Devotion that at a certain point was for its own sake. "Diana," I said again, clutching her upper arm, which had grown strong with her morning yoga guru.

"Okay, okay!" She was trying to shake me away. "I know you want to get going. I know your head is killing you, but it's your own fault. Just let me eat."

Nonetheless, for a little bit, I kept my hand, but softly, on her arm.

When we finished our sandwiches, we turned for the north, leaving the two of them at their places on the deck. The sun was moving beyond the trees and houses, no place in my old town to see it finally slip over the filmy city horizon. Madeline and my father would sit there together until the fireflies appeared and the street lights came on, waiting for the ghostly mothers to ring their bells and sing out the names of their children from the back porches—time, at long last, to come inside.